W9-ACI-441

THE
English Rogue:
DESCRIBED,

IN THE
LIFE
OF
MERITON LATROON,

A Witty Extravagant.

Being a Compleat Hiſtory of the

MOST
Eminent Cheats
OF
BOTH SEXES.

Read, *but don't* Practice: *for the Author findes,*
They which live Honeſt *have moſt quiet mindes.*

Dixero ſi quid forte jocoſius hoc mihi juris
Cum & eniâ dalis.

London, Printed for **Henry Marſh**, at the Princes
Arms in Chancery-Lane. 1665.

THE
English Rogue

by RICHARD HEAD

Critical Introduction by
Michael Shinagel
Harvard University

NEW FRONTIERS PRESS

BOSTON

1961

INTRODUCTION

When the original edition of the <u>English Rogue</u> was submitted to the censors of the press for licensing, the book was promptly suppressed on the charge of "being much too smutty"; consequently, what copies already were printed had to be sold and circulated clandestinely. Only after the author "was fain to refine it"[1] did a legitimately licensed edition appear in 1665. Seemingly none of the unexpurgated copies survive - which may be just as well - for, in Sir Sidney Lee's estimate, "if, as seems probable, the extant editions, with their coarse language and episode, present the expurgated version, Head's original draft must have been singularly disreputable."[2]

The author of this controversial work was Richard Head (1637?-1686?), whose life and literary career typify the wretched existence of scores of hack writers during the Restoration period. The highly autobiographical opening chapters of the <u>English Rogue</u> furnish us with a vivid picture of Head's childhood experiences. Born of English parents about 1637 in Ireland, where his father was serving as chaplain to a nobleman, Head witnessed the murder of his father by Irish rebels during the bloody insurrection of 1641. During that same year his only brother also died. He and his mother barely escaped to Belfast, which afforded them little protection, so they were forced to make their way to England. Later Head was admitted to Oxford, from where his father had graduated, but he soon abandoned his studies and became a bookseller's apprentice in London. In time he married and prospered to the point of opening his own bookshop, which was going well until he succumbed to drinking and

1. William Winstanley, <u>Lives of the most famous English Poets</u> (London, 1687), p. 209.

2. <u>Dictionary of National Biography</u>, edd. Leslie Stephen and Sidney Lee, Vol. IX (London, 1908), p. 327.

i

gambling. Head soon lost his money and his business and was forced to retire to Dublin out of the reach of his creditors. In 1663, however, he returned to London with hopes of a wealthy patron to support his literary endeavors. But this prospect never materialized and Head again turned to bookselling. "Being addicted to play," he again gambled away his business and was ruined. From 1664 on, according to John Aubrey, Head "maintained himself by scribling [sic]," relying on booksellers and printers for his livelihood, which was doled out to him "at 20s. per sheet."[3] Head lead a dissolute life as a literary hack, suffering "many crosses and afflictions."[4] He is believed to have drowned while crossing to the Isle of Wight in 1686.

The English Rogue (1665) was Head's first major work to appear, and it remains the book upon which his reputation rests. A number of other works followed. An enumeration of some select titles will most accurately reveal the audience Head wrote for and the nature of the material he supplied them:

Canting Academy, or the Devil's Cabinet opened. Wherein is shewn the mysterious and villanous Practices of that wicked crew commonly known by the name of Hectors, Trapanners, Gilts, etc., to which is added a compleat Canting Dictionary (1673).

Jackson's Recantation, or the Life and Death of the notorious Highwayman now hanging in chains at Hampstead (1674).

Proteus Redivivus, or the Art of Wheedling or Insinuation (1675).

3. John Aubrey, Brief Lives, ed. Andrew Clark, Vol. I (Oxford, 1898), p. 305.

4. Winstanley, 209.

Nugae Venales, or a Complaisant Companion being
new Jests, domestick and foreign, Bulls, Rhodo-
montados, pleasant Novels, and Miscellanies
(1686).

Head consciously aimed his books at the sensation-seeking
lower class reading public of the time, a class of readers
who delighted in rogue and criminal lives, jest-books,
and descriptions of thieves' practices. Head also es-
sayed into the popular literature of travel and adventure
with such works as The Floating Island: or, a New Discovery (1673) and The Western Wonder: or, O Brazeel
(1674). In short, whatever promised a fair commercial
success fell within the compass of Head's literary ac-
tivities.

But how does Head's hack writing, particularly his
English Rogue, fit into the literary context of his time?
Briefly, the Restoration period was dominated by three
main types of prose fiction: 1) the translations of
courtly French romances and their English counterparts
(as exemplified by such authors as D'Urfé and Roger
Boyle, respectively), 2) the allegorized religious narratives (as exemplified by John Bunyan), and 3) the
rogue and criminal biographies (as exemplified by Head
himself).[5] Each of these three literary types was directed at and primarily appealed to a particular level of
society. The romances provided the aristocracy with a
polite escape into an idealized world of decorum and in-
trigue. The allegorical narratives supplied the pious
middle class with dramatized conflicts of good and evil.
And finally the popular rogue literature pandered to the
coarser appetites of the lower classes. In his Life and
Death of Mr. Badman (1680), for example, Bunyan had
Mr. Wiseman deplore how an apprentice "would get all
the bad and abominable Books that he could, as beastly

5. There were also, to be sure, other types of prose fiction then in
   vogue, such as the philosophical romances or the epistolary narratives, but these constituted minor currents.

Romances,[6] and books full of Ribbauldry, even such as immediately tended to set all fleshy lusts on fire." [7] Undoubtedly, in this censure, Bunyan had in mind the literature of low life, like the English Rogue, so popular in his time.

What makes the English Rogue of such direct interest to us now is the fact that it stands both as a creation very much representative of its age, as well as a compilation of much that comprised the sources for the literature of roguery common to the lower classes. For Head was hardly an inventive artist; he was a hack, and like most hacks he borrowed shamelessly from existing materials to produce his book on such short order. We have little difficulty, therefore, tracing such divers sources as, for example, the jest-books in the interpolated chapters comprising "The Life of a Law-abusing Cheat" (XXXIX-L); the books of characters in "the Character of an Hector or Trapan" (XII); the beggar-books (VI-VII); the conny-catching pamphlets (VIII); the canting catalogues and canting songs (V); the scoundrel verses in "What is a Bawdy-house" (LVII); the criminal lives (XXXIII-XXXV); the prison pamphlets and recantations (LIX-LXIV); and lastly the books of travel and adventure (LXVI-LXXVI). Although Head's English Rogue never realizes the ambitious aim stated in the sub-title, "a compleat History of the most eminent cheats of both Sexes," it certainly does, thanks to its comprehensive approach, afford us a storehouse of source material.

Head harbored no lofty artistic ambition when he "scribbled" his English Rogue; he simply addressed himself to producing an entertaining book for an audience whose tastes he had come to know at first hand as a

6. Bunyan here alludes to the chap-books, not the courtly romances of the aristocracy.

7. John Bunyan, Life and Death of Mr. Badman, ed. John Brown (Cambridge, 1905), p. 43.

bookseller. In this respect Head was eminently successful, as the popularity of the work amply demonstrates. We must approach the work, therefore, primarily for its social significance, for the panoramic sweep of 17th century low life it affords. The author's briskly paced episodic structure and first person narrative style succeed in engaging and sustaining our interest, and we find ourselves ranging with the protagonist among the dregs of society, encountering in breathless succession whores and hectors, pickpockets and footpads, beggars and gypsies, cheats and highwaymen. Yet the English Rogue, while parading past this rogue's gallery of underworld characters, also places them against the appropriate settings of bawdy house and ale house, deserted highway and London slum, waterfront and countryside. This variety of character and scene clearly delighted the contemporary lower class reader, as did the scurrility and eroticism, the sharping and thieving. And understandably so. Because what Head described for them was more than a mere literary convention; it was for many of them a way of life.

But the English Rogue also reflects the low moral state to which rogue literature, as a genre, had by that time fallen. This decline is most sharply evident when we compare Head's English Rogue with the parent of the genre, The Life of Lazarillo de Tormes, which appeared in Spain circa 1554. The protagonist of this story is an engaging yet roguish beggar boy, a picaro, who narrates in the first person his experiences of serving ten different masters, representative of various levels of society and of specific vices or foibles. Existing by his resourcefulness and cunning, Lazaro ranges through society and exposes such ills as are in need of reform.

Lazaro plays tricks on his masters and steals from them, yet he none the less exhibits an exquisitely developed moral sense; for he only tricks those of his masters who are unnecessarily inhuman to him and he only steals from those of his masters out of bare necessity. When, for example, he finally steals from his second master, the niggardly clergyman, it is only after he has been half-starved and realizes: "I was dying of hunger. . . . I clearly saw that I was headed for the grave if God and my wits should not intercede."[8] His wits fortunately do intercede and he thereby averts death by slow starvation.

Lazaro's finer sensibilities, however, his generosity and compassion, are evoked naturally in the service of a squire who sacrifices everything, even subsistence, for his shabby gentility. " 'This fellow,' I said, 'is poor, and nobody gives what he does not have. It is right for me to hate the greedy blindman and the miserable wretch of a clergyman; even though God had provided for them both, the one through his hand-kissing and the other through a glib tongue, they kept me half starved to death. But for this one [the squire] I can feel only pity.' " [9] Even though the squire puts on airs and fails to provide food for his servant, Lazaro's generous sense of humanity responds to his master's plight and, as he concludes: "Many times, in order to bring home enough food to keep him alive, I went hungry myself."[10]

Turning to the character of Meriton Latroon, we immediately are struck by the lack of resemblance he bears to his picaro prototype. Meriton is anything but a moral agent; he is a thoroughgoing knave totally devoid of finer feelings. We may take as representative of Meriton's career the incident where his master's maid, whom he had seduced, "after many heartfetched sighs," told him "she found herself with child." He arranges for her to retire to the country, so his master would not know of

8. The Life of Lazarillo de Tormes, tr. J. G. Markley (N. Y., 1954), p. 22.

9. Ibid., p. 44

10. Ibid.

this matter, and there have the baby. "After her de-livery," he remarks, "I found the keeping of her and the child very expensive. . . . Well, I bethought myself how to be rid both of cow and calf."[11] He persuades her, on pretext of marriage, to travel with him to Virginia, but he slips off the ship as it weighs anchor and puts to sea, the unsuspecting "cow and calf" remaining on board. While Meriton on the dock postures at being remorseful for his dastardly trick, he is accosted by a woman whose husband happens to be on board the ship also, and they lose no time in striking up a sexual liaison. He persuades his new mistress to entrust her money to his safe keep-ing, which she no sooner does than he again slips off, with the practical thought that "it was better for one to want than two." And so it goes. Meriton is consistently depicted as a sort of Hobbesian hero operating in a state of nature, his _modus vivendi_ being governed solely by self-interest and self-gratification.

As Meriton differs from Lazaro as a _picaro_, so the English Rogue differs from Lazarillo de Tormes as a species of the picaresque. The picaresque, in its pure form, has as its protagonist an entertaining yet funda-mentally moral rogue whose serious aim is social ex-posé leading to social reform. Such certainly is the case with Lazarillo de Tormes. The rogue autobi-ography, on the other hand, represents a vulgarized ver-sion of the pure picaresque, the moral distinctions be-tween good and evil becoming blurred, if not blackened, by an oppressive atmosphere of unmitigated villainy and eroticism. With the English Rogue, then, the _picaro_ has become transmuted into the criminal rogue and the genre has degenerated from the level of satire to sensation-alism.

Still, when viewed in the perspective of the broad history of rogue literature, the English Rogue looms as the most considerable work of its kind in the entire 17th

11. The animal imagery is indicative of Meriton's attitude toward people.

century. It is indebted and looks back to some of the best features of the Elizabethan rogue tradition. Consider, for instance, the passage where Meriton describes himself surprised by a hector while in bed with his whore:

> And presently in came a fellow whose very face would have enlightened the room, though in the darkest night; for indeed it appeared to me a blazing comet, and his nose (for miraculously he had preserved it) was the brushy tail. Laying his hand on his sword, he looked fiercer than a Spanish Don insulting over an Indian slave. The bulk of his body began to heave like an earth-quake, whilst his mouth, AEtna-like, belched out all manner of sulphurous oaths, which roared so loud as if his belly had contained a barrel of gunpowder, and the linstock of his nose had fired it.

For sheer metaphoric exuberance nothing can compare with such a passage but the greatest contribution to rogue literature by the 16th century, Thomas Nashe's Unfortunate Traveller (1594), whose work is here unmistakably called to mind. But looking in the opposite direction, after the appearance of the English Rogue, it is clear that rogue fiction had reached a kind of impasse. It had exhausted the inherited lore of jest-books, beggar-books, conny-catching pamphlets, and the like. It had deteriorated morally to its lowest point. From then on, if the genre were to flourish anew, it would have to take fresh approaches, which, after some fifty years of stagnation, it finally succeeded in doing. With the 18th century there came a renaissance in the literature of roguery: Defoe revitalized rogue fiction in England with his low life realism and Le Sage performed that service for the picaresque in France with his artistically and morally superior Gil Blas, which was to find its way across the channel and exert a powerful influence on the English novel, too.

A final word about this edition. In 1665 Henry Marsh of Chancery Lane, London published the first licensed edition of the English Rogue in an octavo volume. The work apparently was an instantaneous success with the public, for the bookseller Francis Kirkman prevailed on Head to write a continuation to his work. When Head refused, Kirkman unscrupulously took it upon himself to write a second part, his action being prompted, as he declares in his preface, "first and chiefest ... to gain ready money." Although Kirkman's second part was licensed as early as 1668, the earliest extant edition is dated 1671. The year 1671 also saw Kirkman issue a third and fourth part, with advertisements for a fifth, which was never forthcoming. In 1680 a uniform edition of the four parts was printed and this edition was reprinted in a four volume set in 1874.

Of the four parts generally associated with the English Rogue, Head's first part is without question the best, the least offensive, while also being the original version. Moreover, Head repeatedly disclaimed any connection with Kirkman's unauthorized additions. I have, accordingly, restored Head to his sole authorship of the English Rogue by limiting this edition to the first part and by using a slightly modernized text of the reprinted edition of 1874, modeled after the 1680 version.

In parting, I wish here only to reproduce the printer's salutary substitution for his usual page of errata in the earliest extant edition of the English Rogue:

To the Reader, Instead of the Errata.

This Rogue hath had his faults, the Printers too;
All men whilst here do erre; and so may you.

MICHAEL SHINAGEL

Cambridge, Massachusetts
January, 1961

ix

The Epistle to the Reader

Gentlemen,

It hath been too much the humour of late, for men rather to adventure on the Forreign crazy stilts of other mens inventions, then securely walk on the ground-work of their own home-spun fancies. What I here present ye with, is an original in your own Mother-tongue; and yet I may not improperly call it a Translation, drawn from the Black Copy of mens wicked actions; such who spared the Devil the pains of courting them, by listing themselves Volunteers to serve under his Hellish Banners; with some whereof I have heretofore been unhappily acquainted, and am not ashamed to confess that I have been somewhat soiled by their vitious practices, but now I hope cleansed in a great measure from those impurities. Every man hath his peculiar guilt, proper to his constitution and age: and most have had (or will have) their exorbitant exiliencies, erronious excursions, which are least dangerous when attended by Youthfulness.

This good use I hope the Reader will make with me of those follies, that are so generally and too frequently committed every where, by declining the commission of them (if not for the love of virtue, yet to avoid the dismal effects of the most dangerous consequences that continually accompany them.) And how shall any be able to do this, unless they make an introspection into Vice? which they may do with little danger; for it is possible to injoy the Theorick, without making use of the Practick.

To save my Country-men the vast expence and charge of such experimental Observations, I have here given an accompt of my readings, not in Books, but Men; which should have been buried in silence, (fearing lest its Title might reflect on my Name and Reputation) had not a publick good interceded for its publication, far beyond any private interest or respect.

When I undertook this Subject, I was destitute of all those Tools (Books, I mean) which divers pretended Artists make use of to form some Ill-contrived design. By which ye may understand, that as necessity forced me, so a generous resolution commanded me to scorn a Lituanian humour or Custom, to admit of Adjutores tori, helpers in a Marriage-bed, there to engender little better than a spurious issue. It is a legitimate off-spring, I'll assure yee, begot by one singly and soly, and a person that dares in spight of canker'd Malice subscribe himself

A well-willer to his

Countries welfare,

Richard Head.

ON

The English Rogue.

What others writ, was ta'en upon the Score;
    Thou art in Re, what they but feign'd before.
They did but lisp, or worse, speak through the Nose:
Thou hast pronounc't, and liv'st in Verse and Prose.
Guzman, Lazaro, Buscon, and Francion,
Till thou appear'dst did shine as at high Noon.
Thy Book's now extant; those that Judge of Wit,
Say, They and Rablais too fall short of it.
How could't be otherwise, since 'twas thy fate,
To practise what they did but imitate.
We stand amaz'd at thy Ephesian Fire;
Such purchas'd Infamy all must admire.

N. D.

On the ensuing Subject.

What more Rogues still? I thought our happy
       Times
Were freed from such, as from Rebellious Crimes.
But such will be: i' th' best of Times we find
The worst of men; the Law can't lawless bind.
It might be so, since Nature thought it fit
To give some nought but Lands, to others Wit
But no Estates, bestowing such a mind
That can't within due limits be confin'd.
Hence Depredations, Thefts, nay worser facts,
Cheating & Whoring, with unheard-of acts:
For Swimming for their Lives, these misrules think,
'Tis better catch at any thing, then sink.
Such was this Rogue, esteem'd the worst of men;
Liv'd by his Sword, his Pregnant Wit, and Pen.
In short, Pray pardon if I speak amiss;
I never read so arch a Rogue as This.

A. B.

CHAPTER I

What his parents were : the place of his own nativity : his miraculous
escape from the hands of Irish rebels : his brother being at that very
time murdered by the merciless hands of those bloody butchers

AFTER a long and strict inquisition after my father's pedigree, I
could not find any of his ancestors bearing a coat ; surely length
of time had *worn* it out. But if the Gentle Craft will any ways ennoble
his family, I believe I could deduce several of his name, professors of
that lasting art, even from Crispin. My father's father had, by his continual labour in husbandry, arrived to the height of a farmer, then the
head of his kindred. Standing upon one of his own mole-hills, ambition
so swelled him that he swore by his plough-share, that his eldest son
(my father) should be a *Scholhard*, and should learn so long, till he could
read any printed or written hand ; nay, and if occasion should serve,
write a bill or bond.

It was never known that any of the family could distinguish one letter
from another, neither could they speak above the reach of their horses'
understandings. Talk to them in any other dialect but that of a bag-
pudding, of a peck, or a piece of beef (in which their teeth might step
wet-shod), and a man were as good to have discoursed with them in
Arabic. But let me not abuse them, for some understood something
else, that is to say, the art of whistling, driving their team and to shoe
themselves as well as their horses ; how to lean methodically upon a
staff and through the holes of their hat tell what it is o'clock by the sun.

The symmetrical proportion, sweetness of features and acuteness of
my father's wit were such (though extracted out of this lump of red and
white marl) that he was beloved of all. As the loveliness of his person
gained always an interest in female hearts, so the quickness of apprehension and invention, and the acquired quaintness of his expressions
procured him the friendship of such as conversed with him. A gentleman at length taking notice of more than ordinary natural parts in him,
at his own charge sent him to school contrary to the desire of his father,
who was able enough to maintain him at school. And to say the truth,
this gentleman offered not my father his patronage upon any charitable
account, but that he might hereafter glory in being the chief instrument
of bringing up such a fair promising wit, which he questioned not, with

3

good cultivation would bring forth such lovely fruit as would answer cost and fully satisfy his expectation. Being admitted into the Grammar School, by the strength of his memory, to his masters' great amazement, in a very short time he had Lily's *Rules* by heart, outstripping many that for years had been entered before him. His master perceiving what a stupendous proficiency he had made, was very glad that this fair opportunity offered itself that he might be idle, and in order thereunto would frequently appoint my father to be his usher or deputy, when he intended to turn Bacchanalian, to drink, hunt, or whore, to which vices he was over much addicted. My father having now conquered, in a manner, the difficulties of that school's learning began now to lay aside his book, and follow the steps of his vicious learned master, the examples of a superior proving oftentimes guides to inferior actions,

Regis ad exemplum——

Besides, his springing age (wherein the blood is hot and fervent) spurred him on, and the natural disposition of his mind gave him wings to fly whither his unbounded, licentious, self-pleasing will would direct. His youth introduced him into all sorts of vanity, and his constitution of body was the mother of all his unlawful pleasures. His temperament gave sense pre-eminence above reason. Thus, you see (as experience can more fully demonstrate) how the heat of youth gives fuel to the fire of voluptuous enjoyments. But without a supply of what may purchase those delights, invention must be tenter-hooked, which ever proves dangerous, most commonly fatal. My grandfather, too indulgent to his son, supplied him continually with money ; which he did the more freely since he was exempted from such charges which necessity required for my father's maintenance.

He having now more than a bare competence, not only consents to the commission of evil but tempts others to perpetrate the like ; and now, following his own natural proneness to irregular liberty, diurnally suggests matters of innovation, not only to his own, but others' reasons, *Lectum non citius relinquens quam in Deum delinquens, non citius surgens quam insurgens.* No sooner relinquishing his bed, but delinquishing his Creator, No sooner rising than rising against his God. In short, I know not whether he prevailed more on others or others on him, for he was facile ; the best nature is most quickly depraved, as the purest flesh corrupts soonest, and is most noisome when corrupted. Yet, notwithstanding these blooming debaucheries, he neglected not his study so much but that he capacitated himself for the University, and by approbation was sent thither by his patron. He applied himself close to his book for a while, till he had adapted himself a companion for the most absolute critic that could be selected out of any of the colleges. In the assured confidence of his own parts he ventured among them, and left such remarks of his cutting wit in all companies he came into that the gallants and most notable wits of Oxford coveted so much his company that he had not time to apply himself to his study, but giving way to their solicitations (being prompted thereunto by his own powerful inclinations) plunged himself over head and ears in all manner of sensuality. For his lewd carriage, inimitably wicked practices, and detestable behaviour, he was at last expelled the college.

Now was he forced to return to his father, who with much joy received him. But he would not tell him the true cause of his coming down ; but to palliate his villainies, he informed his father that he had learned as much as he could be instructed in ; and now and then would sprinkle his discourse with a Greek or Latin sentence when talking with the poor ignorant old man, who took wonderful delight in the mere sound thereof. When my father spake at any time they were all as silent as midnight, and then would my grandfather, with much admiration, beckon to the standers by to give their greatest attention to what the speaker as little understood as his auditors, not caring what nonsense he uttered, if wrapped up in unintelligible hard words, purposely to abuse those brutish plough-jobbers. In ostentation he was carried to the parson of the parish, to discourse with him ; who by good fortune understood no other tongue but what his mother taught him. My father, perceiving that, made ' Shoulderamutton ' and ' Kapathumpton ' serve for very good Greek ; which the parson confirmed, telling my grandfather, further, that his son was an excellent scholar ; protesting that he was so deeply learned that he spake things he understood not. This, I have heard him say, made him as good sport as ever he received in the most ingenious society.

He had not been long in the country before a gentlewoman taking notice of his external and internal qualifications fell deeply in love with him ; and preferring her own pleasure before the displeasure of her wealthy relations, she *incontinently* was married to him. I shall waive how it was brought about in every particular, but only instance what is therein remarkable. Doubtless the gestures he used in his preaching (when she was present) might something avail in the conquest of her affections ; beginning with a ' dearly beloved ' passionately extended, looking full in her face all the while. And being, in the time of the kingdom's alteration and confusion,[1] a temporizing minister, he had learned all those tricks by which those of his sect and coat used to bewitch a female ear. But that which chiefly effected his desires, was the assurance of an old matron that lived near my mother, who for profit scrupled

---

[1] That is, at the time of the Commonwealth.

not to officiate as bawd. This good old gentlewoman contrived ways to bring them together, unsuspected by any, by which means they obtained the opportunity to perform Hymen's rites, *sans* ceremonies of the Church.

My mother finding impregnation, acquainted my father therewith, who (glad to hear how fast he had tied her to him) urged her to the speedy consummation of a legal marriage, which she more longed for than he did himself, but knew not how to bring it to pass, by reason of those many obstacles which they saw obvious, and thwarting their intentions. As first the vast disproportion between their estates ; next, the antipathy her parents bore to his function. Joining these to many other obstructions, which fancy and knowledge presented to them, they concluded to steal a wedding and accordingly did put it in execution. Much troubled her parents were at first, to hear how their daughter had ship-wrecked her fortune (as they judged it) in the unfortunate losing her maidenhead ; but time, with the intercession of friends, procured a reconciliation between them, and all parties well pleased. The old people took great delight in the fortune, hopeful thoughts and expectations of their son-in-law, but he more in the reception of a large sum of money they paid him, and my mother most of all (as she thought) in the continual conversation and enjoyment of my father, which she equally ranked with what might be esteemed the best of things.

His eminent parts natural (and what he attained unto by his country studies, being ashamed to have lost so much time), introduced him as a chaplain to a nobleman, with whom he travelled into Ireland. He took shipping at Minehead, and from thence sailed to Knockfergus, where he lived both creditably and comfortably. Experience had then reformed his life to so strict a religious course that his observers gained more by his example than his hearers by precepts. Thus, by his piety in the purity of his practice, he soon regained his lost credit.

By this time my mother drew near her time, having conceived me in England, but not conceiving she thus should drop me in an Irish bog. There is no fear that England and Ireland will, after my decease, contend about my nativity, as several countries did about Homer ; striving to have the honour of first giving him breath. Neither shall I much thank my native country for bestowing on me such principles as I and most of my countrymen drew from that very air. The place, I think, made me appear a bastard in disposition to my father. It is strange the climate should have more prevalency over the nature of the native than the disposition of the parent ; for though father and mother could neither flatter, deceive, revenge, equivocate, &c., yet the son (as the consequence hath since made it appear) can (according to the common custom of his countrymen) dissemble and sooth up his adversary with expressions extracted from celestial manna, taking his advantage thereby to ruin him. For to speak the truth, I could never yet love any but for some by-respect, neither could I ever be persuaded into a pacification with that man who had any way injured me, never resting satisfied till I had accomplished a plenary revenge, which I commonly effected under the pretence of great love and kindness. Cheat all I dealt withal, though the matter were ever so inconsiderable; lie so naturally that a miracle may be as soon wrought as a truth proceed from my mouth. And then for equivocations, or mental reservations, they were ever in me innate properties. It was always my resolution rather to die by the hand of a common executioner than want my revenge, though ever so slightly grounded. But I shall desist here to characterize myself further, reserving that for another place.

Four years after my birth the Rebellion began so unexpectedly that we were forced to flee in the night; the light of our flaming houses, ricks of hay, and stacks of corn guided us out of the town, and our fears soon conveyed us to the mountains. But the rebels, wandering to and fro, intending either to meet with their friends (who flocked from all parts to get into a body), or else any English, which they designed as sacrifices to their implacable malice, or inbred antipathy to that nation, met with my mother, attended by two scullogues, her menial servants, the one carrying me, the other my brother. The Fates had decreed my brother's untimely death, and therefore unavoidable, the faithful infidel being butchered with him. The surviving servant, who carried me, declared that he was a Roman Catholic, and imploring their mercy with his howling *Chram a Cress*, or St. *Patrick a gra*, procured my mother's, his own, and my safety.

Thus was I preserved, but I hope not reserved as a subject for Divine Vengeance to work on. Had I then died, no other guilt could have rendered me culpable before God's tribunal but what was derivative from Adam. But since, the concatenation of sins hath encompassed the whole series of my life. Now, to the intent I may deter others from perpetrating the like, and receive to myself absolution (according as it is promised) upon unfeigned repentance and ingenuous confession of my nefarious facts, I shall give the readers a summary relation of my life, from my nonage to the meridian of my days, hoping that my extravagancies and youthful exiliences have, in that state of life, their declination and period.

CHAPTER II

A short account of the general insurrections of the Irish, Anno 1641

BUT though the mercy of these inhuman villains extended to the saving of our lives, yet they had so little consideration and commiseration as to expose our bodies by stripping us stark naked to the extremity of a cold winter night, not so much as sparing my tender age. Thus, without shoes or stockings, or the least rag to cover our nakedness, with the help of our guide, we travelled all night through woods as obscure as that black darkness that then environed our horizon. By break of day we were at Belfast. About entering the skirts of the town, this honest and grateful servant (which is much in an Irishman), being then assured of our safety, took his leave of us, and returned to the rebels.

Here were we received with much pity of all, and entertained, and clothed and fed by some charitable minded persons. To gratify their souls for what they had done for my mother's body, and those that belonged to her, my father frequently preached, which gave general satisfaction, and continued thus in instructing his hearers till the sark or surplice was adjudged by a Scottish faction, to be the absolute smock of the Whore of Babylon. Then was he constrained to flee again to Linsegarvy taking his charge with him.

Before I proceed, give me leave to digress a little in giving you a brief account of the Irish Rebellion. Not two years before it broke out, all those ancient animosities, grudges, and hatred which the Irish had ever been observed to bare unto the English seemed to be deposited and buried in a firm conglutination of their affections, and national obligations, which passed between them ; for these two had lived together forty years in peace, with such great security and comfort that it had, in a manner, consolidated them into one body, knit and compacted together with all those ligatures of friendship, alliance, and consanguinity as might make up a constant and everlasting union betwixt them there. Their intermarriages were near upon as frequent as their gossipings and fosterings (relations of much dearness among the Irish), together with all tenancies, neighbourhoods and services interchangeably passed among them. Nay, they had made, as it were, a mutual transmigration into each others' manners, many English being strongly degenerated into Irish affections and customs, and many of the better sort of Irish studying as well the language of the English as delighting to be apparelled like them. Nay, so great an advantage did they find by the English commerce and cohabitation, in the profits and high improvements of their lands, that Sir Phelim O'Neal, that rebellious ringleader, with divers others eminent in that bloody insurrection, had not long before turned off their lands their Irish tenants, admitting English in their rooms ; who are able to give far greater rents, and more certainly pay the same. So, as all those circumstances duly weighed and considered with the great increase of trade, and many other evident symptoms of a flourishing commonwealth, it was believed, even by the wisest and most experienced in the affairs of Ireland, that the peace and tranquillity of that Kingdom was fully settled, and most likely, in all human proba- bility, to continue, especially under the government of such a King as Charles the First, whom after ages may admire, but never match. Such was the serenity and security of this Kingdom that there appeared not anywhere any martial preparations, nor relics of any kind of disorders, no nor so much as the least noise of war whisperingly carried to any ear in all this land.

Now, whilst in this great calm, the British continued in the deepest security, whilst all men sat pleasantly enjoying the fruits of their own labours, sitting under their own vines, without the least thoughts or apprehension of tumults, troubles, or massacres, there brake out on October the twenty-third, in the year of our Lord, sixteen hundred forty and one, a most desperate, direful, and formidable Rebellion, a universal defection and revolt, wherein not only the mere native Irish, but almost all those English that profess the name of Roman Catholics, were totally involved.

Now, since it is resolved by me to give you a particular account of the most remarkable transactions and passages of my life, it will be also necessary to acquaint you with the beginning and first motions. Neither shall I omit to trace the progress of this Rebellion, since therein I shall relate summarily my suffering and what others underwent, the horrid cruelties of the Irish, and the abominable murders committed, as well without number as without mercy, upon the English inhabitants of both sexes, and all ages.

It was carried with such secrecy that none understood the con- spiracy till the very evening that immediately preceded the night of its general execution. I must confess there was some such thing more than suspected by one Sir William Cole, who sent away letters to the Lord Chief Justices, but miscarried by the way. Owen O'Conally (though Irish, yet notwithstanding a Protestant) was the first discoverer of this general insurrection giving in the names of some of the chief conspirators. Hereupon the lords convened and sat in Council, whose care and prudence at that time was such that some of the ringleaders were instantly seized, and upon examination, confessed that on that very day of their surprizal all the ports and places of strength in Ireland, would be taken ; that a considerable number of gentlemen and others, twenty out of each county, were come up expressly to surprize the Castle of Dublin ; adding further, that what was to be done in the country could neither by the wit of man or by letter be prevented. Hereupon a strict search was made for all strangers lately come to town, and all horses were seized on whose owners could not give a good account of them. And notwithstanding, there was a proclamation dispersed through all Ireland giving notice of a horrid plot designed by Irish Papists, against English Protestants, intending thereby a discouragement to such of the conspirators as yet had not openly declared themselves. Yet did they assemble in great number, principally in the North, in the Province of Ulster, taking many towns, as Newry, Drummoor, &c., burning, spoiling, and committing horrible murders everywhere. These things wrought such a general consternation and astonishment in the minds of the English that they thought themselves nowhere secure, flying from one danger into another.

In a very short time, the Irish Northern Papists by closely pursuing on their first plot, had gotten into their possession most of the towns, forts, castles, and gentlemen's houses within the counties of Tyrone, Donegal, Fermanagh, Armagh, Cavan, &c. The chief that appeared in the execution of this plot, within the Province of Ulster, were Sir Phelim O'Neal, Tourlough his brother, Rore Mac Guire, Phillip O'Rely, Sir Conne Mac Dennis, Mac Brian, and Mac Mahan. These combining with their accomplices dividing their Forces, and according to a general assignation, surprized the Forts of Dongannon and Montjoy, Carlemant, with other places of considerable strength. Now began a deep tragedy. The English having few other than Irish landlords, tenants, servants, neighbours, or familiar friends, as soon as this fire brake out, and the whole country was in a general conflagration, made their recourse to some of these, relying upon them for protection and preservation, and with great confidence trusted their lives and all their concerns in their power. But many of these in short time after, either betrayed them to others, or destroyed them with their own hands. The Popish priests had so charged and laid such bloody impressions on them, as it was held according to the Doctrine they had received, a deadly sin to give an English Protestant any relief.

All bonds of faith and friendship now fractured, Irish landlords now preyed on their English tenants ; Irish tenants and servants made a sacrifice of their English landlords and masters, one neighbour murdering another ; nay, 'twas looked on as an act meritorious in him that could either subvert or supplant an Englishman. The very children imitated the cruelty of their parents, of which I shall carry a mark with me to my grave, given me with a skene by one of my Irish playfellows. It was now high time to fly, although we knew not whither ; every place we arrived at we thought least secure, wherefore our motion was continual ; and that which heightened our misery was our frequent stripping thrice a day, and in such a dismal stormy tempestuous season as the memory of man had never observed to continue so long together. The terror of the Irish and Scotch incomparably prevailed beyond the rage of the sea, so that we were resolved to use all possible means to get on ship-board. At Belfast we accomplished our desires, committing ourselves to the more merciful waves.

This relation being so short, cannot but be very imperfect, if I dare credit my mother it is not stained with falsehood. Many horrid things, I confess, I purposely omitted, as desiring to waive any thing of aggravation, or which might occasion the least animosity between two nations, though of several languages, yet I hope both united in the demonstration of their constant loyalty to their sovereign, Charles the Second.

CHAPTER III

After his arrival in Devonshire, *he briefly recounts what waggeries he committed, being but a child*

BEING about five years of age, report rendered me a very beautiful child, neither did it (as most commonly) prove a liar ; being enriched with all the good properties of an handsome face, had not pride in my tender age deprived me of those graces and choice ornaments which complete both form and feature. Thus it happened my father kept commonly many turkeys ; one amongst the rest could not endure the sight of a red coat, which I usually wore. But that which most of all exasperated my budding passion was his assaulting my bread and butter, and instead thereof, sometimes my hands. Which caused my bloomy revenge to use this stratagem : I enticed him with a piece of custard (which I temptingly shewed him, not without some suspicion of danger which fear suggested might attend my treachery) and so led him to the orchard gate, which was made to shut with a pulley. He reaching in his head after me, I immediately clapped fast the gate, and so surprized my mortal foe. Then did I use that little strength I had to beat his brains out with my cat-stick ; which being done, I deplumed his tail, sticking those feathers in my bonnet as the insulting trophies of my first and latest conquest. Such, then, was my pride, that I nothing but gazed up at them, which so tried the weakness of mine eyes and so ſtrained the optic nerves that they ran atilt at one another, as if they contended to share with me in my victory. This accident was no small trouble to my mother, that so doted on me that I have often heard her say she forgot to eat (when I sate at table) for admiring the sweetness of my complexion. After she had much grieved herself to little purpose, she consulted with patience, and applied herself to skilful occuliſts, to repair the loss this face-blemishing had done so sweet a countenance, though for the present it eclipsed my mother's glory and pride. Yet time and art reduced my eyes to their proper ſtation, so that within six years their oblique aspects were hardly discernible. When I was about ten years old, I have heard some say that this caſt of my eyes was so far from being a detriment that it became my ornament. Experience confirmed me in this belief ; for they proved as powerful as the persuasive arguments of my deluding tongue, both which conjoined were sufficient (I speak it not vaingloriously) to prevail even over the Goddess of Chaſtity, especially when they were backed with ardent desires and an undaunted resolution.

But to my purpose. Being driven out of Ireland, there being at that time no place of safety in that Kingdom, my mother taking me with her (being compelled to leave my father behind, barbarously murdered by the Rebels for being a Proteſtant preacher), adventured to sea not caring whither she went. Foulness of weather drove us upon the coaſt of France, where we were forced to land, to repair what damage the ship had sustained in ſtress of weather. From hence we set sail, and landed in the Weſt of England, at a place called Barnſtable in the County of Devon. Here we were joyfully received and well entertained by some of my mother's kindred, at firſt. But lying upon them, they at length grew weary, so that we were forced to go from thence to Plymouth, so called from the River Plym, unto which the town adjoineth. At that time it was ſtrongly fortified by new raised works, a line being caſt about it, besides places of ſtrength anciently built, as the Caſtle, the Fort, of an hundred pieces of ordnance, that commands Cat-water, and overlooks the Sound ; Mount Batten, and the islands in the Sound, well furnished with men and great guns impregnable. Had they been never built or demolished as soon as raised on their basis, it had been much better than to have proved the fomenters of rebellion in the late wars for a whole year, daily thundering treason againſt their lawful sovereign.

We being here altogether unacquainted both with the people and their profession, my mother having an active brain, caſt about with herself how she should provide for her charge, but found no way more expedient than the pretention of Religion. Zeal and piety were the only things she seemed to prosecute, taking the literal sense of the text ; Without doubt Godliness is great gain : but she erred much in the profession and seasonable practice thereof, hers being according to the true Church, the Church of England, whereas the Plymotheans were at that time heterodox thereunto and led away, as the rest of their brethren called Roundheads, by the spirit of delusion. Finding how much she was mistaken, she changed quickly her note and coat ; being a rigid Presbyterian at first, but that proving not so profitable, instantly transformed herself into a strict Independent. This took well, which made her stick close to the brethren, which raised their spirits to make frequent contribution in private to supply her want. Here we had borrowed so much of the sisterhood, who vilely suspected my mother to be too dearly beloved by the brotherhood, that it was high time to rub off to another place, lest staying longer, the holy mask of dissimulation should fall off ; and she being detected be shamefully excluded their congregation, and so delivered up to be buffeted by Satan. Before I leave the town, give me leave to take a short view thereof. Formerly it was a poor small fishing village, but now so large and thronged with inhabitants (many whereof very wealthy merchants) that as it may be compared with, so may it put in its claim for the name of a city. Havens there are many so commodious, that without striking sail, they admit into the bosom thereof the tallest ships that be, harbouring them very safely, and excellently well fortified against hostility. It is situate alike for profit and pleasure ; in brief, it wants little that the heart of man would enjoy, from the various productions of the whole universe.

Now farewell Plymouth. No matter whither we went, for where ever we came we found still some or other that gave us entertainment for those good parts they found in my mother, she being very well read both in divinity and history ; and having an eloquent tongue, she commonly applied herself to the minister of the town, who, wondering to see so much learning and perfection in a woman, either took us to his own house for a while or gathered some contributions to supply our present necessities, with which we travelled to the next town. And in this manner we strolled or wandered up and down, being little better than mendicant itinerants. Staying so little time in a place, and my mother being more careful to get a subsistence than to season my tender years with the knowledge of letters, I was ten years old before I could read. Travelling through many towns unfit for our purpose, we at last took our seat for a while at Bridport in Dorsetshire. Here being ashamed to go to school in this ignorance, I applied myself to my mother, who taught me to apprehend the alphabet in less hours than there are letters ; so that in a short time, I could read distinctly, and was immediately introduced into the Grammar School, where I had not been long before I became a book-worm, securing as many as lay in my way, if convenient privacy served. And to the intent that my thefts might pass undiscovered before I would vend what book I had stolen, I usually metamorphosed them. If new, I would gash their skin, and if the leaves were red, I would make them look pale with the wounds they received; if much used, tear out all the remarks, and paint their old faces, and having so done, make sale of them. This course I followed a long time undiscovered, which cost many a boy a whipping at home by their parents, as well as master. I had various uses for the money I made thereof (you must think) but principally to bribe some of the upper form to make my exercises, which were so well liked by my master that I still came off with applause; and in a short time so advanced that I was next to the highest form, when I understood not the lowest author we read.

I was forced to employ my wits in the management of my hands, to keep touch with my pensioners, lest they failing me for want of encouragement, my master should discover how much my dunceship was abused. Frequent were my truantings, which were always attended with some notorious act, besides small faults as robbing of orchards, pulling the first and seconds of forty or fifty geese at a time, milking the cows or goats into my hat, and so drink the milk. And then for poultry, there was seldom a day escaped wherein I had not more or less. Usually I took them thus: at night I haunted the hen-roosts, taking them off so quietly from what they stood on, that their keckling noise seldom alarmed the rest. If I could not conveniently carry them off, I made their eggs compound for their heads. If I met with any geese at any time, then out came my short stick with a string fastened to a bullet, and tied to the end thereof; with this would I fetch in my game by the neck, the weight of the bullet twirling the string so many times about the neck that they could not disengage themselves from inevitable destruction. I used to fish for ducks, baiting my hook with a gut or some such trash, and laying it on a piece of cork, that swimming it might be the sooner perceived; I could catch in a short time as many as I pleased. Nay, I have not only thus deceived the tame fowl, but the same way, with a longer time, I have caught gulls and other sea-birds.

What I had gotten by these cunning and so much to be approved tricks, I carried to a house that encouraged me in my roguery, participating of the cheer, and so feasting me for my pains. If I had stolen anything, I had my recourse to them, who would give me twopence for what was worth a shilling, and render me good content. I knew my punishment for my rambling and valued it not; therefore little hope of reformation from thence. Nay, for very small faults I wished to be whipped, knowing the rod would then be laid on gently, which carried with it a tickling pleasure. As for my thefts and rogueries abroad, I was careful they should not be discovered. If any boy had injured me whose strength exceeded mine, so that I durst not cope with him, I would exercise my revenge upon him privately, concealing the resentment of the injury he did me. For to grin and not bite doth but persuade an adversary to knock out those teeth that may prove some time or other injurious. One common trick I had, was to stick a pin on the board whereon he was to sit ; in this manner did I serve several, in which fact I was at last taken. The punishment my master inflicted on me was to sit by his desk alone and complete a copy of verses ; there was great likelihood I should perform my task, when I knew not how many feet an hexameter required, and yet I then read Virgil. However, some thing I must attempt, and thinking Sapphics and Iambics too difficult, I ventured upon Heroics, supposing them the easier composition. But Lord, into what an access of laughter did my master fall, when he perused my hobbling strains. ' Surely,' said he, ' these verses are running a race altogether ; the first did not start fairly, or else is a very nimble gentle-man, for he hath outrun all his fellows four feet, the second comes two foot short of him, yet too forward for a true pace. Here is another lame in a foot, and halts most scurvily ; here is another whose quantity is short, and hath gotten upon stilts to seem long, and one (in contra-diction to him) which is long, because he will be short hath cut his own legs off.'

With these and the like speeches did he please himself in his own wit (which I understood but little), and after he had tired himself and me too, with prodigal talk he then spake to me in a harder dialect, making me understand how ignorant I was, and how much precious time irrecover-ably I had lost, which so much seized on my spirits that I was much grieved and troubled, so that he made vermilion tears run down my cheeks. After he had bestowed so much correction as he thought might work in me penitence for my egregious truanting he degraded me, and made me begin anew. The shame whereof and reproach I daily received from my schoolfellows, I could not bear ; wherefore I prevailed on my mother's indulgence to let me regain at home what I had lost, which she consented to. But perceiving my lecherous inclinations by my night practices with her maid, she resolved to send me to a board-ing school. For our family being but small, I lay with the maid ; being so young my mother did not in the least suspect me ; but my too forward lechery would not let me lie quiet, putting her frequently to the squeak.

In fine, I was sent away a great distance to a very severe and rigid master. I no sooner commenced scholar to this tyrant pedagogue but

I was kept close to my book, and lest my wit should be any ways dulled, my stomach was always kept sharp ; which quickened my invention to supply what was deficient. There is no complaint so insufferable as the grumbling of empty and dissatisfied guts. My greatest care was to insinuate myself into the favour of the servant maids, knowing they loved to play at a small game rather than stick out. I performed my business so well that my stomach was always satiated when the rest of the boarders were dissatisfied, often going to bed, in a manner, supperless. Here I was deprived of my old pilfering way, because I had no convenience for the disposal of what I stole, it being but a very small village. However, to keep my hand in use, I daily practised on fruit. Sometimes with a spar sharpened at one end, I picked apples out of baskets ; other times I took with me a comrade, and then thus would we do. I would go to the fruiterer and bargain with him for a pennyworth or more of apples, receiving them into my hat, pretending to draw my money out, I did clap my hat between my legs my partner perceiving that (as we had afore plotted it would be) behind, snatched it through my legs and ran away with it, I thereupon did use to roar out as if I had been undone, and pretending to run after him to regain my hat, we got out of sight and then shared the booty.

One time, coming along the market, I saw a small basket of cherries. I demanded of the woman that sold them what she would have for as many as I could take up in my hand ; she looking upon it and seeing it was but a very small one ; proportionable to my stature, ' twopence,' said she. With that I laid her down her price, and took up basket and all the cherries therein contained, and at a sober pace carried them away. The woman, amazed that she should be thus surprized by such a younker, followed me, and making a great noise, gathered a conflux of people about us, and among the rest a gentleman of quality, who was very earnest to know what the matter was. Holding my purchase fast in my hands (for nothing could persuade me to let go that booty I had so fair obtained) I desired the gentleman that he would be judge of my cause ; whereupon I related to him in what manner I bargained with the woman, and that I had done nothing unjustly, but what was according to our contract. The gentleman wondering at the pregnancy of wit in so tender an age, laughed heartily, and condemned the cherries for my own proper use, but withal paid the woman for them. I was naturally so prone to please my senses that I cared not what course I took that I might obtain my desires. I applied myself more to my wit and invention than I should have done had I had anything allowed me from a friend for a moderate expense.

But my mother thought otherwise, knowing by infallible symptoms the extravagantness of my inclinations, and therefore debarred me, as much as she could, the very sight of money. A river confined within some made bank, deterring its natural course, will (when that is overthrown which impeded its progress) flow with the greater impetuosity. Youth may for a while be circumscribed as to its desires, but if his inclination prompt him to the enjoyment of sensual delights, sooner or later he will taſte their relish, and better early than late. Before the noon of his days approach experience may reform his life and conversation though from the dawning morning thereof till the meridian his aċtions have been nothing else but the extraċt of all manner of debauchery. But as is commonly observed, that man which in the declination of his age tracks the bypaths of vice and licentiousness seldom desiſts till death cuts off his passage ; never leaving off doting on such false and imaginary pleasures, till the grim pale-faced messenger takes him napping. Thus much by way of digression.

Our maſter was very ancient, however resolved that his age should not hinder his teaching ; for if he found himself indisposed, he would send for us all into his bed-chamber, inſtruċting us there. A man of so ſtrange a temper, he delighted to invert the course of nature, lying in bed by day, and walking in the night, the rain seldom deterring him. On a time above the reſt, a gentleman had sent his son five pieces of gold to give his maſter for diet, &c. Our maſter receiving them, called for a small cabinet that ſtood in the room, which I (more officious than the reſt) brought him. Having put in the gold, he commanded me to carry it from whence I had it : which I did, well considering the weight thereof, being, though small, very heavy. The Devil presently became my tutor, suggeſting to my thoughts various ways for the gaining this money. At laſt I resolved to take the impression of the key in wax : which with much difficulty I obtained, and carried it to a smith four miles diſtant. The old fellow immediately upon my proposal suspeċted me (doubtless he was acquainted with such kind of devices), and queſtioning me what I intended thereby, I was forced to betake myself to my legs for safety, not knowing what answer to make him. The smith seeing me run, thinking to benefit himself by apprehending me, pursued after, with a red hot iron in his hand which his haſte had made him forget to lay aside. One ſtanding by me (juſt as the smith had almoſt overtaken me), seeing him come running with a hot iron in his hand, and fearing leſt his blind passion might prompt him to mischief me, ſtruck up his heels. In the fall he gave himself a burnt mark in the hand which no doubt he had long ago deserved ; my unknown friend would not suffer him to rise till I was out of sight.

My firſt ſtratagem not suiting with my purpose, I tried a picklock

c

of mine own invention, but that would not effect my design neither ; so
that I concluded to take cabinet and all. And in order thereunto
watched my opportunity when he should walk abroad according to his
custom at night. It was not long ere I enjoyed my wishes. My master's
custom was to walk abroad at nights, and sleep in the daytime, inverting
the course of Nature. Foreknowing his intention, I got into the chamber
and concealed myself under the bed ; so finding my way clear, I conveyed myself and purchase[1] out of the house ; and travelled all night.
In the morning I found myself near a small town, about sixteen miles
distant from the place whence I came. Thinking myself now secure, I
thought it very requisite here to repose my wearied limbs and solace
myself with the sight of what I had gotten ; but it was not long after
that I was so laced for it that, comparatively to my punishment, Bridewell
whipping is but a pastime. The first bush [inn] I came at I went in and
called for sack, having never tasted any, and hearing much talk thereof.
The people of the house much admired that so small an urchin as I
should call for such costly liquor ; they viewed me very attentively,
but more especially the cabinet, which caused them to suspect me. The
master of the house was acquainted herewith, who, as the Devil would
have it, was a Puritan, and a constable too, officious and severe. Without
craving pardon for his bold intrusion, he desired me I would admit
him into my boyship's society. I confess his gray hairs and sour countenance made me at first sight very much fear what the event of his visit
would prove. However, with a seeming undauntedness, I drank to him,
but what a difference of taste there was in that and the first glass I drank
solus ! At length he came to ask me divers questions, Whence I came ?
Whither I was going ? What was contained within that cascanet ? and the
like. Before I could give the resolution of what they demanded, the
Hue and Cry overtook me ; I was laid hold on, and my treasure taken
from me. That which vexed me as much as my surprizal was, I had no
further time to try what kind of taste the sack had. Various were the
talk of the people, every one spending his verdict on me. ' This is a prime
young rogue indeed, to begin thus soon,' said one, ' could he have seen,
when in his mother's belly, surely he would have stolen something
thence! ' Another said, Forward fruit was soon rotten, and since I began
to steal whilst a child, I should be hanged before I should write Man.
Ready to die with fear, I was sent back to the place whence I came and
from thence to the place of execution, had not the tenderness of my age,
and fewness of years procured pity from my injured master. Confined
I was within his house, locked up close prisoner in a chamber till that he

---

[1] The word ' purchase ' is here used with its signification of booty or plunder ; *pour
chasser*, chase for.

could acquaint my mother with what had passed. In this time I was not debarred of my suſtenance though my commons were epitomized, neither was I altogether deprived of society, for I was daily visited by my maſter, attended with a cat-of-nine-tails (as he called it), being so many small cords, with which he flayed my buttocks ; and when he found me ſtubborn, or not penitent enough as he thought, after he had skinned my podex, he would wash it with vinegar, or water and salt.

Within a week my mother arrived, who hearing of my rogueries, was so impatient that she would needs take me to task herself. But when she had untrussed me, and saw me in so woeful a plight, my shirt being as ſtiff as buckram with blood and my tender breech ploughed and harrowed, she fell down as if she had been about to expire. Recovering, my maſter endeavoured to satisfy her, by telling her that great offences required great punishments, and the way to bend an oak is to do it whilſt it is young. ' I had once when young,' said he, ' a spaniel which would find out the hens' neſt, and breaking the eggs suck them, so that we could never have any chickens. At laſt discovering who was the male-factor ; I bethought myself of this punishment which should hinder him for ever doing the like. I got an egg roaſted so hard till the shell was ready to burn, then did I firſt shew the egg to the dog, and then clapt it hot into his mouth holding his jaws close. This so tormented him by burning, that ever after he could not endure the sight thereof, but if shown, ran away crying as if he had been beaten. Thus, for the notorious faƈt your son muſt be so sharply chaſtised that when he thinks of ſtealing he shall remember those torments he once endured for it, and so frighten him from executing any such crime.'

Many more arguments he alleged to that purpose, which had satis-fied her well in his severity, had not natural affeƈtion interposed. What to do with me she knew not ; wherefore she consulted with my maſter, who told her, he durſt not keep me longer, the country people bringing in daily complaints againſt me. And to aggravate my mother the more, he briefly summed up my faults in this manner ; having had juſtly various accusers who drew up my indiƈtment, Thus.

Imprimis, That one of his maids having crossed me, to be revenged of her (knowing she was a drowsy wench, when asleep, not easily waked) as she slept by the fire I took my opportunity to melt some glue, and gently touched the closure of both her eyelids with a pencil, which well I knew would lock up her sight. Againſt the time I intended to wake her I placed all about her chairs and ſtools. The plot being ripe, I pre-tended her mistress called. The wench ſtarting up running and rubbing of her eyes turned topsy turvy over the chairs, getting up she engaged herself with the ſtools and so entangled herself therein that, endeavouring

to free herself, her coats acted the parts of traitors in discovering the
hidden secrets and arcanas belonging to her sex, and that with much
satisfaction I had seen the execution of my revenge.   That this wench
could not be persuaded but that as a judgment she was stricken blind
for some sin she had committed privately, which then her conscience
did whisper in her ear ; and undoubtedly had turned lunatic had she
not been speedily restored to her sight by taking off the glue, which was
done with much difficulty.   That he, going about to correct me for this
unlucky and mischievous fact, was by me shown a very shitten trick,
which put him into a stinking condition, for having made myself laxative
on purpose I squirted into his face upon the first lash given.   That being
upon boys' backs, ready to be whipped, I had often bit holes in their
ears.   That another time sirreverencing in a paper, and running to the
window with it, which looked out into the yard, my aged mistress
looking up to see who opened the casement, I had like to have thrown
it into her mouth ; however for a time deprived her of that little sight
she had left.   That another time I had watched some lusty young girls,
that used in summer nights about twelve o'clock to wash themselves
in a small brook near adjacent, and that I had concealed myself behind
a bush, and when they were stripped, took away their clothes, making
them dance home after me stark naked to the view of their sweethearts
whom I had planted in a place appointed for that purpose, having given
them before notice of my design.

A great many more such tricks he recounted which he knew, but not
the tenth of what he knew not.   As for example, on Christmas Day,
we had a pot of plum-broth.   I asked the maid to give me a taste to see
how I liked them, ' Ay that I should,' she said (this was the maid I had so
served before with glue) and with that takes up a ladle full and bid me
sup, she holding the ladle in her own hand.   I imprudently opening my
mouth somewhat larger than I should she poured down the scalding
pottage through my throat : at present I could not tell the jade (that
laughed till she held her sides) how I liked them ; but I verily believed
I had swallowed the Gunpowder Plot, expecting every moment to be
blown up.   I took as little notice of this passage as possibly I could, resolving to retaliate her kindness when she least thought on't.   I observed
the maid to carry this plum-pottage pot into the yard, and taking notice
that the weight of the jack was in the same yard, wound up a great height
under a small pent-house, the jack being down I suddenly removed the
weight, and fastened the pot to the line, so going into the kitchin,
wound it up to the top, and then stopped it, for the meat was taken up.
The house was all in an uproar instantly about the pot, every one wondering what should become of it.   The maid averred that she saw it even

now, and none could remove it but the Devil. Others asserted (which were infected with Puritanism) that it was a judgment shown for the superstitious observation of that festival day. But the next day, roasting meat, this seeming miracle vanished by the descending of the pot fastened to the jack-line. Another time my master had reserved in his garden some choice apricots, not above an half-score ; which he purposed for some friends that intended to visit him shortly. The daily sight of this delicate fruit, being forbidden, tempted me more strongly to attempt their rape ; but I made choice of an impropitious hour to accomplish my design in ; for my master looked out of his window and saw me gather them, though he knew not absolutely whether it was I or no. Whereupon he instantly summoned us together, being met, I quickly understood his intention : therefore I conveyed the apricots into the next boy's pocket. I had no sooner done it, but we were commanded to be searched ; I was very forward to be the first, though I was most suspected, but none was found about me, so that I was acquitted. But to see with what amazement the poor boy gazed, when they were discovered about him, how strangely he looked, distorting his face into several forms, produced laughter even from my incensed master, but real pity from me, for he was severely whipped for that crime I myself committed. I could recite many more suchlike childish rogueries, did I not fear I should be tedious in their relation, and burden the reader with juvenile follies ; wherefore I shall return where I left off. Whilst my mother was in a serious consultation with her reason how she should dispose of me, I had not patience to wait the result, but gave her the slip, resolved to run the risk of Fortune, and try whether mine own endeavours would supply my necessities.

CHAPTER IV

How he ran from his mother, and what courses he steered in one whole year's ramble

IT was in August when I undertook this my knight-errantry ; the fairness of the season much favoured my enterprize. Thinking I should always enjoy such weather, and never be pinched with necessity, I went on very courageously. The first dinner I made was on blackberries and nuts, esteemed by me very delicious fare at first, which delighted me so much the more having not my liberty controlled. When night approached it seemed very uncouth and strange finding instead of

a featherbed no other thing to lie on but a haycock, and no other coverlid
but the canopy of heaven. But considering with myself that I had no
task to con over-night, nor fear of over-sleeping myself next morning,
and so be fetched to school by a guard of my fellow scholars with a lanthorn and candle, though the Sun appeared at that time in his full lustre,
I laid myself down and slept profoundly, not without some affrighting
dreams. The last was of the cat-of-nine-tails, which my master laid so
home methought that the smart thereof made me cry out, and so I
awaked. As then the early lark, the winged herald of the morning, had
not with her pretty warbling notes summoned the bright watchmen of
the night to prepare for a retreat, neither had Aurora opened the ver-
million Oriental gate to make room for Sol's radiant beams, to dissipate
that gloomy darkness that had muffled up our hemisphere in obscurity.
In the morning I went on in my progress as the day before ; then began
a shower of tears to fall from my eyes, considering how I had left my
disconsolate, and almost heart-broken mother, lamenting my loss, and
fearing what fatal courses I might take. It was no less trouble to me to
think that I was travelling I knew not whither, moneyless, having
nothing but hazel and brambles to address myself for the appeasing of
hunger's approaching gripes. Now, methought I began to loath my
aforenamed manna, blackberries, nuts, crabs, bullies, &c., and longed
to taste of the flesh-pots again ; but the Devil a bit could I get but what
the hedges afforded me.

All day I thus wandered about, not daring to come near any town,
having had such bad success in the last when I first rambled ; and now
night came on, which put me in mind of procuring a lodging somewhat
warmer than the other. A barn presently offered itself to my sight,
which I accosted, and without delay or fear, entered into the enchanted
castle, where I found accommodation for the most faithful and valiant
knight that ere strode saddle for ladies' sake. Here might I take my
choice of variety of fresh straw, but my weariness would not permit to
complement my good fortune one jot, and I so tumbled over head and
ears. I had not lain there above an hour before I heard a noise, and
peeping out of the straw, being in a great fear, I saw a many strange
creatures come into the barn, for the day was not yet shut in. My
thoughts presently reminded me that I had heard talk of hobgoblins,
fairies and the like, and judged these no other ; and that which confirmed me in this belief was their garb and talking to one another in a
language I understood not (but since, I understand it to be Canting),
I lay still as long as my fear would permit me, but they surrounding me,
I was not able to contain myself longer, but cried out aloud, ' Great
God, have mercy on me, and let not these Devils devour me,' and with

that, started out from among them. They, amazed as much as I, ran for it too, leaving their children behind them, every one esteeming him the happiest man which was the foremost. I looking behind me, seeing them following me, imagined these Devils ran upon all four, and having started their game were resolved to hunt a sinful leveret to death. Concluding them long-winded hellhounds, I judged praying a safer way than flying, and so fell instantly on my knees.

The Gypsies quickly overtook me, and finding me in that posture, soon understood whence their fear proceeded. They then spoke to me in a language I understood, bidding me not be afraid ; but I had heard the Devil was a liar from the beginning, therefore I would not believe them. They would have raised me from my devotion, telling me it was enough, and that made me suspect them the more ; thinking they designed to get me out of a praying posture, that they might have the more power of me. Nothing prevailing with me, they vowed and protested they would not injure me in the least, and if I would go along with them, I should share as deliciously as they did. This was a potent argument to persuasion, and so I agreed to go along with them back again. All their cry was now for Rum-booz (i.e. for good liquor). Their Captain, not enduring to hear so sad a complaint, and not endeavour the supplying the want complained of, immediately commanded out four able maunders (beggars), ordering them to stroll (wander) to the next town, every one going apart. Some countrymen gave them drink, fearing they might fire the houses in the night, out of revenge, others (of the more ignorant sort) thought they could command infernal spirits, and so harm them that way, or else bewitch their cattle, and therefore would not deny them : insomuch that in a short time these four returned laden with bub and food. It was placed in the middle of us, who sat circularly ; then out came the wooden dishes, everyone provided but myself, but I was soon supplied by a young Rum-Mort that sat next me, intended for my sporting mate. A health went round to the Prince of Maunders, another to the Great Duke of Clapperdogeons, a third to the Marquess of Doxy Dells, and Rum Morts, a fourth to the Earl of Clymes ; neither did we forget Haly, Abbas, Albumazar, Arcandam, with the rest of the waggoners that strive who shall be principal in driving Charles his Wain.

Most part of the night we spent in boozing, pecking rumly or wapping, that is drinking, eating, or whoring, according to those terms they use among themselves. Jealousy was a thing they never would admit of in their society, and to make appear how little they were tainted therewith, the males and females lay promiscuously together, it being free for any of the Fraternity to make choice of what doxy he liked best, changing when he pleased. They plied me so oft with their Rum-booz (as they called it) and pleased me so well in giving me a young girl to dally with. Though she was in rags, and with a skin artificially discoloured tawny, yet I was not so ignorant as not to understand good flesh, and what properties went to the completing a votaress for *Venus's* service. I was so tickled in my fancy with this pretty little wanton companion, that for her sake I was very well content to list myself one of that ragged regiment. And that which added to the inducing me to this resolution was my want of money, and what I suffered in those two foregoing hard days' fare among the nut trees. I first acquainted my doxy with my intent, who, glad to hear thereof, gave it vent, and broached it to the rest, who unanimously with joy embraced me ; and to gratify my inauguration tipped to each other a gage of booz, and so went round. The fumes of drink had now ascended into their brain, wherefore they couched a hogshead, and went to sleep.

CHAPTER V

Wherein he relates what manner of people they were in whose society he entered himself : division of their tribes, manners, customs, and language

AS soon as I had resolved to travel the country with them, they fitted me for their company by stripping me, and selling my proper garments, and clothing me in rags, which they pinned about me, giving a stitch here and there, according as necessity required. We used not when we entered our ' Libkin ' or lodging to pull off our clothes ; which had I been forced to do, I could never have put them on again, nor any, but such who were accustomed to produce order out of a Babel of rags. Being now *a le mode Tatterdemallion,* to complete me for their purpose, with green walnuts they so discoloured my face that everyone that saw me would have sworn I was the true son of an Egyptian. Before we marched on, let me give you an account of our leaders, and the ranks we were disposed in. Our chief commander was called by the name of *Ruffler,* the next to him *Upright-man,* the rest in order thus :

Hookers, (alias) Anglero	Priggs
Priggers of Prancers	Swaddlers
Pallyards	Curtals
Fraters	Irish toyle
Swigmen	Dommerars

Jarkemen	Glymmerers
Patri-Coes	Bawdy-Baskets
Kitchin-Coes	Autem-Morts
Abram men	Doxies
Whip-Jacks	Dells
Counterfeit-Cranks	Kitchin-Morts

We mustered above threescore, old and young, and because we were too great a company to march together, we were divided into three squadrons. The first squadron, that led the van, was ordered by our commander to stick up small boughs all the way they went, that we might know what course they steered. For, like wild fowl, we fly one after another, and though we are scattered like the quarters of a traitor, yet like water when cut with a sword, we easily came together again. As the Switzer hath his wench and his cock with him when he goes to wars : or like a Scotch Army, where every soldier almost hath the geud wife and the bearns following him ; so we had every one his doxy or wench, who carried at her back a Lullaby-cheat, and at may be another in her arms. When they are weary of carrying them, they take their turns to put them in a pair of panniers, like green geese going to market, or like fish in dossers coming from Rye. Where note, that each division hath a small horse or two, or else asses to ease them of their burdens.

Some of us were clad anticly with bells and other toys, merely to allure the country people unto us, which most commonly produced their desired effects. In some places they would flock unto us in great quantities, and then was our time to make our markets. We pretended an acquaintance with the stars (as having an alliance to the Egyptian Magi, the founders of astrologic art) and that the ministers of Fate were our familiars, and so possessing these poor ignorant people with a belief that we could tell their fortunes by inspection into either hands or faces. Whilst we were seriously looking thereon, one of our diving comrades picked their pockets, or with a short sharp knife, and a horn on the thumb 'nipped their bungs.' By asking the silly milkmaids questions, we gathered from their own mouths the properest resolutions ; then they would admire, and in their admiration tremble to hear the truth proceed from the mouth of such as were strangers to their actions, by which means, among some we gained a great respect, accompanied with fear. Did not astrologers make use of such stratagems, they could never acquire so much repute among the judicious, as well as vulgar capacities.

And because it falls in so pat to my present purpose, I shall beg so much patience from the reader as to give him a brief account of some fallacies some star-gazing impostors use to work their own ends, and delude credulous people. One I knew who raised his credit (and since

a considerable estate) upon the basis of good intelligence. He kept a
servant who constantly attended below for the reception of such who
came for satisfaction in the astrological resolution of questions. This
man's office was to tell the querent that his master was busy above,
about some grand concern, but if the person would be pleased to wait
a little while, till that business was dispatched he questioned not but that
his master would render him a satisfactory account of what he demanded,
adding farther (to infuse into him faith, to credit what he said) that though
report had spoken largely, (and yet nothing but what this artist hath
merited), yet all came far short of his real desert ; having done such
stupendous things that must needs, without injustice, be commemorized
to eternity, and admired by future ages. In the meantime, this servant
endeavoured to pump out of the proponent what he came about, which
being understood, he gave information to his master by so many times
ringing of a bell. This item being given, the querent is called up, and
before ever he can frame his mouth to propound his question, this profound artist prevents him, saying, ' I know what you come about, Sir ;
therefore save yourself the labour to tell me that which I know already.
You have lost a watch, a horse ; or you would know how you shall
prosper in such a business, whether marriage or an employment ' ; or
any such like common question. This makes the artist to be wondered
at ; and then erecting a scheme, positively and surely tells him what he
must expect, and that he may give answers more exactly concerning
stolen goods, he was in constant fee with thief-takers, who from time to
time made him a report of what persons were robbed, what the things
were, and many times gave him a description of the felon. By these
practices men believed every word he delivered to be an oracle ; so that
his chamber was daily so thronged with the report of people that in a
short time his ambition pricked him on to purchases with the money
he had gained thus fallaciously.

One story, very remarkable, I shall add, and then crave your pardon
for this my digression. One day a young gentleman (but of a mean
estate) who was more credulous than wise, and more inquisitive than
prudent, came to him, and having not that wealth which his prodigality
required, desired instructions what course he was best to steer to arrive
at the port of his wishes and hopes. Viewing him narrowly, he perceived
him to be a man of a sweet complexion, and a body well proportioned ;
and therefore judged him a fit subject for female fancies to work upon.
' Sir,' said he, ' I shall give you my best advice, but I shall crave your
patience for a little while ; for a matter of this weight must not pre-
cipitately be undertaken : wherefore, if you please to see me to-morrow,
what lies in me shall be at your service.' Being just gone it happened

that a stale maid, who had more money than beauty, and less discretion than lechery, came to be resolved of him, when she should be married : for it seems by the sequel she could tarry no longer. Viewing her well (though she knew not him), he knew her to be wealthy, and nearly related to persons of quality. ' Madam,' said he, ' I shall endeavour your satisfaction ' ; and so withdrew into his closet. Having stayed a while bringing out his figure, and with much gravity looking thereupon, he thus unriddled the mysterious meaning of the celestial bodies : ' Madam, you never was much troubled with the importunate suits of amorous visitants (this he gathered from the deformity of her physiognomy), they all knowing your indifferency to change your condition, but upon considerable grounds ; by which means you have almost frustrated what the stars have designed for you.' ' I hope it is but almost,' said she, ' not altogether ' (for it troubled her very much to hear she should leave the world without tasting the sweets of a married life). ' No,' he replied. ' For if to-morrow by four of the clock in the afternoon, you go into Moorfields, and take a turn or two in the usurers-walk, you shall there meet with a person rich and handsome, that at first sight shall fall extremely in love with you. Slight him not, neither deny him his conjugal proposal ; if you do, it will be too late to hope for an husband. You shall distinguish him from others by these signs : His complexion is fair, his eye sharp and piercing, his hair flaxen, and a middle stature.' Her joy had like to have transported her beyond the bounds of modesty, which she could not conceal, but made it appear in a pecuniary expression of her gratitude for such welcome tidings ; and so promising him to follow his counsel, she took her leave.

The next morning the young gallant came, who had his lesson given him : but before he went, he made him give a bond of 200l. to be paid upon the day of his marriage with that gentlewoman ; which he gladly consented to, and paid that very sum within ten days after, for according to the directions was given him, he met with that gentlewoman described to him, as he had been before to her, who at the first sight of each other was incapable of containing themselves, but mutually embraced (after three or four words passed) as if he had been her quondam dearly beloved, returned from some long voyage, and went not to their respective lodgings till their marriage was consummated. But to return where I left off.

Thus we rambled up and down the country ; and where the people demeaned themselves not civil to us by voluntary contributions, their geese, hens, pigs, or any such mandible thing we met with made us satisfaction for their hide-bound injuries. Our revenge most commonly was very bloody, and so merciless that whatever fell into our hands never escaped alive, and in our murders so cruel that nothing would satisfy us but the very hearts-blood, of what we killed. The usual sacrifices of our implacable revenge were innocent lambs, sheep, calves, &c., all which we handled more severely than prisoners are by serjeants, when they are not paid their unjuſt demands ; fees, I should have said, but that by experience I have found they walk not according to the rules of ancient conſtitutions, but are guided by the dictates of their insatiate wills, which is their law which poor prisoners muſt indulge (though they rack their slender credits, or pawn their clothes), or else they muſt expect less kindness from them than a condemned person about to be tied up by the hangman, who will ſtay till he is ready to be turned off. A goose coming among us, we have a trick to make him so wise as never to be a goose again. But let the wiseſt use what tricks they can, they never shall make some serjeants honeſt men. We seize the prey, and leave the tragical part to our ' morts ' or women to act. The ſtage on which they perform their parts, is either some large heath, or *furzebush-common*, far from any house. This being done, and night approaching, we repair to our dormitories, or houses of reſt, which are moſt usually out-barns of farmers and husbandmen, which we make choice of in some poor ſtraggling village who dare not deny us, for fear ere the morning they find their thatched houses too hot to hold them. These barns serve us inſtead of cook rooms, supping parlours, and bedchambers : having supped (moſt commonly in a plentiful manner), we cannot ' Couch a Hogshead,' that is to say, sleep, without good ſtore of ' Rum-booz,' that is, drink ; and having sufficiently warmed our brains with humming liquor, which our ' Lower ' (Silver) shall procure ; if our deceitful ' Maunding ' (Begging) cannot, we then sing a catch or two in our own language, of which we had good ſtore ; which for their bawdry I omit. However, give me leave to inſtance one canting song, and I shall waive the reſt, being loth to tire you too much with one thing.

> Bing out bien Morts, and toure, and toure,
>   Bing out bien Morts, and toure ;
> For all your Duds are bing'd awaſt
>   The bien Cove hath the loure.
> I met a Dell, I view'd her well,
>   She was benship to my watch ;
> So she and I did stall, and cloy,
>   Whatever we could catch.
> This Doxy Dell can cut bien whids,
>   And wap fell for a win ;
> And prig and cloy so benshiply,
>   All the Deusea-vile within.

The boyle was up, we had good luck,
    In frost for and in Snow :
When they did seek, then did we creep,
    And plant in Ruffe-mans low.
To strawling Ken the Mort bings then,
    To fetch loure for her cheats ;
Duds & Ruffe-peck, Rombold by Harman beck,
    And won by Maunders feats.
Ye Maunders all, stow what you stall,
    To Rome Coves what so quire,
And wapping Dell, that niggles well,
    And takes loure for her hire.
And Jybe well jerckt, teck rome confect,
    For back by glymmar to Maund ;
To mill each ken, let Cove bing then,
    Through Ruff-mans, jague, or Laund,
Till Crampings quire tip Cove his hire ;
    And Quire Ken do them catch,
A Canniken, mill quire Cuffin,
    So quire to ben Coves watch.
Bien Darkmans then, Bouse Mort and Ken,
    The bien Coves bings awast,
On Chates to trine by Rome Coves dine,
    For his long lib at last.
Bing out bien Morts and toure, and toure,
    Bing out of the Rome vile bine,
And toure the Cove that cloyd your duds,
    Vpon the Chates to trine.

Having even wearied ourselves with drinking and singing, we tumbled promiscuously together, male and female in straw, not confining ourselves to one constant consort, we made use of the first that came to hand ; by which means incests and adulteries became our pastimes. By this means I grew weary of their practices, and therefore resolved to desert them as soon as the first opportunity should offer itself, which was in a short time ; wherefore at the present I shall say no more of them, only give me leave to give some small account of their language.

The first inventor of canting, as I am informed, was hanged about four-score years since : such gibberish was never heard of before ; since which time there hath not been wanting such who have taken pains in the polishing, refining, and augmenting that language of the Devil's imps. It is a confused invention of words ; for its dialect I cannot find to be grounded on any certain rules ; and no wonder since the founders and practicers thereof are the chief fathers and nourishers of disorder. Yet even out of that irregularity a man may observe some kind of form, and some words do retain something of scholarship, as ' Togeman,' a gown, from *Toga* ; ' Pannam,' from *Panis*, bread ; ' Cosan,' *Caseus*, cheese. The monosyllable ' Cheat ' ; we use as a relative, as *Nab*, a head ; ' Nab-cheat,' a hat, &c. ' Cove ' or ' Cuffin ' is in general terms a man ; but by adding ' bien,' which signifies good or well, or ' Quire,' which is wicked or knavish, you make the word ' Cove ' signify an honest man, or a justice of peace. Pardon the expression, for they call a justice ' Quier Cuffin ' ; that is to say, as before mentioned, a wicked, knavish, or foolish man. To conclude, I shall here insert this little Canting Vocabulary alphabetically,

AUTEM Mort	A MARRIED woman
Abram	Naked
Abram Cove	A tatterdemallion
Autem	A church
Bughar	A cur
Bouse	Drink
Bousing Ken	An ale-house
Borde	A shilling
Boung	A purse
Bien	Good or well
Benshiply	Very well
Benar	Better
Bing	To go
Bing a waste	To go away
Bube	The pox
Bufe	A dog
Bleating cheat	A sheep
Belly cheat	An apron
Betty	An instrument to break a door
Bite the Peter or Roger	Steal the portmantle or cloak-bag
Budge	One that steals cloaks
Bulk and File	The Pickpocket and his mate
Cokir	A liar
Cove ⎫	
Cuffin ⎭	A man
Cuffin-Quire	A justice of peace
Cramprings	Bolt or shackles
Chats	The gallows
Canke	Dumb
Crackmans	Hedges
Calle ⎫	
Togeman ⎬	A cloak
Joseph ⎭	
Couch	To lie or sleep

Couch a Hogshead	To go to sleep
Commission } Mish	A shirt
Cackling cheat	A chicken
Cassan	Cheese
Crash	To kill
Crashing cheats	Teeth
Cloy	To steal
Cut	To speak
Cut bien whids	To speak well
Cut quire whids	To speak evilly
Confeck	Counterfeit
Cannakin	The plague
Cly the Jerk	To be whipped
Clapperdogeon	A beggar born
Culle	A sap-headed fellow
Dimber	Pretty
Damber	Rascal
Drawers	Stockings
Duds	Goods
Deusea-vile	The country
Dommerar	A madman
Darkmans	Night or evening
Doxy } Dell	A wench
Dock } Wap	To —— [lie with]
Deuswins	Twopence
Dup	To enter
Earnest	A part
Tip me my Earnest	Give me my part or share
Frummagem	Choked
Filch	A staff
Ferme	A hole
Fambles	Hands
Famble chears	Rings or gloves
Fib	To beat
Flag	A groat
Fogus	Tobacco or smoke
Fencing Cully	One that receives stolen goods
Glymmer	Fire
Glaziers	Eyes
Grannam	Corn
Gentry-Mort	A gallant wench
Gan	A lip
Gage	A pot or pipe

Grunting cheat	A sucking-pig
Giger	A door
Gybe	Any writing or pass
Glazyer	One that goes in at the windows
Gilt	A pick-lock
Harmanback	A constable
Harmans	The stocks
Heave a Booth	To rob an house
Half bord	Sixpence
Hearts ease	A twenty shilling piece
Jocky	A flail, or man's privities
Jague	A ditch
Jarke	A seal
Ken	An house
Kinchin	Little
Knapper of Knappers	A sheep-stealer
Kinchin Cove	A little man
Kate	A pick-lock
Loure	Money
Lightmans	Morning or day
Lib	To tumble
Libben	An house to lie in
Lage	Water
Libedge	A bed
Lullaby-cheat	A child
Lap	Pottage
Lurries	All manner of clothes
Maunder	To beg
Maunders	Beggars
Margery Prater	A hen
Mill	To steal
Make	A halfpenny
Mynt	Gold
Muffling cheat	A napkin
Mumpers	Genteel beggars
Milken	One that breaks houses
Munns	The face
Nab	A head
Nab-cheat	A hat
Nab	{ To take { Or cheat
Palliard	One whose father is a beggar born
Paplar	Milk-pottage
Prats	Thighs
Prigg	To ride
Peckidge	Meat

Pannam	Bread
Plant	To lay or hide
Prigging	Riding
Prancer	A horse
Pratting cheat	A tongue
Peake	Any lace
Pike on the Leen	Run as fast as you can
Perry	Fearful
Peter	A portmantua
Prigger of Prancers	A horse-stealer
Pad	The highwayman
Plant your whids	Have a care what you say
Quarron	A body
Quacking cheat	A duck
Quier	Wicked or roguish
Quier-Ken	A prison
Quier-Mort	A pocky jade
Quier-Cove	A rogue
Romboyle	A ward or watch
Rome	Gallant
Rome-vile	London
Rome-Mort	A gallant girl
Ruffin	The devil
Roger	A cloak-bag
Ridge-cully	A goldsmith
Ruffler	An over-grown rogue
Ruffe peck	Bacon
Rod-shanke	A mallard
Rom-pad	The highway
Rome-padders	Highwaymen
Rome-Culle	A rich coxcomb
Swagg	A shop
Sundge	One that lies under the bed to rob the house
Shop-lift	One that steals out of shops
Stampers	Shoes
Stock-drawers	Stockings
Stamps	Legs
Scoure	To wear
Skew	A dish
Slate	A sheet
Strommel	Straw or hair
Skepper	Barn
Stow your whids	Be wary
Stalling-Ken	Broker's house, or an house to receive stolen goods

D

Smelling cheat	A garden
Solomon	The Mass
Tour	To look out
Tout his muns	Look in his face
Track up the Dancers	Go up the ſtairs
The Cul Snylches	The man eyes you
Tip the Cole to Adam Tyler	Give what money you pocket-picked to the next party, presently
Tip the Mish	Give the shirt
Tib o' th' Buttery	Goose
Tip	To give
The Mort tipped me a wink	The whore gave me a wink
Trine	Tyburn
Trining	Hanging
Tick-Rome	A licence
Tres wins	Threepence
Win	A penny
Wicher Cully	A silver-smith
Yarum	Milk

This much for a taſte. I think it not worth my pains to insert all those canting words which are used; it is enough that I have here divulged what words are moſt in use.

Having now deserted this tawny crew, I resolved to betake myself to a new trade, which you shall underſtand in the following discourse.

CHAPTER VI

How he went a-begging : what rules he observed therein: what villainies he committed whilſt he professed that myſterious art

NECESSITY is a thing better known by the effeſts than its charaſter, and of all things the moſt insufferable; to prevent which, it puts a man on to venture upon all manner of dishoneſt and dangerous aſtions, suggeſting ſtrange imaginations, and desperate resolutions, soliciting things infamous, and attempting things impossible; the produſt of which is only disorder, confusion, shame, and in the end ruin. But when necessity shall conjoin with an evil disposition, a depraved nature, what horrid and nefarious faſts will it not inſtigate that man to perpetrate? And though he seeth monthly examples of persons condemned and executed for the like crimes he daily praſtiseth, will not

forbear nor desist from such irregular and life-destroying courses, till
they have brought him to the like miserable catastrophe. Necessity had
now deeply fallen in love with me, and the young virgin shame-facedness
(once my mistress) had forsaken me ; for as soon as I had pulled but one
thread out of her garment, all the rest unravelled, and she, not brooking
her nakedness, changed her master, and so totally left me.

Having now obtained more than a convenient boldness I travelled
and begged with very good success. But methought my life was somewhat uncomfortable without a companion (all creatures coveting society,
but more especially man), at length, according to my desires, I met with
one whose long practice in this art, besides the observations of his pre-
decessors, deriving his pedigree in a direct line from Prince Prig, endued
him with so much skill as to furnish me with the knowledge of anything
that belonged to the liberal art of begging. We straight betook ourselves
to the ' boozing ken ' ; and having ' bubbed rumly,' we concluded an
everlasting friendship. Then did he recount to me the most material
things observable in our profession. First, he tuned my voice to that
pitch which might most of all raise compassion ; next what form of
prayer I was to use upon such an occasion, what upon such, varying
according to the humour of those persons that I begged of, gathered
from their habit or gesture ; then he told me when we came to London
he would acquaint me what places were most fit for our purpose, and what
times ; that I ought not to be too importunate to some, always wishing
well, and loudly praying for the health and safety of estate and limbs
of such as denied me alms ; but more especially pronounce a ' God
bless you Master, and let Heaven reward what you have here done on
earth,' if anything is bestowed upon me ; if any should pity my nakedness, and clothe me in garments without holes in them, I should wear
them no longer than in the donor's sight, reserving my rags to re-invest
myself, and sell the other, as unfit and scandalous to our occupation ;
that we should never beg far from one another, and at nights faithfully
share the gains. Moreover, he informed me the way to make all sorts
of seeming sores and lameness ; that within the tattered rags, there be
places provided for private conveyance.

Some of maturer age, if they have no children, rent them of such as
have ; but we had no occasion for this fallacy. That if I saw a door
open, I should go in boldly ; if I met any in the way, I should then in a
very submissive manner implore their help in the assistance of my wants,
never desiring any thing but what was of small value, one half-penny,
farthing, or some broken crust (if at a door), pretending the not eating
of a bit in two days. If the passage was clear, whip away what was
nearest to hand. That the time of rising in the morning be very early,

shewing myself in the ſtreets ; for then will those that pass by judge I have no other lodging but what a ſtall affords, that way procuring relief from pitiful-minded persons, and so continue begging till the evening ; when it beginneth to be duskish, if any then walks singly, accoſt him in a begging form ; coming up so close, as that you may knock him down with a truncheon, ſtill carried about for that purpose ; which is done securely, and many times with a good booty.

Being full fraught with these, and many more precepts he delivered, we set forth on our progress. We had not gone far before we were surprized by the conſtable as two ſturdy vagrants, and as 'handsail' to my new trade, we were both soundly whipped out of town. To avoid this danger for the time to come, we missed all the towns of any considerable note in our way, and only frequented villages ; nay at laſt we were forced not only to avoid them but the highways too ; for travellers observing our garb, countenances, and weapon, which was a baton, suspecting us, would before they came near us, set spurs to their horses and ride as if the devil drove them. Many petty rogueries we performed by the way, not worthy the commemoration, and therefore I shall pass them over ; only this I shall insert.

Travelling the field-way, we ſtumbled on a tinker and his trull lying by an hedge-side. I knew not what to think at firſt, they lay so ſtill ; with much pulling and ſtirring then they awakened. I asked them what they lay there for ? They answered me, that they were lately bitten by a serpent near adjacent, a potent creature, mighty in ſtrength, and of a vaſt proportion, who had lately ſtung several as well as they. It seemed very ſtrange to us, especially having heard not the leaſt report hereof. To be short, I desired them to shew us the place of his residence, which they readily consented to. Inſtead of this venomous animal, they only brought us to its representation in a sign, where a cup of double-brewed beer was sold, notable humming gear. The people liked the tinker and his female comrade well enough, but would not admit of us, till we shewed them money ; for our veſtments looked like the gleanings of a rag-merchants yard. We drank ſtiffly till we laid the woman asleep again ; ſtill the tinker bore up ſtiffly. She had not slept long but up she ſtarted, pulled up her coats, and in our presence pissed in the middle of the room and so sat her self down, yet awaked not ; which action could not but produce much laughter from me and my comrade. At laſt the tinker fell asleep too, having added so much to his former burden that he was no longer able to ſtand under it. Now had my wits enough to work on ; but finding myself very drowsy, for the ſtrength of the drink had almoſt overpowered me, I was forced to advise with my friend what course I were beſt take to make me a little more sober. He was so well known in such matters (being an old experienced pitcher-man), that he quickly counselled me what to do, he himself being not in the least disturbed. This was his advice which he did put in practice, he got a pailful of water, and so taking me up by the heels, he clapped my head thereinto ; holding me in that manner so long that the pail had like to have proved the ferry-boat that should waft me over the Stygian Lake ; this so qualified the heat my head had contracted by my excessive drinking of that strong stupifying liquor, that I found it had wrought its desired effects.

After this, we ransacked their pockets, but found little in the man's ; but searching the woman in a private place between her pocket and placket, we discovered something considerable, which we took. Having so done, we thought it high time to be gone, but first we resolved to make some sport as well as take their moneys, which was thus. I tied to each of their girdles, behind, a flagon-pot, and to each a label affixed, or a paper of verses, and so immediately tripped off. The host seeing us go out of doors with more than ordinary speed, ran into the room where the tinker and his lady were ; he suddenly awaked them, telling them we were gone. Hearing this, they hastily started up, and reeling ran to overtake us. The master of the house seeing his pots dangling at their breech, ran after the tinker, crying, ' Stop'em, stop'em, Stop the thievish tinker, stop the whore with my pot.' We were wiser than to stay to hear how the tinker and his trull came off, or to hear the laughter that we undoubtedly raised by this waggish contrivance, but directed our course for London directly, where we arrived soon enough, nay too soon for some. This out-cry soon alarmed the ears of his neighbours, who with the host seizing on them, and carrying them back, gave us an opportunity for our escape. The lines that were about the tinker's pot, were these, to my best remembrance :

> Serpents but sting, or only bite so deep,
>   To numb the sense, so lay men fast asleep.
> Wit acts far greater things. I'll say no more :
>   Pay first for sleeping, then the Pots restore.

Those that were fastened to the woman's pot, were these :

> 'Twas not the serpent, but strong beer that stung :
>   The *vent* being stopt, the drink wrought through the *bung*.

I had like to have forgot to give you an account of a merry passage that happened upon the road we travelled on. Beating the hoof we overtook a cart, but in the name of Rabbi Abraham, what think you was in it ? In troth even a Squadron of the Tatterdemallion regiment. Some

pretendedly blind, others their legs tied up in a ſtring ; a third sort
having a dead palsy over all one side ; a fourth so lame as if he never had
been ſtrung with sinews. We fell into discourse, asking them whither
they were bound thus carted ? They answered us : ' Every one for his
own country. We have been already jibbed,' said one, that is jerked at the
whipping-poſt, ' and now enjoy the benefit of a pass.' The surly rogue,
the carter, observing our familiar talk made a ſtand, speaking to us after
this manner. ' Why, how now, gentlemen, how dropped you out of the
cart's arse ? what, you go on foot and your brethren ride ? It shall not
be ; ease your legs, come I'll lend you an hand.' I was about to reply
when a fellow came along who knew this carter, and asked him what he
would do, or whither he was going with them cripples. ' Introth ' said
he, ' to tell you the truth, I am going to Killum ' (a town it seems on the
borders of Oxford-Shire). Hearing this, I knew not what to think on't
but consulted with the aspeƈt of the carted crew. Their faces discovered
nothing but sense of danger, so that now I perceived their thoughts
were solely employed about their escape, which they did soon put in
execution. For forthwith the ſtrings were cut that tied up their legs,
who silently slid out of the cart one after another for fear of discovery.
The blind could see their way down too, the paralytic could run as swift
as a ſtag. The fellow drove on ſtill, not missing his company, presently
looking about he saw one running this way, another that way, a third
contrary to either, a fourth was hiding himself in a bush, thus they were
all dispersed. ' D'ee here, d'ee here,' cried the carter, ' reſtore the legs
and eyes you borrowed, and then run to the devil if you can.' I heard
one of them diſtinƈtly answer him, ' I'll see you hanged firſt, you murdering rogue ere I will come near you ; don't you remember that you said
even now that you were going to Killum.' Could you but imagine the
various poſtures their causeless fear put them in you would be a great
sharer with me in laughter I could not retain myself from. This ſtory
put me in mind of the like miſtake, whose effeƈts proved more fatal in the
time of the inteſtine wars in Ireland. A trooper met with a scullogue or
country-fellow, and demanding of him whence he came, he answered
from Killwanium. ' Whither art a-going ? ' ' To Killmore,' said he
(these are two towns), with that the soldier sware he should not kill
more, and so piſtolled him.

CHAPTER VII

*Coming to London, he enters himself into the society of Beggars, distinguished
by these titles, Ben seakers, Dommerars, Clapperdogeons, &c. : with
a short description of their manners and customs : as also a relation of
a piece of theft he committed*

COMING up to London, we straightway betook our selves to
Newington Butts ; but by the way my friend could not forbear
calling on his friends in Kent Street, there they gave me a nick-name ;
and my comrade immediately fell to work to put himself into an equipage
fit for the employment we had undertaken. He needed not to alter his
habit ; but his chief aim was to make counterfeit sores or ' clymes,'
according to the term of art that is given them. With the assistance of
some of the fraternity, he had in an hour's time such a leg that I could
hardly look upon it without even dropping down ; and thus they made it.
They took unslaked lime and soap, mingled with the rust of old iron :
these being well tempered together, they did spread it thick on two
pieces of leather, which they applied to his leg, binding it thereunto
very hard, which in a short time did fret off the skin, the flesh appearing
all raw. Then did they take blood and rubbed it all over his leg ; which
being fully dried, made the leg appear all black, the sore they did only
let peep out of the holes of five or six matterish clouts. He soon got us a
doxy too, with a couple of children (the fitter for our purpose), the one to
carry in her arms, and the other to lead. Providing himself and me with
a good lusty filch or stick, with a hole at the end thereof, to put in a hook
if occasion should serve, to filch anything off hedges, &c., away we went
into Moor-fields. He would have made me a clyme too, or an artificial
sore ; but my stomach would no ways accept of his kindness.

Coming into the fields, he planted me in a convenient place, the
doxy with her ' Lullaby-cheats ' in another ; and himself in a third,
not far distant from one another, that one might catch the others
' Maunding ' at the rebound. I observed my friend and rogue diligently,
what he did, for my own information. One would have sworn he had
been absolutely lame, for (about to lie down) he slid to the earth by his
staff ; being on the ground, the first thing I took notice of was the piteous
distorting of his face into various forms, to stir up compassion in such as
passed by him ; to which he added a most doleful noise to this effect ;
' For God's sake some tender hearted Christians, cast through your
merciful eyes one pitiful look upon a sore, lame, and miserable wretch.
Bestow one penny or half-penny upon him that is ready to perish, &c.'

I knew not how to tune my voice for hearkening to him; which he observing (when all the people were passed by) he held up his ſtick at me, a ſtrong argument of his great displeasure, which leſt I might farther incur, I was forced to tone it out to some purpose. Night approaching, we left off begging, resolving to recreate ourselves with what we had got. In the way home I saw a very fine piece of beef lying on a butcher's-ſtall; the woman that kept the shop was telling a gossips' tale to her neighbour so intently, as I thought I might seize on my prey, and she never the wiser. With that I boldly snatched it up; which an opposite neighbour perceiving, ran after me, and soon took me. I was brought back before the woman, who was so wise (forsooth) that she would not receive ſtolen goods, though they were her own; and so enraged she was, that nothing would serve her turn, but I muſt go before a juſtice; and to add to my punishment, she made me carry the ſtolen beef openly. Coming before his worship, my accusation was read, aggravated by many feigned circumſtances. The pitiful and sad caſts of my eyes, were all the rhetoric I used in my own vindication; which the merciful juſtice perceiving, they were so prevalent as to gain some favour from him. Whereupon he asked the woman what she valued her beef at? 'Why,' said she, 'I would not have abated a penny of five shillings.' 'Take heed what you say, good woman,' said he; 'for should you swear this it is enough to hang him.' 'O Lord, Sir,' said she; 'I would not hang him for a world.' Then said his worship, 'You muſt price it under thirteen pence half-penny;' whereupon the butcher's wife was content to value it at eight pence. The price being set, the beef was conveyed into the juſtice's kitchin, and the woman put to her oath; having sworn, my *Mittimus* was made, and therewith was sent to prison.

The woman now thought she should have her beef surely, and without any danger in the reception, and therefore demanded it; but the juſtice told her he would buy it of her, and so asked her what she would have for it: 'Sir,' said she, 'five shillings; I cannot afford it one farthing under.' 'How, how!' said he; 'did you not swear but even now, it was worth but eight pence, and do you now talk of five shillings? A mere cheat, extortioner, &c. Make her *Mittimus*' (speaking to his clerk), which so terrified the woman, that she cried out moſt piteously; 'good your Worship, do not send me to prison, and do with me what you please.' The juſtice at this looked ſtedfaſtly upon her (who was not so old but that he could discern a handsome woman when he saw her and indeed generally your butchers have jolly handsome wives; otherwise they may be ashamed to serve seven years in handling and choosing good flesh for others, and at laſt know not how to make choice of a fine young plump juicy bit for themselves). I say, the juſtice looking upon

her, smiled, yet seemed to reprove her sharply, and at laſt pretended he
had something to tell her he would not have everyone hear, carried her
into a withdrawing-room, where they ſtayed not long but out she came and
declared openly that she would never desire more juſtice done her than
that good and juſt juſtice (as she called him) had shown her. And as I
underſtood afterwards, he did her so much right, that she sent him in an
half dozen of bottles of canary, and supped with him on her own flesh.
I, in the meantime wished them both choked in the eating thereof;
for never did Roman Catholic endure greater and severer penance for
eating flesh on Good-Friday than I for coveting this. I have loved a
capon the better for it ever since; for I was no sooner gotten out into the
ſtreet, but I had a hundred people about me, crying ' Which is the young
rogue?' ' This, this is he,' said the butcher, pretending to lay his hand
upon my shoulder, but gave me a terrible nip by the ear, which made me
roar out so loud and so suddenly unexpected that my gentleman usher,
that was leading me by the arm to the White Lyon, ſtarting, let go his
hold. There was no dallying with so fair an opportunity, fear and love
of sweet liberty so winged my feet that running inſtantly hereupon,
I was gotten presently a great way before them. The harmanbeck,
huntsman or conſtable seeing this, unable to run himself by reason of
that great load of flesh he conſtantly carried about him, set a pack of
young yelping curs to track the scent, but they were soon all at a loss;
and so I escape their clutches.

CHAPTER VIII

*Whilſt a beggar what cunning tricks he invented to ſteal undiscovered, and
how at laſt served, being caught* ipso faſto

THE next day I went into Lincolns-Inn-Fields, where I saw a company of rogues, cheats, pickpockets, &c., playing at pidgeon
holes (a game much praſtised there and in Moor-fields, by such mischievous and lazy rascals). Growing very hungry, I singled out two or
three of the fitteſt for my purpose in assiſting or contriving roguery; a
little rising grass-plat was our council-table, where we consulted what
ſtratagems would beſt take and were leaſt known. ' Come gentlemen,'
said I (for the liberal science or ancient profession they ſtudied was
enough to gentelize them) ' what money have ye? *Sine Cerere & Baccho
friget ingenium,* we muſt have good liquor that shall warm our bloods,
enliven and unthaw our congealed spirits and make our inventions and

fancies as nimble as lightning.' ' Faith,' said one, ' I have but three pence ; yet that you may see how well qualified I am for your company, I'll have money for you presently.' He was not gone much above an half-hour but merrily he came to us. Sitting down he desired me to put my hand down his neck between his waistcoat and shirt, which accordingly I did, but admired to grope out three rashers of bacon, which I produced to the company. Very importunate I was with him to know what it meant, and how they came there. ' Give me attention,' said he, ' and I will unravel this riddle thus. Walking along the ſtreets leisurely, ſtrictly eyeing anything on which I might seize securely and advantageously, at length I saw a good pitiful old woman (for so she seemed to me by her countenance) selling bacon, who I observed did put what money she took into a pocket made in her apron.

' Upon this sight fancy, methought, suggeſted to me that her money was already as surely mine as if I had already confined it close prisoner in my leathern dungeon. And thus I wrought my design. " Good woman," said I (speaking in a whining tone), " how do you sell your bacon a pound ? " " Seven pence," said she, whereupon I began a lamentable oration, telling her that I would willingly have half a pound but that I had but three pence ; that my maſter was a very cruel man, half ſtarving his servants. " Come give me your money, sirrah," she said, " for once you shall have it so." Weighing it, I desired her to cut it into slices and thruſt it down my back. She asked my reason for it, I told her that my maſter usually searched me, and should he find any such thing in my pockets, he would half murder me. " Alas, poor boy," quoth the good old woman, " lean down thy head towards me, surely I will do thee that small kindness." Whilſt she was larding my back, I got my hands underneath her apron, and with this short knife nipped off the bottom of her pocket ; and thus have I done my part to procure ye both food and money.'

As I looked on this as base ingratitude, so I could not but tacitly within myself, both condemn and abhor such society, remembering the words of Juvenal :

Ingratos ante omnia pone sodales.

Of all persons we should shun moſt the ungrateful. Neither could I forbear (though I was joyful of the purchase) to read him a public lecture on his ingratitude. ' What,' said I, ' shall we find gratitude in beaſts (as in the lion that was healed by Andronicus in the wood, which afterwards saved his life in the theatre) and yet shall we be unthankful ! I have read a ſtory of an asp that was kept and nourished by an husband-man at his own table, feeding him there daily ; at laſt she brought forth two young ones, one whereof poisoned the husbandman's son, the old one (as my author tells me) in the sight of the father killed the offender and as if ashamed of his ingratitude departed the house with the other and was not seen after.' I would have proceeded, but that they told me if I did, they would have no men of morals in their company, and so away we went to Beggars' Hall, hard by, where we called lustily. Fearing we should spend all the money, I desired the company that some small portion might be left in my hands as a stock to trade on, which they consented to.

Having feasted ourselves well, before we departed the next day's meeting was appointed, when and where. Against the time I had made a quantity of serpents, crackers, &c., and brought them with me. When first I showed them they all fell out a-laughing to think I could improve our stock by such devices. ' Have but the patience to hear me,' said I, ' and then condemn me if you see cause. Ever since I parted from you I have been racking my invention to find out some way whereby I might render myself both deserving of, and acceptable to your company, and I think this my first discovery will do it. I would have you Jack, Tom and Will, take an equal quantity of crackers and serpents, and anon at night let us go into the market, where each of you shall observe each of us. Wherever we make a stand be sure you throw a serpent, &c. at that very place ; and then will we take the opportunity of the people's confusion and fright, and so march off with what we can lay hands on.' This plot was very well liked of by all. The evening approaching (it being near November) we went to put what I had contrived to execution. The first that was thrown was where I stood, which fell into the basket on which a market woman sat. The woman starting up to extinguish it, suddenly it bounced in her face, the smoke whereof and powder for a little time so blinded her that she could not see me walk off with a shoulder of mutton ; my comrades had the like success with a pig and a goose. Having done enough as we thought for that time, we went to a place of our acquaintance, where we had the mutton, pig, and goose roasted, giving the landlord the pig for dressing, bread and drink. We were so successful for the first, that we made several trials afterwards not ineffectual.

But in fine, I found the proverb verified, The pitcher goes not so often to the well, but that it comes home cracked at last. One time I went, and having ordered them to do as they had done before, a serpent came flying on the woman's stall where I stood and fell into her lap, which being brushed off, fell underneath her coats, and there burst. In the meanwhile I had gotten a loin of veal and was trooping off with it. The woman missing it suspected me by my great haste, followed me and laying hands on me found her meat under my coat. ' O have I caught you, Mr Thief?' 'Miſtake not, good woman,' said I, 'it is no such matter. For as I ſtood by your ſtall, the wildfire which some unhappy knaves threw, so scared me that having your meat in my hand at that time cheapening it, I was so frighted that I ran away with your veal to shun the danger, forgetting to lay it down, wherefore pray take it again.' Taking her meat, ' Here is a pure excuse, indeed,' said she, ' but this shall not serve your turn,' and with that, gave me two or three such blows on my chops that I verily thought she had made me swallow half my teeth. Another that had heard our discourse takes me to task after this ; ' Come, sirrah, you love the flesh well, but 'tis fit you should pay for it. And it is but juſt if you will have my flesh, I should have some of yours.' Up ſtraight he snatched his knife, and holding me by the ear I verily thought he would have marked me as he used to do his calves. My crying and praying so far prevailed that he only kicked me to his next neighbour and so from one to another, so that though it cannot be said I ran the Gauntlet, yet between the panniers on both sides, I was kicked the Gauntlet from the Standard in Cheapside to the Conduit at the lower end thereof. This unhappy adventure made me betake myself to my old course of begging, resolving as yet not to deal in that trade I had little experience in.

CHAPTER IX

A merchant seeing him begging, took a fancy to him, conduĉts him to his house, and entertains him as his servant

ONE day, I was begging more fervently than formerly, having gotten not one penny that day, so that I found a civil war between my guts and stomach, yet knew not how to salve up the difference, neither would they hearken to anything but a bill of fare. In the midſt of this combustion, a tradesman of no mean quality passing by, took a ſtrong fancy to me, being extraordinarily pleased with the form of my face and body. He asked me whence I came? what my parents were? and what I intended? I answered him with well contrived forgeries that seemed to give him good satisfaĉtion. Liking well both my speech and underſtanding, he bid me follow him, which accordingly I did. Having conduĉted me to his house, he presented me to his wife, my intended miſtress, telling her his resolutions of receiving me into his service. At which she blessed herself, saying, 'Prithee, Sweetheart, from what dunghill didſt thou pick up this *Shakerag*, this squire of the body? This thing dressed up in sippits? This scarecrow, what shall I call him?'

(For I am sure I had but few clothes on, but what were rather fit to dung ground than to be sent to the paper-mill). Said my master, ' Rest yourself satisfied, since it is my pleasure, this shall be so : neither can I give you any reason for my fancy.' Whereupon he commanded me to be stripped, and well washed; in the meantime clothes were provided for me, a suit of one of his apprentices. A great vessel like Cornelius his tub was filled with water to bath me, but so cunningly set by the maids (though privately), that they might see me all over naked. It was my good fortune to observe my mistress standing in a private place on purpose to see me dismantled ; and after I was washed she commended the whiteness of my skin and well-proportioned limbs ; and by the consequent approved within herself of something else, for I was then a stubbed lad. Being new clothed, and raised to this unexpected fortune, how strangely did this vain blast puff up my empty pate ! However, I was resolved to carry myself discreetly, lest I should overthrow the state I was then in, not yet well settled. Wherefore I behaved myself very respectfully towards my master, and served him as punctually as I could, endeavouring that my service should requite his kindness in as great measure as my abilities could perform.

My endeavour was not only to please my master, but my mistress too, even in the meanest services, so officious to her, that I was ready to perform the office of a chambermaid. The maidservants I obliged also, by doing their duty, as making the fires, washing the kitchin, nimbly and willingly doing anything they would have me ; by which I so ingratiated myself among them that I always had their good estimation among themselves, and good word to my master and mistress when occasion served. Very careful I was not to report what I heard, lest I by that means involved myself in the affairs of others, without advantage to myself ; for by meddling in others' matters, I should breed animosity among them, and reap just hatred to myself, when discovered to be the too busy intelligencer. This I looked on as an undeniable maxim, That nothing more recommends a man than a silent tongue (unless necessity required the contrary), a fair complacential carriage, and a faithful heart. My master, in a humour, would sometimes find fault with me, but then it was my chiefest care not to reply, knowing that what should be alleged as to my just vindication, would but aggravate his spirits (being passionate) always punctually performing what was commanded me. To try my fidelity he would lay a sixpence on the counter, or in the window, as if it had been left there forgotten. I was wiser than to be caught so, and therefore would instantly carry him the money. One time sending me out to buy something, instead of a shilling he gave me among other money a piece of gold. I took no notice of it then, but being gone a little way, I came running back out of breath to restore him the piece. This and the like made my master stand amazed at my seeming honesty. A strange alteration, you will say ; but all this was only to get a good esteem, whereby I might gain fast footing. What though I underwent a great deal of pains, and had my patience tried to the height ? Yet I gained much in the end, had God given me grace rightly to use it, and the baseness of my nature not persuaded me to abuse it.

So much credit I had gotten with my master by my civil behaviour, that he raised me *gradatim*, step by step. Being ignorant of arithmetic, he caused a master to come to his house to instruct me, which I soon apprehended, and by that means was capacitated to keep his accompts, which was the thing I aimed at ; intending thereby the prosecution of mine own ends, notwithstanding my pretended fidelity, and his real kindness to me undeserved. Which puts me in mind of the conclusion of an epitaph I have read on a tomb, which the master erected for the perpetual commemoration of his servant's cordial respect and honesty :

> View oft his tomb-stone, since we seldom find,
> A servant faithful, and his master kind.

Now, to the intent I might complete my conquest of his heart, I pretended myself an Independent, not omitting any opportunity of going to their meetings ; and upon all occasions would rail against steeple-houses (as we called them) and tear the bishops' holland sleeves to pieces, calling them the impure rags of the Babylonish Whore's smock, &c. I would pray mornings and evenings so loud, so late, and so early, that my neighbours could hardly sleep for me, much less those of our own family. Notwithstanding all this piety, not a day passed wherein I cheated not my master. Thus did I delude his eyes with pretended sanctity, yet concluded with the poet :

> *Da mihi fallere, da justum Sanctumque videri,*
> *Noctem peccatis & fraudibus objice nubem.*

> Let me seem just ; to cheat the better shrow'd,
> Let my deceits be hidden in a cloud.

How much did I, silly fool, deceive myself, thinking myself secure because no mortal eye saw me. Be not thus cheated as I was, for assure yourself there is no darkness so thick and obscure, which the All-over-seeing and Eternal piercing eye cannot penetrate——

> *Cernit Deus omnia vindex.*

A passage remarkable in Erasmus I read to this purpose, concerning a young gentleman, whom a wanton lady tempted, who used this expression as his laſt and beſt refuge. 'Art not thou ashamed to do that in the sight of thy Maker, and the Holy Angels, which thou art ashamed to do in the sight of men.' We are afraid of disgrace with men, not caring for the Grace of God.

CHAPTER X

How he came acquainted with lewd and vicious apprentices : what trade they drove together : what places and times of meeting

I WAS as officious at home, as reserved from all company, never ſtirring forth unless called out by my maſter's business, till my next neighbour's man intruded himself into my acquaintance; who so far insinuated himself into my affeƈtions that I was in a manner wholly ruled by him. He and I met on a time abroad, and would not be denied but he muſt needs faſten a glass of wine, conduƈting me to a tavern where the drawer (as he said) was his friend. After several congratulations passed, order was given for a pint of canary. Being gone to draw it, this young man began to tell me what an honeſt fellow this Ralph the drawer was; which words he had no sooner uttered, but I heard him cry at the bar, 'A pint of white-wine in the Rose score'; and immediately in he brings it, and in formality a glass, but we made no use of it, for he was fearful his maſter would discover the cheat, and therefore desired us to be speedy in the dispatch, and so we made but two draughts thereof. Away he goes again, and brings in another, not after the same manner, but crying it 'Right,' bringing withal a quart bottle in his codpiece: 'Now, Gentleman,' said he, 'using your discretion, you may sit and talk freely, without either fear or suspicion, using your glass and when your pint is empty fill him again, you shall not want for liquor, lads.' This something amazed me at firſt, till my neighbour Thomas told me that this was frequent, and that he and two or three friends at any time could be drunk for sixpence a piece. 'Come, come, you are but a novice,' said he; 'but if you will be ruled by me, I'll shew you the way to soften the cord of bondage, to make the long time of a seven years apprentice-ship seem short, by living as merry, nay more jovially than our maſters. They may be diſtraƈted with cares how to procure necessaries, pay rent, satisfy creditors, whilſt we have none of these pressures and dis-turbances on our spirits. What though we have an harsh word or a smart blow, it may be a broken pate? We will make his till spring a leak for it, or his goods go to pot, and break him at laſt, too. It may be his provision is neither dainty nor plentiful, nay, reſtrained, from our liberty too : 'tis only by day, then ; we will be masters of our own at night, not wanting anything that may conduce to mirth, or the delectation of our insatiate senses.'

I asked him how could this be done ? He answered, if I would swear to be secret and faithful, and become a brother of the society, he would not only tell me how all this (afore recited) might be performed, but would likewise introduce me into the place where these jolly blades used to congregate. I soon consented, rejoicing exceedingly at this blessed opportunity (as I thought it), wherein I might sail in the ocean of delight, bound for no other port but that of pleasure or profit, never considering the inevitable quicksands which such meet withal, steering that course, having no other compass to sail by than their own fancy. Very eager I was to have him inform my judgment with what at present I understood not, but doubted not in a little time to be as forward as the foremost in any moral wickedness.

First, he informed me, I must insinuate myself into the maid's favour, so that when the occasion should require, she may let you have the key of the street-door, or else sit up for your return, making her sensible that she doth not so break her sleep for nothing. That I must never fail, coming home, to gratify her kindness. If she be modest and continent, only kiss her, and that my behaviour should not be either rude or lascivious, that all my expressions should savour of Platonic, or chaste love, often repeating this to her ; ' O that I was out of my time, if it were for nothing else but to repay thee thy love ! So great an acknowledgment I have of thy civilities, that I hope a time will come wherein I shall make full satisfaction for all, &c.' If she be buxom, or wantonly given, she will never be content with hopes, promises, and protestations, vows, and such like windy stuff ; wherefore you must kiss, hug, and embrace her, telling how dearly you love her ; and then fall to somewhat else. She may put you off at first with a *Pish*, a *Fie*, or *Pray be civil ;* yet be so far from denying, that if you proceed not on vigorously, she will prompt you yourself, to try what mettle you are made of ; if dull, she will make you the subject of her private nay and public laughter and scorn. But be very cautious of procreation, which you may prevent several ways. Now to tell you what manner of persons we are that are confederates. There are few among us but what are of several Trades selected, as linen-drapers, mercers, woollen-drapers, silkmen, hosiers, haberdashers, merchants, grocers, goldsmiths, jewellers, ribband-sellers, exchange-men, to which add a drawer and an oil-man, the one to furnish us with good liquor, and the other to prepare our palates for it. A great many trades there are which signify nothing in our commonwealth as pewterers, braziers, plumbers, &c., we are only for such as will profit the body, please the palate and fill the pocket. Every one brings his several commodities at the place of meeting, then do we exchange or barter one with another for what each respective person wants ; either to supply his own occasion, or his mistress : for it is to be supposed such a thing must be had, when procured, must be maintained, though to the destruction of our master's estates, and ruin of our bodily health. Further,' he added, ' that our masters might not detect us in the purloining his goods, you must not,' said he, ' take too much of one sort of commodity.'

All this I liked wonderfully well, and promised to meet that day seven-night at the place appointed ; and so we parted. Coming home, I immediately put these prescriptions into practice. First, taking notice of what goods we had greatest quantity ; and whatsoever commodity my master forgot he had, I always secured it as mine own ; nay, sometimes I would try him ; ' There was such a person enquiring for such a thing to-day when you were abroad, but I could not find it.' It may be he would say, ' We had it not,' suiting my design according to desire. Having taken a thorough view of the shop and warehouse, I saw so many ways of advantage, if assisted by a cleanly conveyance, that I could snip as well as the most forward of them all.

The next thing I had to do was to endear myself to the chief maid, who was one of those that lay covertly to see me wash myself in the tub, and as she confessed since, took an affection to me from that hour. It required no long time to court her into a compliance, her complexion or temperament, forcing her acceptance of anything amorously inclined. The colour of her hair inclined to red, which colour (though I know not for what reason) I love above any. This may be partly the reason, because as that complexion hath always the concomitant of a very white skin, so it hath two inseparable companions, plumpness and buxomness. Her skin, as the usual attendant of red or flaxenish hair (as I said) was as white as whiteness itself ; her cheeks naturally painted with vermilion ; plump were her cheeks and lips, with a mole thereon, and a dimple in her chin, as the infallible marks of one that is willing to dedicate herself to the service of Venus.

Having a fit opportunity, after some amorous discourse, I desired her she would grant me leave that night to talk with her in private, having business of importance to impart to her. She condescended to my proposition. As soon as our master and mistress were gone to take their rest, her impatience to hear what I would say, made her soon send the rest to bed. The house being thus cleared, and all things silent as the air, when winds into their hollow grots repair, I acquainted her with the greatness of my affection, which I delivered with all the rhetoric I could

E

invent, still touching that string which produced love's harmonious concord. So fervent I was in my expressions, and so ardent and hot in my desires, that I soon melted the congealed iceness of her chastity. But first there were mutual articles reciprocally drawn and agreed unto, *viz.*

That if she proved with child, I should marry her.

That I should devote myself to her service, and none's else.

That we should both endeavour to make use of all opportunities for the enjoyment of each other.

That to prevent discovery, we should often fall out before people, that without suspicion in private we might agree the better ; she throwing oftentimes bones at my head when sitting at dinner, because suspicion should not deprive her of the grissel.

So great was our seeming feud sometimes, that our master was called in to part us.

After this I gave her plenary instructions as to my affairs, which she faithfully and punctually promised to observe. Then did I put my hand to the instrument, and sealed the articles with two witnesses.

The night was come wherein I was to meet according to promise. I acquainted my Amoretta with my intention of going out at twelve o'clock ; and that my master might not in the least suspect me, I went to bed, but arose again at the hour promised. The first time I would not carry any commodities with me, resolving to see first what they did. Being come to the house, I was introduced by my neighbour Thomas into a private back-room, among the associated brethren. I was much amazed to see such variety of wares lie upon a long table, as silks, stuffs, cloth, linen and woollen, stockings, ribbands, muffs, hoods, scarfs, and the like. Some of them came to me, and welcomed me as a brother, drinking to me in a beer-bowl of sack and sugar.

Most of the company being met, they trucked with each other according to their convenience, furnishing themselves with what they either stood in need of themselves or their friends. Several things were offered me ; I told them I had brought nothing to retaliate in lieu. They told me my credit was good, which is the soul of commerce ; telling me they should have occasion to make use of me in the like nature another time. I took with me only such things as might be proper to bestow at home, on whom I had lately engaged my affections ; which I presented her with, accompanied with many expressions and protestations of a never-dying affection. She accepted of my kindness with much gratitude, but thought she could not fully remunerate me without a re-admission into her private and then particular favours ; I could easily discern her inclinations by griping of my hand, kissing as if she would devour me, the palpitation of her heart, and her inflamed eyes. I ran parallel with her in the same desires, so that with much facility we two clapped up a bargain. After which I would have betaken myself to my rest in my own bed, but that was displeasing to her, I perceived nothing would content her, but that we should be bed-fellows. I soon assented to it, though to the hazard of both our credits and fortunes. I desired her to go up first, telling her I would follow instantly after. By that time I thought she was in bed, up marched I the stairs, which creaked as if they had conspired a discovery. Coming up to the highest stair, I raised my foot (being fearful of making any noise) thinking there had been another, it descended with such precipitation, that I made the house echo.

The chamber wherein my master and mistress lay (the maid lying in a trundle bed underneath them), was right against this stair-head. My master had taken a dose more then ordinary of sack, so that this noise awaked him not. My mistress at the first hearing thereof, imagined thieves had broken into the house; she endeavoured to wake her husband by stirring him, but could not, therefore thought it the best way to lie still, expecting the event. In the meantime I lay *perdue*, stirring not till I imagined my mistress asleep again. The maid, concluding I durst not adventure further by reason of this unfortunate accident, fell immediately into a profound sleep. Finding (after a considerable time) all things still and quiet, I entered the chamber, dark as Hell, and in a low voice, groping the contrary way, I cried, ' Where art ? ' ' Here, here,' said my mistress, in a whispering tone. Minding from whence the sound came as near as I could, I directed my footsteps to that place. The same words being repeated, conveyed me exactly to that side of the bed whereon my mistress lay. Taking her about the neck, I kissed her a thousand times : using then all the alluring and loving expressions I could invent. Not perceiving my mistake, I made all the haste I could (and all too little) to undress myself ; which was done in an instant. Opening the clothes to come to bed, ' Hold,' said my mistress, ' I have a bedfellow already ; what I have suffered you to do was only as a trial to understand what you intended. Get you gone to your own bed for this night, and I shall talk with you farther to-morrow.' I durst not reply, not daring to stay longer, but betook myself to my own chamber, possessed with fear and shame, I nothing but tossed and tumbled all that night, taking not the least rest.

In the morning early I was up, shewing myself more than ordinary diligent. But, Lord, what a confusion I was in when I saw my mistress come into the shop ? I made an hundred pretences to stoop behind the counter, and rectify disordered wares. So busy I was with my back towards her that she could not have so much as a sight of me. At length she comes up close to me, and turning me about, said, ' Indeed you take too much pains, you are too laborious ; fair and softly ; there is a great while to-night yet : desist a little, I must have a word with you.' Hearing this, I presumed to look in her face, and was overjoyed ; for from thence I received a most alluring smile, instead of a killing frown. This re-armed me with confidence, compelling from me these expressions :

' Most respectful Mistress, I do with shame confess myself in a great error : but if you will consider that the cause thereof was irresistible ; I hope you will in some measure mitigate my crime. My very youthfulness speaks my apology. You cannot be ignorant of the fervent heat of young blood, which sometimes boils beyond its bounds. Besides the temperature of my body (being of a sanguine complexion), did add much fuel to that fire.'

She admired to hear me speak in such a dialect ; but laying aside her wonder, she bid me tell her the whole truth, and what contract we had concluded. I equivocated in my relation, intending to excuse the maid's forwardness, and that I only designed to surprize her unawares. This sophistry of mine did not in the least prevent my mistress's prying wit and quick understanding from searching out the truth, tracing every meander, finding it out at last, though involved in a labyrinth of obscurities. She told me plainly she knew all, though I endeavoured to conceal it, and *desired* me, instead of commands, to withdraw my affectionate thoughts from her, since her resolution was to divorce our persons. Adding moreover, that if I was so amorously inclined as not content without a female object to exercise my passion on, I should elect such a one whose merit grounded on beauty, birth, wealth, and power, should command my love, and finally eternize my terrestrial happiness, and so vanished from me, leaving my cogitations to their operations.

Forty-five years had not totally destroyed her beauty, but there was still remaining the ruins of a good face. Her birth, though from a high extraction, had little influence over me, had not her wealth (which she had at her own disposal) whispered in my ear more than a common felicity. Her last words left a deep impression on my imagination, which were not so enigmatically delivered but that I could easily interpret them advantageously enough to my purpose. I resolved within myself to acquiesce, leaving this affair to time to bring it to perfection.

CHAPTER XI

What devices he found out to cheat his master ; and what ways he had to spend it lavishly, at unseasonable hours, on wine, wenches, &c.

THE time being come again for the meeting my snipping brethren, I went prepared with what I could conveniently carry with me. Seeing me come well fraught, my merchants clapped me aboard, resolving not to let my commodities lie long on my hands ; our truck was soon agreed on to our mutual contents. Then, like true sons of Bacchus, we trolled the full bowls about, wishing him that pledged not his fellow, in a dark rainy night on a tired jade bare ridged in a dirty lane, with a pocky whore behind him, and his own bones rotten, nine miles from a house, not knowing one step of his way, nor having one penny in his pocket. This, or the like dreadful execration, made us tumble off whole bowls like so many thimbles full. Half a dozen of these a piece were a *preludium* to our supper, which usually was composed of the choicest viands. Neither could we eat, without our female consorts, whom wine and music waited on. After supper, we fell again to our old Bacchanalian sport, drinking, dancing, or privately treating our mistresses at a venereal banquet. When we had drank ourselves to ebriety, and satiated our lustful appetites, we betook ourselves to our respective habitations, our masters not dreaming of our night revellings. Our own expenses were neither valuable nor comparable to what our mad-dames put us to, which were so great (though they made me rack my invention to supply their pretended necessities) that all my various endeavours could not answer their expectations.

I had taken my gentlewoman a chamber, for which I paid three shillings a week, and upon the bare promise of a whore that she would prove constant to me, I allowed her a weekly pension besides. I never came to receive a private favour but I must return her for it some special and particular courtesy ; as a scarf, a hood, a ring, a whisk, or rich lace for her smock. If I failed at any time of paying my promised tribute I should be severely checked, nay, sometimes threatened that I had undone her ; at the least denied my accustomed familiarity. Then she would pretend that she had refused many eminent matches for my sake, that now she saw herself deluded, and would endure it no longer ; and would tell my master our whole proceedings. If I had performed the man, and not presented her when I came with some other gratuity, as a work of supererogation, she would deride my courtship, telling me, I was an empty fellow, that I bestowed my favours on others and that made me so sparing to her. And that she scorned to be a copartner in my heart. When she thought she had sufficiently nettled me (fearing to ſtrain my passion too high), then a little clapping me on the cheeks, calling me smock-face rogue ; ' Come hither sirrah, I know what you would have, I'll save your longing.' Such sweetened words soon overpowered my sourness : and notwithſtanding my intended hardness, I could not forbear melting in her arms. We durſt not take much time in dalliance, my duty calling me home ; but I regarded not that so much as to preserve my maſter's good opinion of me.

Now since opportunity offereth itself so appositely, give me leave to lay open this subtle female, on whom a ſtrong ascendancy of Mercury and Venus had beſtowed so liberal a talent for whoring and cheating that few escaped her circumvention that came into her company. The relation I shall give of this miracle of female subtlety will be much advantageous to all sorts of persons. By this those that are viciously inclined may be advised into a reformation before they have occasion for repentance : and they who, defying all admonishment, are resolved to be wicked in spite, may out of an apprehension of the ensuing danger and punishment, be deterred into caution, &c.

A SHORT SURVEY OF A CUNNING WHORE

When firſt I made myself acquainted with her, I thought my happiness not inferior to the Grand Seignor's ; for although he had in his seraglio the enjoyment of an hundred or more of the moſt seleƈt beauties of the universe, yet did I fancy all those external glories contraƈted into one, and possessed by my matchless miſtress. She was fair, well featured, sprightly and young, four dangerous advantages, when they are accompanied with wit, dissimulation, craft and impudence, with a covetous desire of enjoying of what others are possessed. She could not be ignorant of her trade, since her mother was a professed bawd from the time she brought her into the world. Taking notice of her extraordinary handsomeness, even from the cradle, she resolved to dedicate her to the service of Venus, not doubting but the bent of her nature would render her very capable of that employ. Being about thirteen years of age, her beauty was so much taken notice of that her lovers swarmed about her. The old bawd, her mother, was overjoyed to see so large and goodly a troop of Cupid's lancers, her daughter's life-guard, and doubted not now but that she should obtain the plenary fruition of her hopes, and therefore entertained them all, yet watching them so narrowly that none should taſte her fruit unless they bought the tree at a dear rate. She so well observed her daughter's natural policy that she was well assured her insinuations would in a little time command both the hearts and purses of those who courted her. Her design proved as fortunate as she could wish, inasmuch as among the many that languished for her there was one so wealthy as that he never knew the want of a thousand pound, whose heart was inflamed by her eyes.

She had now assumed the title of madam, which one should think belonged to none but who are nobly extracted ; however, why should she baulk it, since it is an honour costs little or nothing, and as soon conferred as spoken. This gentleman was so ensnared by the witch-craft of a lovely face that though he knew the profession and practice of the mother, and the daughter's want of honour, honesty and wealth, yet he resolved upon a marriage within a few days, without the tedious-ness of treaties. When there was a firm contract concluded between them before witnesses, the charitable bawd, his intended mother-in-law, came to him and told him that if his stomach was raw and could not stay so long till the meat was served up with the usual ceremonies he should have a bit for a stay, and taste beforehand. The proposition was not un-welcome to him, wherefore he instantly took earnest of the happiness he vainly believed would bear him company *durante vita*. Not long after, they had their nuptials celebrated, and that he might not disparage himself in the world's eye as to his inconsiderable choice, he bought his wife at his proper charge, new clothes, splendid enough you may guess, with the appendixes of gallantry, rings, jewels, &c. and so brought her home to his house in much state. She had not long lived with him but she followed the dictates of a luxurious disposition, and a libertine, hating to have her liberty circumscribed or bounded, especially by one so remote to her nature and unsuitable in years ; wherefore, under pre-tence of visiting this friend and that cousin, she so blinded her old husband by this plausible excuse that she made her frequent sallies abroad pimp for her desires.

Her husband observing her gaddings and profuse expenses could do no less than suspect more than he was willing to understand, and there-fore not only abridged the liberty she took, but divested her of those ornaments he had bestowed upon her ; which so animated her to revenge that she resolved not to let slip the first opportunity. She soon got acquainted with one suitable to her purpose, a person as much engaged in debauchery as his credit was in the world, yet so pleasant he appeared in her eyes that a little courting made her wholly at his devotion. Hence we may observe the dangerous consequences of disproportion of age in matching. Surely there can be no agreement between fire and water, between freezing winter, and scorching summer. Besides, when a woman comes once to have mean thoughts of her husband (upon any account whatever) she is then in the way to affect anybody else. She now not only slighted but hated him, which made her launch out into all the excesses that exasperated and vicious womankind can imagine or contrive, from whence she may either derive satisfaction or advantage ; neither could she want assistance or counsel as long as the old experienced bawd, her mother, lived.

This good old dotard finding himself so abused that the whole world must needs call his reason in question if he suffered any longer his loose wife to career thus in luxury and wantonness, resolved within himself to call her to a severe accompt, intending withal to reduce her by kindness, as well as sharpness, and so equally to temper his frowns with smiles that she should not tell which of those two ingredients were most powerful in effecting the cure of his lust-sick wanton.

Returning one evening from her revels abroad, the old cuckold took her to task ; sharply reproving her for her gaddings, her tavern meetings with debauched and licentious persons, her lavish expense in paying the reckonings wherever she came, but especially her supplying the necessities of lusty younger brothers, which resupplied hers. The old man had so spent his spirits and breath in schooling his lecherous truant that he was forced to conclude his wormwood lecture in an excessive cough ; the inseparable companion of him and age. My buxom madam fearing he was straining for more of that unpleasing stuff which had so lately offended her ears, left him half strangled with a cough.

In this interval a female neighbour of his came in, a gentlewoman of such worth that virtue and gentility contended in her for priority. ' How is it I pray Sir,' said she, ' I am much troubled to see you in this condition ? ' ' You lie, you lie, you whore,' said he, his ears being so furred by time that he could not distinguish this gentlewoman's voice from his wife's, neither could he see, his violent coughing having forced down such a torrent of moisture into his eyes that his sight was totally drowned. Continuing his railing, ' See me in this condition ? I believe you would be glad to see me out of it, you strumpet, lump of lechery, cheat, she-devil, what shall I call thee ; there is no name too bad.' And then coughed again so violently that it was in vain to speak to him. But when this violent fit abated, she resolved to say something, though her amazement to hear what she neither deserved nor expected would hardly give her permission. At last she spake to him, and reasoned with him why he should thus stain her honour which was hitherto spotless, undefiled ; that her actions had ever been so far from rendering her what he unworthily represented, that they made her famous, and looked on as a good example for her neighbours to follow and imitate. ' Infamous you mean,' said he, ' and let me alone to make you such an example that you shall have followers enough to see you carted, you bitch whore.' ' Why, who am I,' said the gentlewoman, ' that you thus abuse me ? ' ' Am I,' said he ; ' you are touch-wood, tinder, saltpetre, gunpowder, wildfire, nay, worse than all this, my wife.'

By this the gentlewoman verily concluded him to be mad, and fearing left his frenzy might be converted into fury, was thinking to slip from him just as his cough left him, and his eyes again restored to him with the insight of his mistake ; which made him much condemn his fallacious age, that had put this trick on him.

Apologies (as many as this old man's sterile invention could frame) were not wanting to excuse this absurdity and error ; neither was his wife without the height of mirth behind the hangings, to hear how much her doting fool was mistaken ; who had not patience any longer to discourse with his visitant, but abruptly left her in quest of his abused wife as he now supposed, imagining from this grand mistake that whatever before he had either seen or heard of his wife, was nothing but the genuine product of his own idle and jealous brain. After he had made a strict enquiry through the whole house for his wife, he at length found her cloistered in a garret, into which she had conveyed herself coming softly behind the hangings wherein she had hid herself ; and the better to colour her intended villainy, hearing her husband ascend the stairs, she put herself into a praying posture.

The old man seeing her on her knees had like to have broke his neck for haste, not minding so much the disturbance he would give her (pretended) devotion as the satisfaction he enjoyed to see his mistake confirmed. Being out of breath, his discourse was abrupt and broken, neither did he know which was most expedient, either first to question her, or crave her pardon. At length he threw himself at her feet (for indeed he could hardly stand upon his feeble legs), and hanging down his head (I know not whether he cried) a salt rheum gushed through the portholes of his head, which looked like scalding tears, and so they might be, for by their burning heat any might conclude the loss of the hair of his eyelids, and that thereby the shrivelled skin of his countenance was parched. It was a long time ere he could speak, and no wonder, since this was the second time of his infancy ; but at length with much ado, with a look as pitiful as his rhetoric, he asked forgiveness. She seemed strangely surprized and not only wondered at, but taxed him for the irrationality of his petition. The pretence of her ignorance in what had passed, made him the more eager to discover his ridiculous folly. In short, he gave her to understand that since he was mistaken in a thing so palpable, he might very well question whether all former reports, and his own evil opinion of her might not be posited on the same basis of false-hood. That for the time to come he would never admit of jealousy within his breaſt ; and to give a full confirmation to what he proteſted, he inſtantly delivered her his keys, committing to her truſt what he had of greateſt value. This cunning quean would not accept this kind proffer, but with much pressing, and then sealing his pardon with a kiss, an everlaſting affeƈtion was seemingly agreed upon. For two or three months she behaved herself so well that had her husband had Argus his hundred eyes, he could not perceive anything that might blemish her reputation, or trouble his head.

Her cue being come to enter and aƈt her part on the ſtage of deceit, she appeared and managed her business to the purpose. For having given her mother a catalogue of those rich things she had in her possession, she never left her daughter till they had conveyed all away which might be carried in the day time without any notice taken. And at an appointed night, getting the servants to bed and delivering the key of the ſtreet-door to the old bawd, her mother, she played the part of a woman in general, by lulling her husband in bed by dissimulation and flattery, into a fond opinion of her cordiality to him, whilſt her agents then were leaving him as naked of goods as he was at that time of apparel. In the morning she arose betimes, before the old man was ſtirring, and went inſtantly to her mother, who had provided her lodgings. Then did she change her name to hinder deteƈtion ; and that she might add to her security, she never went abroad but with her vizard mask, and in as many varieties of suits as there are months in the year, which though but thirteen, yet did she make them ring as many changes as Bow Bells.

Not long after she had played this exploit, it was my unhappiness to be acquainted with her, by her coming accidentally to our shop, where, buying some wares, it was so ordered that I muſt bring them to her chamber. According to the time appointed I waited on her, but found myself extremely miſtaken in my chapwoman. For inſtead of paying me for my commodity, she would have trucked with me ware for ware ; which I would no ways assent to. Finding me no fit person for her purpose, she dismissed me by discharging the debt. This passage did so run in my mind that I could not be at quiet till I had purposed a time to visit her, and indeed I was forcibly pricked on thereunto by those matchless features I saw in her incomparable face. My maſter riding out of town I found a very fit opportunity to make my address to her, which I thought would be the more welcome by bringing a present with me.

Her memory was so good that she knew me again and shrewdly

guessed at my errand, and indeed I was not long in the discovery thereof. There were but two words to a bargain, and so we ſtruck up the business. So much delight I took in her at that time, and she in me that we interchangeably promised each other conſtancy of affection.

Mine and my female's extravagancies made me invent as many ways to cheat as we had ways to spend what was this way gotten. If I had heard any friend say they muſt buy a gown, I had my mercer ready for that purpose ; if a suit and cloak, my draper, and the like ; sometimes telling my friend that I was acquainted with one that would sell me a far cheaper pennyworth than any one else : other times, that such an one owed me some moneys, and that this way I could both pleasure my friend, and hedge in mine own debt. Though I drove a great trade this way, receiving ſtill ready cash, yet this would not do alone. As an assiſtance, I gelded the money-box every day, receiving my part firſt, before my maſter should take his, which usually he did every night, putting it into his till. I could not sleep for thinking how I might be intimately acquainted with the inwards of this same till. Several projects I made trial of, but none suited my purpose so well as a barber's pair of curling irons. I got a file from a smith, and to work I went with my curling irons, filing them to slip in easily, and to turn round.

The firſt essay I made thereof had like to have put me into an extasy for joy. I laid them upon their edge, opened them wide, and pinched the money below ; holding faſt, I turned them on their side, and so drew up the money to the mouth of the scotch. Now because there was many times so much that it would not come through, with a knife I would slide away piece after piece till I had fitted the money to the narrowness of the passage. I seldom brought up at a time less than three shillings, a good draught, not ceasing till I had gotten twenty or thirty shillings at a time, or more, according to the quantity of the ſtock. Finding my engine act according to my desires, I could not be content without congratulating my success. My maſter was seldom at home, wherefore I asked my miſtress to go out for an hour, promising her not to ſtay beyond my limited time. She consented, and I overjoyed, picked up a rambler or two, and away we went to honeſt Ralph. Being glad to see us, he planted us in a convenient room fit for his purpose. There was never a pint he scored at the bar but he had a quartbottle in his breeches for it. They all wondered to see me so frolic, but I thought it wisdom to conceal the depth of my practice from them.

After we had drank very smartly, I came home, transgressing but a little beyond my time. My miſtress was very well pleased, telling me, I should have leave another time, since I was so punctual. Those bottles of sack we drank ran perpetually in my mind, for it was the very flower of wine. In the commemoration of my friend's courtesy, and the goodness of that liquor, I gave my contemplative fancy leave to characterize a bottle of canary, thus.

THE CHARACTER OF A BOTTLE OF CANARY

He is a gentleman, I assure you, well extracted, which once lived like a salamander in the midst of the flames ; and had he not been burnt, he have never proved sound. He seems a prodigy ; for that which we live by, decays him ; hating air, as Bacchus hates small beer. He will lie still if you smother him, and is never so well as when his breath is stopped. Bury him, and you make him quicker. As for his habit, it is ever plain, yet neat. Though nobly born he scorns not to wear a green coat with a badge on it ; and you cannot injure him worse than to pick a hole in his coat. Though he wears for the most part one sort of garb, yet he is never out of fashion, acceptable to the best of company, not regarding his outward dress, but valuing his inward worth. However, his suit is made of admirable stuff, for his outside never grows barer, and his linings are the fresher for wearing. So choice he is in his clothing that he rather choseth to have his brains knocked out than to have a rent in his garment. He wears an *à la mode* hat, as light (and almost as little) as a shuttle-cock, which he puts off to none ; but like the quaker when brought before a magistrate, hath it taken off for him.

As for his pedigree, I know not how to derive it ; for he hath had in him the best and purest of the French blood, but will now acknowledge his race only from the Spaniard, whom he imitates, being stately, and standing always upright ; treads for the most part on carpets, and never stirs abroad but when he is carried, yet full of activity. If he runs fast and long, the more wind he gets. If he chance to fall, which is seldom, for many look to him, he will be extremely moved, yet (contrary to all men) the fuller his belly is the less hurt he receives : his credit is large, never paying for what he wears, running on the score perpetually ; his conditions are a riddle, there is in him pure virtue, and notorious vice ; the quintessence of love, and the venom of hatred. He is the beginning and the end of a thousand quarrels in a year, yet a very coward ; for he suffers any to take him by the ear, and never broke any one's pate but when company was by.

He is very facetious in society, and will spend himself freely to the last drop, if a lady's soft and warm hand will raise him. He is a brisk spark, and therefore courtiers adore him ; he is smooth in his expression, and therefore ladies delight in him ; he is filled with nimble fancies, therefore the wits frequent him, exhausting his radical moisture, to distil it into poetical raptures ; for conceits never run faster from the alembic of their brains, than when this gentleman adds fuel to the furnace. He whets wit, yet dulls it ; creates new fancies, and stupifies ; gives the orator a fluent tongue, and makes him speechless ; gives a poet feet till he cannot go ; and as he helps ministers to preach, so he likewise silenceth more than the Spanish Inquisition. He hath a great many tricks in him ; he will make a falconer fly high within doors ; make a huntsman catch a fox by the fire-side. Whatever he holds is made good ; and unless you mind him well, much good matter that falls from him may be lost : for he is often fluent beyond measure. All tongues court him ; and those that look narrowly unto him shall find him no dry fellow. The truth is, he is too profound for shallow brains to meddle with him. He will pour out quaint expressions and hard words so thick that the best scholars are glad at last to give him something to stop his mouth. Yet hold him up fairly, and you may get all he hath out of him. He is excessively beloved, and relishes all company, being pleasant and full of admirable humours.

He is inwardly acquainted with the Lord Mayor and Aldermen, and incorporateth with their wives daily. His kisses are so sweet that they lick their lips after him ; and though his breath be strong, yet it is not offensive. He is a true good fellow, drinking till he hath no eyes to see with. Good liquor is his life and soul, and he is never musty but for want of it. He will drink till he be filled up to the very throat, and gape whilst others put it in. He will bear as much sack as any man in England of his bulk ; yet he will be soon drunk in company. But if you will give him leave to vomit, he will take his liquor and drink fresh till all the company be forced to leave him. Drinking is his hourly exercise, seldom lying out of a tavern. He is the main upholder of club-meetings, without fear of being broke. He picks men's pockets, yet is never made more reckoning of than by such persons. As for his estate, I can only say this, that all he hath he carries about him ; yet generally he is reputed rich. What he hath, he holds upon courtesy ; but what he gives others, is held *in capite*. What he possesseth is commonly upon sale ; yet more for plenty, than for want ; and if you can purchase him you purchase all.

I could never endure idleness, I was ever in action ; either writing, or contriving, or putting in execution my contrivances. I thought it better *male agere quam nihil agere ;* my brains or hands were continually working, and very seldom but effectually. My pen was generally so happy in discoveries that my wit was much applauded by the most censorious. Much respected I was, and my company much importuned by the tankard-bearers of Helicon, by which means I so swelled with pride, that I thought myself little inferior to Apollo. I called Mercury pimp, the Nine Sisters whores, whom I had frequently lain with, and might when I pleased : the best title I could bestow on Pegasus was Hackney-Jade.

In the height of this my opinionativeness, my cooler (our master's maid) came to me where I was alone ; and after many heartfetched sighs, told me she found herself with child ; which news had like to have deprived me of my understanding. But knowing that vexation never remedies but rather adds to trouble, I was resolved to bear it patiently, and study some means to preserve her and my credit. I framed a letter as from her father, desiring her to come down into the country speedily, if she intended to see him alive ; and according as we had laid the plot, she shews it her mistress, desiring her leave to shew her duty to her dying father.

Our mistress most willingly consented thereunto, as knowing that there was more than ordinary love between us. The maid had stayed as long as possibly she might without discovery. Lacing herself very strait, and keeping down her belly with three busks ; but now she made haste to rub off. I had provided a midwife that should be her bawd too ; but this could not be done without extraordinary cost. After her delivery, I found the keeping of her and the child very expensive ; then did I begin to consider what a vast charge, and how many various troubles this momentary lecherous pleasure draws upon a man ; how furiously he is upon the onset, and how quickly satisfied, loathing that object he a little before longed for. Well, I bethought myself how to be rid both of cow and calf. I told her I would get together what money I could, and so marry her, upon condition she would be willing to travel with me whither I went, which I knew was her only desire. I informed her of my intention to go for Virginia, and the reasons that induced me thereunto.

First, her disgrace would not be known there : Next, my master could have no power over me, insisting further on the pleasantness of that continent, and the plenty of every thing, &c.

She assented to all I propounded, relying herself solely on me to dispose of her as I pleased. To palliate my design, I went with her to Gravesend, pretending as if I was then going with her beyond sea, for no other end but to clear myself from her there, knowing that after she had passed examination or search of the block-house, she would meet with no more. Being aboard, I suddenly seemed to have forgot something ashore ; having well laid my plot upon the basis of a good sum of money I had distributed among the seamen, with a considerable present to the master, and telling my Lindabrides I would return to her instantly, I got into the boat, and immediately after, the ship weighed anchor, and quickly was under sail. I confess, notwithstanding the devil had at that time the total possession of me, yet I was much troubled at what I had done so hard-heartedly and cruelly. A flood of tears so overwhelmed my sight that I could not discern the ship in which she was. So sensible I was of the wickedness of this fact, that Dido-like, I could have thrown myself into the sea after her, had not a good woman, whose husband was in the same ship, prevented me. Observing my tears, ' 'Tis probable, young man,' said she, ' you have lately taken your leave of some dearly beloved friend ; and I guess, by your earnest looking after yon ship under sail, the person was in her.' I told her it was truth. ' My husband is in the same vessel,' said she, ' and therefore I have as much cause to grieve as you. Come, be of good comfort, man ; friends must part ; and it is better to part here than at the gallows. Go along with me, and we will wash down sorrow ; and with a glass of neat canary, antidote our hearts against anything that may disturb them.'

With that I looked intentively in her face, and found it correspondent with a jolly temper, an eye black and piercing ; and eye-brows black also, and each as big as a man's thumb comparatively ; a sign that never fails to denote that woman capable of giving a man the greatest delectation. She was every way completely handsome and suitable to the desires of the most curious critic in love-affairs. I thought it a shame to deny so kind a proffer, and a crime in youth unpardonable not to embrace that opportunity that shall lead him by the hand into Venus her bed-chamber. With that I address myself to her (and afterwards undress together), declaring that the force of her rhetoric, assisted by her external beautiful, and altogether lovely form, had forced me to forget my only dearly beloved she-friend, and to become her proselyte, her absolutely devoted convert, and would prostrate my will to be guided by hers and her command. With that we concluded to solace ourselves at the next tavern. I applied myself to my old way of insinuation ; which soon melted her so that I saw I might when I pleased stamp love's impression on her.

Returning to Gravesend we soon lodged ourselves conveniently for our intended purpose. Having so done, I so ordered the matter that there was not anything wanting that might please our senses. Yet fearing lest her love should cool again, there was no art forgotten that might serve to entertain it. Delays in love-affairs are dangerous ; women love not to be too long tantalized ; there is a certain critical time to know their inclination ; which if you punctually observe, you shall assuredly reap the fruits of your desires ; if not, you may perpetually wait but never enjoy the like opportunity. Wherefore the iron glowing hot, I thought good to ſtrike : to enliven my spirits, she sent for a noise of music, ordering them to play in the next room. And in the end we began to think of some repose, agreeing before to lie in two chambers contiguous to each other ; which were accordingly provided. As soon as I thought all the household were in bed, I repaired to my miſtress, who eagerly awaited my coming ; approaching the bedside, she clasped me in her arms. As soon as day broke I arose, bespeaking a fat capon swaddled with sassages, and a quart of buttered sack. I got all ready by the time of her rising : she was extraordinarily well pleased in my double diligence of serving her. Having applauded my induſtry and care of her, we fell to it, interlining every bit with a glass of canary. She told me she would never part whilſt she had a penny left, having about her some thirty pieces of gold. ' Well,' said I, ' my dear, since it is thy resolution, a match ; but let me be ſteward.' Which she agreed unto, delivering into my hands what gold she had. For two or three hours I shewed myself very officious in my place ; but considering that when this money was spent we should not know what to do, I thought it was better for one to want than two ; besides, I had lately surfeited on a medlar, and therefore my ſtomach nauseated the very thoughts thereof.

I had feed the drawer to bring me word juſt as the Gravesend barge was going off ; which accordingly he did, by a private sign concluded betwixt us. I then pretended an excuse to go down, under the notion of providing something novel which should be conducible to our mirth and jollity. I had juſt so much time below to write her these lines inſtead of a solemn leave-taking, leaving them with the drawer to present her, and so went aboard the barge for London :

> Madam, I'm gone, no wonder, for you know,
> Lovers encounters are but touch and go.

Arriving at Billingsgate, I went ſtraight to a tavern where I had an intereſt with the drawer, resolving there to consult seriously with myself what course to follow, being as yet unresolved what to do. After I had raised my dulled spirits with a glass or two, I concluded to hazard my maſter's good opinion, nay, and my miſtress's affeɕtion too ; which though at that present it only smoked, I might easily divine that in process of time it would burſt forth into a flame. Being before confined to my maſter's time, I began to consider what an excellent thing liberty was, equally eſtimable with health ; which two, though they are the greateſt and moſt precious gifts (next our redemption) the creator of the world hath beſtowed on mankind ; yet we poor mortals value them not till we are sensible of their want, by being deprived of them.

This is an infallible maxim, That the deprivation of a thing shall be so much the more evil, as the possession thereof is good. Now if liberty be such an excellent and delectable thing when enjoyed, how miserable are those that want it ?

Having money in my pocket, I concluded to experiment the enjoyment thereof, and to participate in such delights the nature of young men is most inclinable to. Now man being a sociable creature, I thought I should reap but little satisfaction to myself in the expense of my money, without an associate. Wherefore I sent to an apprentice of my intimate acquaintance contemporary with me, and who had often prompted me to ramble with him. This lad was his master's cashier, which I knew would much assist my design. I made him acquainted with my intention of trying the world. Though it had been formerly his own motion, yet he seemed at the first something startled ; but all his doubts I resolved ; adding moreover, that to have our wills inslaved to other men's, was a thing insupportable, since that we were, as well as they, created free denizens of this world ; That since our great-grandfather was emperor of the whole world, we could not style ourselves less than princes, and therefore debased our birth by a voluntary submission to service and slavery. I had no great occasion to make use of many arguments to this purpose ; for his own inclination was sufficient to perusade him. The result of our discourse was a firm resolution to become two knights-errant. I advised him forthwith to go home and bring with him what cash he had in his possession ; which he readily performed, and indeed more then I could expect, being 200l., the fates having so decreed to favour this our first bold exploit, as a trial of what we durst attempt.

CHAPTER XII

How he frequented bawdy-houses : what exploits he committed in them :
the character of a bawd, a whore, a pimp, and a trapan : their manner
of living : with a detection of their wicked lives and conversations

BEING full fraught with money, we undertook our progress, promising to ourselves all delight imaginable, but not considering what the effect would be. We frequented all places of pleasure, but among the chief we ranked brothel-houses, which were our repositories. We seldom were seen in the streets by day, for fear of discovery ; confining ourselves close prisoners to some 'Bubbing-house'; at night (like such as closely delighted in deeds of darkness) we would sometimes

F

flutter abroad. Our paſtime was to hire coaches to any pretended place, and when we came near it, to make our escape. One time leaping out of the boot, my cloak chanced to tangle in the spokes of the wheel. The coachman not perceiving we were got out, drove on ; by the wheels continually turning, my garment was so engaged that I verily believed my sins had now conferred upon me the juſt punishment of being executed on the wheel, which I could hardly have avoided, had I not speedily unbuttoned my cloak. I was loth to bid the coachman ſtop, thinking I should have it at laſt. I ran lacquey-like a long way, but all my endeavours to shift it, proved ineffeſtual ; so that at length I was forced to cry out, ' Hold, coachman.' The coachman coming out of his box, soon perceived the fallacy, and ſtraightways demanded his money for his hire before he would untangle my cloak, which I was compelled to give him. Delivering me my cloak, he told me, I had paid him, but he had not paid me for my attendance on him. And said moreover, that my cloak would not look like a livery, unless it were laced ; and with that, with his whip, lashed me well-favouredly. Another sort of paſtime we used, was to kick the old watchmen's lanthorns about the ſtreet ; and it may be, sometimes confer a blow or two on their sleepy noddles, and then fly for it, but we had worse success with this than the former.

We praſtised this foolery so often, till at length we were met with and rightly served. It was thus : In Paternoſter Row we found a fellow at noddie upon a ſtall, with his lanthorn and candle by him ; having firſt seized on that, and thrown it into the kennel, we prosecuted our abuse by falling upon him, and beating him. As soon as we had done this manful aſt, we betook ourselves to flight ; but here we miſtook our mark, thinking him to be an old decrepit watchman, and one that had little use of his eyes, without those in his pocket ; whereas to our coſt, we found him as nimble and as light footed as a ſtag, who overtaking us, surprized us ; and as he was carrying us before the conſtable, we met with the Grand Round, who, without much examination committed us as rats to the Compter. The chiefeſt thing that troubled us was the apprehension of our maſter's knowing where we were. But we resolved to drown that care : we had not been there long, before other rats, male and female were brought in to bear us company. Some of the men were all bloody, and their mobs' scarfs and hoods all rent, and none of them sober. Damning and sinking were the conſtant flourishes of their discourse ; calling for drink was the argument they held, and roaring in diſtraſted notes was their harmony. Though I was myself comparatively wicked, yet I blessed my God I had not arrived to that height these superlative villains had attained to. Being in their company,

I thought myself in the suburbs, or on the confines of Hell. Sin, if it be dressed up in specious pretences, may be entertained as a companion ; but when it appears in its own shape it cannot but strike horror into the soul of any, though desperate, if not stupified. Wherefore methought I was so far from associating myself with them, that I protest the lewdness of their actions were so represented to me with such deformity that I knew not which I loathed most, them or the prison.

I cannot make appear to the world what they were, nor my resentments, unless I should stuff a page or two with all manner of horrid oaths, execrations, blasphemies and such like soul-infecting and destroying plague-sores ; wherefore I shall only take leave to anatomize the place that detained us from our freedom. Then look upon a prison as in itself, and it may be fitly termed a temporary Hell. For as the other is a receptacle for damned souls, the gates thereof standing always wide open ; so this refuseth the reception of none, though never so wicked a miscreant. Though my durance in this place was but short, yet I could not but take some observations, employing from thence the faculties of my soul to draw up the definition of a prison. Hell is a very proper denomination for it, since it is a place composed of nothing but disorder and confusion ; a land of darkness, inhabited by calamity, horror, misery, and confusion ; a bottomless pit of fraud, violence and stench. A prison is the banishment of courtesy, the centre of infamy and disparagement, the destruction of good wits, the treasure of despair, the fining-pot of friendship, a den of deceivers, a forest of ravenous beasts. Here you may see one weeping, another singing ; one sleeping, another swearing ; every one variously employed ; one eating in a corner, and another pissing just by him ; another lousing himself between both ; it may be heretofore a military man, and therefore loth to forget his art, but rather exercising it in the killing of his bodily enemies, bearing the blood on his nail, as the trophies of his victory.

It is, to speak most properly, a living tomb or grave to bury men alive in, wherein a man for half a year's experience may learn more law than he can in three terms for an hundred pound.

It is a little wood of woe, a map of misery, a place that will learn a young man more villainy if he be apt to take it in six months, than at twenty gaming ordinaries, bowling-alleys, or bawdy-houses ; and an old man more policy, than if he had been pupil to Machiavel.

This place hath more diseases predominant in it than the pest-house in a plague-time ; and stinks worse than my Lord Mayor's dog-house.

It is a little commonwealth, although little wealth common there ; it is a desert, where desert lies hood-winked.

The place is as intricate as Rosamond's labyrinth, and is so full of meanders and crooked turnings that it is impossible to find the way out, except he be directed by a silver clue ; and can never overcome the Minotaur without a golden ball to work his own safety. The next day, paying our fees, and receiving some checks, with good admonitions from the justice, we were discharged.

This misfortune made us not a jot more cautious, but as soon as we were at liberty we went upon the scent to Mother Cr.[1] formerly famous for the good citizens' wives that frequented her house ; who still rides admiral of all the rest of her function about the Town. I hope the next time I go to visit her, she will not get me clapped for the pains I take in praising her. The truth of it is, of all the bawds I know, she merits most, having an house fit for the accommodation of the best. As for her working utensils, they are composed of refined metal, always neatly kept ; which, because they are not used upon all slight occasions, they appear the more delectable to the eye. As soon as we had entered the door, I could hear a rustling of silks in sundry places ; I conceive it was their policy, by seeming modesty to set a sharper edge on our appetites. We were conducted into a large handsome room ; bottles of wine were brought up, both Spanish and French, with salt meats to relish the palate, though we gave no order for them ; but it seems it was the custom of the house, an expensive one ; but without a piece spending, you shall know little of their practices.

At length, up came the old matron ; after the performance of our devoir, she seats herself by me, and began to be impudently acquainted, chucking me under the chin, calling me her Son Smock-face. Having well warmed ourselves with wine, and the good gentlewoman perceiving that our bloods began to heat, ' Well,' said she, ' I guess at the intent of your coming hither, neither shall you go away unsatisfied. Nature will have its course ; and if in youth it be stopped, it will but, torrent-like, flow with the greater impetuosity. Come, I see by your countenances that ye were born sons of mirth and pleasure ; shew then what stock ye came of. If you want subjects to exercise your parts on, we'll have more wine ; and when ye are inflamed, ye shall have the benefit of a cooler.' With that she leaves us ; but another of the same sex, though three degrees different in age, supplied her place. At first view I seemed very well pleased : handsome she was, and very proportionable ; but withal so impudent, that I was antidoted against lechery. *Ista fœmina quæ limites verecundiæ semel excesserit, oportet illam esse graviter impudentem.* If once a woman pass the bounds of shamefacedness, she will seldom stop till she hath arrived to the height of impudence. I must needs deal ingenuously, at the beginning the needle of my microcosm

---

[1] Mother Cresswell was a famous bawd of the time.

was touched by Love's loadstone ; but upon further acquaintance, if I might have had a hundred pounds, I could not have meddled with her.

Though she had baited her desires with a million of prostitute countenances and enticements, yet I looked upon her rather a companion for an hospital, and stood more in need of a chirurgeon's acquaintance than mine. My friend had nibbled at the bait ; but when I heard them capitulating about the price, I thought she wanted a fee for the doctor. Well, had she not over-traded, she had not broke so soon ; for her trade is opposite to all others : for she did set up without credit, and her too much custom undid her ; and so let her go, without either shame, or hope of repentance.

We desired to see another. 'Tis variety that man chiefly takes delight in. One constant sort of food, without participating of any other, though manna, will cause the stomach to long for the flesh-pots. Neither can the crime be greater in the enjoyment of diverse persons then one alone, provided matrimony make not the act legitimate. I do not approve of these consequent lines tending to this purpose ; yet give me leave to insert them, that you may understand how viciously minded some are in this frothy age :

> Born under some ill planet, or accurst,
> Is he that loves one single whore ;
> Who with one draught can always quench his thirst,
> Ty'd to one mistress, and no more.

This nauseating thing being removed, up came one of Venus her chief darlings. Excellent flesh ! and she herself the cook that dressed it, spending most of her day-time about it, that she might with the better appetite be tasted at night. Finding no exceptions in this, I was impatient till I had consummated my desires. Withdrawing into another room, to heighten my thoughts, she declared to me her birth and education ; that as the one was well extracted, the other had occasioned much cost and expense ; that for her part, she associated with none but persons of quality, whose long patience and entreatments first procured a familiarity, and in fine, freedom in the exercise of love-affairs : and so would have (seemingly) put me off upon this score, that it was not usual for her to admit of any to her embraces but such whose long acquaintance had gained her affection. I offered her a crown, which she refused with indignation ; telling me, that she was not yet reduced to so low a condition as to become so poor a mercenary prostitute. At last, with much persuasion, I fastened on her an half piece ; and so striving with her (she only seeming averse), I accomplished my ends.

And presently in came a fellow whose very face would have enlightened the room, though in the darkeſt night ; for indeed it appeared to me a blazing comet, and his nose (for miraculously he had preserved it) was the brushy tail. Laying his hand on his sword, he looked fiercer than a Spanish Don insulting over an Indian slave. The bulk of his body began to heave like an earth-quake, whilſt his mouth, Ætna-like, belched out all manner of sulphurous oaths, which roared so loud as if his belly had contained a barrel of gunpowder, and the linſtock of his nose had fired it. His courteous salutation to me, was, ' How dareſt thou, son of a whore, presume in this nature to dishonour me, in the abusing of my wife, without the expeċtation of an immediate annihilation or dissipation into atoms ? But I have something here shall tame thy insolence ; and now I am resolved to set thy blood abroach.' With that he seemed to make a pass at me. Now I, imagining that he really intended to do what he pretended, for the safeguard of my life, took up a joint-ſtool, and received his point in the seat ; and following it home, tumbled him down the ſtairs ; and not being able to recover myself, fell with him. My comrade came running down at the noise to assiſt me ; but he seeing me rather make use of my heels then hands, followed my example, and so built a sconce, leaving the old bawd to condole her great loss ; for the reckoning was very considerable.

Now, because I have often met with these Heċtors or trapanning villains, I think it will not be unsuitable to this present discourse, to insert their charaċter.

THE CHARACTER OF A HECTOR OR TRAPAN

A bawdy-house is his cloiſter, where he conſtantly says his matins. He is a whore's proteċtor, pretending himself more valiant than any of the ancient heroes, thereby thinking to take off the suspicion of a coward from himself ; for the opinion of valour is a good proteċtion to those that dare not use it. His frequent drawing his sword upon any slight occasion makes the ignorant suppose him valiant ; whereas he durſt not do it but when he is confident no danger will ensue thereon. He never ſtrikes any but such he is sure will not return his blows. In company he is wonderful exceptious and choleric, thinking in the fray some booty may be obtained : but his wrath never swells higher than when men are loth to give him any occasion ; the only way to pacify him is to beat him soundly. The hotter you grow, the milder he is, proteſting he always honoured you. The more you abuse him the more he seems to love you ; if he chance to be quarrelsome, you may threaten him into a quiet temper. Every man is his maſter that dares beat him ; and everyone dares that knows him ; and he that dares do this, is the only man can do much with him. Yet if he knows a coward, he will purposely fall out with him, to get courtesies from him, and so be bribed into a reconcilement. Yet I cannot say but that he may fight (if with great advantage), being so accustomed to the sight of drawn swords, which probably may infuse something of a conceit into him ; which he so magnifies by his own good opinion that he would have people believe that the molehill of his prowess is no less than a mountain. This little he hath, he is no niggard in displaying ; resembling some apothecaries' shops, full of pots, though little contained in them.

His estate lies in contrivances ; and though other landlords have but four quarter-days, he hath three hundred sixty and odd to receive the fruits of his stratagems. He is well skilled in cards and dice, which help him to cheat young gulls newly come to town ; and the reason he usually gives for it, is, A woodcock must be plucked ere he be dressed. If that will not do, he carries him to one of his mistresses, and so both join to plume this fowl. If there be not ready money to answer expectation, a bond of considerable value shall serve turn, attested by two who shall swear anything for half-a-crown. No man puts his brain to more use then he ; for his life is a daily invention, and each meal a stratagem. He hath an excellent memory for his acquaintance ; if there ever passed but an ' How do you ? ' between him and another it shall serve seven years hence for an embrace, and that for money. Out of his abundance of joy to see you he offers a pottle of wine ; and in requital of his kindness can do no less than make you pay for it. Whilst you are drawing money, he fumbles in his pockets (as schoolboys with their points, being about to be whipped), till the reckoning be paid, and says, ' It must not be so,' yet is easily persuaded to it ; and then cries, ' Gentlemen, you force me to incivility.' When his whores cannot supply him, he borrows of any that will lend him aught ; of this man a shilling, and of another as much ; which some lend him, not out of hope to be repaid, but that he will never trouble them again. If he finds a good look from any, he will haunt him so long till he force a good nature to the necessity of a quarrel.

He loves his friend as one doth his cloak that hath but one, and knows not how to get another ; he will be sure to wear him threadbare ere he forsake him. Men shun him at last as infection ; nay, his old companions, his clothes that have hung upon him so long, at length fall off too. His prayer in the morning is, that his cheats may take effect that day ; if not, that he may be drunk before night. He sleeps with a tobacco-pipe in his mouth, and he dreams of nothing but villainy. If any mischief escapes him, it was not his fault, for he lay as fair for it as he could. He dares not enter into a serious thought, lest he hang himself ; but if such melancholy seize him, drink is his refuge, and drunkenness cures him.

Lastly, he commonly dies like a malefactor on the gallows, or like Hercules with fire in his bones. When hanged, if begged for an anatomy, it would serve to convert tobacco-smokers from delighting in the excess thereof : for they will find the funnel of his body, I mean his throat, furred and choked up.

Being freed from danger, we rejoiced exceedingly that we thus so narrowly escaped, resolving to house ourselves in the next bubbing-place we came to, that we might talk freely of this rencounter. A place (pointed out to us by the devil's finger) soon presented itself to our eyes, which we with more than good speed entered ; and coming into the kitchin, I was not a little amazed at the sight of a thing sitting in a chair by the fire-side, with a pipe of tobacco in its mouth, and a quartern of strong waters by its side. This tun of flesh resembled an elephant for the bigness of her waist, had there been the least appearance of a tooth. A nose she had (which with all wonder be it spoken that she had any) so long that it was a fit resemblance of the elephant's proboscis or trunk. But, as I said before, her teeth were fallen out, and as loving neighbours to reconcile them, her chin and nose resolved to meet about it. She bid us welcome as well as she could speak. Go, I think she could not ; but opening her mouth, Lord, what strong imaginations my fancy suggested to me ! Methought I saw Hell gaping to devour me ; and within that bottomless concave I could discern infinite numbers of souls whose damnation she was accessory to ; and coming somewhat too near her, I imagined her breath was bituminous, and smelt of brimstone. She might fitly be compared to old coal that hath been well burnt, that with the least spark will re-kindle, and fire anything near it. But her fittest likeness is the devil, her envy running parallel with his. All that the devil endeavours is to bring mankind into the same state with himself ; and a bawd's aim is to make all fair women like her. Now because their youth perhaps will not admit of it so soon, she hurries them on to it by degrees, by drinking, smoking, painting, and daily excess in venery. I looked about her house very inquisitively, but I could not judge her moveables (setting aside her quick cattle) to be worth an inventory. Her bedding I doubt me, too, is infectious, few coming near it but they are taken with a fit of the falling-sickness.

This old beldam being loth to put her throat to the trouble of calling her white devils about her, had got a whistle, on which she used several notes ; which musical language her girls understood very well. We called for drink ; the old bawd replied she would send for some, though she had it not in the house : this was to be sure of our money. Herein I observed their temperance, not suffering us to have too much measure. Wenches we had plentifully ; one more especially I took notice of, to have the swarthiest skin I have seen English born, on whom an ordinary fellow was very sweet. When I saw my opportunity, I asked him (craving his excuse) what trade he was ? Pat as I would have it, he answered me, that he was a tanner. ' I concluded so, Sir,' said I, ' by your dressing of that calf's-skin there.' This dull-headed fool apprehended me not, but began to be angry, telling me his trade was a good trade, and I need not undervalue it. I told him, I did not, since there was some analogy between my trade and his. ' Why what trade are you ? ' said he, ' I may ask you a question, as well as you me.' I replied, ' that I was a cuckold-maker.' ' How can that be like my profession ? ' quoth he. ' In this,' said I, ' You dress the skins, and I trim the horns.' The bawd at this fell into such an extreme fit of laughter that down fell her pipe, and up came the strong-waters that she had swallowed. But that was not all, for having not her retentive faculty, she let fly. Surely she was overcharged, which made her recoil, and so blew out her breech-pin. She was forced to leave us, and about an hour after returned ; how sweet, I cannot tell you. We fell into discourse again. I asked her how long she had lived in this house ? ' Two years,' said she, ' a longer time then any house I have lived in this twenty years.' With that I concluded she was in fee with the justices' clerk.

My stomach being waterish, I would needs have some eggs and bacon : but Lord, what an agony the hearing thereof put the bawd in ! desiring me to desist, for she should die at the sight of them. I asked her the reason : ' O,' said she, ' it puts me in mind of one Shrove-Tuesday especially, on which the apprentices pulled down my house ; and sick, sick as I was, pulled me away violently from a caudle I had prepared to comfort me. But they gave me one with a pox to them, and the Devil's dam take the rotten eggs in it, with which I thought they would have pelted out my brains. After they had dragged me sufficiently, and worried me (as a mastiff would a cat) till they were weary of the sport ; fearing I should catch cold, they out of pity covered me warm in a bog-house. But the worst was, after this kind usage, I was to go through a long street before I could come to an acquaintance of mine wherein I could safely secure myself from the out-rage of these hell-hounds. All along as I went, a thousand dogs barked at me, the street was filled with people looking and laughing at my sad disaster, but none daring to come near me. They say I left so strong a scent behind me that several of the inhabitants left their dwellings upon it, and that the strong savour remained in that place above six days.' I seemed to pity her much, promising to visit her often ; and so we left her.

CHAPTER XIII

*What a trick he served his comrade : how himself was trapannd : his own
clothes taken from him : the bawd out of pretended pity invested him
with an old petticoat and waistcoat : his admittance into a boarding-
school : his getting many of the gentlewomen with child : his discovery,
and his flight*

FROM one bawdy-house to another, was our daily travel, still
finding out some variety that might please us. About twilight,
coming along by a well-built house, I saw a gentlewoman richly attired
standing by the door, who, as I passed by, very civilly saluted me, and
so withdrew herself. I followed her in, as very well understanding how
to interpret such actions. She brought us into a spacious inner room,
and then with much civility and good carriage, invited us to sit down.
She called to her servant to bring some bottles of wine, resolving to make
us pay dearly for her extraordinary favours. By our habits she took
us for no less than persons of quality ; for we had gallantly accoutred
ourselves ; and I thought that Fortune now had designed me her
chiefest favourite, in throwing this unexpected blessing upon me. She
caused her lute to be brought her, to which she sung so harmonically,
that the music of the spheres are no more to be compared to it than a
Scotch bagpipe to an organ. This so intoxicated my comrade, with the
wine together (not but that they had a great operation on myself), that he
fell fast asleep (*alias* dead drunk). Glad I was to my very heart of this
accident, fearing he might be a rival in my intention : and to the intent
I might remove all impediments that might hinder my sole enjoyment
of this lady, I consulted with myself what to do with him. I was not long
about it, but straight found out this cunning plot ; which was to send
him home to his master. Love to a woman is so forcible that what will
it not do ? to sum up all, make a man betray his friend. I made an
apology to the gentlewoman for his incivility, and requested the favour
to have her servant procure me a porter ; whilst she was gone to execute
my desires, I searched his pockets, and took away all his gold ; for we
had converted all our money into that metal, which we always made
our *Vade mecum*. To ingratiate myself with this gentlewoman, I
acquainted her with my design ; which she heartily laughed at. I
farther desired of her, that I might have a card and a piece of paper.
On the card I wrote a superscription, and pinned it on his back, directing
the thing to his master, living in such a place. With the paper, I wrote a
letter to him to this effect.

Sir,
Lately I found your goose upon the way,
I took him up, as one that went astray.
To recompence my pains, I pull'd his feathers ;
Such precious down will warm me in all weathers.
His flesh I love not ; it belongs to you :
The gibblets though I keep ; and so adieu.

I gave the porter instructions that he should but just put him within the doors, and leave the letter, and so with all speed come away, to prevent examination. He brought me word he had performed my order ; what discants were made hereon I shall leave the reader to imagine.

By this time I had gained my mistress with a shower of gold, which had so far prevailed on her that she protested she was wholly and solely at my devotion. I would have had her to have gone immediately to bed ; but she told me, there would be time enough before morning to sport in, and that we should be both tired if we went to bed so soon. Wherefore, to divert ourselves, we drank and sung together in parts, I myself having indifferent good judgment. Having spun out the time so long till it was time to go to bed, she then conducted me to the chamber where she intended we should lie. Though she made what haste she could to undress herself, yet methought she was purposely tedious. I commended before her vocal and instrumental music ; but then I esteemed no other music sweeter than what the tag made against her bodice when she was unlacing herself. About two o'clock in the morning three or four fellows rushed into our room ; at which I awakened, but made as little noise as a *Perdue*. My mistress leaping out of the bed, they seized on her, gagged and bound her ; and then opening the two leaves of the window that was the entrance into the balcony, they came in all haste to the bed, and in a trice, had rolled up the bed so close, that they had like to have stifled me in the middle on't. Though they dragged me in the bed from off the bedsted, rudely letting me fall on the ground, yet I felt no harm ; every part of me was so well guarded, that in that condition, I might have bid defiance to a cannon-bullet. But when I heard them talk of flinging the bed over the balcony to their companions, I thought I should have died instantly for fear, knowing I must of necessity go with it. Whereupon I cried out as loud as I could, and struggling, I got a little place open, and then I roared like Phalaris his bull. They seeming to be surprized with my unexpected noise, fled, fastening a rope to the balcony, and so slid down into the street.

Perceiving they were all gone, I groped about the room (for it was very dark) speaking very slowly, ' Where are you Madam ? ' repeating it often ; but much wondering I could not hear her answer me. As I was feeling round the room, ſtretching forth my hands, I chanced to run one of my hands againſt her, and one of my fingers into her mouth. I thought my finger had ſtrayed at firſt, miſtaking the place ; but searching farther, and finding teeth, I knew then whereabout I was, and discovered withal a ſtick in her mouth, keeping it wide open, as butchers do their sheep with a gambrel. But having removed this obſtacle of her speech, she begged me to untie her hands ; which having done, she herself untied her feet ; and with that, she would have clasped me in her arms ; but I hung an arse, being sensible of the ſtinking condition that the fear had put me in. She was very inquisitive after my welfare, asking me again and again, whether I had received any harm from the rogues. I told her no : ' Nay, then I care not for my own sufferings, or what loss I have suſtained by them,' said she, and so speedily went for a candle. As I was thinking to apologize for my naſtiness, up she came with a light. Viewing me, and perceiving what a condition I was in, she kept at a diſtance; ' Sir,' said she, ' my fancy suggeſts to me that you now resemble Nebuchadnezzar when metamorphosed into a beaſt, and lying in his own dung. When you shall have reassumed your humanity, I shall presume to approach nearer to you.' I made my sirreverence to her, wishing they had gagged her breech so wide that her guts might have a passage through her poſteriors. For I plainly perceived, not-withſtanding all her specious pretences, she was the foundress of this plot.

Well, she caused water to be brought up, with which I cleansed myself ; and because my shirt had too ſtrong a scent of *Stercus humanum*, she lent me a smock, which presaged ere long I should wear coats too. Having shifted myself, I looked for my clothes, but there was a *Non est inventus* out againſt them ; all my search could afford me not the leaſt comfort. My miſtress seemed much diſturbed at my loss, but when I told her I had loſt such a considerable quantity of gold, her sorrow seemed to be redoubled, and I am sure her inward joy was increased. She comforted me with a great many friendly loving expressions, desiring me to be patient, and indeed necessity forced me to it. I asked her advice what I should do in this naked condition. ' There is no remedy,' she replied. ' You muſt be content to clothe yourself in woman's apparel, as for man's I have none to furnish you withal.' I consented to it, and presently she dressed me up in one of her gowns, with all the appurtenances thereunto belonging. The slenderness of my body, whiteness of skin, beauty, and smoothness of face (having no hairs thereon) added a suit-ableness to my garb. I muſt ingeniously confess, when I consulted with a looking-glass, I thought the transmutation of sexes had been verified in me ; but when I walked, I found something pendulous, which easily persuaded me to the contrary belief of myself. I thought it folly to tax her for my misfortune, knowing how little it would advantage me.

The time was come I was to take my leave of her. Going to salute her, I committed a foul miſtake, endeavouring to pull off my hood inſtead of my hat, and making a leg (as the vulgar term is) inſtead of a curtsy ; but she advising me to rectify that miſtake for the time to come, we bid each other adieu. In this disguise I traversed the ſtreets, it being almoſt impossible for any to discover me, my voice being so effeminate that I was confident that would never betray me. As I walked, I consulted with reason what was moſt expedient. My invention (as at all times) was now ready to assiſt me ; and thus it was. Finding a bill on a door, I knocked, desiring to see what lodgings they had. I was very civilly entreated to come in, and was shewn several rooms with much respeƈt, for my female habit was very gallant, and so it had need, for it coſt me dearer than so much cloth of gold. I pitched at laſt upon a chamber extraordinary well furnished. I never scrupled the price (because they should look on me as a person of quality), but agreed to my landlord's own terms. I told him I was lately come out of the country, and that my trunks were not yet arrived, with a great many more fiƈtions to prevent suspicion. At firſt I intended to take for no longer time than I could contrive a way to dispose of myself, and procure man's apparrel ; but perceiving how agreeable my feature, ſtature and geſture were to my female weeds, I resolved to try some projeƈts in them.

There was a young gentleman that lay in the house, and took special notice of me as soon as I entered it, and as he told me next day, was over-joyed that I had determined to be a lodger there. This young bravo (who had more money than wit) had prepared a banquet for me, and requeſted the favour of me that it and himself might be received into my chamber. I alleged I could not do it in point of honour, and therefore desired to be excused ; but he pressed me so far (getting also his land-lady to intercede for him), that at laſt (though with much seeming unwillingness) I condescended thereunto. Very merry they were, but I thought it prudence to be reserved. My amoriſt so gazed on me that I thought he would have devoured me with his eyes, kissing me some-times, which had like to have made me disgorge my ſtomach in his face ; for in my opinion, it is very unnatural, nay loathsome, for one man to kiss another, though of late too cuſtomary I know it is. Yet I look on such as use it, inclining to sodomy, and have had the unhappiness to be acquainted with several who using that unnatural aƈtion, found it only the preludium to a more beaſtly intention. In three days' time we grew so intimately acquainted that at laſt he became impudent. One time as I passed by him, he catched at me, endeavouring to intrude his hand where he had no interest ; but he did it so rudely that I verily thought he had spoiled me. I believe he imagined that he had caught me by the busk, which some ladies wear very long to hide their rising bellies. I shewed myself much displeased at him for so doing, expressing my resentment in imbittered words for so great a crime.

Next morning, he courted me to a reconciliation with a gold watch. By that he should have been well skilled in gaining female affections, for there is nothing prevails on them more than presents, and nothing gains sooner over them a total conquest than the hopes of enjoying a fair promising fortune. With much importunity I accepted his peace-offering, conditionally that he should never attempt the like offence. Nothing troubled me more, than how to dress myself, when my clothes were off. I durst not lay two things together, for fear I should mistake ; there were so many baubles, I wished for a pen and ink, to write on them what places they properly belonged to. Viewing them on the table together, they represented to my thoughts babel, or a great confusion, and nothing but a miracle could produce order out of them. I had so improved myself by hourly practice, when none was with me, and observation of others, that I had now the knack on't. I new modelled my steps, my former being too large by three quarters ; I could advantageously cast my eye, set my face in a plat-form, and dissect my words ; my feet were my only traitors, and therefore I always kept them close prisoners, for their greatness (like the Devil's cloven-foot) proclaimed me the contrary sex I imitated.

Well, I thought it high time to be gone, not without plucking my widgeon. Having a fit opportunity, there being none present but himself and I, I pretended disappointment of money, and that my rents were not yet due, and therefore desired him to lend me 10*l.* for eight days ; at the termination of which time, I should not fail to return it him with gratitude. He was much joyed that I would favour him so far as to accept his service ; and with that flew like lightning, fearing he would have fractured his leg-bone for haste to bring me the money, which I received from him thankfully. I caused a coach to be called, pretending I had business in the City. My cully would have waited on me, which I utterly refused, telling him that without privacy my affairs would prove ineffectual ; whereupon he desisted.

Coming into Burchin Lane, I went to a salesman, and bought (pretendedly for my maid) an ordinary yet handsome petticoat and waist-coat, furnishing myself with all the appurtenances requisite for a servant-maid.

Instead of returning to my lodging, I caused the coachman to drive me to one of the principal nurseries of Venus, Whetstone Park. For I looked upon it as a matter of small import to take my leave either of my young gallant at home, or my landlord, since I had not left the least mortgage behind me for sleeping.

Mother Cunny (to tell the truth) was the nickname of that corpulent matron that with much demonstrations of joy received me into her house ; neither could she forbear expressing her great satisfaction in that her civil and honest deportment was so generally taken notice of as that it should be an inducement to strangers to shelter themselves under her tutelage, preferring her as a guardian or tutress, before so many thoroughly tried and long experienced ancient gentlewomen, both in City and suburbs. She highly applauded both the features and complexion of my face, not forgetting the right colour of my hair, which was flaxen : the stature of my person infinitely pleased her, which was somewhat of the tallest. In short, nothing disliked her but that she said I looked as if I had a greater mind to beat, than buss ; and to fight than delight my amoretes with smiling insinuations.

I had not been long in her house before a roaring Damme entered the house (a constant visitant), who meeting with my guardian, was informed that there was a rich treasure discovered in her house, and that none should attempt to spring the mine till he had made entrance by the first stroke. In short, he was brought into the chamber where I was, who at first behaved himself indifferently civil, and treated me nobly. But O Heavens ! how great was my confusion and distraction when strength of arguments and force of hands would not repel the fury of his lust, and that nothing would serve his turn but lying with m.. I defended myself manfully a long time ; but seeing it was impossible to hold out any longer, and that I must be discovered the next assault he made, forced me to cry out. This so alarmed my gentleman (concluding this outcry proceeded not from modesty and chastity, but out of some trapanning design) that he drew his sword, and made toward the stair-case, and running down with more haste than good speed, overturned my kind governess (that was puffing up the stairs to my relief) and so both tumbled down together. Fear had so dispossessed this huffing fellow of his senses that he mistook my old matron for the bravo he thought did usually attend me, and so without once looking behind him, made his escape into the street, leaving the piece of antiquity not so much defaced by time, as by this dismal accident so near extinguishing, that she was half undone in the vast expense of her strong-waters, to bring her tongue to one single motion.

Coming to herself, you may imagine how I was treated by her. But to be brief, I told her I could not brook such a course of life, wherein all enjoyments were attended by ruin and destruction, although habited and clothed in the seeming ornaments of real pleasure ; adding moreover, that I would speedily leave her house, investing myself with a meaner garb, bestowing those I wore on her in part satisfaction for what she suffered through my means. This proposition so well pleased her that I had free liberty to do as I thought most convenient herein.

Exchanging my fine Madamship for plain Joanship, my equipage being suitable for service, I resolved to apply myself to a boarding school; and the rather, having observed it to be more thronged with beauties, than any other. My address proved as successful as I could desire, for instantly upon my motion, I was received in as a menial of the house. But when I came to use the tools of the kitchin, I handled them so scurvily, it made those teething gigglers, my fellow servants, even split with laughter. To add to my misfortune, those varlets one time when we had some meat to roast, on purpose got out of the way for a while, to see how I could behave myself; and then I did spit the meat so monstrously strange, that coming into the kitchin, they could not tell at first sight what those joints were called at fire. My actions had proclaimed my ignorance in all domestic affairs, so that my mistress could not but take notice of me; and told me, that I was altogether unfit for her service, and that she could do no less than discharge me.

Fearing that my design was now frustrated and my fair hopes of delight annihilated, I could not contain my tears from bedewing my face. My blubbered eyes wrought so powerfully with my mistress that I judged it now the fittest time in broken accents to mollify her anger, and still reserve my place in her service. Whereupon I told her a great many formal and plausible lies, well methodized; that I had all my lifetime lived in an obscure village amongst rude and ill-bred people, and therefore knew nothing; that it was my desire to learn, not so much valuing wages as experience, and that it was for that intent I had tendered my service. The good old gentlewoman being much pleased with my freedom, ordered the maids that without their grinning and giggleting, they should shew me anything I understood not.

By diligent observing, I gained shortly an indifferent knowledge. Though I lay with one of my fellow-servants every night, yet I judged it no prudence to discover to her my sex (though much against the hair) till I had by external kindnesses endeared her to me. I went through my business pretty handily, giving a general satisfaction, gaining daily an interest upon the loves of the young gentlewomen.

O the fine inexpressible petulances that daily, nay, hourly passed between me and some other of them; and so crafty I was grown that I perfectly did counterfeit a modest maiden. Sometimes we would retire three or four of us into a private corner, yet not so obscure but that we intended to be seen by some man or other we had afore discovered;

and then, as if affrighted by an unexpected surprize, squeak out, and then with strange haste endeavour to hide our pretended shamefacedness. Thus concurring and suiting myself to their humours, I had all the freedom I could desire.

And now I thought it high time to handle the matter for which I came about; for indeed flesh and blood could hold out no longer. One night I perceived my bedfellow could not in the least close her eyes, continually sighing and tumbling to and fro, sometimes laying her leg over me, and at other times hugging me within her arms, as if I had been in a press. At first I thought this commotion of perturbation proceeded from sympathy, as questionless in part it did; for I found experimentally by myself that my heart did beat as if it would have forced its passage through my breast.

I thought I could do no less than ask her what she ailed that she was thus restless. At first, sighs were her only answers, till at last (I pressing her much) poor thing she melted into tears. As soon as her eyes had given over deluging, and that her heart would give her leave to speak; ' Joan,' said she, for so I called myself, ' if thou wilt keep my secrets, I will tell thee my whole heart.' Having promised to do that, whereupon she began thus to relate her story. ' Our coachman for several years hath shown me more than common respect, and indeed, though I have concealed that affection I ever bore him, yet I could not but now and then give him slight occasions of hope. As the months wherein we lived together added to our age, so did it add true life and vigour to our loves, which increased so much and fast, that I could hide mine no longer. But herein consists my misery, that our affections aim at different ends. I fain would marry him; he is only for present enjoyment; and finding me obstinate, and not in the least yielding to his amorous solicitations, begins to slight me, and toys with such before my face that I know will surrender their maiden forts upon the first summons. Now, dear Joan, let me tell thee, I can hold out no longer, but am resolved to give him all the opportunity of privacy I can invent, upon the least motion offered, I will entertain it.'

I dissuaded her from this rash resolution with as much reason as I could utter; inculcating the danger of being gotten with child, with all its aggravations; that having obtained his ends, his love would be converted into loathing; and he having rejected her as his object, none that knew her would choose her as an object that may make an honest wife; for who would marry a whore, but to entail the pox on his progeny? Whatever I alleged, she valued not. Seeing she was fully bent, I thought this the critical hour to discover myself to her, ' Come, come,' said I. ' I will quickly put you out of conceit with *John*, and cure this

G

love that so much troubles you ; ' and so I did, after which I enjoined her silence ; which I thought she would have done, for her own interest sake ; as she did for a while.

I came at length to be very much beloved in general. It was the custom almost every night for the young gentlewomen to run skittishly up and down into one another's chambers ; and I was so pestered with them that they would not let me sleep. But I had an excellent guardian in bed with me, that would not let any of them come in to us, resolving to monopolize all the sport to herself. It was good sport to observe how this maid always followed me as my shadow, and whatever I was doing of, she would have a hand in it with me. What an endless work we made in making the beds ! Our mistress saw her work very much neglected, laying all the blame upon my bedfellow ; and indeed not without cause : for her mind was so employed about thinking on night, that she did little all day ; which my mistress perceiving, turned her away ; which was no small joy to me, if for no other consideration than her extreme fondness, which I knew would betray us both in the end.

After the departure of my bedfellow, the young ladies pitying my loneness in the night, redressed that solitude by their welcome presence. The first that came had like to have spoiled all, by her squeaking ; but some of her associates running to know what was the matter, she readily told them she *thought* there was a mouse in the bed. Thus satisfied, they departed ; and I enjoined her as I did the other, silence. But alas ! all injunctions on women to keep a secret are but as so many persuasions to divulge it. Notwithstanding I had so enjoined her secrecy, yet she made it known to some that she entertained a peculiar respect for, intending they should participate with her in the pleasure she enjoyed. This discovery did put me to an extreme hard task. I should never have undergone it, had not variety of such sweet smelling rose-buds encouraged me.

> Thus frequently each night did I repeat
> My uncontrolled passions ; and for heat,
> And active liveliness, I thought that none
> Could stand with me in competition.
> Twas then, forgetful wretch, that I a kiss
> Did oft prefer before a greater bliss.
> What did I care ? my carnal joys did swell ;
> So slighted Heaven, and ne'er feared Hell.
> But let me henceforth learn to slight those toys,
> And set my heart upon celestial joys.

In the very height of these my jollities, I could not forbear thinking sometimes on my eternal condition ; but custom and opportunity had so absolutely enslaved me that good thoughts, which were but seldom, wrought little good effects upon me. But if my soul's welfare would not deter me from these foul and wicked acts, yet love to my present mortal condition compelled me for a while to desist, and by flying those embraces I lately so hotly pursued, shun those complicated mischiefs which were appropinquant, the undeniable effects of my immoderate and destructive wantonness. My approaching danger was too visible, for I observed that some of the gentlewomen began to find strange alterations in their bodies, with frequent qualms coming over their stomachs, which made me sick to be gone ; and in this manner I did plot my escape. My mistress having a son much about my stature, and one time finding a fit opportunity, I got a suit of clothes of his, with other perquisites, which I put on, reassuming my proper shape and habit, and so with flying colours marched off, insulting over the conquest of so many maidenheads, leaving the *quondam* possessors thereof to deplore their ensuing misery, and condemn their own rash folly.

CHAPTER XIV

What a trick he served a young man of his acquaintance, whom he met withal accidentally : how he was pinched with hunger, and what ways he invented to kill it

I MADE all the speed I could to London, knowing the largeness of that vast city would afford conveniency for my concealment. But then my clothes much troubled me, knowing nothing would betray me sooner than they. Whilst I was studying all imaginable ways for my preservation, such an opportunity presented itself that therein it was plainly seen the Fates had decreed of old to favour my enterprizes. As I said, walking the streets, and ruminating what was best to be done, I met with a young man of my acquaintance, who seeing me, ran and caught me in his arms, and with very much joy we congratulated each other, and so as is usual when friends meet, we must drink together. Over our cups, I began to enquire after his condition. He shook his head, and so related to me a sad story, which in effect was to this purpose in his own words.

Dearest Friend, since last I saw you, never was young man so unfortunate as myself. The cause thereof I can impute to nothing more than self-conceit, and over-much credulity ; which by the sequel you will plainly understand. For perceiving that my mistress shewed me more than a common respect, I concluded that she had entertained some private favour for me within her breast, so that I began to be puffed up with conceit; neglecting my duty, and now despising the chambermaid, who was before the only saint I made nightly my orizons too. Withal, I carried myself so imperiously, that my master was not very well assured whether he durst command or no. My mistress would sometimes heartily laugh, to see how ridiculous I carried myself; which I looked upon as a singular favour, mistaking her smiles for tokens of her love, when they were no other than the apparent symptoms of her derision. Observing how affable and pleasing she was, I never considered the generality of it, so that my self-flattering noddle supposed this carriage particular to me, and thereupon interpreted this her complacency strong affection; and by reason she was frequently merry and jocose, I concluded her salacious or lecherous. Thus by the false lights of misconstruction and easy belief, I was led into love's labyrinth. My master's affairs was less regarded than my mistress's supposed affection. In fine, I judged it absolutely necessary to make her acquainted with my amorous passion, and no expedient better than by letter. My mistress (as it is customary with citizens' wives to light the candle of their husband's estates at both ends) had her country-house, to which I was sent by my master, with some bottles of wine, preparatory for a feast intended for the accommodation of some special friends. Arriving, I found my mistress had sent her maid to London about some business, at which I blessed my propitious stars, to direct me thither in such a fortunate and most desired hour.

After I had delivered my message, I began to talk very familiar with my mistress. She with a smiling countenance, asked me, what I meant? not in the least checking my presumption, which made me more arrogant and bold; telling her, I was her eternally devoted servant. She answered me, I was bound to be her servant for a time, and that I must, when commanded, obey her pleasure : to which last word, I added in my thoughts the epithet 'Venereal,' supposing she meant not to have left it out. With that I replied, 'Mistress, I should not deem myself worthy to be your servant, if my resolution had not engaged me to be so perpetually; as for my affection, it shall daily anticipate your desires; you shall not need to lay your commands on me, since my thoughts shall be solely employed in contriving ways how we may enjoy each other, to the mutual satisfaction of us both.' At which words, she fell into an excess of laughter (which I judged the effects of joy), and then asked me whether I was mad? I answered, No, unless too much love had made me so; 'Dearest Mistress, read but this paper, and I hope that will better inform you.'

Dearest Mistress,

Frequently revolving in my thoughts the condition I now am in, despair ſtands ready to seize me. But the consideration and knowledge of your commiserating nature draws me out of its ruinating jaws. When I reflect again on the disparity of our fortunes, and that it is your indentured vassal that thus proſtrates his affection at your feet, I fear one blaſt of your just indignation will suddenly shipwreck all my hopes. I confess my error is overmuch confidence, for which I may expect ruin which commonly attends rash attempts ; especially daring to sail in the narrow seas, without any other pilot than blind Love ; and if I should arrive at my desired port, I cannot deliver my goods without ſtealing cuſtom. But waiving all difficulties of this nature, consider that love muſt needs be quintessential, that is not drawn from any other intereſt than reciprocal enjoyment ; and it muſt needs be exceeding ſtrong and eminent too, that will force its way through the greateſt hazards. Signify my pardon by one gracious smile, for what I have so boldly (yet forcibly) discovered, and I shall esteem my condition little inferior to what is celeſtial ; which is no happiness to me, without the auspicious beams of your favour shine on me. And so subscribe my self according as your sentence shall be, either the

Moſt happy, or moſt miserable.

The verses that were annexed to the letter, I got a rhymer to compose, which afterwards I found stolen out of several authors ; a line out of one, and a half out of another, and so with the coarse thread of his brain botched together ; which were these :

Cupid did wound my heart ; I hid the grief
Long time, but durſt not seek for your relief ;
I found the smart increased on that score,
For wounds, if not well search'd, but rankle more.
O cure me quickly then, or else I die ;
Deny not, since there's none but you and I.

I withdrew as soon as I had delivered my paper, giving her leave to read in private what my love had dictated. About a quarter of an hour after she called me to her, assuring me in a day or two I should receive an answer to the purpose ; and so absconding her displeasure, she sent me with all expedition home again. After the expiration of three days she came home to her City-house. At night she pretended some indisposition of body, and desired to lie by herself ; which hearing, I thought my joy would prove a traitor to my supposed happiness. She takes an occasion to tell me, About twelve at night I might come to her bedchamber, the door whereof she would leave open for me on purpose. In the meantime, she shewed my maſter the letter, acquainting him with the whole business. According to the time appointed, I entered the chamber in my shirt. Approaching the bed, I began to pour out my amorous expressions ; and I had one leg upon the bed-side, ready to enter the bed, where I thought my miſtreſs had attended my pleasure, when I thought the Devil had waited on my poſteriors, correcting me for not making more haſte. The firſt lash was seconded with three or four more in an inſtant, which made me caper up and down so nimbly about the room, that for my life I could not find the door. At laſt I did ; speed was now the only guardian I had left, and so without pausing long upon it, I made but one ſtep of the firſt pair of ſtairs from top to the bottom, which had liked to have lamed me. Before I could recover myself, my maſter was with me again, which put fresh expedition into me ; and so ſtarting up, I leapt down half the next pair, and tumbled down the reſt. By this time he had loſt the cord of his whip, and fearing leſt he might spoil me with the ſtick, desiſted, bidding me go to bed leſt I should catch cold after so great a heat.

So with two or three parting blows I got into my chamber, where I fell into a deep consultation with myself. The result of it was this. I took my curtains and sheets and tied them together, and then faſtened one end thereof to the window ; after this I went out of the window, and so slid. By the time I was within an half-ſtory of the ground, the knot of one of the curtains slipped, so that falling from that height, I thought that every bone in my body had been absolutely broken. Knowing it was no ways safe to lie there and cry God help me, I raised myself as well as I could. But I had not walked far before I found myself in no condition of going, wherefore I resolved to lie under the next ſtall. As the Devil would have it, I found a cobbler's ſtall newly broke open that very night. Never queſtioning the place, I crept in, and notwith-ſtanding my bruise by the fall, and whipping besides, I fell faſt asleep, so soundly, that I awaked not till I was forced to it with an horse-pox. For the cobbler coming to work early in the morning (according to his cuſtom) found his door broken open. With that, he made an hideous noise, crying out he was undone ; for the day before he had laid out three shillings four pence, which was all his ſtock in leather ; all which was ſtolen, with many old shoes, nay his very working implements. Doubtless it was done by one of his own fraternity, that had informed himself of his late great purchase. The cobbler entering his ſtall, found me in one corner faſt asleep. He took no other course to awake me, than dragging me by the heels out of my den, into the ſtreet, crying out that he had got one of the rogues ; and without any more ado, fell upon me, buffeting me with his fiſt, and treading me underneath his feet, making himself both my Judge and Executioner. Thus you see one mischief attends the other's heels. I begged him in a pitiful manner to let me alone, and I would confess to him all I knew, desiring him to go with me to the next ale-house, which accordingly we did. I vowed to him I was no ways accessory to his wrong, informing him as much as I thought convenient of my sufferings, shewing him what a woeful plight I was in ; relating, it was my master's cruelty that was the cause of all this, and no other fault of mine than staying the last night out a little too long. The cobbler seemed to commiserate my misery, asking me forgiveness for what he had done, and so we parted. Since, by the kindness of a good-natured widow where I lie I have recovered my hurts and strength, and now am overjoyed we should so happily meet.

After this we drank very smartly, but I forgot not all this while my design on him. After that I had pitied him, and lamented his sad misfortune, I thought it high time to put my plot in execution. In order thereunto I demanded what difference he would take between my hat and his, his cloak and mine. There being small matter of advantage in the exchange, we agreed to go to handicap. In fine, there was not anything about us of wearing clothes but we interchanged. Scarce had I uncased myself, and put on my friend's clothes, but in came one that had dogged me, attended by the constable, with a warrant to seize me, who they knew by no other token but my boarding-mistress's son's garments I had stolen for my escape. They forthwith laid hold on my companion, (finding them on him), telling him he should severely suffer for the wrong he did his mistress, in the abuse of her house. Full of horror and amazement, he beseeched them not to carry him before his mistress, knowing how much he had offended her, she would have no mercy on him ; this confirmed their belief that they had found out the offender. The more he entreated the more deaf and inexorable were they ; and whilst they were busied about their mistaken criminal-prisoner, I took an occasion to give them the slip, knowing that a little further discourse would rectify their error. What they did with him I know not, neither durst I be so inquisitive to understand. Wherefore, leaving him to the mercy of such as would shew but little to him, I shall proceed forwards in my own story.

My stock was now very small, how to increase it I knew not. My invention was daily on the rack to find out expedient ways to supply my necessary expense. But my money being all spent, my belly began to grumble out insufferable complaints against me, seeming to charge me with want of ingenuity and industry, since I enjoyed my liberty ; for want that man cannot, which wants not that. Alas, what should I do ? I used what means I could, having no better experience. There was not a billiard table, boards end, or nine-pin-yard that I did not daily visit, frequenting such as had the greatest resort. In a short time I learned the art of spunging so perfectly that I had the title of *Spunge-Master General* conferred upon me. In those places I learned to take tobacco, which was the chiefest part of my food, living in a manner by smoke as the camelion by air. I fed so lightly that I durst not stir abroad in a high wind ; neither durst I fight, lest one single stroke should have hazarded my dissolution. Continued drinking had so washed me that my body was transparent, you might have seen within me (without dissection) the motion of the heart ; you could have observed but little as to my liver, it long since had lost its use in the conveyance of the blood, for my stomach had nothing therein contained to supply it ; like an Inns-of-Court kitchin out of Term-time. In short, I appeared like a walking skeleton.

I had several suggestions within me to proffer myself again to my master ; but the shame to be seen in that condition, deterred me ; wherefore, I resolved to weather it out a little longer, and try whether Fortune would once more be favourable to me. My clothes were indifferent good, which could not but procure me credit, if I would make experiment. By means thereof I got an handsome lodging chamber. It was a public house of entertainment, so that here I thought I should have meat, drink and lodging for chalk, and chalk for nothing. I called freely for what was in the house, which was readily brought me ; but when the servants beheld with what celerity (Hocus like), and cleanly conveyance I had disposed of what was before me, they verily believed in one week I would cause a dearth in the house if I stayed. Wherefore, one of the servants acquainted her mistress with what she had observed, alleging further invectively against me, that I looked like one of those lean beasts which have nothing given them to feed on but virtuous and honest women ; that she believed I was the genius of some hunger-starved wretch, or a shadow without a substance (which was very true as to my pocket).

When I thought it was time to go to bed, I called for a candle, not mattering whether I called for a reckoning. But my landlady did, for, said she, ' Sir, it is our custom to reckon with our lodgers every night what they have that day, and once a week to discharge their lodging.' In truth I did intend to have discharged myself of it before the week had been out. I knew not what at present to answer her, but I was seldom to seek in such cases. I desired her to be content for that night, on the morrow I would have my trunks brought to her house, making it my quarters for some time. And that she should find me a boon companion, drinking freely. ' I believe,' she said, 'you will be here for some time, or maybe you will make this your refuge or sanctuary for one night ; and then you say you will drink freely too ; give me leave to tell you, you meant at free coſt. Sir, give me my reckoning now, or you shall have no lodging here this night.' 'Do you suspeᐸt me, Landlady,' said I? 'Respeᐸt you,' said she (miſtaking the word). 'For what grounds, unless I knew you better ? And yet I doubt I shall know you too well. That's a good one indeed, respeᐸt a skinful of bones ; a bag of chessmen ; a bundle of small faggot-ſticks. Why, thou haberdasher of small wares, doſt thou think I will respeᐸt thee otherways than for thy money, unless I should be so mad as to fall in love with Famine ? Come, give me my reckoning firſt, and I shall talk with you in another dialeᐸt ; if not, I shall set my curs at thee (the tapſter and hoſtler) that shall worry thy gibbed catship.' Hearing her say so, and thinking the passage had been clear, I betook my self to flight ; but running through the entry, I ran my belly direᐸtly againſt the tapſter's leg, that lay over the bench on which he slept. I ran so fiercely that I shoved his head so violently againſt the board raised at the end of the bench that I made his neck double ; the knock likewise had like to have turned what little brains he had within his head. As for my own part, I thought that his foot had run quite into my belly, and that pulling it out he had left his shoe behind.

Before I could rise, I had three or four about me, which I thought would have limbed me, as boys falling-out do their cocks on Shrove Tuesday. At that time I would have spared them one limb, provided that would have contented them. But there was no mercy to be had at their hands, especially the shrill note of their miſtress's perpetually moving tongue sounding a charge in their ears. Being tired with me, they would be revenged of my clothes. They would have ſtripped me, I think, ſtark naked for my reckoning, but that one said, ' Let his cloak suffice ; ' at which another pulled so furiously at it that miraculously, without rending that thin transparent garment, he got it all but the cape. In this condition I was brought before my new landlady. I asked her what was to pay ? ' Sirrah,' said she, ' more than thou haſt in thy pocket, two shillings and fourpence.' As well as I could speak, I demanded how it came to be so much. ' Why,' said she, ' there is for beef 1s. for bread 4d. six pipes of tobacco, and three pots of ale ; all this thou hadſt in less than half an hour.' I would not contradiᐸt her, though I knew it was near an hour ; I desired her to keep my cloak for the reckoning, but durſt not threaten her for her abuse.

Being about hay-making time, I walked out into the fields, resolving to spend that night in contemplation. I had now time to consider the damage I suſtained in this skirmish. They had carried away all my ribbands with their fingers, otherwise my clothes received the leaſt harm. My nose resembled a black pudding before it is boiled, and my eyes were fled into my head for fear of such melancholy meat. My cheeks were so puffed up with swelling pride that they were resolved to close up the portals of my optics, that they might not be eye-witnesses of the height of their ambition. My ears were so mauled with their fleshy hammers that I heard a peal within my head for joy, I suppose, that my eyes had taken up their residence within my brains. At laſt I felt something about my shoulders ; at firſt I thought it had been the weight of the blows, but feeling, found it a part of my friend that ſtill hung about my neck, and would not leave me ; which put me in mind of that faithful cloak that would never leave its maſter, although his maſter had attempted all ways imaginable to leave it. I muſt needs say, I loved my cloak so well that it grieved me much to be compelled to part with it. It had been a servant to servants, ever since the setting up of the firſt billiard-table, whence it derived its pedigree. Being deprived of its employment, and dispossessed of its ancient habitation, its heart-ſtrings were ready to break, and being not able to take a nap for grief, turned changeling. The young man I had it of told me that from the fifteenth successively, it was descended to him : but they were unworthy to him that having had his beſt days, would turn him off in his extreme old age. I have him so fresh in my memory, that I cannot but condole his loss.

> Cloak, if I may so call thee, though thou art
> Thus ravished from me, don't abruptly part.
> Thou didst not take diſtaſte, and so art gone,
> Cause once I called thee a mere hanger on.
> 'Twas but in jeſt ; for had I now my will,
> I'd have thee for to hang about me ſtill.
> Now I may tax thee juſtly, for I see
> That now th'art nothing else but levity ;
> Nay when I had thee, scarcely did I know
> Sometimes whether I had thee on or no.
> Thou wert so thin, and light, that some have thought
> Thee made of that same web *Arachne* wrought,
> And say th'art useless now, unless men put
> Thee like a cobweb to a finger cut.
> I love thee ſtill, for better and for worse ;
> He that divorced us, let him have my curse.
> Sure 'twas a red-nosed fellow, for I know,
> He coming near, it was but touch and go.
> But let him keep thee, for thou'lt useless be
> To him ; thick clothes suit beſt with knavery.

Day appearing, I got me a ſtick out of a hedge, and so walked into the City. I walked up and down, but met with none of my acquaintance

on whom I might faſten on as a bur. Noon approaching, my belly
began to chime ; I thought all the meat in Eaſtcheap would not lay the
spirit hunger had raised within me. Coming by a baker's shop, I pretended to be ignorant of the city, and as I was asking him the way to such
a place, not caring what, I happily secured a penny loaf, which I carried
off undiscovered. I thought it not good to cumber my pocket with it,
wherefore at two bits I gave it my belly to carry. Surely at that time I
had an oſtrich's ſtomach ; every thing I put into my mouth passed
through me like quicksilver. Going a little farther, I came to an ordinary,
where I saw two sitting in a lower room expeéting their meat. I sat me
down in the next little box to them. Immediately there was brought to
them powdered beef and turnips. The young man that served them,
came to me, demanding what I would have ; I bid him let me alone,
and not speak too loud, for those two which were next me were my very
good friends, and I would ſtartle them by and by with my unexpeéted
appearance ; at which he left me. Finding my opportunity, I slipped
my hands through a hole in the form of an heart, which was in the
partition that divided us, and laying hold on the turnips, I spake aloud,
' You hogs, are ye at the roots ? I will make one among you inſtantly,'
and so brought out my handful. Having devoured them in a trice, I
presented myself to their view, and sat down with them. ' Gentlemen,'
said I, ' excuse my frolic ; I am in a merry humour to-day.' They concluded what I said to be a truth, and bade me welcome. ' Nay,' said I,
' meat will come inſtantly as a supply ; ' and so it had need, for we made
a clear board immediately. Seeing this, they called the boy, taxing him
for sloth that he did not bring my meat. ' Sir,' said he, ' the gentleman
did not order me to bring any ; ' at which they frowned, and began to
charge me with incivility. ' What, are ye angry ? ' said I. To which
they replied affirmatively. ' If so,' I answered (laying my hand upon a
full pot of ale), ' I value your anger no more than the drinking this pot,'
which I swallowed at two gulps, and so bid them farewell, leaving them
to call for another ordinary.

CHAPTER XV

How he had like to have been transported, being taken up by kidnapper,
vulgarly called a spirit

HAVING satisfied my ſtomach, I walked along with much more
courage than before ; which had been to little purpose, had I
not had a ſtick in my hand. For there was hardly a dog in the ſtreet

which I went through that gave me not his grinning salutation and would,
when my back was turned (knowing else I would never have suffered
their humility), have kissed my very heels, had not my stick prevented
their sneering dogships' mouths. I have wondered often why dogs will
bark so incessantly at the sight of a tinker, pedlar, Tom-a-Bedlam, nay,
any suspicious fellow, till I found it myself by experience, that by
natural instinct they know and hate the scent of a rogue. My course of
life appeared so idle (by my lazy stalking and gaping this way and that,
sometimes standing still and seriously viewing what deserved not a
minute's observance) that the beadle took hold on me, telling me it was
great pity that such a lusty young man should want employment, and
therefore would help me to some. But understanding from him that it
must be in Bridewell, my legs failed me, shewing thereby how unwilling they were to be accessory to the punishment which would
be inflicted on my back. At length, by pitiful looks, and many
entreaties, I got clear of him, but fell immediately foul with an evil
spirit or a seducer of persons to the Indies. Well may he be called a
spirit, since his nature is like the devil's, to seduce any he meets withal,
whom he can persuade with allurements and deluding falsities to his
purpose.

After he had asked me many impertinent questions, he invited me to
drink with him. I ingenuously told him I had not a penny, otherwise
his motion would be acceptable to me. At which he cast up his eyes to
heaven, and laying his hands on his breast, ' alas poor young man,' said
he, ' what pity it is such a fellow as thou art shouldst want money ;
which argues thou art both destitute of friends, and an employment
also. Well, I'll say no more for the present, but before we part I'll
study some way or other for thy advantage, which I shall do merely out
of commiseration to the miserableness of thy condition, as also out of
respect to thy father, whom I am confident I have heretofore known,
by the resemblance thou bearest him in thy countenance.' I could but
smile to myself to hear how this rascal dissembled. Not discovering
my thoughts, I willingly went with him to drink, resolving to see what the
event would be. After he had paused a while, ' Well,' said he, ' I have
found it. There is a merchant an intimate friend of mine, that wants
a store-house-keeper. Now if you can cast accompts ever so indifferently,
you shall find entertainment from him, and 40 *l. per annum* for encouragement.' I told him that I joyfully accepted his kind proffer, and that I
should refer myself to be disposed of as he should think fit. With that he
embraced me, saying ,within two days I should go aboard the ship where
the merchant was, who would go along with me to Virginia (where he
pretended the merchant's plantation lay). ' In the meantime you shall

go along with me to my house, where you shall receive from me what your necessities require.'

I had heard before how several had been served in this kind, so that being forewarned, I was forearmed : *premonitus, premunitus*. He carried me away presently to Wapping, and housed me. To the intent he might oblige me to be his, he behaved himself extraordinary friendly ; and that he might let me see that he made no diſtinction between me and his other friends, he brought me into a room where half a score were all taking tobacco. The place was so narrow wherein they were that they had no more space left than what was for the ſtanding of a small table. Methought their mouths together resembled a ſtack of chimneys, being in a manner totally obscured by the smoke that came from them ; for there was little discernible but smoke and the glowing coals of their pipes. Certainly the smell of this room would have out-done assa-fœtida, or burned feathers in the cure of ladies troubled with the fits of the mother. As to the sight, the place resembled hell, so did it like-wise as to its scent, compounded of the perfume of ſtinking tobacco and tarpaulin. So that I concluded the resemblance moſt proper.

> In Hell damn'd souls, fire, smoke, and ſtink appear.
> Then this is Hell, for those four things were here.

I was seated between two, leſt I should give them the slip.

After I had been there awhile, the cloud of their smoke was somewhat dissipated, so that I could discern two more in my own condemnation. But alas, poor sheep, they ne'er considered where they were going, it was enough for them to be freed from a seven years' apprenticeship, under the tyranny of a rigid maſter (as they judged it, coming but lately from sucking the breaſts of a too indulgent mother) and not weighing (as I know not how they should) the slavery they muſt undergo for five years, amongſt brutes in foreign parts, little inferior to that which they suffer who are gally-slaves. There was little discourse amongſt them, but the pleasantness of the soil of that continent we were designed for (out of a design to make us swallow their gilded pills of ruin), and the temperature of the air, the plenty of fowl and fish of all sorts ; the little labour that is performed or expected having so little trouble in it, that it rather may be accounted a paſtime than anything of punishment. And then to sweeten us on the farther, they insiſted on the pliant loving natures of the women there ; all which they used as baits to catch us silly gudgeons.

As for my own part, I said but little but what tended to the appro-bation of what they said. For all my aim (as I related before) was to underſtand the drift of this rogue, and then endeavour to get what I could from him. By this time supper was talked of by our masters ; so choice they were in their diet, that they could not agree what to have. At last, one stands up and proclaiming silence, said that a dish of bruise[1] was the most princely dish of any. And to tell you truly, by his looks, I thought he had been begot just as his mother had put a sop into her mouth of that stomach-murdering stuff, the grease running about her chops, which pleasing her fancy, struck so deep an impression in the imagination upon her conception that the face of that thing she brought forth, looked much like a toast soaking in a cook's dripping-pan.

That he might persuade the rest this way to indulge his appetite he added, farther, that it was a dish would not be expensive, and soon ready. My landlady, to back him on, said she had some skimmings of the pot which she had been collecting these three months, some whereof she questioned not but to procure, and let her alone to order it so that we should say we never had a better dish aboard in our lives.

Another contradicting him, preferred a bowl of pease-pottage before the chiefest meat whatever, that he could never look into the pot and see them boil round but that his heart leapt within him, and kept time with their motion. My master (that was their senior) scorned to be controlled in his fancy ; and therefore positively determined to have some Poor John,[2] swearing that the Great Mogul did eat nothing else thrice a week, and that Atabalipa (that Indian king whom Cortez conquered) caused a sacrifice every day to be made of them to his idol, commanding them to be laid on an altar made of some coals of fire, then the fat of some beast rubbed thereon (because they had no butter), and so presented to the idol, afterwards to the king, which he did eat with inexpressible satisfaction. Order was given that this delicate fare should be provided. Though they did beat it most unmercifully, yet it would not yield, resolving rather to be broken in pieces, than to become unlike its *master's* heart, or shew anything of a tender nature. There was one allotted me for my proportion, which I used as they had done, laying it on the coals a little while, and so committing it to my teeth's disposal. I never found till now that my teeth could be thus shamefully baffled. They made several assaults upon it to little purpose. My teeth at length fearing a total conquest, desperately and enragedly seized on the thinnest and weakest part, and holding it as fast as a vice, at last in the conflict overpowered one small flake. But not being able to stay the swift backward motion of my head, the hinder part thereof (the seat of memory) flew so violently against the wall that I instantly forgot what I was doing and where I was, and all but the pain I sustained by the knock.

[1] Slices of bread soaked in boiling fat pottage from salt meat.
[2] Salted and dried hake—a very coarse dish.

Strong water they poured down my throat to revive me, but there was nothing did sooner fetch me than a small flake of the Poor John, which sticking in my throat had wellnigh choked me, which caused a struggling, and summoned the spirits together to oppose what might be destructive to nature.

Now did I really imagine myself at sea, where, for want of provision, I was forced to feed on cordage, or the ship sides. Had this poor creature been ground small, I might have made as hard a shift to have swallowed it as those seamen did the saw-dust of deal boards coming from Norway, and destitute of other food. That night I slept but little, neither could I, had I swallowed opium for that purpose, for the innumerable quantity of bugs (as some call them) that had invaded my body, being weary (I suppose) of inhabiting any longer the dry mansion of that old rotten bedsted on which I lay. In the morning I found the ruins of a looking-glass in the window, which I took up to discover what knots or nodes those were I felt o'erspreading my face. The sight whereof struck into me a panic fear, verily believing I had been infected with a spotted fever.

I began to curse the bed and sheets, imagining the contagion pro-ceeded from them. To be satisfied herein, I drew aside at the bed's feet the curtain (that is to say, part of a tilt) pinned there to keep the wind off, which otherwise would have fanned us to death, coming in so furiously through the portcullis of the window (for glass there was little). At first sight I questioned whether I was not lately risen from the dead, since there was visibly before my eyes the black cloth that covered my hearse. Had not we gone to bed without a candle over-night I should sooner have chosen a bulk than this bed to lie on. It might have been a good quære, whether those sheets had ever been washed since weaving, and continually since employed by whores and bawds, successively, to sweat out their contagious humours, and matter proceeding from their ulcerated bodies.

My pretended friend perceiving my amazement, bid me be of good courage, for those marks in my face were only occasioned by a stinging sort of vermin, who seldom meddle with such as are accustomed to them, only giving their welcome to such as were new-comers. I took these sufferings as patiently as I could ; thinking it was an ill coming for me to either of them ; and it should not be long before I would take my fare-well. We had scarce breakfasted, before a messenger came into the room, and with much seeming respect pretended to deliver a message to my friend. I guessed it was to inform him how the tide served, and so it proved. My friend told me we must be gone instantly, for the merchant attended my coming. Wherefore we went down to the stairs to take boat. By the way he told me that he would go with me in the same ship,

and take as much care of me as he would of his own son, whom I understood afterwards he had too sure, above a year since, stolen away and sold
as a slave. One while I thought to have ran for it, another time I thought
to have cried out, ' spirit, a spirit,' but that the thought of the watermen
being his accomplices, deterred me.

I was at my wits' end, not knowing what to do. Coming into the boat,
being now destitute of all relief, I asked him according to his former
pretence, whether he resolved to go to sea with me ? ' Yes,' replied he,
' I question, Sir,' said I, ' whether you ever told a truth in your life, but
I am resolved you shall now ; ' and with that I flung myself with him
overboard. Those which were in the boat immediately endeavoured at
our rising to pull us up into the boat ; but I, clapping my hands unfortunately on the side of the boat on which they within leaned, overturned it
upon me. The first thought this accident produced in me was that a
whale had swallowed me, and that I was in the dark concave of his belly ;
or that death had arrested me, and clapped me up a close prisoner for
my sins, in Hell's deep and black dungeon. But by the industry and
expedition of many watermen, eye-witnesses of this passage (which
had like to have proved tragical), the boat was recovered, and I the first
person taken up and set on shore.

Multorum manibus grande levatur onus.

Many hands make light work. I ne'er stayed to see what was become
of my good friend (a pox take him), but with what speed I could, attended
with a great number of little hooping owlets (I mean the young fry of
scullers) I secured myself from this *Anthropopola*, or man-seller. A
charitable woman seeing me in this pickle (for it was salt water, which my
soused guts may testify, if they please, in their grumbling manner of
speaking), told me that she would entertain me till to-morrow. This was
the greatest cordial could be applied to this cross ; and without many
compliments, I thanked her for her great love. Now because she saw
what condition I was in, she immediately put me to bed.

CHAPTER XVI

*How under the pretence of begging, he stole a cloak, and with that went to a
gaming ordinary : what a bold adventure he made there, and the
success thereof*

PARTING from this good woman, I began to think that the art of
stealing might be reckoned amongst the liberal sciences ; for
though it may be called an handicraft, yet it cannot be looked on as

mechanic. This is the art, the right practice whereof is the true philosopher's stone, the elixir of life ; with which many turn poison into medicine, coarse cloth into cloth of gold, hunger into fulness and satiety, convert rags into satins, and all this done by a quick wit, and slight of hand.

The antiquity and dignity of this profession I shall relate elsewhere, and shall proceed in my adventures.

The evening of twilight being come, I chanced to look in at a door ; and perceiving none at hand, I went in boldly, resolving if I met any to beg an alms of them, having before premeditated what I had to say, *viz*, that I was a poor distressed young gentleman, my father, mother, nay, all my relations I knew, being dead ; and that not knowing what to do, was forced (under cover of the night) to beseech the assistance of charitable-minded persons. But in my way I found none that should occasion my using this form.

I found in the parlour a good camlet cloak, which I made bold to put on, and so very gravely walked out of the house ; but coming to the door, you must think there was wild-fire in my breech, that hastened me out of the street. Being gotten a bow-shot off I thought myself indifferent secure, so that I slackened my pace, but could not (if my life lay on it) forbear looking this way, that way, sometimes over one shoulder, sometimes over the other. Thinking of what dangerous consequence this might prove, I resolved to walk more confidently, and not let my eyes discover anything of fear, by reason of guilt. This loose garment had so of a sudden metamorphosed those thoughts I had of myself but a little before, my eye being continually on my cloak, I could not conceit myself less than the best of the young Templars that walk the streets to shew themselves. Coming into Bell Yard, I observed several gallants go into an house, and others to come out, which put me to the curiosity of enquiring what or whose house it was. One told me it was a gaming ordinary. Nay, then, thought I, it is as free for me to enter as others, and so went in.

I looked on a while, but my fingers itched to be at it. Why, thought I, have I not adventured a gaol, a whipping, or an hanging, and shall I now fear a kicking, a pumping, or a bog-house ? These considerations made me resolutely take up the box, and I threw a main, which was 7. A great deal of money was set me ; I knew it was but to little purpose to baulk them, so that confidently I threw at all, which I nicked with eleven, and so continued holding seven hands together. Perceiving I had got a considerable quantity of money, and fearing I might lose that which I had so boldly adventured for, I thanked my propitious stars and the gentlemen, who had rather lose their money than suspect any that hath the garb of one well extracted ; and so bade them good night. A privilege too many skarking ubiquitarians use without interruption, being most commonly in fee with the waiters and box-keepers, who will be sure to speak in the behalf of such confident cheats. If they lose, pretending great knowledge of them, that they are men of repute, civil and responsible ; which frequently so prevails upon a mouth, that he hath not a word to say more. Questionless, ordinaries were first impartially founded, interdicting all play but which was upon the square ; but since, by the connivance of the box-keepers, when the table grows thin and few at it, let the stranger beware : for the box-keeper shall walk off, pretending some speedy dispatch of a business concerning the house of office, &c. whilst your antagonist shall put the change upon you, or make use of his own Jack-in-a-box. And then had you 500 *l.* (would you set like a gamester) he will have it to a penny in a short while : with whom the waiter goes snips. If at any time such they know want an high flier, &c. they know how and when to supply him.

Full fraught with this good fortune, and so laden I was ready to sink, I resolved to moor my vessel in the next harbour. The landlord whence I came, was very loth to entertain me, his lodger having served him a scurvy trick the night before, conveying out of the window the furniture of a room that cost him 40 *l.* besides a great silver tankard which the gentleman would have filled with stale beer and sugar, to stand by his bed-side all night, pretending it was his custom. But I desiring him to lay up a parcel of money for me till the next morning, quite put out the eye of his jealousy. I shewed myself that night very exceeding noble, concealing my success at play that he might conclude the greatness of my expense proceeded from the nobleness of my nature, having a good estate to back it. I was conducted to bed with many ceremonies, and abundance of respect. Sleep I could not, for thinking how to dispose of myself.

I had experimented the various exigences and extremities an unsettled condition is accompanied withal ; and knowing how securely I could purloin from my master, if I would moderate my theft, I concluded to supplicate my master by a letter for my reception into his service, not forgetting my mistress's *quondam* kindnesses. If my master should refuse to re-entertain me, I had by me what might supply my necessities, till I had re-considered how to improve my stock, or bestow myself. Not to delay time, the next day I wrote him this letter.

Sir,

Having seriously considered the greatness of my folly in running from so good a master, (whom I may more rightly entitle father) with tears I beg mercy from Heaven, and forgiveness from you. Mitigate my offence by revolving in your mind the fewness of my years, which makes me (as it doth moſt others) prone to rambling fancies ; look then favourably on my long absence from you, as a mere exiliency, a youthful lapse, which maturity of age may reĉtify. If you can forgive my follies, I will ſtudy to forget them, and daily endeavour the propagation of my fidelity in the remainder of my time. By the bearer hereof you may signify your pleasure.

Sir, I am
Your cordially penitent Servant, &c.

With much joy my maſter read this letter, and haſtened the bearer away to bring me to him. Having converted my silver into gold, sewing it in my collar and waiſtband, and putting myself into a garb convenient for his sight, I went to him.

CHAPTER XVII

His maſter sheweth him more kindness than formerly : the ill requital he made him by cuckolding him : an accident that fell out thereupon, which produced two remarkable ſtories, deduced from the ſtrength of imagination

MY maſter, upon my reception, told me he had freely forgiven me, and if that I would henceforward endeavour the prosecution of a more regular course of life he would forget too my paſt follies. I promised him more than the ſtriĉteſt zealot ever yet did, and begged him pardon aforehand, if he found a defeĉt in performance.

As my expressions gave my maſter much content, so my return (I perceived by my miſtress's eyes) gave her the greateſt satisfaĉtion My maſter began to dote on me again, seeing I daily trebled my diligence, and so aĉtive was I in everything that concerned his affairs, that it was hard for any to anticipate me in my intention.

This gained so much upon his facile good nature, that I had liberty to wear my hat, and sit at table with him, neither would he command me anything servile. I had (as formerly) the same solicitations from my brother snippers ; but fearing leſt one time or another I might be snapped by the timorous nature of some, who, if once taxed, will confess, not only as to themselves, but likewise deteĉt the whole knot of a brother-hood, I resolved to have no more to do with them, but would snip securely by myself, knowing, that in any secret design, if many are concerned, their business cannot be long kept private. Wherein, by the way, I cannot but commend the craft and policy (though I absolutely disclaim the actions) of modern padders, whose providence instructed them to rob singly, by which means their booty came to them entire without distribution, or if apprehended (as it was very rare) they knew how to make a better plea for themselves in a court of judicature. I now kept close to my business, not harbouring the least temptation to any extravagancy, and had sequestered myself from what might render me publicly notorious and only studied by what means I might raise my fortune, intending to build my future estate upon the ruin of other men. Having nothing of mine own but my late purchase at play, my only way was (as I thought by some success therein) to make the world believe I was really reformed, and so create to myself a credit, whereas I was only a devil converted to an angel of light, or a wolf in sheep's clothes.

Now did I begin to cant religiously, and not omit one Sabbath wherein I did not take sermon notes, judging this religious cloak to be the best expedient, to screw myself farther into my mistress's favour, who doted on Morning Exercises, and monthly Fasts. If my master had forgot to do the duty of the day I would with much respect put him in mind of the neglect, desiring that I might repeat what had been delivered. As they looked upon my conversion more miraculous than that of St. Paul, so they gave me the greatest encouragement lest like weak women, I might prove a back-slider. There were few private meetings my mistress heard of but, by the leave of my master, I must conduct her to them, which were as many portents of our private meetings afterwards, where Venus should appoint.

I am sorry that I am so uncharitable as to say that the zeal of her spirit was not so hot as that of her flesh. Every day I had some remark of her love, which I received with much submissive respects, pretending I understood not her meaning, which added but fuel to the blazing flame of love within her. I could not be ignorant that since she began to court me she would prosecute it to the end. Her courtship, methought, was very preposterous ; she might have first received the charge from me, and by that means she would have found me prepared, whereas otherwise she might have been deceived in her expectation.

My mistress gave me so many opportunities, and signified her desires by so many tokens and dumb expressions that I began to condemn my fears, which rendered me unworthy of her favours. The besieger deserves not the honour of possessing that city whose gates are freely opened to him, yet dares not enter. Whilst I was thus ruminating, my mistress came to the counting-house where I was writing ; and leaning upon my shoulder asked me what I was doing. I told her nothing but writing. ' Nothing, I believe,' said she, ' nor never will do anything, but draw up blanks,' and so abruptly left me. She knew the quickness of my apprehension, and so left the interpretation hereof to my own construction.

Not long after, thinking her words had left a deep impression, as they did, and withal concluding I would give her the sense of them when I had an opportunity, she informs my master that she had a great desire to visit a gentlewoman she had not seen a long time, and requested that her man Thomas (for that was my name) might wait on her ; to which he assented. Though I led her, yet I wondered were she led me, through one street into another till we arrived at the water-side. She bid me call for a pair of oars, which I accordingly did. The watermen were very inquisitive, according to their custom, to know whither we intended. ' Well, well,' said she, ' put off and then it will be time enough for you to understand.' Said she, ' Row us up to Fox-hall.' I, for my part, was somewhat amazed, yet I partly guessed what she drove at. I kept at a distance, shewing her the respect of a servant ; which she taking notice of, laughed, saying, ' Come Cuz, why dost not sit nearer ? ' To which I replied as familiarly (for by this time I had much improved the stock of my confidence) ' I were best to sit a little nearer you, since I shall be the best expedient to balance the boat even, or trim it, for you are but light on your side.' This expression I doubt nettled her, for presently thereupon she shot a piercing dart from her eye (which I fancied to have penetrated my very soul). ' How now Cuz,' said she, ' I thought you had a better opinion of me. I understand the riddle. Your expressions may be very dark to some, however I have too much light in it.' I would have made an apology for myself but that she hindered me by whispering me in the ear, to this effect, that if she was light, there was no other cause but myself, and that if I abused her love any longer, she would sit the heavier on my skirts. Landing, we went straight to Spring Garden. By the way she told me I must lay aside all formality, and for the better carrying on the design we went upon she would have me as afore assume the title of Cuz. We were conducted into an obscure bower where, without a clue, it would be hard for any to find us. There was not anything wanting that might delight the appetite, which with much freedom we enjoyed together.

' Now,' said my mistress, ' I shall take off the veil of my modesty, and discover to thee the very naked secrets of my heart. The first time that ever I saw thee, I had more than a common respect to thee, and there was not a time since wherein I had the sight of thee, but that it added new fuel to the flame of my affection. I used all possible means to smother or blast it in the bud, but could not ; I summoned my reason to confute my passion, and notwithstanding I alleged that there was a disproportion in our age, and unsuitableness as to our condition, and lastly how great

a strain it would be to my religious profession ; yet love got the victory
over these, and would have been too strong for ten times as many ' ;
the rest she supplied with kisses, which were infinite.

Having gained a little breath, and she again having lent me the use
and disposal of my own mouth, I returned to this her amorous oration,
something suitable to it by way of retaliation ; protesting with invoca-
tions that since she had so completed my happiness by her love, I would
perish before I would be guilty of the least abuse therein. That had it
not been for the sense of my unworthiness, and fear of hazarding her
love, and so gained her displeasure, no other difficulty should have
deterred me from declaring and discovering what she had prevented me
in ; adding, that were the quintessence of all loves contracted into one
body, it could not equalize mine.

' Come,' said she, ' let us leave off talking in such idle phrases, let
future constancy make apparent the reality of our affections, and let
us not lose any time wherein we may mutually enjoy each other. It
is but a folly for me now to mince the matter, or by my coldness endeavour
to recongeal that water where the ice is too visibly broken and thawed.
Yet let not your prudence be questioned, or reason forfeited, in making
any unhandsome advantage of this my freedom. But above all, blast
not my reputation by the unsavoury breath of any ostentatious boasting
of a gentlewoman's favours, nor let not my love cause any slighting or
disrespect in you to your master ; neither let it so puff you up with
pride as to contemn your fellow-servants. In company, shew much
more reverence to me than formerly. In private, when none sees us but
ourselves, be as familiar and free as actions can demonstrate. Be constant to me alone, for true love will not admit of plurality. Be secret and
silent, and follow not the common practice of vain-glorious fools that in
requital of those favours they have received in private of some credulous
female, will make their brag of them in public ; as if it were not enough
for them to rob them of their chastity but must likewise murder their
reputations. Have a special care you slight me not (as some squeamish
or curious stomachs use feeding too long on one sort of food, though never
so delicious), for a woman's love despised will turn into extreme hatred,
and will be ever restless till malice and revenge have consulted with
invention how to be more than even with the slighting injurer.' She
propounded more articles, which I have forgot now, but I remember I
sealed them without a witness. We made an end of our business for that
time, with much expedition, to the intent the tediousness of our staying
might not be suspected by the ignorant cuckold at home. I have reason
now for so calling him.

Coming home, I applied myself to the business of the shop as before, enjoining my eyes a severe penance not so much as to look towards that object they so dearly loved. According to my usual time I went to bed, but sleep I could not, for thinking on what I had done. About one o' clock I was much startled to hear something come into my chamber ; but before I could give my eyes the liberty for a discovery my mistress had gotten within the sheets, not daring to speak, because my master lay in the next room, most commonly by himself, and her chamber was the next to that (and in a trundle-bed underneath my mistress's bed lay the maid). Near upon day-break my sweet bedfellow left me ; at an unhappy time, for then was my master awake, which might have ruined us both, which had so fallen out had he been resolute or courageous. But on the contrary, he was exceeding timorous, but more especially, childishly afraid of the supposed walking of spirits. For hearing the boards crack twice or thrice, with the weight of her body ; besides, by the help of starlight, perceiving something to move all in white, he shrunk underneath the clothes, not daring to put out his head. Now did his imagination work as strongly almost as his breech, suggesting strange and ridiculous things to his fancy. But I shall give him leave to tell his own story.

A little after it was day, being almost stifled for want of fresh air, and choked with the stink that was in the bed, he boldly and valiantly put his head out of the coverlid, and after he had thrice exorcised the devil, or the supposed evil spirit, with ' avoid Satan,' repeating as often that Scriptural Sentence, ' *Resist the Devil and he will fly from thee*,' he called out as loud as he might for me to come to him. I leapt out of bed, and ran to him, asking him what was the matter. ' O Thomas,' said he, ' light a candle quickly.' I running in haste to light the candle, fell (by mistaking the first step) down the stairs, which made a terrible noise. My master hearing me, cried out, ' O God, what will become of me ? ' thinking the Devil indeed had mistook me for himself, and that he was horsing me on his back to carry me away. With that he fell to prayer so fervently loud that up starts the mistress and the maids, running to know what was the matter. Fear had so possessed him that he could not be persuaded but that they were some of the devilish crew.

At first they thought him to be fallen mad ; but finding out the cause of this distraction, with much ado my mistress made him sensible of his mistake. Being fully assured, that they were not damned spirits, he related what he had seen, in this manner. My mistress afterwards told me that had it not been for laughing, which so busied her that her sense of smelling for that time had left her, she could never have endured to hear him out, for that notorious stink which came from the bed, when he stirred ever so little.

' I wondered,' said he, ' that contrary to my usual custom I awaked

about four o'clock, whereas I used to sleep soundly, thou knowest, till
eight.   I hearkened ; at firſt I perceived only the boards to crack, but
presently after I heard chains rattle, and the ſtools flung about the room,
the bed, and I in it, danced up and down, as if a Scotch bag-pipe had been
played upon by a Northern witch, and the Devil the while had danced
with me and the bed a morrice (supplying the bellows with wind).
Sometimes they pulled me out of bed, and laid me on the cold floor, and
then tossed me in again like a dog in a blanket.

' Hearing no noise, I attempted to peep out ; but scarcely had mine
eyes recovered the top of the bedclothes, when I saw ſtanding by me, a
composition of mere bones, with a shroud thrown over his shoulders,
like an Irish brachin, or a Scotch plaid, with a light taper in one hand
(I knew not what use he could make of it, for there were only holes in his
head inſtead of eyes) and an hour-glass in the other. He grinned at me
with his teeth (for he had no lips), and shaking his chains left me,
which sight so terrified me that I had like to have shot out (like a pudding
in a bag) all that was within me.' My miſtress had like to have broken
out into extreme laughter, had not the consideration of danger that might
have ensued thereon hindered her.

After this, it was a long time before he would be persuaded to lie in
that chamber again, which made me curse his ſtrong conceit, for by
this means he would lie with his wife, which interrupted our sweet
venereal paſtime.   As for my part, I believed he would never have returned to his own chamber again, for he trembled when he passed through
it in the day time ; and if alone, he would so thunder down the ſtairs
(fear giving wings to his feet) as if (Vulcan-like) he had been sent by
Jupiter head-long in a message.

Another accident happening not long after cured him in part of his
ridiculous belief, grounded on nothing else but fancy.   In the cellar, on
a certain beam that went cross, there were great quantity of tenter-
hooks placed there, some to hang meat on, others of a smaller sort for
other uses.   Our cat being somewhat ravenous, was following the
scent, and had gotten upon the beam ; her foremoſt feet slipping, she
was ſtrangely caught by the tail, and not able to recover herself. Being
terribly pained by the hook, she made a moſt hideous noise, which made
our dog fall a-howling.   This ſtrange din firſt approached my maſter's
ears, who awaking my miſtress, asked her now whether she would believe
her own ears.   At firſt she confessed to me she knew not what to think,
her conscience being yet tender (which having no long time accuſtomed
herself to sin was not hardened and seared up) put her in mind of what
she had lately committed, so that she had like to have concluded that it
was Satan was sent to buffet her.   But she having a martial spirit, and

not easily daunted, she hearkened further, and then judged that thieves had broken into the house.

My master all this while was breathing his last at both ends, whilst my mistress leaped out of bed, and came to my chamber door, bidding me in all haste to rise, for there were thieves in the house. I confess I had no great mind to be killed, and therefore I was in no great haste to rise, sometimes buttoning my doublet, and anon unbuttoning it again. Perceiving that I delayed, she came again, taxing me with cowardice, and meanness of spirit, which put new life into me, making me to resolve to adventure my life, rather than hazard the loss of her good opinion.

Finding my mistress in her smock, I thought it a shame for me to have any clothes on ; and so naked as I was, we marched on. Coming to the stairhead my fancy troubled me a little too, for the noise had so amazed me that I would fain have my mistress to go first. She could not forbear laughing, to observe how complimental and ceremonious at that time I was. Having scattered my fear by resolution, 'How do I abuse myself,' said I, and with that boldly went on.

By this time a light was produced, and then those bug-bear thoughts which darkness possesseth the fancy withal, began to vanish. There was not a hole big enough to contain a man, but what I probed. Descending the cellar-stairs, I there plainly saw the original cause of our fear and distraction, hanging by the tail. I called my mistress to the sight, and now the maids too would be spectators, understanding the danger to be overpast.

Well, the general vote was that the cat should be carried upstairs to our master, to shew him the wound in his tail, for evidence to prove his guilt in being seduced by fancy.

He hearing some come up, thought we were all destroyed, and that they were coming up to dispatch him too. Wherefore he cried out, 'Save my life, and take all I have.' His wife (not to increase his perplexity) bid him quiet himself, there was no harm, not any like to be done ; and withal so convinced him of his folly, both past and present, that he had not a word to say in his own defence ; he enjoining us all silence, we were dismissed.

The next night, to shew how much he was altered from his former temper and belief, he did lie in his chamber aforesaid, supposedly haunted, and that same night with much joy, my mistress and I renewed our pleasures.

CHAPTER XVIII

How his mistress supplied him with money, even to superfluity : what ways he had to spend it : he is tempted to destruction by correctors, alias clippers, and coiners alias matter-men

I FOUND my estate to increase abundantly, for I was half sharer myself with my master ; my mistress she put in for one too, which I had likewise ; so that the good man received but the fourth. I had been (since my return) very sparing in my expense, having laid up my money securely. But now finding out another rich mine, I thought I should be too rich, unless I contrived ways to draw out, as well as put in.

In the first place, I thought good to buy a brace of good geldings, for by that means I could meet whom I pleased, though a dozen or sixteen miles distance, and so by the quickness of return come home undiscovered. If occasion should serve, they might very well serve for the High Pad. These I bought, and where they stood I had four or five several suits, either to ride withal (using variety that I might pass *incognito*), or to wear when I did intend to appear splendidly to peculiar friends ; and then the prodigal himself did not spend his money more profusely than myself.

I judge it unnecessary to relate how, and in what manner I disbursed great sums, since there are few that are addicted to pleasure and have money, but know how to lay it out to the satisfaction of their desires, that is, to please all their senses. My mistress seldom saw a piece of gold in her husband's hands, or some large and great piece of silver, but she would be begging it of him, for no other intents but to give it me ; which she took delight in, withal, knowing that frequent presents very much engage the affection.

My master seldom denied her (for like a cuckold he doted on his wife), but if he did, she would take pet, and would not eat, have the forehead bound down with a cross-cloth, look pitifully, and the like. If he asked her what she ailed, or what she was troubled at, she would say, ' At nothing more than your unkindness,' and then weep bitterly. For, like a right hypocrite, she had tears at command. The dotard would melt too, sometimes the great calf crying and sobbing, like a child that hath lost his bread and butter. Then to make his atonement, he must procure her two or three pieces, if he hath them not in the house ; otherwise it shall cost him as much more wealth on the doctor, of whom she would often pretend to take physic, but it should be only

rich cordials, strengthening jellies, with such like provocations to
venery.

For my own part, I was not idle in the mean time, laying up like the
careful bee for winter. We returned great sums of money every day,
which an acquaintance of mine knew very well; and he being daily
in the company of a fellow, who was both coiner and clipper, it seems a
decayed goldsmith, undone by the study of chemistry, but now lived by
some particular part thereof, as the transmutation of metal, or so forth.

This man he informs that he knew a young cashier that he thought he
could work to their purpose, who was very well qualified for it. An
appointed time for meeting was agreed upon between them, which was
made known to me. I thought of no other design but to be merry.
Being met, we drank stiffly, but ever and anon the stranger would beseech
me to favour him with my future acquaintance, that he should think
himself very happy if I would admit him into a familiarity. I could do
no less than promise so much, and so, laying aside ceremonies, we entered
into a very familiar discourse. But for that night there was nothing
propounded, neither was it thought convenient. Several times we met
(not without great expense), so that now we were grown intimately
acquainted. Our discourse happened on a time to be about chemistry;
I was forced to be mute, as not understanding anything thereof; yet I
could not but admire to hear my new friend relate what admirable
rarities he could perform in that mysterious art, and thereupon shewed
me a piece of gold, demanding my opinion what I thought of it. I told
him I could judge no less but that it was what it seemed to be. He
smilingly replied, ' No wonder that this should deceive you, since it
will do the like to the most critical goldsmith about the Town. No
doubt,' said he, ' you have heard of the Philosopher's Stone, and what
vast estates some have misspent in the search thereof, how ineffectual
the labour of such hath been the miserableness of their condition makes
apparent. Others, and not a few, have pretended they have obtained the
mastery thereof for no other intent than to delude some wealthy credulous
person, making some ridiculous experiments to confirm his belief, and
at last extract him to the very lees of his estate. I shall not deludingly
pretend to anything but what I will perform, which your own eyes shall
attest.'

Hereupon he shewed me various pieces, both gold and silver,
' which are the effects,' said he, ' of my own labour and pains, employed
in an art I have found out by the curious search and industry of my
brain, with which I can convert copper into that metal which current
money is composed of, either of which, according to the tincture I shall
give it. And to be plainer with you; out of that great love I have borne

ever since I first saw you, and that my actions shall make it apparent, see here this piece. According to the term of art given, it is called a black dog, with Queen Elizabeth's head thereon, which is only pewter double-washed. This here is a George plateroon, being all copper within, and only a thin plate about it. Another called compositum, which is a mixed metal, and will both touch and cut, but will not endure the fiery test.' He gave me the sight, likewise, of pieces-of-eight, half pieces and quarter pieces. ' Then again,' said he, ' our own coin we usually call English cloth, the other Spanish ; the prices whereof are several, according to their goodness and fineness. The best you may have for 15 sh. the yard, i.e. five shillings in the pound profit ; the worser for eight, ten, or more. Now to the intent that I may complete your happiness here, if enjoyment of wealth will do it, I would advise you to take some of every sort, and so mingle it with the rest of your good cash, proportionably to the sum. Let me add one thing more ; if any large money comes to your hand, lay it aside for me, which after I have corrected a little (for broad brimmed hats are not now in fashion), I will return it, allowing you 18 pence per pound interest.'

I gave him all this while great attention, without the least interruption ;· but he here making a stop, I thought he expected my replication ; which was to this effect, That I thanked him cordially for his respects, which I believed were real, having used that freedom with me ; that I did not in the least question the greatness of profit that would redound by the acceptance of his profer ; but it being a matter of the greatest consequence, and highest concern, I desired I might have some time for consideration. This answer made him look blank, fearing lest I made a demur only to betray him, so that I saw by his countenance he wished he had been more sparing in his expressions. I must needs confess, I trembled all the time I was in his company, wherefore I made all the haste I could to be gone, giving him to understand that after serious consultation with myself, I would send him an answer by my friend, and so I took my leave of him. The whole night following I spent in weighing his proposals in the balance of profit and preservation. I quickly found that life's preservation outweighed all other interest, and that honour, riches, and pleasure would avail little to that man that was riding post to the gallows. Besides, how could I expect to escape better than others, who were frequently made wretched spectacles of rash imprudence and folly, who, having forfeited the king's high and just displeasure, did usually betray their own selves to the severity of the law, which hath as little commiseration on such as on the worst of offenders ? Though I had committed several things that might come within the verge of an indictment, yet I always shunned such actions as bore the inscription in their front, *Memento mori.* To be as good as my promise, I sent my chemist these consequent lines :

Sir,

You seemingly do proffer fair, but know,
Hanging attends such kindnesses you shew.
The hope of profit tempts me ; loss of life
O'erpow'rs persuasions, and so ends the strife.
Had I two lives, my deeds should make it known,
How little I would care to hazard one ;
But having solely one, I will not try
Its loss ; *as yet I have no mind to die.*
Should we proceed then, and be taken in it ;
Death and damnation seize us in a minute.
Cease then, and let your fancy's suit with mine,
We'll plot no *treason,* but to get good *wine :*
That being had, let each man's *face* declare
Th' *Indian mines* not so rich as ours are.
If we want coin, the best way, I suppose,
Is to transmute the *metal* of my *nose.*

I never received any answer to what I wrote, neither did I ever see my new friend after, which was according to my own desire ; but I heard of his sad destiny, whereof I should have participated had I listed myself in that mettle-simulating regiment. Some were found out operating in the obscurest thickets of woods ; others were detected clipping in dark concaves on Blackheath, and their ringleader discovered in his own house, in a deep vault befitting his purpose ; who, though he had timely notice to remove his tools, yet, by his seizers they were found hid in a chimney-mantletree, hollowed to that intent, with a shutter at the end. After the dismal catastrophe of these hazardous fools, I had like to have been put to a great trouble, though not in the least guilty of the accusation. Thus it was ; an indigent hanger-on, having taken notice of my being once or twice in the company of the chief of those lately executed, came to me one evening, and requested some private discourse. I consented. Being together (laying aside several formalities that ushered in his discourse) he told me that I was taken notice of as a notorious disperser of counterfeit money, and that there was a warrant out to apprehend me, and that out of pure love to a man so young and fairly promising as myself, he thought himself bound in duty to preserve, if he could, by giving timely notice, to shun that which, if neglected, might prove destructive. I immediately saw the rogue peep through the vizard of dissimulation, and therefore instead of giving thanks I gave him a blow over both the eyes, to the intent he should not see how I would beat him, which was in such a manner that he could not see himself for three days afterward.　This fellow, I underſtood, to be a dun for the prisoners of their confederates abroad ; and if they would not continually let down their milk, impeach them, and were often condemned.

CHAPTER XIX

He breaketh his maſter (by the help of his miſtress) and so sets up for himself with that money he had unlawfully gotten in his apprenticeship, and credit besides : what a trick he served his maſter at laſt : his maſter and miſtress soon after died

BUT to proceed ; now I had served my time, and was accordingly made free ; but was solicited by my maſter to ſtay some longer time as a journeyman, which I consented to, knowing it could not be long : for we had so purloined from him that it was impossible for him to subsiſt any longer.　His creditors visited him daily, so that now his whole time was taken up in ſtudying fair promising words to satisfy them for the present, and tell them when they should come again.　My maſter perceiving the danger he was in, would neither ſtir abroad, no, not so much as come into the shop.　He now ſtanding upon the brow of a very high hill, and being forced to descend, I resolved to save him the labour, and so threw him down headlong.

By this time I had conveyed away a sufficient quantity of his goods, intending them for my own use ; and ſtowed them in a warehouse which I had lately taken privately for my purpose.　My maſter one night told me his intended design, that he was resolved to pack up all his goods, and to gather in what moneys he could, and so take his wife with him for Ireland.　I thought I should have dièd at firſt when I heard him talk of carrying his wife with him, and could not forbear dropping some tears ; which he perceiving, his trickled down his cheeks to bear mine company. ' Well now,' said he, ' I see thou loveſt me too, as well as thou haſt hitherto proved faithful.　But the deareſt friends muſt part ' (and with that he wept again like a child) ' however my comfort is, I hope we shall see each other in Heaven.'　I thought with myself, I had rather see him in the Compter.　And from that minute I contrived how I might effeét it ; for at that time I should never have been able to have brooked a separation between my miſtress and self, especially at so great diſtance. ſ She and I often consulted what to do.　Sometimes we were in the mind to take what money the old fool had, and so run away together, with many ſtratagems which we propounded ; but were rejeéted as no ways expedient nor convenient. At last I resolved on this, that she should acquaint herself of the exact time and way he intended to go, and so inform me thereof. I received information, a short time after, that before break of day, at such a time he would take horse at Islington, and so for Winchester. I immediately sent away word to one of his chiefest creditors, making known to him the sum and substance of everything, and that if ever he expected to receive what was due to him, he must at such a time have officers ready to waylay him, in order to his arrest. This was punctually done according to what instructions I sent him in a letter, without a name subscribed thereunto. He had not been long in custody before I was sent for, to advise with him what was best to be done in this his great extremity and perplexity. I could do no less than seemingly condole his misfortunes, and withal seemed to be very active as to his assistance, running up and down to his creditors to bring them to a compliance ; but he had been better to have sent some person else as solicitor in his business, for by my means I made his wound incurable. Seeing there was no remedy but patiently to endure his inevitable imprisonment, he got an horse (as some men term it) *alias* a *Duce facies*, and so removed himself to Ludgate, where he had not been long ere he died for grief.

In the meantime my mistress had secured what he had, which I enjoyed. I had now a house and shop of mine own, very well furnished ; but withal I was grown so deboist and profusively lavish that I seldom was at home but at night, and then in bed with my mistress, who was very importunate with me to marry her. I confess I loved her entirely as my mistress or whore, but I hated her as my wife, knowing very well that if she would be an whore to me, and have an husband, she would be so to another when I was in the former's place. She now found herself with child ; whereupon (taking upon her my duty) she daily pressed me to save her credit. But I delayed, putting her off continually with specious pretences, which her love and facileness easily swallowed. The time of her delivery approaching, I went down into the country with her ; and because it was at hand, I stayed to see the event. Within a short while she fell in labour, because we were known for no other than man and wife when her throws came upon her, she would not let me stir out of the room. Her pain growing intolerable, she called me hastily to her, and getting my hand within hers, ' Farewell,' said she, ' I die for thee. Thy last unkindness in not performing thy promise, and not returning love answerable to mine, hath untimely yielded my days.' With that she groaned, and then using her former expressions, cried out, ' Love my memory, however, since I die for thee.' She uttered not one word afterwards, being as good as her word. The good women looked ſtrangely on me, every one passing their verdiƈt, and all concluding her none of my wife. The firſt Chriſtians under the great persecution, suffered not in 500 years so many several ways as I did in five hours, by people's tongues. I muſt needs say, I took it very much to heart that report, which made Richard the Second alive so often after he was dead, should kill me as often whilſt alive. Desiring them at laſt to waive their censures (which they expressed publicly) I entreated them with all the rhetoric I could produce to endeavour the reviving of my wife, which if paſt recovery, to use means to preserve the child. In a short time they told me that was dead likewise. At firſt I shewed much grief, which was unfeigned, being not so much afflicted for the loss of her as affected with those words she uttered when she breathed her laſt. I was too conscious of my own guilt, and therefore they made the deeper impression in my very soul.

But all these perturbations of mind I dissipated with a glass or two of canary, which was the common antidote I used againſt care, sorrow, and vexation, &c. I now provided things necessary for her funeral, which were not vulgar ; which I might the better do, having made myself her executor before, taking all she had into my cuſtody. In memorial of her, and her fidelity, I wrote this epitaph on her tombſtone.

> Women, they say, will *lie*, but now I see
> 'Tis false, to th' laſt she spake the *truth* to me.
> ' Farewell,' said she, ' I thought my grief t'have hid,
> *I die for love of thee*,' . . . and so she did.
> Here with her lies her child, that ſtrove in vain
> To untomb itself, to be entomb'd again.
> But reſt my babe, thy cares with life are gone,
> *Thou'lt rise again*, though now a setting sun.
> Though wonders cease, thy mother's death doth prove
> They may revive, for she did *die for love*.

CHAPTER XX

His credit becomes suspeƈted by his exorbitant manner of living in drinking, whoring, gaming, &c. : he thinks to solder up that crack by marriage : he is deceived both in person and portion

RETURNING to my own habitation, I found that my so long absence had raised a suspicion in my neighbours' breaſts that I was run away ; which reſted not there, but spread like a canker, so that this flying report came to some of my creditors' ears, which made them both impatient and importunate with me for their moneys. I wondered whence proceeded their unexpected haste. Some that would not be put off with promises, I was forced to pay ; from others I obtained a little longer forbearance, which gave me but liberty to prosecute my former courses. If I was at the tavern, I was either drunk, engaged in a quarrel, and so involved in blood ; or else at play, if not at a bawdy-house, which places I could not refrain from frequenting, though I kept one of my own at home. For I would not entertain a maid but what was more than ordinarily handsome, whom I commonly vitiated either by presents, or promises if I got them with child. When I was weary of one, I paid her off, with some additions to her wages, and entertained another, who would in a short time be wrought upon as well as her predecessor ; being ambitious to lie with her master, and vainly hoping that to be the first step to her preferment, thinking of nothing but marrying, and so being mistress. In three years that I lived as a master I had nine illegitimates which I knew, four whereof were begotten of my maids, which put me to a vast expense. Two of the mothers would have forced me to have married them, or allowed them competent maintenance (for they were subtle cunning baggages) had I not by a wile got them aboard a vessel bound for Virginia, and never heard of them since. Besides two of three terrible claps, which cost me a considerable sum in their cure. This distemper, as it caused a consumption in my pocket, so it impaired my wonted strength, and almost spoiled my natural talent :

> For now it is much like Paul's Steeple turn'd
> A stately thing before the top was burn'd.

I now began to be sensible of my folly, and so resolved to take up in time, and redeem by degrees my lost credit by a temperate sober life. But I found I had wasted myself extremely, by which means I became less capable of reacting what I had before done, and my mind in a manner satiated, I question whether I should have had now such penitent thoughts. For a while I kept my shop diligently and constantly ; I would not drink with any but at home ; my sudden alteration made people admire, and the suddenness of my reformation was the common discourse of all my neighbours. The parson of our parish hearing of my strange alteration, came to me, which I admired at ; for before, he that had the least care or respect of his reputation would avoid all occasions of being seen in my company, lest they might be suspected extravagant and deboist.

> *Pares cum paribus facsimile congregantur.*
> Birds of a feather will flock together.

I

The shortness of his hair declared him a member of the Circumcision, but his triple cap, or three caps on his head, shewed, though he hated the very name of Rome or Babylon, yet he loved formerly a whore in private, though common.   His cloak was faced down with zeal before, and his band appeared but as a broad hem, to shew that a hem, with two or three formal spits, or a feigned cough, was the usual supply of his discourse, when he had thrashed himself in his cloak out of breath in the pulpit.   His looks resembled the bleer-eyed printing at Geneva and his face like that sort of ragged paper on which they work off their impressions.   After he had set his face into a platform, he delivered himself.   I shall not relate exactly his canting words, or what he borrowed from Scripture, being sensible, *non est tutum ludere cum sacris*, but give you the substance, which was first a reproof for my extravagancies : secondly, some general instructions (picked out of a common-place book) for my future practice : and lastly, some encouragements drawn from various motives to proceed (without looking back) toward a good life : on which three points he ran divisions strangely till dinner-time, and then his stomach petitioned him to shut his mouth, lest it should be deprived of its appetite by receiving in too much air.

In this seeming strictness of life I lived two or three months, and now some began to have charitable thoughts of my soul : and that I might regain my runnings out by future diligence and industry.

I had several matches offered me, which I saw, but liked them not ; for I had always been a general lover, and could not now come to particulars.   At last it was my misfortune to see one whom I was wished to ; and which at first sight robbed me at once, both of myself and good company.

Formerly I was pleasing and affable, desirous and desired of good society, but never lived till now an anchorite on earth.   Neither did I ever, till now, tie up mine eyes to one particular face, giving them free liberty to wander.   But now at last I fell from my primitive liberty, losing it totally, by dotage on a creature, and that a woman, too : a just judgment on me for my manifold sins, to throw this thing in my way for me to stumble at.   And it will appear in its due place that she was a bowed token of my Maker's displeasure sent me, for she was crooked.

CHAPTER XXI

How he was married, and what kind of thing was his wife

I MADE ſtrict enquiry after the condition of my intended wife's parents, and found by report they were very wealthy. In a short time we had conference together about the portion, and my eſtate, and therein we were all satisfied. My courtship was very noble, yet not prodigal, for fear of giving offence ; and in a little while we were married. By her looks I thought her so modeſt that an unchaſte thought durſt not enter into her head, since all immodeſt expressions she banished from her ears.

The firſt night I thought to have had the firſt taſte, but my experience told me the Tarriers had been there before. This ſtruck me into an amazement that there should appear such virgin whiteness, and the extract of innocence in her face, yet be guilty of a crime so notorious. Much perplexed I was, but durſt not vent myself what was more than bare suspicion. In one half year's time what I intended to conceal could be hid no longer, being brought to bed three months before her time ; and yet the bawd her midwife would make me believe this was usual ; and that children brought forth at six months might live.

Now began our domeſtic Civil Wars, which was carried on with such fury between us that there was hardly a utensil in the kitchin that could reſt in quiet from flying about our ears continually. My wife acted the *Silent Woman* to the life, whilſt in a single ſtate ; for before we were married all her answers were very short, comprehended within the two monosyllables of Aye, and No ; and those two muſt be forcibly extracted from her. But now her tongue wagged in a perpetual motion, and her voice so shrill and loud that it would be heard diſtinctly, though a piece of ordnance were discharged near her at the same time, or ſtanding at the bell-room door whilſt the bells were ringing. Frequent were her complaints to her father and mother, which alienated their affection from me, so that their only ſtudy was how to be rid of me. Her forgeries (to excuse her own devilry) had so inſtigated them that they sought my ruin by all ways imaginable. Besides, they laid an embargo on the reſt of my wife's portion unpaid ; advising her withal to secure what she could, for her own self-preservation. She followed their inſtructions so exactly that in a short time I found myself in a very declining condition, yet knew not the cause, till it was too late, conveying away both my goods and money, some whereof went to supply the necessities of her ſtallion.

I was all along suspicious of this, though I could not conclude her altogether so culpable. But my doubts and fears which of all are the sharpest passions, could not turn this distemper into a disease (although they looked through false optics, making things appear like evening shadows, disproportionable to the truth, and strangely longer than the true substance) till knowledge hereof (confirmed me by the witnesses of my eyes) had banished bare suspicion.

Which was thus : One night I caused myself to be brought home by a porter as dead drunk ; my wife received me in that condition (I perceived by peeping out of my eyelids) with much satisfaction, and I was immediately carried up to bed. With much difficulty they undressed me, pretending myself asleep all this while, and so they left me. It seems by the story that my wife sent away the maid (which was her pimp) to her friend to come at such an hour. About nine of the clock the maid was posted to bed; and about ten I heard one small knock at the door. He needed not to knock there any longer, for there was one below that was ready to receive him. When I judged they were encircled in each other's arms (which I understood by hearkening at the bottom of the stairs, and thereby knew whereabout they were), I ran in upon them with my sword (which I had prepared ready) and thinking to have run them through the body, intending to make a passage for their souls' escape, I passed my sword through the fleshy part of both their thighs. At which they made a most hideous outcry, so that the maid came running down : and a watchman that stood just at my door hearing the noise, knocked at the door to know what was the matter. The maid apprehending the danger, let him in, who by the help of his candle never saw so strange a sight ; for I had so pinned them together that they could not stir. As well as they could speak, they both begged their pardon for their lives only, which I granted, as looking on my revenge somewhat satisfied.

My gentleman I dismissed, but as for his mistress I was forced to send for a chirurgeon, whose wound needed no probing, but tenting, for it was through and through. There was no concealing of what was done ; wherefore in the morning early I acquainted her parents with what had happened last night, insisting further, that since she had instead of putting off handsomely the chain of matrimony, rudely broke it, it should be her own damage ; neither would I be at the cost of a visitation to repair the breach. To which I added, that had I denied her things requisite and necessary, or not performed duly my duty, she might have had some pretence for her slighting me, and look upon me only as a false crow set up in a garden to keep others from the fruit it cannot taste itself. But since it was otherwise, and that she had nothing to object against me but only sometimes curbing her inordinate desires ; I wished them to save me the labour of having the law to tear her from me, but that they would remove her elsewhere.

They replied but little, haſtening to their daughter; and fearing worse mischief might ensue, they inſtantly conveyed her into the country. She had not remained there long before she was cured, and not enduring to be confined to solitariness, repaired again to the city, where now she lives, as such do that keep civet-cats; but I hear she is very reserved to all but such she knows she may entruſt herself with. But let her go with these lines pinned to her back.

> There never yet was woman made,
>   Nor shall, but to be curſt;
> And oh! that I (fond I) should firſt
>   Of any lover
> This truth at my own charge to other fools discover.
>
> Ye that have promis'd to yourselves
>   Propriety in love;
> Know women's hearts like ſtraws do move,
>   And what we call
> Their sympathy, is but love to men in general.
>
> All mankind are alike to them;
>   And though we iron find
> That never with the loadſtone joined,
>   'Tis not the iron's fault,
> It is because the loadſtone yet was never brought.
>
> If where a gentle bee hath fallen
>   And laboured to his power,
> A new succeeds not to that flower,
>   But passeth by
> 'Tis to be thought the gallant elsewhere loads his thigh.
>
> For ſtill the flowers ready ſtand;
>   One buzzes round about,
> One lights, one taſtes, gets in, gets out.
>   All always use them,
> Till all their sweets are gone, and all again refuse them.

However, I muſt confess my own faults as well as condemn others; which was, I was too inquisitive after that which the more I knew would the more diſturb me. Of all things the less we know, the better. Curiosity in this renders a man as ridiculous a coxcomb, as that cuckold Sir John Suckling mentioneth, who made diligent enquiry whether he was made in a bed, or on a couch, and whether his duty-officiating cavalier pulled off his spurs firſt or not, &c.

Well, it was my hard fate to marry thus like one doomed to prison, who expecting to lie in a private room, is confined to the hole. Had I married the best, I believe I should have found myself in the stocks. 'Tis strange that I, of all men, should be deceived by this thing that was like a box bearing drugs not suitable to the inscription. Had not my passion hung in my eyes, when I looked into her disposition and carriage, I might have easily understood that her behaviour in the presence of me was only like action on a public stage, and that the evil of her natural inclinations were hid from me under the veil of silence and seeming modesty. And, indeed, my palate was bed-ridden, and so scarce sensible of sauce, much less of meat. But since I have had such ill-luck in marriage, which some vainly and falsely account a merry-age, I shall in the ensuing discourse give you some instruction or advice as landmarks. For having split upon this rock, I may the better be a pilot to another that would sail this way.

CHAPTER XXII

Some observations concerning love and women, selected out of the choicest commentators on their nature, together with his own experimental reflections

LOVE, 'tis confessed is a natural distemper, a kind of small-pox; most have either had it, or is to expect it, and the sooner the better. Surely I was never well cured on't, or else I had not thus fallen in a relapse. Want of knowledge misguided me at first, and so I fell into a quagmire; but I knew not what possessed me to ride afterward into another on purpose. Love-seeds, when it grows up to matrimony, is good for nothing, like some fruit-trees which must be transplanted before they will bring forth anything. And when love in this nature doth feed, the increase thereof is dissatisfaction, sorrow and vexation multiplied. This afore-mentioned is not truly love but lust; for I cannot believe that that noble passion can be the ruin of its subject; neither would I have it disparaged by so unworthy an object as a woman. If there be love, it should be to Heaven, a male friend, relations, or our country's preservation, and not to a female piece of imperfection. And yet nothing will serve the turn, but monopolizing it by marriage, because we would make it surely our own, and nevertheless our own till then. For if she be young, she is like an hawk upon her wing; and if she be handsome, she is the more subject to go out at check. Faulkners that can but seldom spring right game, should still have something to take them down. The lure to which all stoop in this world, is either garnished with profit or pleasure, and when you cannot throw her the one, you must be content to shew out the other.

Consider again that woman (besides the trouble) is a rent-charge, which though the curiosity of man hath often enclosed, yet he cannot for his life stop so well one gap, but it will lie open for any straggler; by which means it seldom improves or becomes fruitful. And why should a woman be denied the liberty of breaking a pane in her own window, or not admitted the freedom of regress to her own sally-port, letting in whom she esteems as friends? If you will not give them the permission, you must be forced to wink when they take it, or do worse: cross them, and they will endeavour the not leaving a cross in your pocket. Take it which way you will, marriage is the dearest way of curing love. Faring with such, as it doth with those for the most part that at great charges wall in grounds and plant, who cheaper might have eaten melons elsewhere, than cucumbers in their own garden. Besides, it is a gross piece of ignorance to be bound up to love for an age, when the cause of love may perish for a month, and then the effect will follow. If it be Nature's paint in the face, that doth induce you, those beautiful flowers of red and white, a disease will quickly wither; if not, ravishing Time will deflower the choicest beauty.

But the ill consequences of marriage are more to be considered, which are commonly drawn from the evil inclinations of that sex. Eve by stumbling at the Serpent's solicitations cast her husband out of paradise; nor are her daughters surer of foot, being foundered by the heat of lust and pride. It were something if marriage could answer the expectation of all she boasts the cure of; for instead of quenching the hot coals of concupiscence, it aggravates the simple sin of fornication, making it sprout into adultery. What might be said more as to this subject, I shall refer the reader to the writings of that ingenious gentleman Mr Francis Osborne. If any more (like boys stripped and stand shivering about the brink) are ready to leap into love's whirl-pit, and so endanger the loss of themselves, let them first look upon love to be an idle fancy, and wedlock a dangerous consequence. If I could persuade you from loving, one would think the other then would be disregarded, but some to their cost can speak the contrary.

In the first place, marry none but whom you love: for he that marries where he doth not love, will love where he did not marry. If you are prone to love one particular person, some are of opinion that travel is an excellent remedy; for absence doth in a kind remove the cause, removing the object. Others think that frequent visits (whereas the rarity of them endears the affection) may by a surprizal discover some defects, which though they cure not absolutely, yet they qualify the vehement heat of an amorous fever, and as near as can be, let it be unseasonably, either when she is in sickness or disorder, by that a man may know she is but mortal, and but a woman ; the last would be enough to a wise man for an antidote. Enter into discourse with her of things she daily hears not, and it will confirm the cure. Neither will it be amiss to contrive yourself into the company of variety, especially such beauties which are generally cried up ; and if you can, taste them all (but now I think on't, it is no matter, one is sufficient for a surfeit), for this malady is better remedied this way, than by abstinence ; good jovial company will much conduce to the cure.

But I like not the prescription of marriage, since it is the last and most dangerous receipt ; like a kind of live pigeon applied to the soles of the feet, which remedy to say truth, is worse than the disease. Were it possible for a woman to be constant to one, something might be said, but I never yet tried any which did not very much shew their displeasures when offered some kindness, but never found any to refuse them, if opportunity and privacy of place admitted their reception ; which hath made me often in my own thoughts question my mother's honesty and fidelity to my father.

What I now utter is not derived from prejudice to that sex, grounded on my own wife's disloyalty ; but experience tells me this, which most past sixteen very well understand, that there are few women, let them pretend what they please, but will yield to the temptations of the flesh, and so much the sooner by how much she professeth some new light, which is *Ignis fatuus* that leads them into the quagmires of all sorts of erroneous tenets. With this dark lanthorn-light they dazzle the eyes of such as would pry into their actions, while behind in the dark they sensually satisfy themselves undiscovered.

Experience dictates what I here express ; for I have had converse with several of these religious pretenders, that in the very act would very much inveigh against adultery with their tongues, whilst their blood willingly consented to the commission of that sin, and then immediately after seem extremely pensive, using these and such like formal expressions : ' Fie, fie, I wonder how you durst sin thus, even before the face of your Creator. Do you think he saw you not ? yea verily, and you shall answer for what you have now done ; ' whereas it could never have been done without a mutual consent.

They will make it their daily discourse, speaking against such whose natural inclinations have prompted them to unlawful satisfaction of their lust, and yet they themselves are at the same time studying how they may secretly and securely accomplish the same thing.

To conclude, Woman in general is the very extract of inconstancy, and therefore it is but a vain thing for any to think she can absolutely love one man. Such who are found constant to their husbands, preferring their welfare before the indulging of their own by-respects, ought to be looked on no less than miracles of their sex, by such who are acquainted generally with female dispositions and actions.

CHAPTER XXIII

He cheats his creditors by knavish breaking, and runs away from Ireland : *he is shipwrecked on the Isle of* Man

WHILST my credit was good I thought good to make use of it, lest that failing, I should want an opportunity to march off with flying colours. To raise my repute amongst my neighbours (whom I knew would spread abroad what they had seen) I caused a porter (whom I could trust) to carry out privately an hundred pound, and a little while after to come with a trusty friend of mine with that, and five or six hundred pound bags more on his back, openly carrying them. Upon receipt hereof, I tumbled the money out of the bag (which had really money in it) on the counter, purposely making a great noise. Having told it over (my friend standing by the while) I put it up ; and pretending to lay that aside and take another, I took up the same again, so doing till I had told it over five or six times ; then writing in public view a receipt, with much civility and respect I dismissed my gentleman. And this did I thrice in a month's time ; so that by this means without suspicion I conveyed away a great quantity of my goods, which people thought I had sold, and therefore thought me to have a great trade. Report hereby rendered me a man of vast dealing, so that now I had goods daily offered me, some whereof I received, promising to them payment at three months, others at six. What wares or moneys I could take up, I did, not mattering at what rate. To some of the more wary sort I confessed a judgment for their security. I needed not to have spoken in the singular number, for I deluded four with my judgments. What commodities I had I converted into money by a Bill of Sale, and so went away, leaving my creditors to sue out a Statute of Bankrupt if they so pleased ; which I valued not, if once out of their reach. To my chiefest creditor I sent these lines, to the intent he should not tax me with incivility for going away and not sending him word :

> Credit doth ſtrengthen such whose trades are weak,
> But too much credit, Sir, did make me break.
> Credit to sinking tradesmen is a prop,
> But had you kept your wares, I'd kept my shop.
> Pray do not blame me, Sir, because I shew
> A way to pay those many debts you owe :
> Which you may do, if you'll advised be,
> Which is in short, prepare to follow me.
> Believe me, faithful Sir, in what I say,
> I went before, but to shew you the way :
> But you will not, don't lament your loss,
> For in your money I do bear the cross.
> Grief will diſtract you, and deſtroy your wit ;
> Good Sir, preserve it, for y' ave paid for it.

I rid poſt for Holyhead night and day, so that I arrived there in a very short time. Going to dismount, I tumbled off, neither could I rise again ; continual and unaccuſtomed riding had almoſt dislocated every bone in my body, notwithſtanding it was swathed for that purpose. The next day I made a shift to walk abroad to view the rarities of the town, but found nothing rare but handsome women, civility, and good drink. In two days' time we set sail. We had not ran above three leagues before the sky darkened ; the wind blew hard at a South Eaſt, and the waves rose mountain high. In an hour's time we were forced to cut our maſts by the board, and lightening the ship as much as we could, let her drive. Every man fell to his prayers, expecting every moment when they should be swallowed up by the sea. As for my part, I now thought divine vengeance had overtaken me, and would reckon with me for all my rogueries; I looked on myself as Jonah, and was much troubled that others should suffer for my iniquities. About three o'clock in the morning we heard a hideous noise occasioned by the beating of the sea againſt the rocks, which was echoed by the loud and lamentable cries of the seamen, who now knew there was no hope for us. Now could I pray heartily, that had never prayed in my life before ; but my devotion was soon spoiled, for the ship ſtruck in between two rocks. I looked out, and me-thought the dashing of the waves looked perfectly like flashes of fire. Here she ſtuck a little while, which gave five of us opportunity to leap out upon a rock. We were no sooner there, before a wave fetched her off, but brought her on again, and split her all to pieces, we five, in the meantime, riding aſtride on a rock behind one another, like so many criminals on a wooden-horse. Sometimes a wave would ſtrike clear

over us, which endangered our washing off. Sometimes we thought to
let go our hold, as looking upon our preservation to be impossible ; and
withal imagining that the tide was coming in. At laſt the hindmoſt
could hold no longer, but crying, ' Lord have mercy on my soul,' committed himself to the merciless sea. Immediately came a tumbling sea
and washed off the next ; now did I expeſt that every wave would prove
my executioner. But it was not decreed, I suppose, that I should be
drowned. Day broke, so that we could discern we were not a quoit's
caſt from shore, and that the sea was ebbing. We waited not above an
hour before we crawled to shore, for go we could not, our joints were so
benumbed by the cold. We got up the beach, and could discern a little
way diſtant a small cottage ; thither we repaired with much difficulty,
and were kindly entertained, pitied, and informed where we were.
We ſtayed about a week in this Isle of Man, without one farthing
expense. For the inhabitants are generally very civil, and courteous.
and especially to ſtrangers. From thence we embarked for Dublin.

CHAPTER XXIV

His arrival into Ireland : he changeth his name : what trick he served his
firſt landlady, all his money being spent, and those goods and coin like-
wise shipwrecked which he expeſted to follow him

WE landed at a place called Ringsend about a mile from Dublin.
I was asked whether I would have a coach. ' Where are there
any,' said I, for I looked about me, and could see nothing like a coach.
The fellow looked upon me to be a very ignorant person, because I underſtood not what he meant, and angerly spake thus : ' By my gossip's
hand, thou canſt not see very much well, arre look here is one by thine
own side.' It was a great while before I could tell what language he
spoke, he did so tone his words ; neither could I underſtand him, till
one ſtanding by interpreted him. As for his Ringsend coach, as he called
it, it was wheel-barrow fashion, only it had two wheels not much bigger
than a large Cheshire cheese. The horse that drew this princely pygmy
chariot, I at firſt mistook for an over-grown maſtiff, but viewing him
narrowly, found him the extraſt (by his shape) of a Scotch hobby.
Well, up I mounted, but could not invent a name for the manner of my
riding, for I was neither coached nor carted, but I fancied myself
(and that juſtly) as I was riding, to be some notorious malefaſtor drawn
on a sledge to the place of execution, which afterwards experimentally

I found Dublin to be. Many of its inhabitants call this city Divlin, *quasi* Divels Inn, and very properly it is by them so termed ; for there is hardly a city in the world that entertains such variety of devil's imps as that doth. If any knavishly break, murder, rob, or are desirous of polygamy, they ſtraightway repair thither, making that place, or the kingdom in general, their asylum, or sanctuary. My firſt care was to plant myself conveniently ; the next day I sent for a barber to shave all my hair off, ordering him to bring me a periwig of an absolute contrary colour to my own hair, to the intent that if I should meet with any of my former acquaintance, they might not know me, whereby I should prevent their sending notice to any where I was. The truth of it is, in this disguise I hardly knew myself. The greateſt difficulty I found, was to make myself familiar with my fictitious name. At firſt, when my landlady called me by that name, I either ſtared her in the face, or looked behind me (not answering thereunto), thinking she had spoke to some man else ; but had I not pretended to be thick of hearing, and so that way apologizing for my silence, my design might have been marred. I daily met with several I knew, but would not take the leaſt cognizance of them.

In this manner I spent a month, but all this while no tidings of my goods and money ; that which I had brought with me was all consumed. My landlady (as it is cuſtomary there, having as little truſt or faith as they have religion) called upon me for what I owed her. For a little while, I ſtopped her mouth by telling her I had a considerable quantity of goods and money coming, which I expected by every fair wind. A little while after I heard the ship in which they were was caſt away. Now did I absolutely conclude God's juſt judgment attended my fraud and knavery. My loss I did not in the leaſt discover to any, knowing I should reap at firſt only some pity, and afterwards be undervalued and disrespected. My hoſtess again was very importunate with me to have her reckoning. I endeavoured to put her off, saying, I expected daily Bills of Exchange ; but she would not believe me, for I perceived that she had been often cheated with such delusions.

Now did I not know what to do. I thought good to try another way ; she being a widow, I fancied I could work upon her female frailty. I used all means possible to get her alone ; which I did but seldom, and then did I make use of all my rhetoric to persuade her into a belief how dearly I loved her. She replied little, but would laugh at me till she held her sides again. I verily believe she underſtood my drift, which I might argue from her expressions. Sometimes she would say, ' Come, come, away with these love fooleries, and pay me what you owe.' Then would I tell her, all I enjoyed, and myself too were properly hers, and that she might take them when she pleased into her possession. ' No, no,' she would say, ' my youthful days are paſt, and it is time for me to look Heavenwards ; wherefore let fall your suit,' &c.

Since words would no ways prevail, I resolved to try something else, knowing how difficult it is for a woman when in bed to refuse a venereal proffer. To that purpose one night I came softly into her chamber, and groping with my hand for her face, I caught a man by the beard : at which he awaked, and thinking the devil was come to trim him, or rob him of his wash-balls, would have cried out aloud, but that fear had so locked up his voice that his higheſt note was little louder than whispering. I could but juſt hear him say, ' In the name of ——— what art ? ' ' I am,' said I, and then she waked too, ' no ghoſt, but a living witness of your lechery ; to that intent I came hither, to be fully satisfied of what I have a long time suspeſted. As for you Madam, your youthful days are paſt, but your luſt will endure for ever. If this be your way to Heaven, why were you so uncharitable as not to let me go along with you ? As for your part, Sir, I believe that you are travelling that way too ; for if I miſtake not, you lately came out of purgatory.'

To be short, they both entreated me to be silent and retire to my own lodging, and that in the morning they would treat with me to my full satisfaſtion. This was what I aimed at, though brought about otherwise than intended. Early they both came to me : the pious gentlewoman being very tender of her credit, would forgive me my debt if I would not blemish her reputation by my report ; her gallant gave me ten pieces to bind the bargain. Having gotten a discharge under her hand, I sealed our contract with an oath and faithful promise never to divulge their shame. The gentleman (though his eſtate much exceeded hers) out of spite, I think, or vexation to be so caught, incontinently married her, though all former solicitations (which I underſtood were many) proved ineffeſtual.

CHAPTER XXV

He is driven to extreme necessity : he describes what it is to be indigent, by what he suffered in that condition

THIS ten pound I received from my old lecherous dotard made its exit almoſt as soon as its entrance into my pocket. By that sum I thought to have purchased mountains in Ireland (and indeed there is too great plenty of them there) by gaming ; but experience told me afterwards that my design was hazardous, and so it proved, for I met with a person that bubbled me at hazard, not leaving me a penny, and engaged besides for my proportion of the reckoning. My gamester dealt too hardly with me ; yet it was but juſt, for I intended to show him as little favour, if compelled to lie at my mercy, which I verily thought would be, having various utensils about me to that purpose, but I was over-matched.

> I thought myself secure, for I could top,
> By which I've forc'd some cits to leave their shop.
> I palm'd, and put the change upon them too ;
> I only ſtudied how I might undo.
> But now I'm met with, 'tis but juſt I see,
> That he which others cheats, should cheated be.

I returned to my lodging (which was none of the beſt), with what anxiety and perturbation of mind I shall give any loser leave to imagine, whilſt the remembrance thereof enforceth me to speak ; and I hope the reader will give me that liberty, since the proverb entaileth on the loser that privilege. I acquainted my landlord with my misfortune, who seemed very much to condole me for the present, but it was afterwards the occasion of his not crediting me. From hence, I will advise all to speak as little as they can of ills that betide them ; but we cannot dis-course too much of the good that happens to us. Perceiving my land-lord grew cold, my spirit was too high to be any longer beholding to him but for my lodging ; wherefore I seldom came home till night.

Neither would I make known my condition to any that knew me. Sometimes I should meet with some in the ſtreet, who would ask me to drink with them ; my usual answer was, I came from it but even now : insiſting farther, that such a gentleman, with two or three more besides myself, had drank so much, and that I admired at myself for being so sober ; whereas to deal ingenuously, I had not drank one drop that day. Another seeing me, would ask me whether I would dine with him at the ordinary ? Then would I pretend that my lord —— Gentleman over-persuaded me to dine with him, and that we had such variety that I doubted my ſtomach had received some detriment thereby ; and there-fore begged an excuse ; whereas a dry cruſt taken out of my leather cupboard, was all the varieties the Gentleman-Usher of my ſtomach, my throat I mean, had taken cognizance of that day. So hard it was too, that I would look this way and that way, not daring to commit it to the engine of my chops, unless there was none near me within a furlong ; for had there been any near me, they would have sworn I was eating walnuts, shells and all. Now did I learn to drink water, which necessity made me to commend as the moſt sovereign liquor, and moſt suitable to the body of man ; otherwise Adam in Paradise would not have been without a cup of ale.

Every morning I offered up my devotions either to St. Patrick, or St. James, each of which have two excellent wells dedicated to the honour of their saintships. Thither did I repair constantly twice or thrice a day : after I had offered up the fumes of smoke (most commonly of none of the best tobacco) I kneeled, not using the common way of drinking out of the chained iron dish, but with greater adoration sucked it as it came through the conveyance. After a walk to Kilmanum (about a mile from Dublin) or some other place to prepare my stomach, I returned to Christ Church, frequently dining there with Sir Richard Strang-bow. Reflecting on his cheer, and the liquor of those two saints, I cannot but tell you my thoughts of both.

> Sir Richard Strang-bow keeps an house where wine
> And bread some sup on, but few seldom dine.
> Ask yet an hungry rambler, and he'll say,
> (Though not one bit came near his mouth that day)
> He plentifully din'd with him, so let him still
> Till he hath found his empty belly fill,
> Where I ne'er could, which made me hate in fine
> Sir Richard Strang-bow's feasts, St. Patrick's wine.

I fasted so long, I had now almost forgot how to eat : for if casually I came where meat was, I often made a proffer to convey something to my mouth, but my lips understood not my meaning ; for having been so long unaccustomed to their duty, knew not how to perform their gaping office. It was impossible at this time for the greatest fright to have made me foul my breeches, because I seldom used anything that might cause excrements. And therefore I wondered to hear any enquire for an house of office, since I had now left off going to stool. Once in five days I thought I stood in need of evacuating ; but I was mistaken, for by discharging a blast of wind (whose fury scattered small stones underneath me) I found it only a fit of the colic. I shall deal plainly, should I have found a propensity, I would have been very unwilling to let anything go out, since so little passed into my belly. Some moveables I had left, which I was forced to dispose of, to keep the passage of my guts open, which would frequently grumble against my stomach for detaining too long what was received, challenging a propriety therein. I thought it good policy not to buy any belly-timber of a quick concoction, because it should stay the longer within me. To this purpose I looked on old cheese to be food convenient ; knowing that though it will digest anything else, yet it cannot digest itself ; and as it closeth up the mouth of the stomach, so by its respective quality it locks up fast the postern of the microcosm. Flesh again (if I got any) I would swallow by whole-sale, fearing lest by chewing it, my stomach would too suddenly give it a passport to my hypo-gastrium ; by which means it would be immedi-ately ready again, nay restless in the craving more. I seldom slept for the gnawing of my stomach and the anguish of my guts, and for want of those fumes which proceeding from meat ascended into the head, and so the causers of sleep. If I chanced to nod at any time, I dreamed of nothing but eating, my fancy feeding that while as voraciously as an hunger-starved hound on a shoulder of mutton. I was driven to that pass, I could not justly tell whether I was alive or not. Sometimes I was of the opinion that I died in our shipwreck on the Isle of Man, and that I was now a soul in Purgatory.

Immediately after my arrival in this place, the itch and bunniah, or flux (the two grand epidemical distempers of Ireland), gave me their welcome into their country, attended by a great number of six-footed gents clad in a gray livery, with on single list down the back ; who all promised to stick to me and be my bosom friends, neither would they for-sake me as long as life lasted. But they, like the rest of the best and fairest promising friends, left me when fortune committed me prisoner to the merciless cruel hands of that accursed gaoler, poverty. I was grown so lean that the mongrel Scotch and Irish gentleman the itch, finding not flesh enough to feed on, gave me the French compliment, ' Adieu pauvre Gentilhomme.' The flux stayed with me as long as anything was left in my belly, but finding no substance from my guts, took his leave also, un-kindly carrying away all that was within me. Their retinue perceiving they were like to feed on hard meat, there being little left but bones, whose teeth were incapable of fastening thereon, resolved to follow after ; some making more than ordinary haste, broke their necks off the cape of my cloak, missing their footing, the threads thereof being spun out at times as fine as those of Arachne's working.

To conclude, I was a mere walking skeleton, my skin only served as a mantle for my bones. But for wind, my belly would have contracted an approved philosophical axiom, proving a vacuum.

One time passing by the castle gate, a soldier fired his musket, and I protest methought my belly sounded like a drum at the report. Should I relate every particular wherein the malevolence of Fortune afflicted me, I should much tire the reader, as well as perplex myself with re-membrance ; wherefore I shall desist, and give you leave to imagine the deplorableness of his condition, who hath neither money, friends, nor credit, and in a place where he is neither acquainted with the people nor their language.

CHAPTER XXVI

*He falling accidentally into a strange house, endeavours to build a sconce,
but is frustrated of his intent : the old hostess pities him at first, and
relieves him, and continually after feeds him for her own peculiar diet,
further insisting on the misery he then endured*

I WAS by this time grown so feeble by fasting, or by the manner of
my feeding, which was either cheese or hard eggs (there being great
plenty), that I could hardly go ; and so light I was by continual smoking
that I questioned often whether I was not a mere fume myself ; fearing
still when I walked abroad, to be extracted by the sun for an exhalation.
Fortune so favoured me one day that I found a groat, which put me into
an extasy of joy.   I know not what magical power there was in that vast
sum of four pence, for in an instant, not knowing by what means, I
found myself in a victualling-house, so speedy was my conveyance, as
if I had been riding some Dæmon through the air.   I called for some
meat, but my voice sounded so hollow as if I had spoken in a vault.
Some said it was the echo of some person speaking in the next house :
others of the wiser sort believed me to be some spectrum, or apparition ;
and that the Devil had assumed a body speaking in that *mortuum cadaver.*
The truth of it is, 'twas something hard to determine whether I spake or
no, but that they might perceive my lips to open.   There was a physician
in the house at that time, who looking on me narrowly, openly proclaimed that I was the workmanship of some mortal, who having first
gotten the skeleton or bones of a man, had artificially skinned them over,
and that German clock-work caused my motion.   I would have laughed
heartily at their ridiculous apprehensions but that I had forgot how.   I
had some gall left in me still, which made me start up in as great a rage as
my feeble body was able to declare, intending to demonstrate to them
how grossly they were mistaken, but perceiving me to approach, they all
fled but Mr Doctor, whom shame retained, otherwise by a fit of an
ague (which just then possessed him) I knew he would willingly have
been gone too.   'Speak,' said he tremblingly, 'what art?'   I was
somewhat puzzled at his question, for I knew not well what I was.
'I am a living man,' said I.   'Why then thou wouldst have flesh,'
said he.
     After several discourses to this purpose, I at length made him partly
believe that I was no such thing he imagined, and yet he would be asking
me still a many impertinent questions, as whether I could see ; and his
reason was, because he could discern no eyes ; whether I was born

K

without eyes, or loſt them since accidentally, &c. I was forced to tell him at laſt that it was the country disease that had reduced me to this condition. Hearing me say so, he pitied me much, and told me he would fetch inſtantly something that should do me much good. I thanked him, and away went Mr Doctor. The good woman overhearing our discourse drew near then confidently, and demanded what I would have? I told her, anything which was eatable, as far as a groat would go. She brought me some hot meat, and setting it before me, went for some drink, but before she could return I had swallowed it all. She fetched me more, which went the same way with as much celerity. But like quick-silver it wrought quite through me, not ſtaying a quarter of an hour.

The manner whereof was thus. About to pay my reckoning, my groat got into a piece of paper; I fumbled a great while in my pocket, but found it not, which put me even to my wit's ends. At laſt drawing out some papers and shaking them my groat dropped. Perceiving its fall might be dangerous, there being many holes in the floor, I catched after it; notwithſtanding it fell upon the very brink of an hole. What with haſte to recover it, and the fright the danger put me into, I discharged myself of every bit I had eaten. There was nobody could say I had fouled my breeches, or that I ſtunk; which I made appear to my land-lady by showing her what I had evacuated, but little differing from what I had eaten a quarter of an hour before. The good old woman persuaded me ſtrongly to eat it again; 'for,' said she, 'it cannot be much the worse for juſt passing through you, and I will fry it if you please.' I thought I should now have died with laughter at her ſtrange proposition; but the woman ſtared upon me, not knowing whether I grinned or laughed. 'Well, well,' said she at laſt, 'if you will not eat such good victuals, somebody else shall.' I offered her my groat, which she refused, telling me there was as much more to pay. I told her that was all the money I had about me, and that I would pay her the reſt the next day.

> But she for her part thought it was unjuſt,
> To liſten to the arguments of truſt.

And therefore told me plainly she would have her reckoning. I bid her ſtay a while; then as soon as she had turned her back I attempted to march off, but my ſtrength failing me, I wanted swiftness, and so was brought back. I made her acquainted with my condition how miserable it was; I needed not many arguments to persuade any into that belief, for my person was the true emblem of misery. She gave a serious attention to what I expressed, and at laſt melted into tears, commiserating my misfortunes. She caused inſtantly a bed to be warmed, where being laid, she ordered a caudle to be made, and in fine shewed a world of kindness to me, not imagining what she aimed at. She would not let me ſtir out of my bed but whilſt it was making, for above a week; at the conclusion of which I began to recover a little colour in my cheeks, and grew indifferent ſtrong. She gave me money in my pocket, and told me I muſt walk into the fields with her. I blessed myself and that angel that directed my feet to the finding that loſt groat which was the occasion of my reſtitution to a condition of living again. By this time I imagined what my old gentlewoman expected; wherefore, in the firſt place I acknowledged how much I was obliged to her matchless civilities, and that it was impossible for me to return her answerable satisfaction. Rolling her pretty pigs-eyes to and fro in her head, ' I require,' said she, ' nothing but your love.' If it muſt needs be so, thought I, there is no way better than to let fancy form her beautiful, and so by the force of imagination I shall enjoy as much pleasure as if lying with Venus, though in conjunction with this Succubus. We used not many ceremonies (like puling-whining lovers that are always saying grace, but never fall to), but taking the convenience of a ditch underneath a bushy-topped hedge we conferred notes. Had any seen us in this poſture, they would have concluded old winter metamorphosed into an old woman lying in a dike, and that Flora was converted into a young man, and both in an unnatural conjunction; or that youthful Phœbus had contracted his rays to court a lump of ice, but with shame was forced to desiſt, finding his powerful endeavours ineffectual in the production of a thaw.

Whenever I wanted a small sum, a kiss or two, or the saying I loved her, extracted so much as supplied my present occasions; if I wanted a sum considerable, why then a quarter of an hour's discourse in private effected my desires. Moſt that knew me wondered what politic ſtratagems I used that I so suddenly wound myself out of that labyrinth of all sorts of miseries, and that I appeared both in feature and garb so different to my former condition. I had as many pretences to blind the world as there were various suspicions of pragmatic persons. In short, I was now very well apparelled, well furnished with money, I kept my horse, nay my whore too; this I made use of for what she was, the other for what she had. So seemingly happy was the present ſtate of my life that I deemed it impossibly unalterable by any decree of fate.

CHAPTER XXVII

He makes a ramble into the country ; takes some observations as he travelleth ; and is soundly beaten for attempting to board a small Irish pinnace

I BEGAN now to be somewhat weary of the city, and therefore resolved to refresh myself with the country air. I acquainted my patroness therewith ; who with much regret condescended, conditionally two days should be the utmoſt time of my absence.

That morning I set forth there was such solemn leave taken between us as if my voyage had been intended for the Indies. About to mount, she retrieved my intentions, clasping me in her arms ; I should rather have chosen the embraces of a she-bear, as thinking her breath far sweeter ; and truly I have often wondered at my recovery in so impure and unwholesome air. Being on horse-back she so bathed her cheeks with tears (wanting no moiſture, derived from an everlaſting spring of humours diſtilling from her head) that you would have sworn she was the representation of the pig-woman in Ben's *Bartholomew Fair*. Had not her watery flood-gates drowned her eyes, I think she would have ſtood looking after me that way I rid till my return. Well, there is no fool like the old doting fool ; and were I again to love for intereſt, I would choose such a person. Your young skittish things that only mind their pleasures, think they have done a man a courtesy that merits reward, if they admit him into their private familiarity, because they find fond man so passionate and impatient in the prosecution of his desires. And then again, having variety of courtiers, they are too sensible that if one will not meddle with the bait, a second will nibble at it so long till he is caught with the hook. Whereas a woman ſtricken in years, and having loſt her beautiful allurements is disregarded, and looked on as no fit subjeʒt for love to treat on ; not but she may have as youthful desires as any, and if that way inclined, none so prone as she. For knowing she hath nothing but her wealth to attraʒt withal, she will freely part with it for her self-satisfaʒtion ; and that she may not lose her ſtallion, conſtantly encourage him even to the exhauſting of what she hath. Moreover, finding the man to answer her expeʒtations, she ſtudies all ways imaginable how to please him in everything, that he may please her in that one thing.

But to my purpose. Coming to Balle-more-Euſtace, a little beyond the town (which is in the County of Wicklow), there is a small river in the summer-time not above knee-deep. I perceived a young woman about to cross it ; drawing to the water, she ſtood not on the niceties of modeſty, but pulling up her clothes to the waiſt. The sight hereof ſtopped me, and as near as I could opposite to her. She minded me not, but came ſtraight over to me, and at about three yards diſtance let down her coats. I observed so many excellencies that my blood began to boil, and my flesh was all of a flame. For her hair which naturally curled, and was plaited, was of a bright flaxen, each hair in the sun glittered like a thread of gold.

Here take notice by the way, that the maids for the moſt part, winter and summer, go without any coverings on their head, which they wash all over every night ; the meaner sort as soon as married wear kerchers. She had an angelical countenance, only somewhat brownish by the sun's frequent kissing of it ; I know not whether I may adjudge that a deformity. The skin of her body might vie with snow for whiteness. I dismounted, and addressed myself to her in English ; she answered me in her own language, she underſtood me not. Then did I make use of that little Irish I had learned, which were some fragments of lecherous expressions, to which she replied, but I underſtood her not. To be brief, I so far prevailed that I got her into a small wood, in which the thick and spreading tops of the trees seemed to lay their heads together in conspiracy to keep not only the sun's entry, but also the curious search of any mortal's eye. She permitted me to kiss, dally, lay my hand on her thighs, &c., which were the only preludiums of what should follow. But herein I miſtook, for their dispositions are much different from the English. We use to say that where we gain over any woman the liberty to use the hand, we cannot fail of doing what we moſt desire ; whereas, quite contrary, they will without the leaſt opposition permit the firſt, but with the greateſt difficulty admit of the laſt. For as soon as she saw me ready to engage, she cried out incessantly, ' Whillallalloo ' ; and I could hear this ululation echoed.

I had juſt recovered my horse when two or three fellows came running to me, the one with a flail, the reſt with long poles. The firſt salutation I received was from the flail, which failed but little of doing my business. The next my horse's crupper received ; the poor beaſt being civilly bred, could do no less then return them a congee with his leg, which made one of them fall on his knees to his maſter, as if he had been monarch of that soil. These two rogues ſtood ſtiffly to me, insomuch that I knew not what course to take. The villains were so nimble that one of them was continually before me hindering my flight, whilſt the other drubbed me forward. I bethought myself of a piſtol I had in my pocket, charged without a bullet. I drew it, presented, and pretended I would fire if they desiſted not. These ſtupid fellows apprehended not the danger ;

perceiving how stupidly senseless they were, I fired it full in the face of
him that fronted me, who verily believed he had been shot, and so out
of conceit (for they are naturally very timorous) fell down as dead. The
other seeing that, ran away as swift as lightning, whereby I had leave to
ride on, which I did (you may think) with no ordinary speed. Lovers
may talk of their sufferings by their mistress's frowns or obdurateness,
but let any one judge of mine by the blows I received ; sighing is nothing
to fighting, and a few tears are not to come in competition with dry
basting. Pox on them, they made me out of conceit with love for six
weeks after. I never thought of enjoying a woman since but the remembrance of those three bog-trotters converted the hot fit of my amorous
fever into a cold one.

A little way from Baltinglass I took up my quarters for that night.
The inn I lay in was one story high, about the height of an extraordinary
pigsty, and there was one chimney in it, too, more than there is to be
found in one of an 100 such hovels. The good man welcomed me after
his fashion, but I think an Anthropophagus or Indian man-eater would
have done it as civilly. I bid him set up my horse, by signs (for that was
the language we conversed in), but alas, there was no other stable but
what was at the end of our kitchin ; our dining-room, bed-chamber,
pigsty, pantry and buttery being all one, without distinction or separation. Some few wattles (as they call them) were placed above, that was
our hay-loft. The only door of our inn was a large hurdle, much like
a sheep-pen. The Bannette, or good wife of the house, could speak a
little broken English. I asked her what I should have for supper ?
' Thou shalt have a supper,' said she, ' for St. Patrick a gra.' I stayed
an half-hour expecting when she would lay down something to the fire,
but instead thereof she brings me, in a wooden platter, a great many
leeks, in the bottom whereof was a good quantity of bay-salt, and
withal a loaf as black as if the meal had been wetted with ink. ' Seest
tou tere, Chreest himself nor St. Patrick did ever eat better ting.' I
could not forbear smiling, which put her into a great passion ; for if a
man eats not what they set before him, they think themselves highly
affronted. Because I would please them (not knowing but that I might
find as bad sauce here) I pretended to eat, conveying it into my boots.
After supper I asked them for a clean pipe ; the woman brought me
one about an inch long, telling me it was very clean, for her husband had
not smoked it above ten times. I judged it to be the ruins of the first
pipe that was made, which was conveyed from one of that family to
another, conditionally they should constantly smoke in it without burning it. They offered me some snuff too ; which is one of the greatest
kindnesses they can either shew or be shewn. I called for some drink

(to try whether that corresponded with the rest), and so it did, for there was no swallowing it without chewing.

Finding but little satisfaction I desired to go to bed. That I should instantly, they said, but I wondered where they intended to lay me. In a little while in came a lusty wench with a bundle of rushes on her head (my bed it seemed by the sequel) which she spreading on the ground, covered them with a caddow or rug. Here I must lie or nowhere, patience was my only comfort; wherefore, stripping myself to my drawers and stockings, I laid myself down. About two hours after came in two cows, three or four pigs, some ducks and geese (which they brought not in before, out of civility to me). All their family being within doors, the good man, his wife, and two daughters, stripping themselves stark naked, lay down altogether by my side, which seemed somewhat strange to me. I could hardly forbear the two young ones, but that my late misfortune was so fresh in my memory.

I could not sleep all that night, wherefore very early I discharged my reckoning, and so set forward for Dublin with all the expedition I could, not liking the country entertainment. I would not ride the same way back as I came, to avoid my bone-breakers. But it had been as well, for coming to a river that I must ford, I asked a fellow which was the safest place. He pretended no knowledge of what I said, wherefore making signs to him, he answered me again with his hand, directing me to such a place. At the first step my horse and I plunged over head and ears; and had not my horse been strong, we had both perished. With much difficulty we got up the bank on the other side, and looking behind me, the villain was e'en almost out of sight. Such causeless revenge they frequently exercise towards the English, naturally hating us with a perfect antipathy. I returned at length to my old hostess, resolving when next I undertook such a journey I would steer by the compass of other men's experience.

CHAPTER XXVIII

The manner of his stealing an hogshead of French *wine from the Custom house*

TRACING the street, I chanced to cast my eye on a fellow, the slowness of whose pace informed me of the idleness of his condition. His garb was so preposterously unsuitable that a man could not possibly look on him without excessive laughter. To the intent you may participate with me in the same sport, I shall open his wardrobe. In general there was not anything he did wear that had not some time been another's property, and of which one might derive another pedigree. The hat he had on was divested of all royal dignity, having lost its crown, and yet his crime would not be allowed of as capital. But what it wanted in one place was supplied in another, the brims whereof being so large they might have conveniently served as a pent house for another besides himself. But this ingenious squire politicly had pinned up the brims on one side, that he might have some light to discern his way. His hat thus pinned up on the one side looked much like a trap-door pulled up. His band was so torn and dirty as if he had but just come from some fray ; and lest passion should prove obnoxious, time had done him that courtesy to purge away his choler. In what condition his doubtlet was behind, I could plainly discover through the holes of his cloak, which generally was so transparent that the rents and patches of several colours of his clothes were as visible as if you had looked through lawn. The forepart of his doublet and his breeches, I am confident, were the offspring of the furniture of a billiard-table. His cloak proceeded from a boat-tilt, whose grandfather was an horse-cloth ; and I could not look on his breeches but it put me in mind of the Scotch flags that hung up in Westminster. His skirts were so liquored and greased, that in case of extremity they might have served for belly-pieces, not using anything but their own fatness to fry them in.

By his countenance he seemed like a man of courage and ingenuity, and so I could not choose but endeavour his relief. Wherefore I accosted him, pretending I had seen him somewhere, but could not for the present call to mind the place. His necessity made him assent to whatever I said ; and desiring his company to an ale-house, he readily granted my request. By what unhappy accident he became thus miserable, I know not, but the man was well furnished both with natural and acquired parts. Having had various discourses of several matters, and that we began to be familiarly acquainted, I asked him why he wrapped himself up so close in his cloak ? ' O Sir,' said he, ' to be plain, I have a maimed doublet, and I have heard some say, there is nothing more prejudicial to a wound than the intromission of air.' ' Which that network garment of yours,' said I, ' will never be able to keep out.' He replied, ' 'Tis true, Sir, I find it so, but I wish it were a net, for then I might employ myself by fishing.'

I was so well pleased with my new acquaintance that bidding him stay there till my return (which should be speedy) I went and procured him all things necessary for to cover his nakedness. The last thing he put on was his shoes ; finding them to have soles, they added new life to him.

> But did before in one condition roll,
> And both appear'd as if they had no sole.

Having thus cast (colt-like) his ragged coat, I was not ashamed to walk with him in the streets. Coming to the Custom-house we saw several pipes and hogsheads of wine. Viewing all the places belonging thereunto, said I, ' Methinks it is no difficult matter to steal one of these hogsheads, had I but assistance.' ' You shall not want mine, Sir,' said he, ' even to the hazard of my life, which I shall never look on as a sufficient requital for this singular favour you have now conferred on me.' Having walked there a while, we went down to a place called Lazy Hill, where I found out two or three pure rogues more, one whereof had a boat. I informed them of my design ; they willingly promised their helping hand, and the time appointed for effecting our intentions was that night about twelve. Accordingly we all met, and having procured an empty hogshead, we filled it with water, and away we went in the boat. The tide ebbing had left dry ground underneath the quay, where I planted three of our company, instructing them that as soon as they found the coast clear above, they should with slings (which they had for that purpose) leave the hogshead of water, and exchange it for one of wine ; which done, they should march off immediately. I and my new comrade marched up the Custom-house stairs, where we encountered with two old watchmen. They asked us what our business was, we told them we had no other design but to drink with them, having been a little frolicsome the other side of the water. The old watchmen were very joyful at this news, and so giving one of them money to fetch some drink, the other carried me to the lodge. The drink being come, they minded that so much, they had forgotten their duty ; and I plied them so close with whole ones that they were incapable of holding one more. In the meantime my comrogues were gone. Pretending our boat was adrift, we took our leave, for then we could go along by the shore side ; leaving this paper on one of the hogsheads, I left them.

> What *Moses* did in the Creator's name,
> By art Egyptian magic did the same.
> Since I have read of water turn'd to wine,
> This miracle is opposite to mine.
> For I (though never yet a Rhenish hater)
> Have by my art converted wine to water.

I have often heard these very lines (with some real circumstances of this our exploit, but more fictitious) repeated to me as a very good jest, which pleased me near upon as much as our purchase.

Being five of us concerned, we scorned to sell our wine, but contracting with some to find sugar, with others Westphalia hams, or such like relishing meats, and with others to be at the expense of music, but every one to be at his own charge for wenches, we never gave over ranting and roaring till we had drained the hogshead dry.

CHAPTER XXIX

His landlady dieth, and so he is left again to live by his wits : his comrade is hanged, with some hints of his desperate, irreligious, and atheistical tenets

IN the height of our jollity, word was brought me that my landlady was dangerously sick, and that she desired to speak with me instantly. Thinking it was only a fit of lecherous and salacious itch, I made no great haste, but at length I went. As soon as I entered within her doors, I received the sad tidings of her death. I ran up stairs (not believing this report, because I would not have it so) but found it too true. Viewing her as she lay, I perceived her hand fast clenched. I took it into mine, and wrenching it open, there dropped ten pieces of gold, which I conceive she intended to have bestowed on me whilst living, as her last legacy. I conveyed them privately into my pocket, and presently made enquiry how she had disposed of her estate, but I received little or no satisfaction herein, only to my great vexation, I heard she often to the very last called much upon me.

I stayed not above two or three days in the house, but I was forced to leave it.

I met with my obliged friend, to whom I communicated my late misfortune. He, like an experienced Stoic counselled me to bear my loss patiently since it is below a man to repine at any sublunary casualty, much more to sink under the burden of any vexatious cross, or remediless loss. We discoursed what expedient we were best to take, and to increase our small stocks by some witty exploit. We propounded many things which we approved not of. We thought of turning highwaymen, but I dissuaded him from that, by informing him that money was very scarce, and that men of 500 *l.* per annum usually travelled 30 or 40 miles with a single cob, or piece of eight, not so much for fear of robbing as for want of coin, and that is the reason that all sorts of provisions are very cheap, because there is so great a scarcity of them that should purchase them. 'Why then,' said he, 'there is money enough in the Exchequer.' 'But,' said I, 'it is so difficult to come at, that I will not hazard my life in the attempt.' Hearing me speak in this manner, he looked upon me in derision, saying that fear was a passion unworthy to be lodged in the soul of man, and that there is nothing here which a man either should or need to fear, *secundem religionem stoici :* And that man deserved not the fruition of the least happiness here that would not, rather than go without it, venture his neck.

We had so hot a contest about this, that we parted in anger, and I never saw him afterwards till I heard of his condemnation, which was occasioned by the prosecution of what he propounded to me. Two or three more besides himself combined to rob the Exchequer, but were apprehended in the enterprize, committed, arraigned at the Bar, convicted and condemned. Hearing hereof, I gave him a visit in prison, expressing much sorrow for what he was to suffer, but he only laughed at me for my pains. I desired him to be more serious, since three days would put a period to his life, and then he must give an account of what he had done on earth, and that though we might sooth up our selves in all manner of debauchery here, yet without cordial repentance we must suffer for it hereafter. 'Prithee,' said he, ' do not trouble thy head with such idle fancies. That there is a God I cannot, nor will not deny, since there are regiments of arguments levied both from the stately fabric of the arched heaven, and from the inimitable embroidery of the flowery earth which are sufficient to conquer that infidelity, and render men tributaries to the all-forming Essence. But that this God should be so unjust (who is all goodness) as to make the intent of my creation damnation, it shall never come within the verge of my belief. If there be any punishment for criminal commissions, it must be annihilation, or nothing. Quote not me the Scriptures for my conviction if I err, since they are full of contradictions, and contain many things incredible.

' Neither do I know (since we are forbidden murder) why Abraham should kill his son Isaac, and the same person commit adultery with his maid Hagar (which is largely described), and yet we are commanded the contrary. If we borrow or steal, we are enjoined to make restitution, notwithstanding, the Israelites were permitted to borrow the Egyptians' earrings without giving satisfaction. In this manner I could cavil ad infinitum, and yet this Book is the basis of Christianity. Let me tell you plainly. Religion at first was only the quaint legerdemain of some strong pated statesmen, who to overawe the capriciousness of a giddy multitude, did forge the opinion of a punisher of all human evil actions.

What was Mahomet but an impostor, whose palpable cheats grew up in his successors into a religion, and whose inventions were and are received with as much adoration by the wisest of men, as is the Orthodox Veneration (as they term it) to a Deity, which is the object of Christian worship. The Pope's piety is only pride and ambition, and yet he pronounces damnation against all such as are not of his belief, &c. If you will know the diversity of religions (all oppugning on the other), take a view thereof in Mr Ross his Pansebeia. Now seeing the rational soul hath failed so oft and so absurdly in its discoveries, how or why should we submit ourselves slavishly to its determinations. For that which doth at some times err, can never at any time be concluded infallible.' He would have proceeded, but I desired him to desist.

Now his profane and irreligious discourse did so bore my glowing ears, that notwithstanding the wickedness of my own nature, I could not endure to hear him blaspheme. Wherefore, instead of endeavouring to rectify his erroneous judgment (for to speak the truth, my knowledge at that time was but slender in the doctrine of Christianity), I durst not discourse longer with him, but left him to his own conscience for conviction, which I judged would be powerful with him at the place of execution.

The day being come, I resolved to see the final end of my friend. And there did I enjoy the fruits of my hopes and wishes. For as soon as the halter was about his neck, he roared so loud with his voice, that it could not but awake the most lethargic conscience that ever the Devil lulled asleep. There I might see and know by the urinal of his eyes, and the water standing therein, what convulsion fits his soul suffered, his own mouth confessing how grievously his diseased soul was stretched upon the rack of despair. Then it was that the voluminous registers of his conscience, which did formerly lie clasped in some unsearched corner of his memory, were laid open before him, and the Devil, who hitherto gave him the lessening end of the prospect to survey his licentious courses and damned opinion, now turned the magnifying end to his eye, which made him cry out at last for mercy, and so was turned off.

CHAPTER XXX

*He passeth for a bachelor : courts several under the pretence of marrying
them, by which he persuades some out of their maidenheads, others out
of their money, with which he goes for England : at Chester he cheats
his landlord, where having all things requisite to complete an highwayman, followeth that trade : he is met with by some of that gang, who
intending to rob him, he discovers his intentions, and they admit of him
into their society*

BEING left now to shift for myself, having lost the main prop that
sustained me in all conditions, husbanding well the advantage of
this contrary wind, I presently set the engine of my brain to work, and
thus it was I addressed myself to courtship. Beauty was not the mark I
aimed, the purchase thereof producing little profit, since itself is most
commonly the sole reward. Neither can a man attain to it but by great
expense, outvying all therein, lest any interpose. Either wealthy and
aged widows, or thrifty maids, who had laid up what they had gotten in
service as a bait to procure an husband, such did I daily hunt out and
visit by turns. I was not sparing of amorous expressions, shewing therein
the height of zeal, by which means I deluded several. Some I was forced
to give earnest to for their goods, before they would trust me with what
they had. This course I followed till I was generally taken notice of for a
grand deceiver. Having now gotten a round sum of money by me, I
borrowed wherever I could, so crossing St. George's Channel, in twenty-
four hours I landed at Chester. I took up my quarters in a very graceful
inn, and gave out immediately that I had an hundred head of cattle
coming. The master of the house taking notice of my extraordinary
garb, and believing the report which I had caused to be spread abroad,
lodged me with much respect in one of the best chambers of his
house.

The wind favoured my design as much as I could desire, for it blew
east-north-east, by which no shipping could come out of Ireland. One
day I came to my landlord, telling him that by reason of the non-arrival
of my cattle I was disappointed of money, and therefore I desired him
to lend me ten pounds, and he should satisfy himself in the first choice
of the best of my beasts when they came, and swore to him I would perform my promise to him upon the word of a gentleman. So that without
any scruple he lent me the money. Being market-day, I bought an
excellent gelding with furniture thereunto belonging, with sword and
pistols, and in this equipage I mounted, taking leave of my credulous

landlord without speaking a word to him. I had not rid far before three well mounted rid by me (I found them afterwards to be the vanguard), having as many more in the rear.

At the bottom of an hill they before faced about, and bidding me ſtand, those in the rear reinforced the van. One of them clapping a piſtol at my breaſt, commanded me forthwith to deliver, swearing three or four full-mouthed oaths. I saw it was now to little purpose to resiſt although I was so well armed, and therefore endeavoured a conqueſt some other way, viz. by smooth expressions. ' Gentlemen,' said I, ' ye are all miſtaken. Neither do I greatly wonder thereat, since I verily believe ye are freshmen, men of a day's ſtanding in the ſtudy of this noble science, otherwise you might have diſtinguished me from an honeſt man. For I think in this garb and poſture I look as suspiciously as any of ye. Only I think I take a better course than ye to avoid apprehension, and reap to myself greater satisfaċtion. For ye rob in companies, and if any one be taken, his juſt fears frequently betray himself but oftener the reſt to deſtruċtion, whereas I robbing singly, I rob securely. Now, Sirs, freely examine my pockets,' where finding ſtore of coin, they demanded how I came by it ? I invented a lie to their general satisfaċtion, which was, I had met with a booty a little before I met with them, which was the occasion of my being so well furnished. But that which confirmed them moſt, was my being so well provided with piſtols in my holſters, pockets and boots. Inſtead of doing what they intended, they were then of another opinion, and all of them caressed me in a very high manner, resolving to be merry at the next inn, and there to admit me as a brother.

Having set up their horses, they went into a room before, whilſt I ſtayed some time after for the benefit of easing nature. Coming in among them I thought myself miſtaken in my company, and made a proffer to go out again, but they laughing heartily called me back. I knew not one person, for they had pulled off their false beards, vizards, hoods, patches, wens, mufflers and periwigs, together with those other disguises that obscured the natural proportion of their faces, so that they appeared as other men. ' Come,' said the chief (as I guessed him to be by the sway he bore over the reſt) ' you are a freshman, and therefore want some of our inſtruċtions which in due time you shall receive from us. In the firſt place it is fit that you take an oath which every young thief muſt observe that is admitted into the brotherhood, or at his inveſtation into the honour of one of the knights of the road,' which was to this effeċt. Firſt, they read a charge of secrecy, that whatever misfortune happened to cloud their freedom by rendering them as an objeċt to juſtice and the law, they should conceal their complices to the death, or againſt any other jeopardy whatsoever, burying in oblivion not only his confederates, but also his manner of entrance into this way.

And further, they proceeded to swear me, that if the judges should press me to a discovery of particulars, that then I must cunningly create some men in my fancy, devising not only names, but to give each man a particular feature, describing their stature, complexion and age, as also their dwelling place, still provided that the place of their abode be far enough off. And then, before enquiry be made the danger of the trial may be over or passed ; and then again this pretended discovery may purchase favour from the Bench.

Further, if I should be examined why and how I fell into these courses, I must then tell them that I was born a gentleman, and well educated, but being a younger brother, I had not wherewithal allowed me for a subsistence, and rather than I would live beneath my birth, or disparage the stock from whence I came (here fetching a deep sigh, and looking very sadly) necessity constraining me to supply my wants, I fell into these wicked courses. ' Which will make them think you are some misled young man whom temptations had drawn aside, and so cause them to take pity of your condition, and if their mercy extend to the remission of your guilt, it shall not only rest you from the punishment of the law, but from the persecution of your past evils.

' By this means we may have liberty to fall to our old courses, nor must conscience trouble us, but dispense with every impiety, and glory in the greatest iniquities, counting him most honourable who is grown the oldest and most exquisite experienced practitioner of all manner of vice.' Much more was committed to my memory for future observation, which for brevity sake I shall omit.

CHAPTER XXXI

Some instructions given me by our grand master thief

AFTER I was sworn, and full bowls of sack had trolled round, our grand master thief, composing his countenance and looking very gravely. ' Come my new and young knight of the road, be ruled by me, whose long experience makes me able to command and my love to you willing to instruct you. Ever lurk or lie in some by-place most advantageous and least suspicious which yields the eye the prospect of the road. So strictly view the booties that other men's misfortunes may enrich your condition, and the honest man's loss be your gain, and be sure you draw every advantage that may promote your cause to the longest extent. For your masks and chincloth, thus must you place them and fit them at a moment to disguise your face, thereby to blind the intellects of such as by constraint pay tribute to your wants. Who then can know and with considerate heed directly swear you are the man, when these artificial vizards are withdrawn, and so the visible tokens vanish that might inform men's knowledge what you are? And that your words may have a different sound, alter your voice, that so as your habit, face, and hair obscure your discovery, your speech (reputed undisguisable) will add to your concealment and security.

'Be sure you ingeniously contrive a watchword to yourselves that may occasion no suspicion. As we are like to have a fair day or a foul, according as the weather is like to prove, which being named, let every man fall to his work. Those that are strongest at the grasp and have hearts accordingly, let them seize first, always duly observing this, to catch the bridle by the left hand, and with the right draw your sword. If he or they resist, the one prevents his flight, the other cuts, and so cools his courage. The weaker sort's charge is to bid stand, and confronting the horses' heads, present a pistol fit for to discharge. If they deny delivering patiently what they have, but contend, you must waive all niceties, but cut them soundly. If that will not qualify their foolish presumption, be sure you fire not without doing execution, and then with all speed fly, after you have with expedition taken the pillage of the field.

'If you are pursued by an Hue and Cry, obscure yourself in some place or other, and let it pass by you, and then to be sure it will never overtake you. If a prize comes by, or in your sight, if up the hill, meet him. If down, follow close at the heels, and having more in company than yourself, let each man single out his choice which he likes to deal with. The coast being clear, fall up all to your close order and side, be sure that you jointly seize your prize. But here observe, let not any baseness of spirit unman you. For (speaking to me) Nature hath bestowed on you the full proportion of limbs and thou seemest a man of courage, suitable to the largeness of thy manly size, but be not surprized with fear or cowardice if the assailed boldly assaults thee.'

Full fraught with the documents which I received from my old experienced master, I resolved upon some achievement. Between two and three in the afternoon, I with four more set out. We planted ourselves in a convenient place, only I was sent out for a discoverer. Not rightly understanding my trade, I wandered too far, but in my digression I met with a single person whom I bid stand, which he would have done, and as willingly have surrendered his purse, but that he was mounted on a stone horse, I on a mare. As soon as I had given the word, his stone horse wheeled off and came in the rear of me. I thinking he intended to crupper me, endeavoured all ways imaginable to prevent him, for there was something it seems under my mare's tail more powerful, which at that time I dreamed not of. I led him round and round several times circularly. The poor harmless gentleman fearing he should provoke me too much by delays, the unruliness of his horse hindering my seizing the booty, cried out, 'Worthy sir, take what I have and spare my life.' At that very inſtant his horse reared his two fore-feet upon me and my mare, in so much that I thought he said, ' I'll take both life and money too presently,' fear had then rendered me so incapable of performing the office of a thief. With that I put spurs to my mare, and flew through the air for the procuration of my safety.

Notwithſtanding I made what speed I could, the other was close at my heels ; ſtriving and kicking with both my legs, one of my piſtols went off in my pocket. The apprehension of the present danger had bereft me of the true use of my sense, for I imagined that my back-friend had discharged at me, which made me roar out for quarter. He on the contrary concluded I fought Tartar like, flying, and that I had fired it at him, which made him with much eagerness echo out with repetition this expression, ' As you are a man, shew yourself merciful.'

Sometimes he would say, ' For heaven's sake hold, good sir ſtop,' which made me ride more furiously, thinking he called to the country, hold him, ſtop him. At laſt do what I could, his ſtone-horse leapt up upon us, at that inſtant (by what means I know not) we all came headlong to the ground. I expeĉted now that my imaginary adversary would be upon me, and cut my throat before I could recover my legs, wherefore I ſtarted up, and found my mortal foe up before me, and upon the run. I could have hanged myself to think I should be reckoned among the number of men, and yet want that spirit and courage which completes a man, but losing no time, I pursued him, and easily made ˑmyself possessor of what he had. ' Sirrah,' said I, ' if ere I meet thee again, and find thee so obſtinate, or durſt resiſt, as now thou haſt done, I will tie thee to a tree in some obscure place, where none can hear thy doleful cries, and there for six days thou shalt have no other food but what I shall bring thee. Once a day during that term I will visit thee, and each day's meat shall be either a piece of thine own sword broken into small bits, or those bullets (which thou intendeſt for the deſtruĉtion of honeſt men) dissolved, and mingled with gunpowder, which shall be conveyed to thy mouth through the muzzle of thine own piſtol.' It pleased me exceedingly to see how pitifully and submissively he looked, for verily I durſt not have uttered half so much if he had shown an auſtere countenance.

As I was framing a lie to delude my comrades (when I should meet them) into a belief how valiant I was, and dexterous in prosecution of that design I had newly undertaken, I looked about me and saw them all at my elbow. I now believed (which I easily perceived by their flearing looks) that they were all eye witnesses of my dangerous encounter. ' Oh brother,' said one, ' how is't, are you well ? ' I asked him the reason of his impertinent question. ' Because,' said he, ' we took notice of the great danger you were in even now narrowly escaped of being shot by a pocket inkhorn. Without doubt, brother, you are very hard-hearted to fly (riding full speed) at the very naming of, " Good sir be merciful," the poor harmless soul making frequent repetition thereof, but you stopping your ears from all entreaties, his stone horse seemed to be his advocate, and to that intent ran after your mare, endeavouring to court her into an intercession for his master.'

I should never have stopped their mouths had I not shewed them what I had gotten, which was not inconsiderable.

It was twilight as we met with another prize, which was of a different temper from the former. For though he and his fellow traveller were (comparatively to any of us) but pygmies, yet of so undaunted resolution and unresistible courage, that neither threats of death, or torture (I am confident) could dull the edges of their courageous spirits, which might be in part understood by their deportment to us. For had we not slashed, carbonadoed, and forcibly bound them, rather than they would have yielded willingly, they would have stooped to death. Our power having subdued them, we withdrew them into a secret place, leaving them not anything valuable. Then did I learn to search with so strict care, that sooner might the Grand Turk turn Roman Catholic than conceal a penny from me. Here was I taught to be deaf when the poor traveller cries he is undone, and to be more flinty than adamant, not to be moved with sighs or tears. Having engaged them by oath not to follow us by Hue and Cry, or by means of a general rising of the towns adjacent, these two fellows robbed, rifled and amazed, we left wrapped up in woes, and hasted away to secure ourselves.

I shall conclude this chapter with a relation how I was quit with my comrades upon the account of fear or timorousness. Neither could they justly tax me with it, since they are things entailed upon the profession. For every crow that flies extracts a fear, and every thing that doth but stir, or make the bushes rush, seemed to our fearful fancy a constable to apprehend us for our theft. I cannot forget how strong a confusion arose amongst us by a trifle. The means were so small, and the occasion so ridiculous, that whenafter I thought thereon (though by myself) I could not forbear laughing excessively, and condemn the temerity of such minds so meanly spirited. 'Twas thus in short. An owl who to gain shelter from the troubles of a sunshine day, when all the airy tribe (wandering) flock to him, screened himself in the obscure retired residence of an hollow tree. No sooner had he cloistered up himself, but between discontent and something of a pleasing satisfaction he first uttered his amazing screeks, being in a slumber, and dreaming of the assaults were made at him by his feathered enemies of all sorts, and then again awakening, whooped for joy that he was delivered from them. Thus did he whoop and hollow incessantly, which infused such a terror into our distrustful minds, that whips, switches and spurs were all too few to expedite our haste. For we absolutely thought those hollows were the outcries of the country following us for what we had committed. We at length took sanctuary in an inn, where we had some interest and confidence in our security.

Understanding that our day's work had been prosperous, our host calls lustily for sack, which the drawer doubles in the bar. The hostler must be one of our company too, and hail fellow with us, who knowing what courses we take, presume we dare not cavil, lest they betray our practices. *Sic nos non nobis.* So we rob for them, and not for ourselves, for by that time we have profusely frolicked (a bill whereof shall be brought in of twice as much as we called for) and have bestowed our largesses to the servants, and offered up our (expected) sacrifices to our landlady, or her daughter, for some private favour received, we find ourselves to have the least share, and so betake ourselves to our trade till apprehension take from us that liberty, and the law sentenceth us to pay our lives as a just debt we owe to justice.

CHAPTER XXXII

Scouring the road, he lights on a farmer's house which he intended to rob, but desists from that resolution, falling in love with his daughter, who was exceeding beautiful : gets her with child, under the pretence of marriage, but afterwards refusing it, she and her parents tax him with the undoing of the young woman : whereupon he leaveth them, giving them no other satisfaction than what they could gather out of a copy of verses he sent them

RIDING along the road, I met with a young girl with a milk pail on her head, but I was amazed to see such perfection in one mortal face. I rid up to her very near, purposely to entertain some discourse with her, introductory to a future acquaintance. Considering the ground, you may imagine the questions I propounded to this pretty rural innocent were frivolous enough, as, which was the readiest way to such a place, &c. which with much respect and modest confidence she resolved. She opening a gate to milk her cows, I followed, and tying my horse to an hedge, I begged her an excuse for being so rude, and beseeched her charitable opinion of my present actions, assuring her I would not offer the least injury nor prejudice to her chastity. Being over-persuaded with my protestations and vows to that purpose, she admitted me to sit down and discourse with her whilst she performed the office of a milkmaid. I could hardly contain myself within bounds when I viewed her pretty little hand stroking the dugs, which indeed so heightened my amorous passion that I soon forgot my oaths and promises, but after some dalliance, what by entreaties and love persuasions, and what by corporal strength, I obtained my desires. We then grew somewhat more familiar, but the burden of the song was, I had undone her ; let him that reads judge the truth thereof. We concluded at length that she should go home to her father's house, and that near night I would come thither likewise, according to the time appointed, as if I had never seen her before, and that I casually rid that way for information in the steering of my course regularly in the prosecution of my journey.

She subtly goes in, and acquaints her father and mother that there was a gentleman without whom by his countenance, garb and gesture, shewed himself no less ; that fearing to travel farther, being night, knowing not the way, desired to rest himself there till morning. With much respects from her parents to her own great satisfaction (which I discerned in her eyes) I was kindly entertained, and nobly treated. That night we intended to be better acquainted by the renovation of our late enjoyments, but our unlucky stars were impropitious to our amorous designs. Next morning I seemed to be very ill, that I might have some pretence for my staying, which I acquainted the daughter withal.

The old people were very loving and courteous, so that as soon as they heard thereof with much pity they visited me, and with as much care they provided what was necessary for me. I offered them money, shewing good store of gold, that they might have the better esteem of me. Thus I lay for at least a fortnight, several doctors had been with me, but none knew my distemper. All this while I nightly had the society of my fresh country mistress who deviated from the common customs of her sex, did not coyishly refuse that which was the centre of her hopes, wishes and desires. Fearing lest I might be suspected, I left off counterfeiting, and shewed them some recovery of my strength. When at any time the good old people would come into my chamber to sit with me, the main subject of my discourse would be the resentments of their favours, and that if I lived I would gratefully repay them. Being restored to my former healthful condition, I one day told them I could never recompence their love and care of me but by marrying their daughter, whom I told them I loved most affectionately. Her parents made many excuses. As that she was but a poor country girl, and the like, but glad I perceived they were to hear such an overprized motion. Enquiries I made in a neighbouring town what this farmer was, whom I understood by all to be very wealthy, and that time was not more careful to furnish him with silver hairs than he industrious to maintain them by the procuration of a plentiful estate. My wanton was his only darling, for whom he furrowed the surface of the earth, and for whom he chose rather to sell than to eat his better sort of provision, that he might add to her portion. It was now he thought he had well bestowed his labour, since he had met with such a blessed opportunity wherein he should add gentility to his daughter's riches. O the slaughter of pigs, geese, capons, which as to some idol were sacrifices diurnally offered to procure my favour ! And as he was liberal in his food, so was not I sparing in the sending for wine, six dozen of bottles at a time. So that the old man was brought to this pass, that he cared not whether he spent his estate on me, or gave it, and that young girl so well pleased with her imaginary paradise here, that I am confident she would never have been induced to have exchanged this for any other on equal terms.

Inexpressible was our satisfaction on all hands, but nothing gave them greater content than to see us together, by which we had as many opportunities as we listed. My main aim was still to know of my young mistress what store of coin her father had, and where it lay, but to my great grief and vexation she told me he had not five pound within doors, having lately bought a purchase. I now thought it was to little purpose to stay longer, since I could not glean from her father's harvest, though I had reaped the crop of her mother's labour, and so resolved to be going, but not without one night's solemn leave-taking of her. The night being come, she purposely stayed up till all the rest were gone to bed. But we being too imprudently hasty in the kitchen, stumbled against two barrels piled one on the other and fell ; and we both were so entangled, that we could not disengage ourselves so soon but that her father came out crying, ' In the name of goodness what is the matter ? ' And groping about caught me by the naked breech. Seeing there was no remedy, I desired him to be silent ; and not spread his daughter's disgrace. If so, I would make her shortly a recompence. The old man was very much perplexed, and could not forbear telling his wife of what had passed. They both cried out that their daughter was undone : The daughter was in the same tone, unless I would speedily marry her.

I ſtayed afterwards about some three days to colour the matter, and at laſt marched off *incognito*, sending her twenty pieces of gold, and a copy of verses, which, although I knew they underſtood not, yet I could not but express myself by writing, if for nothing else but mine own satisfaction.

> Is it not ſtrange thou and thy friends should say,
> Thou art undone by me ? Let's see which way.
> Have I not done to my great toil and pain,
> What all thy friends cannot undo again.
> Call but to mind the pleasures thou haſt taſted,
> The hours and minutes which with thee I waſted
> To bring thee to perfection ; and to teach
> Thee learning, far above the sex's reach.
> Have I not taught thee oft' aſtronomy,
> Within thy mother's garden, shew'd thee all
> The ſtarry course, and spheres celeſtial.
> Did I not teach thee poetry that night
> And how in tripped dactyls thou shouldſt write.
> I taught thee then *geometry*, the notion
> Of *length* and *breadth*, *egality*, *proportion*
> Of *quadrant triangles ;* the way to enter
> *Circles*, or *semi-circles ;* how the *centre*
> Stands ever *fixt*, how that every *line*
> *Direct*, or *oblique*, *circular*, or *trine*
> Hath ſtill its *ending ;* how to take the *height*
> Of any *blazing bearded ſtar* by night.
> I taught thee *music's harmony* to know,
> To keep *true time*, where thou shouldſt *reſt*, and how :
> Learned thee likewise thy notes, *large, long*, & brief,
> Prickt minom, with a crotchet, and the chief
> Of the lov'd art, good discant for to make
> Upon a plain-song, *discords* also take
> With a sweet close, and meltingly to fall
> Into a treble, ravishing withal.
> I shew'd thee why artiſts hold six *cliffs* beſt,
> And why 'tis prized far above the reſt,
> Because it keeps the midſt ; the very *heart*
> And soul of music is the inner part.
> Yet art undone thou saidſt ? Is to impart
> The hidden secrets of myſterious art
> Undoing to thee. Hadſt thou ever spent
> Thy means upon me, or thy money lent,

And had not paid the int'rest back to thee,
Thou and thy friends might then have rail'd at me.
What wert thou before I knew thee, but an ass,
A rude neglected home-spun country lass,
Knowing not how to speak, to go or look,
But hide thy self when seen in every nook.
And blush, nay tremble if thou wert found out ;
Strive to be gone again, scratch, cry, and pout
If one but touch thy apron, and wouldst spit
In's mouth should come to kiss thee : for thy wit
It did extend but unto no, and aye,
Confess this truth, or else in faith you lie.
This was thy eloquence ; why did I love thee ?
Young, plump and fair thou wert, and that did move me.
I took thee and refin'd thee, made thee new,
Alter'd thy nature, chang'd thy former hue :
Taught thee to kiss, embrace, and entertain
A lover with that sp'rit and catching vein,
The goddess of delight in her own sport
May strive to equal thee, but must come short.
Where hadst thou all thy *breeding* but from me ?
Who *bound* thee first, and now have made thee free ?
Thy petulant discourse, and apish toying,
A change of humours, now a sullen coying,
All which I taught thee, which do make thee rare,
Now are thy attributes as well as fair :
And what content is in a simpering fool,
A squeamish thing, she doth man's spirits cool ;
Beats back the flowing current of his blood,
And ebbs it in the very spring or flood,
'Tis harsh to hear a school boy in one tone
Repeat his lesson like a bagpipe's drone,
But it doth ravish with delight the ear
Well worded and sweet languag'd lines to hear,
Pronounc'd by one hath skill and art to know
When he should raise his voice, when bring it low.
For though a poet write good lines, it is
The speaker that doth make them hit or miss.
So though a wench be ne'er so fair, so neat,
Or well proportioned, if she want the *feat*
Of acting well upon love's theatre,
It will not make man's loving passion stir.
She's like one handsome in a splendid suit,
Only to fit a stage and play the mute
And shall not go clapt off with frequent kisses,
The lover's *plaudit*, but distasteful *hisses*.

And such wert thou, when firſt I met with thee,
Now have I brought thee to thy *excellence*
With my excessive toil, and dear *expense*
Of my beſt blood ; and added to thee more
Than was in all thy *anceſtors* before
Gentility.   I have enricht thy mind
With the chief ornament of woman kind
Behaviour : Taught thee to live and spend
Of thy own gettings, without help of friend.
And have I this ungrateful *girl* for all
That I have done to thee.   Why doſt thou call
Me thy *undoer*.   How ere I will forgive,
For I'm in charity, and do believe
The only cause why I am taxed so sore
With thy undoing, 'cause I do no more.

CHAPTER XXXIII

*From this farmer's house he rides he cared not whither : on the road he is
ſtrangely surprized by a woman robber in man's apparel : he discovers it by unbuttoning her breeches to search for private pockets
within : they two conclude a perpetual friendship*

ABRUPTLY taking my leave of the farmer and his loving daughter,
I rid a long time, but met with none worthy of my taking
cognizance. Being wearied, I ſtruck into an inn, and by that time I
had thoroughly refreshed myself, the evening began to approach. Whereupon I mounted, and so put on. Passing by a small coppice in a bottom
between two hills, a gentleman (as I then supposed) well armed, and
handsomely accoutred, ſtarted out upon me, and bid me deliver inſtantly.
Hearing him say so, I told him if he would have but the patience I would,
and with that drew out a pocket piſtol and fired it at him, without doing
any execution. ' If you are for a little sport,' said the gentleman, ' I
shall shew you some inſtantly,' whereupon drawing a piſtol he shot me
into the leg. Having so done with his sword (which hung ready at his
wriſt) neatly at a blow he cut the reins of my bridle, so that I was not
able to guide my horse. But he being good at command, and used to the
charge, with the winding of my body I gave him to underſtand what he
was to do. ' Come sir,' said my adversary, ' have you enough yet ? '
' In faith sir,' said I, ' I'll exchange but one piſtol more, and if that prove
unsuccessful I shall submit to your mercy.' Whereupon I shot, but

missed my mark. However I killed his horse, which instantly fell. My gentleman was so nimble that before I could think what to do, he had sheathed his sword in my horse's belly, which made me come tumbling down too with a horse pox. 'Once more,' said my antagonist, 'we are upon equal terms, and since the obscurity of the place gives us freedom, let us try our courages ; one must fall.' And thereupon with his sword (which was for cut and thrust) he made a full pass at my body, but putting it by I closed in with him, and upon the hug threw him with much facility. I wondered much at it, which I need not have done, since his nature (as afterwards I understood) was so prone to it.

Having him down, ' Now, sir,' said I, ' I shall teach you to be careful on whom you set. You have as imprudently undertaken this enterprize as a pickeroon did once, who seeing a man-of-war high built, and but few men aboard her discoverable, her portholes being likewise fast, clapped her aboard immediately, thinking she had been a merchantman ; but they found the contrary, the deck being instantly filled with men that were below, and running out her guns there could be no wisdom in resistance. Wherefore now sir, yield, or I shall compel you.' With much reluctancy he did. With cords I had ready for that purpose, I tied both his hands and feet, and so fell to rifling him. Unbuttoning his doublet to find whether there was no gold quilted therein, I wondered to see a pair of breasts so unexpectedly greater and whiter than any man's ; but being intent about my business, that amazement vanished from my thoughts. Then did I come to his breeches (which I laid open) my curious search omitted not any place wherein I might suspect the concealment of moneys. At last proffering to remove his shirt from between his legs, he suddenly cried out (and strove to lay his hand there, but could not) ' I beseech you, sir, be civil,' said he. I imagining that some notable treasure lay there obscured, I pulled up his shirt (alias smock) and found myself not much mistaken.

The sight so surprized me as if I had been converted into a statue by the head of a Gorgon, but after a little pause, I hastily unbound her, and taking her in my arms, ' Pardon me, most courageous Amazon,' said I, ' for thus rudely dealing with you ; it was nothing but ignorance that caused this error ; for could my dim-sighted soul have distinguished what you were, the greatness of love and respect I bear your sex would have deterred me from contending with you. But I esteem this my ignorance, my greatest happiness, since knowledge in this case would have deprived me of the benefit of knowing there could be so much prowess in a woman. For your sake I shall ever retain (since you have restored it) a good esteem of the worst of females.' She begged me not to be too tedious in my expressions, nor pump for eloquent phrases, alleging this was no proper place to make orations in. ' But if you will enlarge yourself, let us go to a place not far diſtant from this, better known, but to few besides myself.' I liked her advice very well, and returning what I had taken from her, I followed it, by following her through divers obscure passages till we came to a wood, where in a place the sun had not seen since the firſt deluge, ſtood an house. At our approach the servants were all in a hurry who should firſt obey Mrs Virago's commands, for they all knew her, being no way eſtranged to her disguise, but wondered to see St. George, and his truſty esquire on foot, neither durſt they shew themselves inquisitive presently. With much respect we were conducted into a véry ſtately room, where embracing each other, we knit an indissolvable tie of friendship.

CHAPTER XXXIV

After supper they enter in discourse, wherein she giveth him a short account of her life, and the cause of her undertaking such an extravagant and dangerous course, relating how notably she revenged herself on her husband for his unworthy and base carriage towards her

HAVING refreshed ourselves with what the house afforded, and bottles and pipes had supplied the place of dishes, we dialogued as familiarly as if our acquaintance had bore equal date with our nativities. And now it was she laid herself open to me, not concealing anything, having before made myself acquainted with her greateſt secret. Frankly she called for bottles of wine, which we smartly drank together out of beer glasses. Had not supper been speedily provided, which required a cessation for some time, I should not have been in a condition to discern the dish, nor him that brought it to the table. Having taken some repaſt, I began to be refreshed, she not in the leaſt diſturbed all this while. I pressed her to tell me what she was, and what manner of life she led.

Sir, said she, I cannot deny your requeſt, wherefore to satisfy you, know that I was the daughter of a sword cutler. In my younger days my mother would have taught me to handle a needle ; but my martial spirit gain-said all persuasions to that purpose. I could never endure to be among the utensils of the kitchin, but spent moſt of my time in my father's shop, taking wonderful delight in handling those warlike inſtruments ; to take a sword in my hand well mounted and brandish it, was reckoned by me among the chief of my recreations. Being about a dozen years of age, I ſtudied all ways imaginable how I might make myself acquainted with a fencing master. Time brought my desires to their complement, for such a one as I wished for casually came into our shop to have his blade furnished, and fortune so ordered it, there was none to answer him but myself. Having given him that satisfaction he desired, though not expecting it from me, amongst other talk I demanded of him whether he was not a professor of the noble science? (for I guessed so much by his postures, looks, and expressions.) He told me he was a well-willer thereunto. Being glad of this opportunity, desiring him to conceal my intentions, I requested him the favour as to give me some instructions how I should manage a sword. At first he seemed amazed at my proposal, but perceiving I was in earnest, he granted my petition, allotting me such a time to come to him as was most convenient. I became so expert at back-sword and single-rapier in a short time, that I needed not his assistance any longer, my parents not in the least mistrusting any such thing.

I shall waive what exploits I did by the help of a disguise, and only tell you that when I arrived to fifteen years of age, an inn keeper married me, and carried me into the country. For two years we lived very peaceably and comfortably together, but at length the insolent and imperious temper of my husband made me begin to shew my natural humour. Once a week we seldom missed of a combat between us, which frequently proved so sharp that it was well if my husband came off with a single broken pate, by which means the gaping wounds of our discontents and differences being not presently salved up, they became in a manner incurable.

I never was much inclined to love him, because he was of a mean dastardly spirit, and ever hated that a dunghill cock should tread a hen of the game. Being stinted likewise of money, my life grew altogether comfortless, and I looked on my condition as insupportable. Wherefore as the only remedy or expedient to mitigate my vexatious troubles, I contrived a way how I might sometimes take a purse. I judged this resolution safe enough (if I were not taken in the very fact), for who could suspect me to be a robber, wearing abroad upon such designs man's apparel, but at home only that which was suitable and agreeable to my own sex? Besides, none could have better encouragement and conveniency than myself, for, keeping an inn, who is more proper to have in custody what charge my guests brought into my house than myself or if committed to my husband's tutelage, I could not fail to inform myself of the richness of the booty. Moreover, the hostess is the person whose company is most desired, before whom they are no ways scrupulous to relate which way they are going, and frequently what the affair was that led them that way.

Courage I knew I wanted not (be you my impartial judge, sir), what then could hinder me from being successful in such an enterprize? Being thus resolved, I soon procured necessary habiliments for these my contrivances, and never miscarried in any of them till now. Instead of going to market, or riding five or six miles about such a business (the usual pretences with which I blinded my husband), I would when out of sight ride a contrary road to this house (wherein we now are) and here metamorphose myself, and being fitted at all points, pad uncontrollably, coming off always most victoriously. Not long since my husband had about one hundred pounds due to him some twenty miles from his habitation, and designed such a day for its reception. Glad I was to hear of this, resolving now to be revenged of him for all those injuries and churlish outrages he had committed against me. I knew very well which way he went, and knew the time of his coming home, wherefore I way-laid him at his return. And happily as I would have it, he did not make me wait above three hours for him. I let him pass me, knowing that by the swiftness of my horse I could easily overtake him, and so I did, riding with him a mile or two before I could do my intended business.

At last (looking about me) I saw the coast clear on every side. Wherefore riding up close to him, and laying hold of his bridle, I clapped a pistol to his breast, commanding him to deliver, or he was a dead man. My imperious don seeing death before his face, had like to have saved me the labour by dying voluntarily without compulsion, and so amazed at his sudden surprizal, that he looked like an apparition, or one lately risen from the dead. 'Sirrah,' said I, 'be quick.' But a dead palsy had so seized every part of him, that his eyes were incapable of directing his hands to his pocket. But I soon recalled his lost spirits by two or three smart blows with the flat of my sword, which so wakened him out of that deep lethargy he was in that with much submissiveness he delivered me his money. After I had dismounted him and cut the reins of his bridle and girths, I basted him soundly, till that I had made jelly of his bones, and that his flesh looked like Egyptian mummy. 'Now, you rogue' said I, 'I am even with you; have a care the next time how you strike a woman (your wife I mean) for none but such as dare not fight a man, will lift up his hand against the weaker vessel. Now you see what it is to provoke them, for if irritated too much, they are restless till they have accomplished their satisfactory revenge. I have a good mind to end thy wicked courses with thy life, but that I am loath to be hanged for nothing, such a worthless man. Farewell, this money shall serve me to purchase wine to drink healths to the confusion of such rascally and mean-spirited things.' And so I left him.

She was about to have proceeded in such agreeable relations of her rencounters, when word was brought her up, two gentlemen below desired to speak with her. Craving my excuse, she went down, and in a little time returned with them. She made an apology to me for so doing, adding that if she had committed a crime herein, my future knowledge of those persons would extenuate it. By their effeminate countenances I could not miss of judging rightly what they were, *viz.*, females. After several discourses we grew so familiar that the longest continued friendship could not boast of more freedom.

Having talked and drank ourselves weary, we concluded to lie all in one chamber, there being two beds. What our nocturnal passages were, I'll give the reader leave to imagine.

CHAPTER XXXV

Here he relates (modestly) what satisfaction he received from his new female acquaintance, and what occasioned the two last come Amazons to attempt the hazardous enterprizes of the high pad : with their character and course of life

THOUGH melancholy night had drawn her sable curtains about her hemisphere, yet the coverlet of our optics was not yet laid down to admit our active senses to their usual rest and repose. Obscured darkness had everywhere proclaimed silence about us on penalty of distracted incomposedness ; yet we feared not the breach of those binding laws, by breaking our minds to each other interchangeably. My conquered foe (now my new friend) first began to relate to her old associates the rise of our late rencounter, and the success, which she expressed with so much life and ingenuity that they knew not which to value most, her wit, or my courage. But when she came to relate the manner of the discovery of her sex, so petulant and facetious was her discourse that it occasioned a great deal of laughter and mirth among us. Having thoroughly discoursed varieties for further diversion one of these late incomers undertook to give us a summary of her comrades (or sisters) being therewith intermixed ; now I must give her leave to tell her own tale.

Sir (for to you I apply my discourse particularly, being wholly ignorant of what these two inseparable companions of mine well understand), I shall not trouble your ear with anything but what is absolutely necessary. Laying aside therefore superfluous preambles, let me tell you I was the eldeſt daughter of a vintner in London, a man looked on so wealthy that he was called upon for alderman, having no more children than a son, myself, and this my dear siſter, my metamorphosed follower. My brother I think was begot out of degenerate wine, and that made him so degenerate from virtue and a good spirit a hot fiery fellow, always on the fret, till his cask or carcass was pierced, and so I leave him as I found him, an empty hogshead.

This obſtacle being removed (the Remora to our fair promising fortune) none were more extolled and courted for wealth and beauty (rarely seen together) than my siſter and self. Men of all sizes, both of wit, eſtate and ſtature, daily frequented my father's house, pretending they came for the goodness of wine there vended, till they had got an intereſt in our acquaintance, and then they unmasked their meaning. Several overtures were made to our parents who, like good domeſtic politicians, seemed to like to encourage them to continue coming for their expense sake. Frequently they bespake dinners, vying who should exceed in prodigality, thinking thereby to gain eſteem, while the old fox did but laugh at them in private for their pains. My mother had her trade at her fingers' ends, for when she would oblige any of them to any treaty, it was but calling him son, or ' sirrah you are a wag, my Benjamin muſt have the largeſt portion, &c.' By this means she chained them to the house, and to engage them the more, permitted us to bear them company. But fearing leſt we might glut our idolators by too long ſtaying (for we sooner surfeit on delicates than coarser fare) our mother would call us, pretending business, and would then supply the place herself, then would they charge afresh, till they had blinded one another.

I muſt needs say, my mother's company was deservingly desirable, for though she had passed her age's Æquinox, yet her beauty appeared but a very little declining. In her youthful days she was the wonder of her sex, and was so generally talked of among beauty hunters, that our tavern was never empty, and happy was he that could procure the drinking of a glass with her at the bar, but transported, if they could obtain the favour to have her company in a room. Which for profit she sometimes permitted, and something else, which my father winked at gladly, because he could not find the like expedient to enrich himself. She was comely, tall, and of a beauteous blushing brown ; her hair proper to her complexion, neatly put into curls and folds by nature. Her face was made up of excellent parts, as a quick eye and full, her circled brows graceful and big, her nose not over Roman with a full mouth ; the largeness of the lips commendable, because plump and red, her dimpled chin (which Nature had drawn, with a wanton touch of her pencil) did singularly set out her looks most comely. Her neck was round, rising, full and fat ; her body well fed, not fat ; an Italian don's delight. When any gentlemen came in, methinks I now see how she leered out of her enticing Italianated eyes, able to confound a saint. In short, her hair was enough to enchant you into those mazes, but that her looks were so near, which hooked yours into her eyeballs, full, black and rolling, and when she had you, she held you there. Neither was she a niggard of those gifts so liberally bestowed on her, but communicated a taste thereof to divers, for as she was naturally prone to whorishness, so she gave her inclinations the reins, and at last became so impudent that she did frequently that in our sights which, though we understood not, being too young, yet forcibly drew a blush into our tender cheeks. Being in her prime, she gave herself so much liberty that she was a shame to her sex ; there was not any vice that was attended either by pleasure or profit, but she would be sharer therein. And now being gulled with shadows and impostures, she drew up the portcullis of her heart, and laid the gates thereof wide open to her own ruin.

Who would imagine, that a pleasing countenance could harbour villainy, or that a smile could sit upon the face of mischief ? But therein she shewed herself a courtezan of the right stamp, that for her own advantage can entertain man's appetite with wanton dalliance, but will never make assurance of settled love. When men think themselves most interested in her, then was it frequently that they were farthest from her. I am somewhat the longer in my mother's character that I might the fuller demonstrate what was the original that I so exactly copied in the actions of my own life. Did parents consider how prevalent their wicked examples are with their issue, they would be less curious to cleanse their houses of dirt and dust against the coming of their friends, and more careful not to see them hung with vices in the presence of their children. You see I know the difference between good and evil, because I talk so well, though I act so ill.

But to proceed. How is it possible the daughter should be chaste that cannot reckon up the adulteries of her mother, though she be ne'er so well in breath, without a dozen stops or intermissions at the least ? Such as are conscious to these faults in others cannot but be capable of them in themselves. The hearing of them told begets a willingness to try them ; the seeing of them done, a wilfulness to do them. She presumed, I believe upon our indiscretions as children, persuading herself we had not wit enough to discern it. But alas ! she erred in her cyphers, and was much mistaken in her accounts : for we coming to years, did not stick to that in her sight, which she before would not forbear in ours. And with what face could she reprove us ?

The crooked wretch muſt not upbraid the lame,
Nor muſt the Moor the tawny Indian blame.

Her house did daily swarm with such as pretended more than common kindness to me. Several my parents approved of as wealthy, and propounded them to me, whom I only disliked for want of comeliness. One I confess I could have fancied highly for his wit, had not his formation been so extravagant and prepoſterous. Oh, the innumerable quantity of poetic brats which Pallas-like sprang out of his head, and so peſtered my chamber, that I could hardly sleep for the trampling of their feet; some whereof appeared so fair unto me from a father so foul, that I have carried them in my bosom to converse with them among the solitary shades. I proteſt civility could scarce keep me from laughing outright every time I saw him, his whole composure appeared to me so ridiculous. For firſt, his head seemed to sink down into his breaſt, his eyes ſtaring affrighted at the danger, whilſt his mouth continually gaped, as if it intended to cry out for help: his back and breaſt bunched out, as if a wallet ſtuffed at both ends had hung over his shoulder behind and before. Though extravagant enough, you could not say he shewed much waſte. Had you seen him on a rainy day, by the length of his legs (yet of dwarfish ſtature) you would have thought him mounted on ſtilts, and wading through the dirt with a boy at his back. Now let me skip over his person, and only tell you how I served him, and then I have done with him. That day I saw him not, I had his representation sent me, which was good diversion, but his presence was insufferable: to the intent therefore that I might be rid of him, I sent him these lines.

> Sir,
> You are the son of *Esop*, for I find
> Legitimation by your shape and mind;
> Deform'd ye are alike, thence 'tis thought fit
> That such defe&ts should be supply'd by wit.
> Your aspe&t's monſtrous foul, yet don't complain,
> Your issues fair, the produ&t of your brain.
> But ſtay, I muſt recall myself, for know
> My praises are like to ourself, too low:
> Troth when I view you well, my fancy muſt
> Imagine you much like a capon truſt,
> Or like Sir *Hudibras*, nick-nam'd *All-feather*,
> Or like one ty'd both neck and heels together:
> Nor do not think Pygmean sir that I
> Will fall in love with mere deformity;
> Then court some Succubus, a fiend will be
> A fitter match: so think no more on me.

These lines so nettled him, that having belched out some execrations against me and our sex, I never heard more of him. To be short, there was none could get any interest in me, but our head-drawer, a neat flaxen-haired dapper fellow. So passionately we loved one the other, that we could not forbear holding some private correspondence at nights. My father at length suspecting us, turned away his man, whose absence I could not brook, and therefore resolved to follow after, which I did, taking with me what ready money my father had in his custody, and finding out my dear comrade. This was the result of our consultation, that I should clothe myself like a man, and so travel together.

It will be too tedious to relate how and whither we went, but let it suffice to tell you, that after we had run through France and Italy, and wearied ourselves in foreign parts, we concluded to return to England. We landed at Dover, having made an end of our voyage and money together, saving so much as would purchase horse and arms, for padding was the way we agreed on to recruit our decayed stock. Many were the robberies we committed, taking such a course that the devil could hardly detect us. Sometimes when we had robbed, and fearing lest we should be taken by the Hue and Cry, it was but turning my horse loose, and then would I put on woman's apparel (which I always carried in my portmantle in such expeditions) and getting up behind my dear friend, I passed unsuspected as his wife. This stratagem frequently proved a safeguard to us both. By this means we several times robbed houses, under the pretence of my friend taking lodgings for himself and wife.

To tell you in what manner and how often we played our pranks under a double disguise, would take up more time than is convenient. Wherefore I shall now wind up my story. My comrade, in an unhappy enterprize, received a shot in his shoulder, which proved mortal, for not long after he died. Being then destitute of my dear companion, I had several thoughts of returning home, but that I liked my trade so well, I could not be induced to leave it. However, I went to my father's house frequently with roaring blades, but they knew me not, though sometimes they would stare upon me, as if their eyes would have started out of their heads for joy to see their old acquaintance. At last I took a convenient opportunity under the veil of courtship to discover myself to my sister (here present) who understanding my course of life, and knowing well her own constitution, for my sake resolved to hazard all, and run one risk with me. Having instructed her how she should rob her father, as I had done before her, we met at a place appointed, and so took our journey hitherward. Now if our conversation may be any

M

ways pleasing, and our service advantageous, we are both your devoted servants.

She uttered these words with such a grace, that I could not forbear embracing her. After we had plighted faiths, and mutually caressed each other, we betook ourselves to rest, which you may imagine was little enough.

CHAPTER XXXVI

How he with his new female padding comrade contrived notable subtle and safe ways to rob together ; with a relation of some remarkable stories which were the effects of those consultations

ANGRY I was when I perceived the appearance of day, which I knew would unavoidably rob me of my present delight and pleasure. But it was only my fear of being deprived of so much bliss made me so grossly to mistake, for I quickly found my happiness enlarged by the approaching light, my sense of seeing being now made co-partner with that of feeling. Love had now his eyes restored him, who before only groped for the naked truth in the dark. Now did we begin afresh to renew our late sweet nocturnal pastime, and could our bodies have any ways answered our boundless desires, our bed would have been the sole concern we should have minded, till that time which must put a period to this transitory life.

But to avoid the censure of sluggishness, we all resolved to rise, and unanimously strive and contend who should make the best proof of the greatest ingenuity in contriving what may give the largest satisfaction both to mind and body. As a præludium to our intended purpose, and a restorative to our decayed strengths, we first resolved upon buttered sack, with other things of like comforting natures, and now finding ourselves by this first essay so much beyond expectation revived and fitted for mirth and pleasure, we straight gave order for a dinner to be speedily prepared, whose composition should be of the choicest viands. And that the time might not seem tedious in the interim, it was put to the vote what pastime we should make choice of for divertisement. Some were for bodily exercise, but I was clearly against that, having so lately tired myself with it : besides my lameness, which was occasioned by the shot I received in my leg from my valiant rencountress. It was at length agreed on by all that we should entertain ourselves with music and discourse. 'A match,' said the eldest sister, ' and to the intent you may see

my freedom and forwardness to propagate your proposition, I shall
give my assistance first to heighten your spirits by vocal and instrumental
music; having thus broken the ice, I question not but you will prove
ready followers, and swim with me in the same streams of delight.'
Whereupon she took up a lute, and having praised that instrument above
all other for its sweet ravishing harmony, ' I will now try ' said she
' how my voice will agree with it,' and thus sang :

What need we to care ?
W' have enough and to spare,
What we gain we will drink and spend on't ;
But when all is gone,
We will get more anon ;
Then make it all fly, there's an end on't.

We will rob, we will steal
For our own common weal.
Let the miser be damn'd with his treasure :
Our designs we will shape
For the juice of the grape,
Thus spin out our lives in our pleasure.

We think it more fit
To live by our wit,
And hazard our lives on adventure ;
We are sons of the blade
Never bred to a trade,
We scorn'd to be bound by indenture.

Not for flattery, but due merit, we could give her no less than
applause. Though that word may favour of something of a compliment,
yet I will assure you there was no such thing passed between us ; we knew
how to improve our time to a far greater advantage, leaving such empty
vain expressions to such who have little else to do than to play with a
lady's fan, or to consume their times in combing their periwigs, not only
in the streets and playhouses, but even (irreverently) in the holy places
of divine worship.

The pertinency of this song to the practice of our lives did as much
please us all as the sweet harmony of that voice did ravish our delighted
ears. And lest our satisfaction should any ways cool or abate, more
musical fuel was laid on, to warm our benumbed spirits, if any such
unlikely thing should happen.

Whereupon her sister (not making use of any instrument to assist her voice, being sensible it was good and natural) frankly, and with a becoming freedom, sang to this purpose.

'Tis liberty which we adore,
It is our wealth and only ſtore ;
Having her we all are free,
Who so merry then as we ?
'Tis she that makes us now to sing,
And only she can pleasure bring.

Chorus.
Since we then such freedom have,
We'll purchase pleasure, or a grave ;
'Tis better so, than live a slave.

As I am free, so will be ſtill,
For no man shall abridge my will :
I'll pass my life in choiceſt pleasure,
On various objeſts spend my treasure :
That woman sure no joy can find,
Who to one man is only join'd.

Chorus.
Since we then such freedom have,
We'll purchase pleasure or a grave :
'Tis better so, than live a slave.

What pleasure is in full cram'd bags ?
No more than is in beggar's rags :
Unless made use of, what is cash ?
A fine new nothing, glittering trash :
Being well employ'd, it is a thing
Which doth delight and honour bring.

Chorus.
Since we then such freedom have,
We'll purchase money, or a grave :
'Tis better so, than live a slave.

About to have proceeded in this manner round, we were interrupted by dinner coming up, which came as seasonable as our ſtomachs could require. Waiving all ceremonies, we inſtantly fell to it without the tediousness of long-winded graces ; neither were we long at it, our hands and appetites being alike nimble and quick to give the body its required satisfaſtion.

After dinner we had various discourses about the vanity and imbecility of the female sex ; winding up our argument, one said, she would not be a mere woman for the whole universe, and wondered that man, so noble and rational a soul, should so unman himself in his voluntary inslaving himself to a woman's will. I wonder how they dare boaſt of conqueſts, when they muſt acknowledge they are daily overcome by a weak and feeble creature, woman, a thing which for want of heat sunk into that sex.

With suchlike prattle we entertained ourselves for an hour or two, and now it was put to the vote what course we should ſteer, and what deſign·we should next put in execution. Different were our opinions for a while, but at laſt we concluded unanimously about the evening to set out and rob jointly, the manner which we laid down was thus. The youngeſt siſter should ride behind the eldeſt siſter on a pillion in her own proper apparel, and my Virago behind me in the like female garb, and this we judged to be the safeſt projeƈt we could propound, for who could be so senseless to imagine us robbers, riding in that manner double-horsed, and attended with the greateſt symptoms of innocency?

Hereupon we fell to work, that is to say, endeavoured to get such necessaries as were moſt convenient for our enterprize, as pillions, safeguards and short swords for my females, pocket piſtols they had already. Having gotten what woman's attire we wanted, and all things ready, we mounted with boots, which we dirtied on purpose, to the intent those which saw us might not suspeƈt but that we had rid many miles that day. It was about six of the clock in the evening when we did set forth; we had not rid above two hours, but there overtook us four horsemen, and demanded whither we were travelling? I answered them, to such a place. Now did our two subtle queans which rid behind us play their parts to the life, pretending a great fear of being robbed, and carried their business so craftily that they gave the gentlemen to underſtand their pretended fear and jealousy, and the better to cloak our design, 'Pray thee my dear,' said I, in a voice not over-loud, but juſt so that they might hear me, 'do not be afraid, I am confident they are no other than what they appear, that is, honeſt civil persons.'

Hereupon, one of the gentlemen over hearing, rode up close to me, and comforted my supposed wife behind, proteſting they were no such persons as she imagined, that they were gentlemen of good eſtates all, and so far they were from offending any, that they would with the hazard of their lives defend the injured on the road. We seemed hereat to be much satisfied, returning them many thanks, and desiring their company, which they kindly granted, saying, 'Come follow, we'll lead the way gently on, and ſtand between you and danger.' I was glad to hear them say they would ride before, for now I judged our business to be facile, and easily done. I now whispered behind me, telling her, as soon as ever she saw me give a blow, she should immediately leap off the horse, and make use of what weapons she had. Her sister had the like instructions given her.

My brother, as I called him, riding up close with me, received directions from me that when we came to the bottom of the hill, he should at the same time with me directly discharge his truncheon on the head of his foregoer, with all the force he could sum up together.

When they least suspected us in the rear, we executed what we designed with such exact time and so successfully, that a divided minute did not difference their fall. Our women were as swift as lightning upon them, depriving them of all the advantages of rising, whilst we set spurs to our horses, and overtook the other two afore, who insensible of what was done, were strangely surprized and amazed, to see our swords and pistols ready to dispatch our hellish commands. Fear on a sudden had so chained up their tongues as that they could not utter a word, till we forced them to it by threatening their unavoidable deaths if they did not instantly deliver. Being willing to ransom their lives by their money, they gave us what they had, as not to stand in competition with a matter of eternal concern. Having reaped our desires, we dismounted them, and cutting their girths and bridles, we took their pieces with the saddles, and threw them into an obscure place. The horses were whipped over into a field. Our prisoners we led into a little wood, where we bound them, as the rest of our gang did, who were more expeditious than we in our work. Having finished our business to our hearts' content and security, we mounted, and so rid back again to our old quarters. Our landlord wondered at our speedy dispatch, but had like to have expired for joy when he saw our booty was so considerable, for you are to understand he had a quarter share with us. Here did we carouse and feast for a long time, not so much as thinking on any prize, and the truth on't is, my leg grew so bad by my shot, that I could not ride but in great pain. Wherefore I resolved to lie still till its cure should be effected by my loving and skilful landlady. My wound being healed, I resolved to follow my custom, and rob alone, not so much that my profit would be greater, but I began to be tired with my three former dainties ; nay more, they were so insatiate in those pleasures they enjoyed that my strength could not cope with such excesses. Wherefore pretending business of privacy a little way off, I gave them the slip, knowing how difficult it would be to part from them knowingly.

CHAPTER XXXVII

Being now upon the pad *alone, he baits at an inn with which he was acquainted, and there by the hostler is informed of a booty, which he pursued, but was soundly banged for his pains, losing both his horse, and what small matter he had left*

VERY loath I was to part with these Amazons, neither should I, had not scarcity of money called me away to look out for more. For no man could ever be better pleased with society than I was in theirs, enjoying such persons whose courage and fidelity might vie with the most approved male friend, and reaping at the same time the choicest favours Venus can confer on her chiefest favourites.

One remarkable passage concerning this female robber I had like to have forgot, which was this. She would frequently pad or rob on foot in woman's apparel, but so disguised, that she could not easily be known. Getting a cushion, or some such thing (by putting it under her clothes to make her seem big with child), she would usually walk abroad, it may be three or four miles at length, near some beaten road. Thus had she the benefit of viewing all that rid by. If she saw any single person by whose equipage she might imagine him to have his pockets well furnished, before he came near her, she used to feign herself both exceeding sick and weary, groaning in a most pitiful manner. What man's heart could be so obdurate as to pass her by neglected, and without taking any notice of her? Who would not proffer a big bellied woman (tired and indisposed) the courtesy of riding behind him for a little way to refresh her? As she told me, she met with very few that did not take her up behind them, seeing her in that deplorable condition. Having rid a pretty way, seeing the coast clear, and coming to a convenient place to execute her design, she would pretend the gentleman's hat that rid before her offended her eyes. Most in point of civility would put it off, though they immediately put it on again. Then would she with a cord with a nooze which she had ready for the purpose, clap it over his head, and so whipping off the horse pull the man after her, oftentimes half strangling him, serving him as the mutes do the Bassas with their black box and silk string therein, when they are designed for death by the Grand Senior's appointment and command. Taking the advantage of their being half suffocated, she could easily first bind their legs, making them so secure, that they were so far from resisting that they were totally at her devotion.

But to return where I left off. Before I took my leave of her, perceiving the temper of this brave noble spirit, and that it was poetically inclined, out of my true resentment of her due merit, I gave her these lines, which she thankfully received, though modeſtly denied to concern her in the leaſt.

> Stand back ye *muses*, *Mars*, come guide my pen,
> To rank this female hero 'mongſt thy men.
> So, so, 'tis well. Now let us to the matter,
> 'Tis such a subjeƈt that I cannot flatter.
> The pantalooners ſtrut, and muffetoons ;
> Taking great pains for to appear buffoons.
> They do seem men, and like 'em wear their swords :
> But dare not draw ; such may be kill'd with words :
> These love a lady, and affeƈt perfumes :
> Who *lighter* are (than what they wear), their *plumes*.
> Thou scornſt such shadows, or *chimæras*, which
> Are good for nothing, but a woman's itch.
> Thou loveſt that man alone, that dares in spite
> Of fate, scorn *death* himself in fight.
> Thy aƈtions speak thee *man*, who dares deny it ?
> Believe this truth, or if you dare, then try it ;
> 'Twill be a favour to her, for they'll find.
> That never man enjoy'd so brave a mind.

Bidding this my Minerva and her associates adieu, I rid on in the next road, without meeting any I thought requisite to faſten on. At length I came to an inn where I was very well acquainted, and intended there to have refreshed myself ; but the hoſtler prevented it, not suffering me to alight, telling me haſtily, that there was a gentleman not an hour since baited there, who had in his portmantua a considerable purchase, that he was a poor spirited fellow, whom he knew, and that he ever had an absolute antipathy to a naked sword, and that he was gone such a road, &c. I ſtayed not so long as to drink, but with all possible expedition made after him. Ascending a small hill, I discovered him who rid an ordinary pace, wherefore I slacked mine to cool my horse ; however I soon overtook him, and rode by him, not without viewing him well. Riding down the hill I did alight, purposely that he might overtake me, which he did ; being paſt I mounted, and at the very bottom I bid him ſtand and deliver inſtantly, or he was a dead man. ' Sis, sis, sir,' said he lisping very much, ' I-I-I-I am going home.' I bid him not make these proposed delays, leſt he smarted, and therefore wished him to dispatch and give me his money, for I was informed (I told him) that he had a sum behind him. ' T-t-t 'tis true,' he replied, ' b-b-but it is my father's m-m-money.' ' Hang your father and his stuttering coxcomb too,' said I, ' I must have what you have.' ' W-wh-why then you shall,' said he, and with that drew out a pocket pistol and fired it at me which made my horse start, and very much surprizing me, expecting not the least resistance from such a seemingly ignorant and cowardly fellow. By that means he had time and liberty to draw his sword (which was almost as broad as a chopping knife) and came upon me so furiously, that I am sure I had not time to defend myself : he so laid about him, that I soon lay at his mercy.

I was forced to beg very hard for my life, which I obtained with very much ado : then he fell to my pockets, not leaving any suspected place for money unsearched : by which I guessed him to have belonged to our profession, and was not mistaken, as you shall understand by and by. He went to my horse, and viewing him, he seemed to like him very well. Wherefore coming to me (for he had cut me off my horse) ' Ha-ha-hark you,' said he, 'you are but a raw thief, a me-me-mere child, and it is but fit that you should be sent to a ma-ma-master to be ta-ta-taught knowledge, and be whipped for your foo-foo-lishness. You said you must have my fa-fa-father's money, but I tell you I must have your hau-hau-horse, and so farewell.' He was so kind as to leave me his, which was a pitiful jade ; however, necessity compelled me to mount him, and anger spurred me on to be revenged of the hostler, but I better considered with myself, that probably that horse was known there, and so I should be detected ; wherefore I rid a contrary way, and took up my lodging in a place I never had been in before.

As soon as I alighted, abundance of people flocked about me, seeing me all bloody, to know the cause thereof. Whereupon I related in a very doleful manner how this sad accident befell me. That travelling to such a place with about 150 pieces of gold, I was set upon by five or six lusty rogues, who robbed me, and because I made what resistance I could, to save what I had, it being my whole estate, they had thus barbarously mangled me, hacking and hewing me till I grew weary, and at last with much difficulty escaped with my life. There was a general sorrow for me, pitying me so much that the inhabitants strove one with another, who should shew me most kindness. A chirurgeon was presently sent for, who (as he was a barber too) barbarian like, dressed my wounds ; some were employed in procuring me cordials, and getting me things necessary ; others were sent out to make inquisition after the thieves.

This gentleman that served me this trick, was (as I understood afterwards) an highwayman himself, who being well born and bred, but his father being either at that time unable or unwilling to supply him with what money his lavish expenses required ; nature having bestowed on him a stout resolute heart, and strength answering his courage, betook himself to the pad. In which profession he behaved himself so gallantly that he was styled the father or governor of his tribe. But his attempts proved not always successful, so that there was hardly a county in England, wherein he had not been in prison, being frequently arraigned for his life, but having eminent and potent friends, he still came off. This did his father and kindred so frequent, that they grew weary, and he narrowly escaping with his life one time, and finding that his kindred mattered not much if he were hanged, he submitted himself to his father, making a solemn protestation that he would never follow the like courses again. Whereupon his father settled an annual estate upon him, on which he now liveth very orderly. Thus much briefly of my overcomer.

I had not laid above a night in this place for the cure of my wounds, before I was questioned about my horse by some persons that knew him well, and taken on suspicion for murdering the gentleman, the right owner, which seemed more than probable by various circumstances. First, this gentleman was not to be found, which well might be his late success having conveyed him on the wings of speed to an obscure place, there to revel and congratulate his good fortune by the speedy spending his late purchase. Next, my many and dangerous wounds sufficiently declared the great hazard of the two combatants' lives ; but that which chiefly committed me, was the gentleman's horse, which I like an impudent insipid coxcomb must ride on, which reason must needs say was the ready way to ride post to the gallows. Notwithstanding the miserable condition of my carbonadoed body, I was inclosed between a pair of walls, and had undoubtedly been hanged for being robbed, had not the gentleman appeared again amongst his friends ; then did my accusers slip their necks out of the collar, and none prosecuting me, I was discharged.

Staying a little while in the town for refreshment, an old acquaintance there found me, of whom I cannot but give you a character, since the passages of his life hath been so remarkable and notorious, and from the short relation of which I question not but the reader will reap much benefit and satisfaction. For indeed examples have so great an influence and power upon the actions of man's life, as that we find men are more wrought upon by precedent than precept. To this intent, preceding generations have made it their grand care and labour, not only to communicate to their posterity the lives of good and honest men, that thereby man might fall in love with the smooth and beautiful face of virtue, but have also taken the same pains to recount the actions of criminal and wicked persons, that by the dreadful aspects of vice, they may be deterred from embracing her.

CHAPTER XXXVIII

He here reneweth his acquaintance with a cunning fellow, that formerly studied the law, and since made it his sole business to practise the abuse thereof

ABOUT four days after I was discharged, there came into the same inn where I lay a gentleman, who hearing some of the house discoursing of the robbery that was lately committed, he desired to be particularly informed, which they did, adding that the robbed gentleman lay wounded in the house ; he enquired of them my name, which they told him, as I had told them, having a name for every month in the year. Very desirous he was, if it might be no disturbance to me, to give me a visit, unto which I condescended, a servant to that intent desiring to know my pleasure. As soon as he entered the room, I verily thought I knew him, though I could not for the present call to mind where I had seen him. I was so muffled about the chops, that it was impossible for him to have any knowledge of me. He sat down by me, and asked me various questions, to which I gave him convenient satisfaction. At last I recalled my memory, and asked him if his name was not so ——— ; he answered me affirmatively. ' Dear friend,' said I, ' I am glad to see you : come, be not amazed ; my right name is so ———' With that he embraced me, and was overjoyed that he so casually found me out. Laying aside all formal niceties, I unbosomed myself to him, not mincing the truth in the least ; for we know ourselves birds of a feather, rogues together.

He condoled my wounded condition, and comforted me, by telling me that he would not leave me till I was well, and that he would procure me such a plaster for the wounds I had received that should prove very effectual. In short it was this ; by following closely the footsteps of his crafty advice I got of the country the one hundred and fifty pounds I pretended to be robbed of. He stayed with me above a fortnight, enjoying what pleasures the country was capable to afford us. Being by ourselves (for so we designed the major part of every day) we discoursed interchangeably of nothing but our adventures, &c. how we might lay new plots for our advantage. I gave him the epitome of what I had done, since I left him, who took more pleasure in the relation of my rogueries, than the Quaker did in courting his mistress mare near Rochester. But when he began to relate his villainies, I was struck dumb with admiration ; and what cannot a man do if endued with the strength of his natural parts, sharpness of wit, quickness of apprehension, depth

and solidness of judgment, with a tenacious memory? Now because
he ever had a smooth and insinuating tongue, with the command thereof,
I shall give him leave to tell his own tale.

CHAPTER XXXIX

The life of a law abusing cheat

Dear friend,

FOR what am I beholding, it is to Nature alone; for as I am
ashamed of my birth, so I cannot condemn my father for not
bestowing education on me, since his condition was so low. Yet his
spirit was so high, that he would not beg himself, though ready to starve,
however would permit me, who was the sole support of his and my life.
I was ten years old before I could meet with any preferment. One day
fortune favouring, she offered to my view a commodity which, with
confidence and dexterity I might carry off undiscovered. My hands
successfully effected what my mind suggested; it was but of small
value, the utmost I could get for it was a link, with which that night I
more than trebled what it cost. This course I followed by night, and ran
errands by day, so that I had furnished myself both with clothes and
money. In process of time I was admitted as a servant into a scrivener's
house; my master taking a liking to me, put me to a writing-school,
where being capacitated for his business, he put me into the shop, and
instructs me in his employment. I had not been there long before I
made myself very eminent by studying the law, the rudiments whereof
I understood so well, as I knew how to ingross an indenture. This made
my master esteem me, and that estimation made me proud, and being not
yet bound his apprentice, I thought I knew better things than to be his
servant any longer, and so left him. Then was I with an attorney a
while, afterwards with a counsellor, till thinking I had law enough, I
took an house, resolving to see what I could do with it myself. I solicited
several men's businesses, giving a general content, insomuch that my
credit and reputation increased daily.

Now did I marry for wealth, having not the least affection, for her face
looked much like a gammon of bacon with the skin off. Some time I
lived with her, too long for any delight I took in her, and being resolved
to be rid of her, this stratagem I used. I shewed her more kindness than
formerly, pretending I would do nothing but what I would consult with
her about; which so wrought upon her love that she would have been

content to have sacrificed her soul to my interest, and made her withal so opinionative, that she judged every silly and unsavoury expression she uttered was no less than an oracle. Having brought my business thus far to perfection, I came home one evening very melancholy : very inquisitive she was to know the cause. 'My dear,' said I, ' I will not conceal anything from thee ; such a gentleman hath injured me, and I cannot rest till I be revenged. Thou knowest my nature, if wronged I am implacable, it is a fault I cannot help.' ' Come, come,' said my wife, ' let us go to bed and there we will consult.' Being there she asked me how we should bring our revenge about ? I seemed to study awhile,— ' I have it now,' said I, ' thou art with child ; he is one tender of his reputation ; tax him for being the father of it, and that will do the work to my full content.' Very loth she was, because of the talk of the people, but I satisfied this poor silly harmless soul by telling her that as long as I knew her chaste, it was no matter what others said of her. Whereupon she condescended, and had the person before a justice, where she swore positively that she was got with child by that gentleman. I took advantage of her confession, turned her off, leaving them both to the disposal of the spiritual court. This was my first prank.

One of my clients another time, having bought a good handsome tenement, had so much confidence as to put me in possession. My client having purchased an estate in the country, was forced to be there to look after the management of his rural affairs, for some certain time ; I took this opportunity to forge a lease to myself, at an easy rent from him that constituted me his trustee. I soon found a chapman for it, and sold this lease, receiving a good round fine, which had been a penny-worth indeed, had the title been good. Unto this man I delivered possession, who dwelt in it till the return of the right owner, who coming to his said house, wondered to find every thing so contrary to his expectation, and demanding of the tenant by what power he inhabited in that dwelling, the poor man shewed him his forged lease, declaring that he had paid his fine to such a man, nominating me, who at that time was not to be found. The landlord could do no less than eject him his house, but finding him so grossly abused, required nothing for the time he was in it, but left him to the law to require satisfaction of me. The abused being very much troubled he should be thus deceived, made so strict enquiry after me, and so unwearied in his search, that at last he found me out, who said, nothing should serve his turn, but he would for this cheat have the rigour of the law executed upon me. Knowing of what a dangerous consequence it was, I got my adversary arrested in an action of a thousand pounds, who wanting bail was committed to Newgate, where grief released me by his death from ensuing prejudice.

I afterwards forged a deed of sale of an house hard by the former, which would have made more for my advantage, had not this man discovered my design, which made me the more inveterate against him and his. For this was always my temper, though nothing could provoke me to express my anger in company (as having a perfect command over my passions in that nature) yet if any durst prosecute his own or friends' right in opposition to me, I seldom left him till I had either absolutely undone him, or so impoverished him that he should be in no condition to hurt me, or help himself, making him at last confess that he had been better to have sat down with his first loss. And this I effected the easier, having a conscience that scrupled nothing, and instruments that would swear anything. These contrivances of mine made me generally reputed a subtle and knowing man, which brought me in multiplicity of business, with considerable incomes. Neither did I alone solicit for such as were concerned in the law, but I had my concernment with lifters, who did put so great a confidence in me, that what they got was left solely to my disposal, either by sale or pawn, for which I had my brokage, and something else besides. Now was I grown so famous (my garb adding much to my fame, which was very splendid) that if any intricate controversy, reference, or law suit arose among my neighbours, they knew no person fitter to make their appeal to than myself for arbitration. If any again wanted either money, goods, nay a cooler of concupiscence, I was adjudged the best procurer. By these means I tumbled in money, and to let the world know it, I wore several suits every day, having besides habits suitable to any design.

Now did those that knew me not even adore me ; those that were acquainted with me, out of fear were forced to shew me more than ordinary respect. I confess had I now walked in a medium, this had been the time (as they say there is a time allotted to every man) to have made myself for ever. But knavery was so implanted in my nature, that I could not forbear cheating the dearest friend I had, if he entrusted me, circumvent every man that had more honesty than myself, and though I was sure to damn soul and body, yet I must attempt the destruction of my adversary, and to speak the truth, I did not stick to betray my friend, if any advantage would accrue to me thereby. For one trick I served an ancient widow, I now and then find some internal gripings. I cannot tell whether they proceed from conscience because I never knew what conscience was, and this it is. A gentlewoman of my acquaintance, whose sole dependance was upon lodgers, having taken up a great many goods to a considerable value to furnish her house befitting the reception of any person of quality for which she was indebted, and having too often put off her creditor, came to me, desiring the favour of me to procure her fifty pounds, telling me, that such a knight, and such a squire would stand bound with her. ' That will not do,' said I, ' for the gentry have so many tricks to keep citizens out of their money that they will have better security.'

Perceiving her present necessities were very urgent, I knew I could do anything with her; wherefore I persuaded her to confess a judgment: she agreed to it. I told her such a day it should be done but I would speak with the party first: according to the day prefixed I came, bringing with me a warrant of attorney, with a friend or two to attest it; she confided so much in me, as to seal before she received the money. That being done, ' Now come along with me,' said I, ' to such a place, where the money lieth ready.' As we were going, there was a stop in a lane by carts and coaches, and by the help thereof I dodged her she seeing me no more till it was too late, for I came with an execution a while after and carried away every pennyworth of goods she had. Yet so civil I was, that I would not let her see it done knowing it could not but be a great trouble to her; to that intent about half an hour before, I sent for her in my name, far enough distant from her own habitation. In this nature with some variations as to the manner, I served several. Knowing I had a plentiful invention, which seldom failed me, I scorned to be so idle as to make use of one trick only to bring about my ends, and as I had several, I never made use of one trick twice, for fear of being smoked. I seldom went abroad, but I had some of my complices at my heels, rarely going together, unless necessity required it. I went into a coffee-house one day, and sat me down at a common table (as the room is to all comers); a little after came in one of my imps, and sits himself down too. I had then a very curious ring upon my finger, which a gentleman opposite to me perceiving, ' Pray sir,' said he, ' do me the favour as to lend me a sight of that ring on your finger.' I presently delivered it to him; having viewed it and commended it, my rogue must needs desire a sight of it too from this gentleman, who thinking no harm, gave it into his hands; after he had looked on it a while, he fairly marched off with it. I saw him, but would not in the least take notice thereof, knowing where to find him. The gentleman imagined nothing to the contrary, but that the right owner had received it again.

A little while after, I demanded very courteously my ring, excusing his detention thereof upon the account of forgetfulness. The gentleman starting, replied, ' Sir, I thought you had had it long since.' I told him I had it not, and as I delivered it unto him, I should require it from no other person. He pished at it, and in the conclusion bad me take my course, and so I did, having first taken witness of the standers by, I sued him, and recovered the value of my ring twice over, producing two in court that swore point blank, that one of them sold it me for so much—. One thing I confess I frequently made use of, which was this. If any person died, and none durſt adminiſter, but leave the deceased's goods to the creditors, then would I be sure to make myself a principal creditor by a forged bond, and thereupon sue out letters of adminiſtration, and sweeping all away, I wiped the nose of other creditors.

CHAPTER XL

What a notable revengeful trick he served the turnkey of Ludgate

I WENT on a time to see a prisoner in Ludgate, but thinking to come out again as easily as I went in, I found myself juſt as the piĉture I have often seen upon the Exchange, wherein is represented a man plunging himself with much ease into the great end of the horn, but with the greateſt difficulty can hardly squeeze his head through the other end. Hell's gates ſtand ever open to let all souls in, but none are suffered to go out. Here I waited two hours for the return of the turnkey, fretting myself even to death for being detained from my urgent occasions. At length he came : I told him what an injury he did me. Inſtead of excusing himself, he returned me very scurvy language which provoked my passion so much, that though I said little, yet my invention was presently at work to be revenged. Not long after I got a poor fellow to be arreſted for an inconsiderable debt, advising him to turn himself inſtantly over to Ludgate. In a short time the poorness of this man's condition was generally known, and he himself pretending he was almoſt ſtarved, got liberty to put in what slender security he could procure for his true imprisonment, and so had leave to go abroad. In the mean time I had got a bond of the prisoner of fourscore pound for the payment of forty, and so went privately and entered an aĉtion of debt. I told the prisoner the next time he went out he should run away, which he did, neither was there any security to be found ; then did I bring my aĉtion againſt the keeper, with my Knights of the Poſt, and so recovered the money.

CHAPTER XLI

What a freak he played upon a jeweller

I WAS intimately acquainted with a jeweller in Foster Lane, whom I often helped to the sale of rings and jewels, so that my credit was very good with him. Being one time above in his workroom, I chanced to spy a very rich jewel, whereupon I told him I could help him to the sale thereof, my lady such a one having lately spoke to me about such a thing. He gladly delivered it to me at such a price to shew it her. But I only carried it to another to have one exactly made like it with counterfeit stones. Before I went, I asked him if the lady dislike it, whether I might leave it with his wife or servant ? ' Aye, aye,' said he, ' to either will be sufficient.' I was forced to watch one whole day to see when he went out, and being gone, presently went to the shop and enquired of his wife for her husband. She answered me he was but just gone. ' Well, Madam,' said I, ' you can do my business as well as he ; 'tis only to deliver these stones into your custody,' and so went off undiscovered. Not long after I met him in the street, carrying displeasure in his looks. ' Sir,' said he, ' I thought a friend would not have served me so ; ' but I denied it stiffly. Whereupon he was very angry, and told me he would sue me. I valued not his threats, and so left him. I had not gone many paces before I met with a friend that complained to me he had lost a very valuable locket of his wife's, it being stolen from her.

Glad I was that this should fall out so pat to my purpose ; I asked him to give me a description of it, which he did punctually. ' Now,' said I, ' what will you give me, if I tell you where it is ? ' ' Anything in reason.' ' Then go to such a shop in Foster Lane (the same shop where I cheated the man of his ring) and there ask peremptorily for it, I was there at such a time and saw it, and he would have had me help him to a customer for it. I'll stay at the Star tavern for you.' Away he went and demanded his locket. The jeweller denied he had any such thing (as well he might). Upon this he returned to me (by this I had another with me), and told me what he said. Whereupon I advised him to have a warrant for him to fetch him before a justice of peace, and that I and my friend (which saw as much as I) would swear it. The goldsmith was instantly seized on by a constable, and as soon as he saw who they were that would swear against him, desired the gentleman to drink a glass of wine, and then tendered him satisfaction. But I had ordered the business that it would not be taken unless he would give us all three general releases. He, knowing the danger that might ensue to life and estate if we persisted, consented to the proposal.

N

CHAPTER XLII

He puts a notable cheat upon a gentleman concerning his house

WALKING one time in the fields with an attendant or two, who would be constantly bare before me, if in company with any persons of quality, but otherwise, ' hail fellow well met,' I was got as far as Hackney, ere I thought where I was ; for my thoughts were busied about designs, and my wit was shaping them into a form. Casting my eye on the one side of me, I saw the prettiest built and well situated house that ever my eyes beheld. I had a covetous desire to be master thereof : I was then, as fortune would have it, in a very genteel garb ; I walked but a little way further and I soon found out a plot to accomplish my desires. And thus it was. I returned and knocked at the gate, and demanded of the servant whether his master was within. I understood he was, and thereupon desired to speak with him. The gentleman came out to me himself, desiring me to walk in. After I had made a general apology, I told him my business, which was only to request the favour of him, that I might have the privilege to bring a workman to supervise his house, and to take the dimensions thereof, because I was so well pleased with the building, that I eagerly desired to have another built exactly after that pattern. The gentleman could do no less than to grant me so small a civility. Coming home, I went to a carpenter, telling him I was about buying an house in Hackney, and that I would have him accompany me to give me (in private) the estimate. Accordingly we went, and found the gentleman at home, who entertained me kindly as a stranger. In the meantime the carpenter took an exact account of the butts and bounds of the house on paper ; which was as much as I desired for that time.

Paying the carpenter well, I dismissed him, and by that paper had a lease drawn with a very great fine (mentioned to have been paid) at a small rent ; witnesses thereunto I could not want. Shortly after I demanded possession. The gentleman thinking me out of my wits, only laughed at me : I commenced my suit against him, and brought my own creatures to swear the sealing and delivering of the lease, the carpenter's evidence, with many other probable circumstances to strengthen my cause ; whereupon I had a verdict. The gentleman understanding what I was, thought it safer to compound with me, and lose something, rather than lose all.

CHAPTER XLIII

How he cheated a scrivener under the pretence of bringing him good security for an hundred pounds which he would borrow

ATTIRING myself in one of the richeſt garbs I had I went to a scrivener in Bow Lane, and acquainted him I had an occasion for an hundred pounds. He demanded the names of my security. I told him where they lived, two persons of eminent worth (whom I knew were gone into the country) and desired him to make enquiry, but in it to be private and modeſt. The scrivener according to my desires went and found them by report to be what they were, real, able, and sufficient men : two or three days after I called upon him to know whether I might have the money upon the security propounded. He told me I might, bringing the persons, and appointed me a day. According to the time, I came with two of my accomplices attired like wealthy grave citizens, who personated such persons so to the life that the scrivener could not entertain the leaſt suspicion. The money being ready, I told it over, and putting it up in a bag, I and my insignificant bondsmen sealed, leaving the scrivener to another enquiry after us, whom, if he did not meet, I was confident he could never find out by reason of our feigned names.

It chanced that my forged and fiĉtitious name shook hands with that of a gentleman in Surrey, who was a great purchaser, which I came to know by being accidentally in his company the next night after I had cheated this credulous scribe, understanding likewise from him the exaĉt place of his abode ; and as the devil would have it, his chriſtian name was the same, as well as his surname, with that of mine I had borrowed. Whereupon I went to the scrivener again, and told him that now I had a fair opportunity to benefit myself very much by a purchase, provided he would assiſt me with 200 pounds more. ‘ But sir,’ said I, ‘ take notice (in a careless and generous frankness) that it is out of a particular respeĉt to you, that you might profit by me that I come again, neither will I now give you any other security than my own bond, though I did otherwise before. But if you will desire to be satisfied as to my eſtate, pray let your servant go to such a place in Surrey, there is a piece of gold to bear his charges, and I will satisfy you further for the loss of your servant’s time.’ He being greedy of gain, very officiously promised me to do what I required, and would speedily give me an answer. Imagining what time his servant would return, I repaired to him again, and under-ſtood from him by the sequel that he received as much satisfaĉtion as in reason any man could require. Hereupon I had on my own bond the money paid me. I cannot but laugh to think how strangely the Surrey gentleman was surprized when the money becoming due was demanded of him, and how like the figure of man in hangings the scrivener looked when he found himself cheated.

CHAPTER XLIV

How he was revenged on a broker for arresting him for some goods he had passed his word for upon his friend's account

NOTWITHSTANDING I daily thus, almost, cheated one or other, procuring thereby considerable sums of money, yet, by my drinking, whoring, and defending myself from such as I had wronged, I seldom kept any money by me. One day as I walked the streets securely, as I thought, a fellow fastened his flesh-hooks on my shoulder. Looking about to see what this sudden clap meant, I saw a fellow behind me, whose face looked ten times worse than those Philistines that are pictured on chimney pieces, seizing upon Samson; his mouth was as largely vaulted as that within Aldersgate; his visage was almost eaten through with pock-holes, every hole so big that they would have served for children to play at cherry pit. His nose resembled an hand saw; take both head and face together, and it appeared like the Saracens on Snow Hill; questionless some Incubus begot him on a witch. Having a little recovered myself from my amazement, I asked him what his business was with me. He spake but little, leaving his errand to his mace (which he shewed me) to relate. Away they carried me to Wood Street at the King's Head, from whence I sent for bail, which speedily came to me: having put in bail to one action, I found another entered: having done the like to that I found another, half a dozen more bearing it company; wherefore thanking my friends for the trouble I had put them to, I desired them to leave me, resolving to go to Ludgate. The two serjeants that arrested me conducted me thither, having my name entered in the paper house, as horses in Smithfield are in the toll booth. Cerberus turned the key, and set the door as wide open as Westminster Hall gate in the term time to country clients, to receive me from my hell guides, which puts me in mind of that old verse,

Noctes atque dies patet atri janua ditis.

I no sooner was entered into this enchanted isle, where some lie wind bound sometimes seven years together, but a fellow (whom at first sight I took to be a gardener, because he had a kind of reddish beard, and turned up withal) came to me, and understanding I was a prisoner, seemed mighty courteous, proffering me his chamber for my garnish sake. I accepted his kindness, and went with him to view this cobweb hung chamber, for so it proved. I demanded of him who should be my bedfellow. ' That gentleman there sir,' said he, ' that sits by the fireside : ' I could not forbear smiling, for he was a fat squobby fellow, though his brain seemed to be lean. I believe he was his own barber, and was forced to make use of a knife instead of a razor, for his beard it was cut round like a rubbing brush. Certainly, had all the skin of his body been like that of his face, it would have served excellent well when he was dead to make cloak-bags of. Not content with this lodging, I sought out another, liking it somewhat better than the former, I pitched on it. As soon as they understood my resolution, they worried me presently like angry mastiffs, barking for their garnish. I told them they should have it to-morrow, at which they grumbled like the greatest strings of a base viol. Before I went to bed I must pay for a pair of sheets, that never came nigh Holland by three hundred miles, and out of much civility my bedfellow brought me a candle not so long as his nose to light me to bed.

The next morning I made it my business to get out as soon as I could ; some I paid, others I nonsuited, and so got clear. Being out I resolved not to rest till I had revenged myself on this broker that had thus troubled me. I needed not means, for the devil seldom failed to help my inventions. I pretended to go into the country, and in order to it packed up a trunk of what I had most valuable and portable, and getting a porter, sent it to an inn where a Norwich carrier used to lie, but I knew him to be gone the day before. Going along with the porter, I enquired for such a carrier, but they told me he was gone, and would not return till the next week.

I asked them where I might lay my trunk safe ; they shewed me a room where bidding the porter sit down, I called for some ale, telling the porter, moreover, that I would have him be a witness of what there was in the trunk, lest I should be dishonestly dealt by. Whereupon I unlocked it, desiring him to take notice, which he did, and to be more sure took an inventory in writing. Having paused a little, ' Now I think upon it,' said I, ' porter, it will not be safe to leave this here in a public house, as in a friend's, wherefore prithee, go buy a cord, and thou shalt carry it elsewhere.' Whilst he was gone, I took out the chiefest things and put in rubbish, or what I could get, and so locked it again. The porter returning, we corded the trunk, and carried it to this broker, who took it kindly from me, that I would entrust him after our controversy, and received it. The next week I told him I would call for it, in order to the sending it into the country. The time being come, I took the same porter with me, and demanding the trunk, it was forthwith delivered me. 'Come, porter,' said I, 'you muſt uncord it again, for I have present use for something therein contained'; which being done, I seemingly amazed, cried out I was robbed, taxing the broker for so doing, vilifying him for his knavery. He proteſted that he never looked on it to his knowledge since the receipt thereof. 'Well sir,' said I, 'this shall not serve your turn, this honeſt porter knows how differently it is fraught from what he saw it at firſt.' In a great seeming heat I left him, but before he slept I sent a couple of serjeants to him, who arreſted him; coming to trial by the assiſtance of two (resolved jurors) and this porter, I overthrew him, and recovered above forty pound, besides coſt of suit.

CHAPTER XLV

How he cozened a rich usurer, and a young tradesman

BEING resolved to go and look out some of my consorts to rejoice together for my good success in my advantageous revenge, I met with an old comrade that had lately heaved a booth, Anglice broken open a shop, who told me he had a quantity of good commodities, and desired me to put them off for him, knowing that I dealt in brokage in goods indireſtly come by : I promised him I would. The next day he delivered what he had into my hands, I inſtantly carried them to an old usurer that would grasp at anything, telling him I only desired to mortgage them for such a time, requeſting to lend me fifty pounds thereon. He, looking upon them to be thrice the value of that sum, lent me freely the quantity of money propounded, and in my sight took the goods and laid them in a place next his bedchamber.

The same day I met with this friend, who demanded of me whether I had done his business ? 'No, not yet,' said I, 'it will be to-morrow firſt : However let us drink a glass of wine,' which he readily consented to. Having drank pretty smartly, he could not contain himself (so powerful are the operations of wine, as it frequently makes a man divulge that which carrieth in it inevitable ruin) I say he told me whose shop it was he robbed, and at what time. I seemed to take little notice then, though I intended to make good use of it. Parting with him, I went ſtraightway to the person robbed, and told him that accidentally I was informed of his late loss, and that my intent of coming was out of a principle of honeſty, to assiſt him in the recovery of what was ſtolen from him. But before I acquainted him with anything, I required of him a bond of 10 *l.* if I helped him to his goods, which he granted me. I advised him to get the Lord Chief Justice's warrant, which he did and taking some friends with him, I directed them where they should go, and in what place they should find them. He would have had me go with him, but that I excused myself, alleging it would be inconvenient. Taking a constable with them they went and found what they sought for according to my direction, which they seized, leaving the old man to condole his loss, which had been no great matter, had not his life lain in his purse.

Having thus carried on my mischievous contrivances with continued impunity, the next I fell on was a young merchant, to whom I went genteely habited with a footboy waiting at my heels. I looked out several commodities, and laid them aside, assuring him that I would ere long lay out a considerable parcel of money with him. We discoursed upon the price, and in the conclusion closed. The next day I appointed the goods to be sent home to my house, and in the interim desired him to go along with me, and accept of what poor accommodation my habitation would afford him, under the pretence of being better acquainted, but my design was to raise in him a good opinion of me, for I had one room (especially) very richly hung with costly furniture. My motion was entertained and away we went, where I treated him nobly ; the next day the commodities were sent in with his servant, who expected his money, but I pretended that my cashier was abroad, and so desired him to call the next morning ; he did, but then I was not to be spoken with. Thus he did so often till the young man was weary. At last the master himself came, who met me just as I was going out, who had not the patience to ask for his money, but railed most bitterly, calling me cheat, knave, &c. and that he would not put himself to the trouble of posting me up, but would have a warrant for me instantly.

Being gone, I was as nimble as himself, having a couple of my emissaries ready for him against his return. It was not long before he came strutting with a constable. Perceiving him coming, I sent my two friends out with their warrant, and putting it into the constable's hand, charged him in the King's name to execute it upon such a one, meaning the merchant who dared not deny it, but carried him before a justice, before whom my two rogues swore flat felony, and so was committed. Sending for friends, they advised him to make an end thereof. Whereupon I was much solicited, and upon consideration I consented to cause my friends to forbear prosecution.

As yet I have not fully unbowelled the huge bulk of my villainy, that hath proved so burdensome to the world, and destructive to so many families. Wherefore give me leave a little farther to anatomize my own vicious nature, and I shall so lay open the ulcers and sores of my impoſtumed machinations, apparent to the sight of every one, that the moſt ospray and owl-eyed speǎator shall confess there never was a more necessary and commodious discovery revealed.

'Brother,' said I, 'for so I muſt call you now, your flagitious deeds claiming that title, and muſt be compelled I see to give you superiority, for I am confident the line of other men's inventions never sounded the sea of a more deep and dreadful mischief. When I consider how powerful and imperious vice is of late grown, and what horrid faǎs are committed every where by licentious and wicked men that swarm in all places : I admire that the fabric of the earth is not continually palsied by earthquakes, since there is a Creator above that oversees such aǎions. That the Earth herself (though an indulgent mother) doth not receive into her womb her offspring, and therein for shame hide them : that the air is not choked with frogs, and that black pitchy miſts do not perpetu- ally masque the face of Heaven, and leave the world in obscurity ; and that the sun doth not hide his face from seeing such enormous crimes blacker than is the eclipse of his countenance : and laſtly, that the sea is not turned to blood to put us in mind of the cruel and remorseless usages of one another ; our kindness being commonly attended with discourtesies of a vermilion hue. Thus brother you see I am sensible of my miscarriages, but want the power to regulate my life.' I would have proceeded, but that I found this discourse grated in his ears ; wherefore I desired him to prosecute his ſtory, which he did in this manner.

CHAPTER XLVI

He discovers the subtlety of some citizens he had to do withal by broking for them, relating his own craft and cunning, and what the consequence was, the ruin of young gentlemen

LIKE an hawk as I told you, I flew at all game, not confining myself to any one thing particularly : where I could abuse the law, I did, and if I had an opportunity to trepan, I seldom failed, &c. Some part of my time I spent in the enquiry of what young heirs were arrived, into whose society I was sure by one means or other to insinuate myself. These country woodcocks I knew how to catch with a city spring ; whom I very well underſtood would rather be out of the world than out of the fashion, who would be brave for the present time though their gallantry coſt them all their future fortunes. I commonly laid my plot thus : ' Sir, you undervalue yourself by the meanness of your habit, it being so unsuitable to your quality. If you want money, you cannot want credit, having a fair promising estate in reversion ; if you are willing, I will find you out a believing mercer.' Returning me many thanks, it may be he would be in such haste as to send for me presently. He could not be so eager to have his gaudy desires satisfied, as I forward to accomplish them. I knew where to go readily to one, with whom I went snips ; in so saying, I would not have any think I throw dirt upon that noble profession. If I discover the fraud of any particular person, as long as I name him not, I do him no wrong ; but if I detect by what deceitful and sinister means he worketh upon the infirmity of the youth of a green-witted gallant, it may serve for an use of instruction. In the most famous Universities there are some dunces resident, that by disgracing themselves, disgrace also their fellow students. In the most virtuous Courts there will be some parasites. So in the most goodly and glorious city under Heaven's canopy, there are some asps lurking, that sting the reputation of their brethren by their poisonous and corrupt dealings. There are knaves in all trades but book selling.

But to my purpose : a young gentleman coming out of Norfolk to see the City and finding so many (beneath him in estate) gallant it so much above him, he grew very melancholy. Happening to be in his company, and indifferently well acquainted with him, I asked him the cause of his sadness. After I had pressed him very much, he ingenuously confessed the true origin of his pensiveness. ' Pish,' said I, ' is that all ? Let me alone to effect what you desire ; neither shall you wait longer than the morrow.' Leaving my gentleman, away I went to a person fit for my purpose, and gave him an account of my business : glad he was, thanked me for my pains, promising me a reward, and would needs have me to a tavern to consult this affair. Having concluded every thing, I repaired the next day to my gentleman, who overjoyed to see me was impatient to know whether his wishes were consummated. ' Come along with me,' said I, ' and we will try what we can do. I have been very importunate with the mercer, but as yet I cannot mollify him ; it may be your presence may do much.' Finding him in the shop, I called him aside, and told him this was the gentleman. My young gentleman, that would be a gallant presently, fell aboard him, and (with much fervency and protestations) he wooed the mercer to credit him for 30 *l.* worth of commodities.

I called him aside, saying, ' What will 30 *l.* worth do ? Take up 100 *l.* worth ; and what you use not, I'll dispose by sale, to furnish your pockets with money.' He thanked me kindly for my advice, and returned to the mercer, who asked him if he should credit him with so much, what security would he propound? This struck my young gentleman as mute as a cod's head. The mercer perceiving he had nothing to say, played the rope maker, being extreme backward to trust him. Bonds he refused, judgments he would not hear of, statutes he scorned. 'For,' said he, ' gentlemen of late have found out so many tricks to cozen their creditors (I by the same means having had several collops cut from the body of my estate), that I will not credit any more ' : whereas he spake this only to grind the blunt appetite of my commodity taker into a sharper edge, and make him more greedy, of his own ruin, imitating in this a cunning and deceitful, though petulant and wanton courtezan, who is nice when a sick brained young gallant importunes her to admit of his amorous kindness, only to make him more fierce upon his own confusion : holding him off like a fencer a month or two, that he may come up the more roundly to her purpose. But to the matter. My gentleman being as it were denied, I seconded him thus: ' Sir, you know not what you do in refusing to credit this gentleman ; he is his father's heir, a man of a vast estate, and very aged. This his son is about a very great match, a rich heiress, and though he hath not money for the present, yet let him have an hundred pounds worth of commodities, you need not doubt your payment ; and it will do him at this present a thousand pounds worth of good.'

The mercer began to hearken to this, and protested to my green goose that he would be glad to do any a pleasure, so as not to injure himself ; that if he could but possess him with a belief that he should have his money in six months, he would freely let him have 100 *l.* worth of what he pleased. The young gentleman protested it, and I warranted it, and the mercer (though seemingly loth) condescended, upon this proviso still, that he should procure some man else to be bound with him, as good as himself. ' For,' said he, ' we are all mortal, and not having a lease of our lives, we may die before to-morrow ; where then is my 100 *l.*? ' Signior Unthrift is once more put to his *non-plus* ; but at length he fell to entreat me to do it, who would not by any means, and so we parted. He would not let me rest for two or three days together, so that at last, provided he would give me 10 *l.* I agreed ; and so we went again to the mercer, and entering into bonds we had the commodities. Having made my young gentleman an absolute gallant, I went to sell what was left, of which I made 40 *l.* but I made my gallant to be contented with 30 *l.* alleging that when goods came once to be sold, they will not yield the moiety of what they cost, though new, and out of that 30 *l.* I had my 10 *l.* for suretyship. Thus I persuaded him to be very well satisfied. He revels about, whilst I was contriving to leave him as bare of means as brains.

Now doth my mercer dream of nothing but his payday, which he hoped would be broken. The time being expired, and my young novice not minding it, the mercer invited him to a dinner in Fish Street. Dinner being almoſt ended, for a third course came up a couple of serjeants ſtewed with mace, who arreſted him at the suit of the founder of the feaſt. Not procuring bail, he was carried to the Compter, where he lay some time. His friends hearing of it, endeavoured to get him out, by suing out an *Audita querela*. My mercer hearing of that, advised with me what was beſt to be done. ' Agree,' said I, ' with some officer in the Exchequer, and turn the debt over to the King, pretending you owe him so much money, for the Chancery will not or cannot allow any thing in such a case againſt his Majeſty.' He so doing, did his business for the present. Thus have I read, when Jews have bought a red-haired boy, at firſt they clothe him in silks, ravishing him with all the delights that can be thought on, never have music from his ears, or banquets from his taſte, and thus use him, till they see he is plump, fat, and fit for their purpose. But when the poor boy leaſt thinks of his imminent ruin, he is taken by a brace of slaves, and tied up by the heels, so beaten by degrees to death with cudgels, purging the rankeſt poison out of his mouth, and making mummy of his flesh. I shall leave it to the Reader to make application.

In short, I persuaded the mercer to take a bond of 500 *l.* of his prisoner, to be paid after his father's decease. This widgeon being in the nets, sealed to any thing for his liberty. He was not the firſt so served, by thousands, and that is the reason there are so many creſted citizens : for gentlemen being beggared by their extortion, they have no other means than to fall in with their wives, purchasing from them a supply. This is it that makes the road everywhere so full of highway-men, who will borrow of men when they have little mind to lend, but not without giving them bonds. This makes Tyburn the Metropolitan, and other petty gallows have so many hangers on ; and this is the cause so many such citizens' sons are plagued after their fathers' deaths, as their fathers when living have plagued others. These are the boars that plough up whole acres, nay fields of gentlemen's lands with their snouts : these are the swine that eat up whole orchards ; and these are they, whose fiery consciences drink up whole fishponds at a draught ; and laſtly, they are the hurricanes that root up the trees of whole woods together. From such *libera nos Domine*.

To conclude, take this as an infallible maxim, that the worſt of creditors are either very rich, or very poor men. The rich man can ſtay for his money, and so will have all or none ; the poor will have no pity, not indeed can he, since the debt may be all he is worth.

CHAPTER XLVII

*How he insinuated himself into the acquaintance of all he thought he could
prey upon, and what tricks he used to build his interest upon their ruin*

HOW can that tyrant flourish in his commonwealth when the
foundation of his reign was built on the sepulchre of the right and
lawful heir he murdered? And how can that man prosper whose rise
he reared from other men's ruins? Such was I, who having oftentimes
been gulled by knaves turned knave myself, and did as greedily hunt after
such I could make a prey of (to repair the damages I had sustained by
others), as the devil doth after usurers' souls, being on their death beds,
resolving to live like a bandit on the spoil. Like an old soldier having
been beaten to the world (or indeed more properly beaten by the world),
I began to summon up all my senses and my idle brains to a strict
account, how to get that up again, my riot and folly had spent; and thinking I had no way to recover myself, but by what ruined me, I did cast
about me and fished after this manner. I prepared my lines, provided
baits, and made ready my hooks, which had such constant and firm
barbs, that after I had struck a gudgeon in the gills, I was sure to hold
him, though I suffered him to play a little in the stream. The floods
I daily frequented, were either the Temple, ordinaries, playhouses,
cockpits, brothels or taverns, leaving no place unsearched, wherein
there might be anything worthy of bait. If such I found, like a shadow
I was never from his heels, but followed him close, especially if he was a
young country gentleman, whom his father had sent up to see fashions
in the City: and rather than he should go out as raw as he came in, I
failed not to season him in one of the City's powdering tubs.

First, I made it my business to know what his father allowed him;
then would I study his natural disposition and inclination, and accordingly suit myself to him, so that by my behaviour towards him, he should
look upon me to be his masculine sweetheart, his bosom-friend, and
that like Hippocrates' twins we must needs live and die together. Having
accordingly by much sweat and industry adapted and fitted him to my
humour and purpose, and wrought him to such a soft and waxen temperature that I could make what impression I pleased on him, I brought him
acquainted with some of my accomplices, who all vailed bonnet to him,
invited him from tavern to tavern, not letting him expend a penny;
or if he wanted money, I would supply him with four or five pounds.
This innocent (not having yet scented the City air) all this while thinks
himself in Elysium, fancying he enjoys more delights than the Turk's

paradise affords, and withal imagineth himself not a little graced, to be entertained among such seeming gallants. For my rogues (give me the liberty to call them so) looked on it as the greatest piece of policy to wear good clothes, though their pockets were worse furnished than a chandler's box, that seldom hath any greater money in it, than twopence, threepence, groats, &c. Sometimes my cully did meet with some that knew me, who would advise him to have a care of me, and not to keep me company, for I was a dangerous person, and in the end would be his ruin. Whereas it was but to little purpose, for when youth is in its full vigour, and height of desire, neither wholesome counsel, not lamentable examples, will give them warning of their future destruction.

Still I continued my seeming respects and kindnesses to him, which I only intended as the præludium or prologue to that play which was to come after : for my country cock brain being honeyed with these sweet delights, thought that whatever he could return, was not able to give an answerable satisfaction. Watching a fit opportunity (when he was well warmed with wine), then would I persuade him (which was no difficult matter), to be bound with me for so much, &c. which I promised I would repay at the day, without putting him to any inconvenience : but he knew not, that what I borrowed for an hour, I borrowed for an age. When I could squeeze no more juice out of him, then I left him to the mercy of his creditors, to be dealt withal as the popinjay in the fable, who being summoned to appear with the rest of the winged tribe before their king the eagle, borrowed of all the finer sort of birds feathers to adorn him, and make him appear splendid before his sovereign.

After he was dismissed, he proudly fluttered up and down the woods with his borrowed gallantry, which made the little titmouse, wren and hedge sparrow adore him. They to whom he was obliged for his gallantry, hearing thereof, demanded again their own, and so deplumed him, whereby he seemed ten times worse then those small birds that lately did admire him. Such popinjays are they, who borrow of every citizen, to make themselves shew glorious in the world's eye ; but when the creditors shall come and claim their own, and get it, they will seem more foul, than lately they did fair. So various and villainous were the pranks I committed every day, that I was forced now, like an owl, to appear only by night in the City. If I did at any time transgress that custom, I did then like the dogs of Egypt, which when they come to drink of the river Nilus, lap here and there, not daring to stay long in one place, for fear the crocodiles that lie lurking within the banks, should pull them into the current : so did I, skulking here and there, first to one tavern, and then, not daring to stay longer there, shifting to another. But to proceed.

CHAPTER XLVIII

How he could make ink that would disappear from the paper, accordingly as he pleased, by the ſtrength or weakness of the composition : his imitating exaƈtly both hand and seal : a remarkable ſtory thereupon

READING one time a book that an Italian writ, I found therein a description of several sorts of ink, and how to make them ; but more especially, an ink that should laſt a week, a month, or two, according to the composition. I made an experiment, and found it hit indifferently well. Perceiving how beneficial this would be to me, I resolved not to reſt till I had found out the true recipe ; which I did at laſt, by much ſtudy and induſtry. Having obtained it, I so highly valued it, that methought I would not have parted with it for the Philosopher's Stone. Not to be tedious, I did abuse therewith many persons with bonds, leases, deeds, acquittances, &c. there appearing in such a time nothing but the bare seal, the paper remaining as white as if never writ on. By the help of graving, I could counterfeit seals exaƈtly, insomuch that I have often cheated the grand cheater, Oliver, the late hypocritical and bloody tyrant, and by an exaƈt imitation of an handwriting his council was too sensible of what cheats I put upon them. That I was no bungler at it, I shall give you this inſtance.

Accidentally coming acquainted with a gentlewoman, very beautiful and well featured, her sparkling eyes set me all in a flame, so that I resolved to attempt the enjoyment of her. Oftentimes I visited her, and by the modeſty of my carriage towards her, she perceived not my burning luſt. One time having a fit opportunity, she being alone, I communicated my thoughts to her. Waiving what amorous discourse passed on my side, I would have fallen roundly to the matter, but she underſtanding my intent, cried out ; whereupon I desiſted, seeing it was to little purpose if I proceeded. Sitting down by her, she expressed an absolute hatred to me for my incivility, and vowed she would neither see nor endure me more. The vehemence of her utterance and countenance fully declared she was in earneſt, so that I saw 'twas time to be gone. Looking about (unperceived by her) I took up half a sheet of paper of her writing, and clapped it into my pocket ; and so took my leave.

Coming home, I found my love converted into hatred, and therefore vowed my revenge, and thus it was. I underſtood from her whereabout her husband lived, and what his chriſtian name was, with something of her concerns ; that her husband's mother could not endure her (because her son married her without a portion, though a wise, discreet, virtuous,

and handsome woman), and whereabout he lived, with name, &c.
I counterfeited a letter, as from this virtuous gentlewoman, to a gallant
of hers, taxing him with want of love, and that if he proved not more
conſtant, she had no more to say to him, &c. The contents you shall
have in the letter itself, as followeth.

MOST BELOVED BY ME OF MEN!

I cannot blame you so much as myself ; it is cuſtomary for man to proffer,
but then it should be a woman's duty to refuse : but alas ! how could I with-
ſtand the powerful persuasions of your eloquent tongue, especially when they
carried with them so much seeming reality of affection and conſtancy? I
find you now like other vow-breaking men, who having obtained the fruition
of their desires, their appetite nauseates that which before it so eagerly craved.
Call to mind those many endeared and melting expressions you did voluntarily
utter, when I was encircled in thine arms, and if that will not reduce you to
your former ſtation, and good eſteem of me, now so much slighted by you,
consider that I have preferred you in love before my husband, not caring how
much I wronged him to pleasure you. If nothing will prevail, know then,
this shall be my resolution, that since you have alienated my affeƈtion from
my husband, and you thus unworthily desert me, I will procure a subjeƈt
elsewhere shall out-do you in every thing, as much or more as you have out-
done my husband. I am young, plump, handsome, and buxom ; what then
should hinder me from enjoying such a person, my heart will not reſt satisfied
till I have found, which having done, he shall lead me in thy view, and then it
is probable you will desire, but never shall reassume your place again within
my breaſt.   *Farewell.*

This letter was sent to her mother in law in the country, who was glad
she had matter to impeach her daughter to her son. As soon as he saw
the letter, he very well knew the hand, he thought, and would have sworn
it to be his wife's : but reading the contents, the poor man was ready to
sink down for grief. Perturbation of mind would not let him reſt in
his country dwelling, but rid up poſt to London, where he soon found
out his wife. The unexpeƈted sight of him at firſt surprized her, not
hearing of his coming, and knowing that his occasions were very urgent
in the country : however, like a truly-loving wife, she was overjoyed
to see him, and would have kissed him, but that he rudely thruſt her off ;
which aƈtion ſtruck her to the heart, and overwhelmed her in amazement. ' Prithee, sweetheart,' said she, ' what is the matter ? '   ' There,
read it,' said he, throwing her the letter. She read it, and swooned.
He let her lie, not caring whether she lived or died ; and had died indeed,
had not her maid come up accidentally. Being recovered, he asked her
whether it was her hand. She could not deny it : which made the man
rage, ready to run out of his wits, whilſt she was silent with astonishment, taking such inward grief that she betook herself to her bed.

Nothing could comfort her, neither would she take anything to sustain life. Hearing how powerfully my forgeries had wrought, to the hazard of some lives, in the same hand I sent him a letter, wherein I gave him an account of the design, proclaiming to the world this gentlewoman's honesty, unspotted and unstained. The gentlewoman recovered in a little time after; but this trick had too much seized upon my gentleman; for like a fool he fell distracted in a sneering posture, as pleased to think his wife was honest notwithstanding. I have been somewhat long in this relation, because it was a passage very remarkable. Now I shall tell you how I cheated a young citizen and an upholster.

CHAPTER XLIX

How he cheated a young citizen newly set up, and an upholster

A YOUNG citizen about to set up, and wanting some money, was directed to me, to procure so much as his present occasion required. I treated him very civilly, promising him very fairly; and in order thereunto, appointed him a day, which being come, contrary to my expectation or desire, he brought a crew with him, to see the receipt of the money. Judging this time inconvenient for my designs, I told him I expected the money this very day, but if he pleased to seal the bond, and have it witnessed, he might keep it himself, and bringing the bond with him the next day, he should not fail to have his money. The next day he came to the place appointed, where I was ready to wait him. As good fortune would have it, he came alone. I discoursed with him a while: at last I desired him to let me see the bond; which he delivered into my hand, being signed and sealed before. I took this as a good and lawful delivery, and put it up into my pocket. He asked me what I meant. I told him he should know when the bond became due. 'Why sir,' said he, 'you will not serve me so.' 'Dost thou think I am such a fool,' said I, 'to lend thee so much money upon a piece of paper which next shower of rain will wash away with thyself into the common shore? Shall I trust thee, when thou canst not trust thyself?' At this the young man began to be clamorous, but one of my accomplices soon stilled the clapper of his mouth, by a sound knock on the pate, which laid him asleep; and in the meantime we marched off. Just as the money came due upon the bond, my flock pated cit was gone to tell his friends in the country the danger of compters and prisons in the city.

At another time I wanted money to supply my present occasions, but could not instantly think of any other means of assistance in this necessity but to sell my featherbed, together with its appurtenances. Whereupon I packed them up, and desired a friend to go with the porter, and sell them to an upholster. My friend did so, and brought me half their worth ; but withal, that which was more than their worth, the man's name. A week after I wanted my bed, and resolved to have it again. To that end, I went to him that bought it, and asked him before a couple that I took with me, whether at such a time he had not such commodities sold him. He acknowledged that he had. I desired to see them, and he as readily granted it. ' Sir,' said I, ' these are my goods. I was lately robbed, and now I know you are the receiver. I must have you before a justice, to know how you came by them.' The naming of a justice so terrified this silly fellow, that he bid me take them if I would swear they were mine, and put him to no further trouble. I swore they were mine (and therein I was not perjured), but told him I could not receive stolen goods safely, though they were mine own. In short, I recovered my bed and furniture, with money to boot.

CHAPTER L

He is at last met withal, and laid up in prison by one of his creditors : the abuses and tricks serjeants use to arrest men : lastly, he escaped, by putting a trick upon his keeper

HAVING gone thus far without any remarkable check or control, at least any such as might bear a proportion with the villainies and injuries I had done, I absolutely thought that nothing was dishonest or difficult that had in it either pleasure or profit. Meeting with no molestation or hindrance, I took my freedom to do even what I listed. One time thinking myself most secure, I then found myself in the greatest danger, being arrested in an action of 5000 *l.* Several times there were attempts made to take me, but I was still too cunning for them : yet at last they overreached me ; it will not be amiss to relate in what manner.

They had information, that every week I had letters come to me out of Essex, and that the porter which brought them had still free admittance to me : wherefore the serjeant provided himself a frock and a rope about his middle, which would better have become his neck, and with letters in his hand directed to me, trudged to my lodging. Knocking at my door, and being demanded his business, he told them he had letters for the master of the house, nominating me. Looking out, and seeing

o

no one but a seeming porter, I ordered that he should be let in. As soon as he was entered, he bid my worship good morrow, and instead of delivering me his letters, shewed me his mace; which I wished might be the only spice and meat too he should eat for a twelvemonth. Seeing how I was betrayed, I went quickly along with him to the compter and afterwards, finding I could make no composition with my creditors, turned myself over to the King's Bench. Various are their tricks and inventions to ensnare whom they intend to arrest. Sometimes I have known a creditor seem to comply with his debtor, telling him that paying some inconsiderable matter, his bonds should be renewed with longer time : then appoint him a place of meeting, where he saith he will bring a counsellor and scrivener, a counsellor to advise them in management of their business, and a scrivener to write what they determined. He acquainted a serjeant and a yeoman with his plot, who were as hot upon it, as an Italian on a wench of fifteen. The serjeant going with a barrister's gown on his back and the yeoman with his beard cut as close as a stubble field with a pen in his ear and some parchment in his hand, effected their design without suspicion.

A merchant I knew that intended to break and go beyond sea, was betrayed by his servant, who informed his creditors that just at such a time his master would be gone, that on the morrow he would send for coopers to hoop some dry vats to pack his goods, and that if ever they hoped to have their money, they must make that their time. Some serjeants were presently acquainted herewith, who attired like coopers in red caps, canvas breeches, with adzes in their hands and hoops about their shoulders, went to the merchant and were entertained whilst he was giving them direction; but instead of hooping the dry vats, they hooped him in their arms, and arrested him. Before they parted with him, they made him part with so much money as would satisfy his creditors and them, and made him fee them besides, not to enter any more actions against him. They will change themselves into as many shapes as Proteus, to bring about their designs; sometimes like a grand wealthy citizen, othertimes like a country fellow newly come to town, with boots and spurs all dirty. Now as I have related their manner of arresting, so let me in short inform you of their using (or rather abusing) prisoners. First they enquire of the person whether it be the first time he was arrested : if so, then they know the better how to deal with him. Perhaps they will carry him to the tavern, pretending to do him kindness, where they will advise him to send for some friend, and one of them will be the porter himself; but instead of fetching the friend, he only enquires out his creditors, and persuades them to use this opportunity to recover their debt : meanwhile, the other that is left behind doth milk him.

The messenger returning, sorrowfully tells him his friend is not at home. Getting as much as they can by spunging, and sucking the very heart blood of his pocket, the compter must be his refuge at last.

Sometimes, when they see a man in fear of arresting, they will without warrant of the creditor give him a cast of his office, which they often do before they enter their action, and have ways to prevent any mischief that can come by search of the offices. Other times, for a fee, they will send to the party to keep out of the way, as was concluded beforehand. Oftentimes, upon an arrest, if the creditor stand not by, they will let the party escape for a brace of angels or so, and tell his adversary that he cannot set eye on him. And whereas their fee for an arrest is to be but 1 s. yet will they hardly be persuaded to do their office under a crown : and albeit the statute say that the party arrested shall pay but one groat, he will not excuse him for an angel. If a man oppose them, or endeavour an escape, they will both gripe and pinch him, and afterwards clap an action of assault and battery on him at their own suit. I could say more of them, but that for fear I must be favourable, who am now, as I tell you, a prisoner in the King's Bench, which may be called the bankrupts' banqueting house, where he feasts himself on dishes borrowed from other men's tables, or the prodigals' purgatory, and a pesthouse for decaying citizens. Weary of this place, wherein are as many maladies and mischiefs as flew out of Pandora's box opened by Epimetheus I invented this strategem.

One day I pretended much business abroad, and so got leave to go out with my keeper, resolving not to return with him. Having been from tavern to alehouse and so to tavern again, pretending the dispatch of much business, I at length told my keeper, that I would visit a very dear friend of mine, but that I thought it requisite to be trimmed first. He consenting, we went to a barber's. I sat down in the chair first, and being dispatched, I desired the keeper to sit down too, and I would pay for sprucifying his phiznomy. Whilst he was trimming I talked of one thing or other, to hold him in discourse. At last said the barber, ' Shut your eyes, or else my ball will offend them.' Shutting his eyes, I took an occasion to slip out, planting myself in an house hard by, the barber not imagining I was a prisoner. The keeper not hearing me talk, valued not the smart, but opened his eyes and seeing me not in the shop, rose up, and that so hastily, that he overthrew Cutbeard, and the bason on him, running out into the street with the barber's cloth about him, and Don Barberoso's turban on his head. The people seeing him thus with the froth about his face, concluded him mad, and as he ran gave him the way. The barber with his razor ran after the keeper, crying, ' Stop him, stop him, that I may be revenged on the rogue.' The other ne'er minding the outcry, ran ſtaring up and down as if his wits had lately ſtole away from him, and he in pursuit of them. Some durſt not ſtop him, others would not, thinking the barber by his poſture intended to have his teſticles for abusing his wife. To conclude, the barber at laſt seized him, and having recovered his clothes, and made him pay 6 d. for shaving, the keeper was dismissed with a kick or two in the arse, the barber not suffering him to speak a word in his own defence. Thus freeing myself, I resolved to take the country air, where I happily met with you. Many other things worthy remembrance did he relate, which now I have forgot. Some while we ſtayed together ; but at laſt his business called him one way, and my padding trade invited me another.

CHAPTER LI

He is laid up in Oxford *gaol by his hoſt : he is cheated at Cheſter, and after some time is ransomed thence by some of his comrades, knights of the* road, *they paying his debts*

OUR crew having been abroad, we had got a valuable purchase ; which after we had divided, I told them that I would but visit a friend at Oxford, and repair to them again within two or three days. My old acquaintance being overjoyed to see me after so long absence, treated me very gallantly, introducing me into the society of the wits ; who would frequently drink too, till they had loſt them. The company pleased me so well that I thought it a solecism in civility to be sober, when they made any appointment for mirth ; and they being true Bacchanalians, in the uppermoſt classes of Ariſtippus's school, scorned to be outvied by a junior sophiſter. And therefore, do what I could, they would be drunk before me. They never contended about any argument that tended to ebriety, but swallowed them all. I thought they would never have done speaking of sack ; every one endeavouring who should express moſt in its praise. One said, that Diogenes was but a dry fellow ; and the only reason he could give for it, was, that it is shrewdly suspeſted by the commentators on his tub, that that wooden-house of his was given him by a beer brewer, who being a enemy to all good wits and learning, gave him this cask, which formerly had contained that pernicious liquor, beer, that by the mere scent he might deſtroy his underſtanding. But Bacchus is so witty a philosopher, that he never fails, night nor day, to pour forth his inſtruſtions, till he hath filled his auditors out of measure ; it is he that makes us speak fluently, and utter our minds in abundance.   For my part, I am commonly so overjoyed in his company that I have often feared I should never be my own man again.

Said another, it is sack was the Promethean fire, not stolen from Jove's kitchin but his wine-cellar, to increase the native heat, without which we are but cold clay ; but that celestial liquor applied even to the dead, will cause a revivification : this is it which gave Ganymede beauty, and Phoebe youth.   Can you think that ever Aristotle would have been taken notice of, had he drank ale or beer ; or that Alexander's conquests had been heard of, had he been sober ?   To make his captains famous to posterity he taught them how to muster quarts and pottles, and by accustoming them to be dead drunk shewed them the way to contemn death.

' All this is true,' said another, so drunk that what he spake could hardly be understood, ' but pray take my opinion with you too.   Do not all light things ascend ?   What better way is there to understand high matters, than a light head ?   Copernicus, by the lightness of his head, claimed alliance with heaven, and by that first found out the motion of the earth ; which he could never have done had not sack been his instructor.   Hence grew the proverb, *In vino veritas*, as if sack were the only butt truth shoots at, the piercing of which causeth the other to be drawn out with it.'

' For my part, Gentlemen (said I) my passion was never more stirred than the other day, coming by a red-lattice, unto which I have a natural antipathy.   There did I hear a tapster aver that Helicon was nothing more then an hogs-head of march beer, and that Pegasus was anciently a dray-horse ; and then speaking of French wine, in derision, called him frisking Monsieur ; and the Spanish, Don Rhodomontado ; swearing that if ever he met with either, he would challenge all the drawers in the Town to dash him as he would.   Then tumbling out two or three small-beer oaths, he wished that he might never look through his red-lattice portcullice, if he did not verily believe he should see Monsieur burned, with a pox to him, and Spanish Don mulled to death with butter and eggs.

> It is a thing beyond my reason,
>   That we strong ale for sack should quit ;
> Since 'twould have blown us up by treason,
>   Had not ale bestirred our wit.
> Then give us ale, but banish sack ;
> That *Spanish Don* must have the rack.

I could do no less for his malapertness, but broach his hogs-head, which to convince him of his error, ran terse claret.   I heard afterwards, this accident converted the infidel.'   We spun out various discourses of this nature, as long as we could see, and then each man reeled to his respective lodging.

The next morning, walking abroad to find out some of my laſt night's associates, unfortunately my Cheſter landlord (who having some business to do in Oxford, was newly come thither to dispatch it) espied me, and without accoſting me (like a subtle sophiſter) watched me whither I went. Being housed, he fetched two officers, and coming out into the ſtreet napped me. I sent to those friends that had been so merry with me ever since my coming to that city ; but they underſtanding the business, came not near me, one pretending indisposition of body, another that he was not within, a third that he was about urgent occasions, which having finished, he would wait upon me. In fine, none came to my relief, shewing themselves right pot-companions, whose courtesies, it may be, shall extend to the payment of a reckoning, when their friend wants it to discharge it himself ; but who disappear and vanish when their assiſtance is implored to draw him out of prison.

Seeing no remedy, I patiently suffered myself to be confined. My adversary visiting me, I treated with him about my releasement, offering him what I had, which was near upon half ; but his resolution was to have all, or there I muſt lie. Though I could not much condemn him, yet I could not but complain againſt the inconſtancy of Fortune ; and ruminating within my mind the miseries that attend all sorts of prisons, I judged that of debt to be the moſt deplorable. And though I wanted liberty, which commonly doth depress the mind, yet by the virtue of canary (which I could not be without) my fancy scorned to be fettered, but would in spite of fate, use her freedom. 'Tis some kind of pleasure and comfort for a man sometimes in adversity to descant on his own miserable condition ; which because I found experimentally true, I applied myself to my usual cuſtom, the use of my pen, differencing these metropolitan prisons thus :

> To *Bedlam* men are sent bereft of wit ;
> When 'tis reſtored, then they are freed from it.
> Confin'd to *Newgate* long, men can't complain,
> For once a month they're clear'd from it and pain ;
> In a short time their bolts wear off, and then
> They may be sure ne'er to come there again ;
> Discharged thence their fettered souls shall be,
> Only an hour confin'd, and then set free.
> *Bridewell*, no wiseman yet did e'er dispraise thee,
> For thou doſt feed the poor, correct the lazy ;
> The expiration of a little time,
> Forgives offenders, and forgets their crime.

Hereafter from the prison, Heav'n defend me ;
Rather to *Bedlam, Newgate, Bridewell,* send me ;
For there wit, work, or law doth set men free,
Nothing but money here gets liberty.

Having lain here above a week, I sent away a letter to my brethren, informing them of my misfortune, and acquainting them with the sum I was imprisoned for ; which was sent me by them, and brought by one of our trusty knights. Paying my debts and fees, I returned again to them.

CHAPTER LII

He returns to his brethren, the knights of the road, *whom he finds with two or three gentlemen, strangers : he cheats one of them of a very fair and rich watch*

MY companions took little notice of me at my return, which made me think there was some design in hand ; but according to their usual course, fell to drink high. Observing two or three faces, I tipped a wink to one of my brethren, being in another room. I asked him who they were ; he replied, gentlemen that were travelling into the North ; to which he added, ' We have been pumping them ever since we did thrust ourselves into their company, to know what store of cash they had about them ; but we find little more than will defray their necessary expenses on the road ; only,' said he, ' there is one of them hath a very rich watch.' I bid him return to his place, and I would warrant to have it before he stirred. I came in again to the company, not taking the least cognizance of any, but shewed much respect and civility to them all, as a stranger. I purposely asked what it was o'clock. One of the gentlemen, and both my friends, pulled forth their watches, striving who should first give me satisfaction to my question ; after this, they viewed interchangeably the workmanship of one and the other, both praising the seeming goodness of each other's watch.

At last my friend makes a proposition : ' Come, Sir, if you please we will make an exchange upon sentence and repentance.' The stranger desired to understand his meaning. ' Why, Sir,' said he, ' we will commit them both into the hands of any one indifferent person, and what difference he shall judge there is between them, shall be given in money by him whose watch is least worth.' It was concluded upon ; but they could not agree into whose hands to put them. At last it was mutually agreed upon between them that I, being a stranger to them both, should be the decider. I seemingly refused it, but they would not hear me allege any arguments to the contrary; whereupon I went out, and immediately causing my horse to be brought forth, without the least delay I mounted, and away I rid. My comrades knew where to meet me at the next stage. The next morning they found me out, telling me how they all stormed to be so cheated, to avoid suspicion; and now did they all embrace me, promising to themselves great hopes in me from this adventure.

CHAPTER LIII

He puts a notable trick upon a physician

NEAR adjacent to our general rendezvous I was informed of the habitation of a wealthy physician, who had shewed himself fortunately expert in divers cures, where it seemed that human art had not sufficient power to give a remedy. The fame of his great skill, and of many admirable cures, which to the shame of other physicians, he had performed, made him so generally beloved and sought after that in a short time he purchased by his sanatory industry, above 500 *l. per annum*, and seldom had less by him than a thousand pound. Thus much I casually understood from one accidentally, speaking of this his rich neighbour. But that which pleased me most was, that (as he said) he seldom carried less then an 100 pieces of gold about him constantly, proceeding from a fancy derived from an extreme love he bore that metal. I could not sleep for contriving a way how I might disembogue this urinal of what it contained. Sometimes I waylaid him in his return; but he was so well esteemed of, that he seldom returned home without two or three gentlemen to accompany him. At another time I thought to have pretended some distemper, and so have applied myself to him for cure; and imagining that he would privately discourse with me about my malady, that then I would present a pistol to his breast, swearing, that should be his immediate and unavoidable executioner if he did not without the least noise or resistance, deliver such a quantity of gold. But this way I could not approve of, it being accompanied with so much hazard.

At last I thought of this stratagem, which safely produced its effect. One day after dinner I rid to his house seemingly in extreme haste, which he might perceive not only by my own affrighted looks, but by my horse, which was all of a foam. I asked his servant, with much quickness, whether Mr Doctor was within. ' Yes, Sir,' said he, ' if you please to walk in, I shall call him to you.' I waited some time (for most of that profession must take some state upon them) and then Mr Doctor came. ' Sir,' said I, ' the report of your great experience in your happy practice hath brought me hither, humbly imploring your assistance, and that instantly, if you have any respect to the preservation of life. The trouble I shall put you to, shall be gratefully recompenced to the utmost of my ability.' The doctor inquired of me who it was, and what manner of distemper the person laboured under. I readily told him, it was my wife, who for some continuance of time had been extremely troubled with the flux of her belly ; ' the more that is applied to it by us, the more it increaseth ; wherefore, our help failing, I beseech you lend us yours, and favour me so far as to ride with me to her.' The seeming sincerity of my words prevailed upon him, as they would have done upon the most distrustful. This doctor (who as I was informed, was accustomed to be induced more by gain, than fair words) gave me this desirable answer. ' Sir, far be it from me that I should refuse to do my endeavour to any person whatever, much less to a gentleman of your rank and quality, in that little skill which I have in the knowledge and practice of physic. If I can effect anything for the good of the good gentlewoman, your wife, I will attend you thither with a very good will, which at any time my charge requireth.' Without attending any further discourse, his horse was made ready, and so we rid away together.

As we rid through a small wood, leading him the way, I turned my horse about, and clapped a pistol to his breast, shewing him withal an empty bag. ' See here, Sir,' said I, ' my wife, which hath a long time been troubled with a flux or vomiting, which you please, the last I think more proper ; for she no sooner receives anything for her and my sustenance but she immediately brings it up again at her mouth. Now, Sir, if you do not find out some means to mitigate this distemper (the cure I shall never expect, as knowing it impossible) this pistol shall send you to Æsculapius, to consult with him what is most fit to be administered. Come, Sir, let me advise you, and save yourself the trouble of so long a journey ; your gold (an hundred pieces as I am told) are the constant attending esquires of your body. I say, that is the best and only recipe for a remedy.' The doctor perceiving there was no help, in much amazement and fear delivered me what gold he had about him, which was near upon the sum expressed. There was a rich diamond ring on his finger, which I desired him likewise to give me, which should serve for a perpetual memorandum of his kindness to me. I commanded him, as he tendered his life, to ride back again without so much as once looking behind him ; and that if he offered to raise the country, if I was sure to die that instant I would be the death of him first. The doctor followed my dictations so exactly that I never heard more of him.

CHAPTER LIV

He falls in love with a wealthy widow, who is poetically inclined : he courts her, and in a short time enjoys her, and after that ungratefully leaves her, carrying away what ready money she had

HAVING gained so much money by my own industry and sole procurement, I resolved neither to acquaint my brethren therewith, nor associate myself any longer with them, being so encouraged by this success, that I concluded I might achieve gallant things by myself. Being belated one night, and some miles from any town, I knocked at an house that stood in my road, imagining it at first a public house for entertainment. One of the servants coming to the door, I found it no such thing. She demanded my business ; ' Prithee, sweetheart,' said I, ' acquaint your master that there is a gentleman requests the civility of a night's lodging.' She goes in and informs her mistress what I said, who came to me with much respect, telling me she questioned not but I was a gentleman, and therefore should be welcome to the mean accommodation she was capable of shewing. I rendered her many thanks, and so alighted. Strict order was given to the groom that he very carefully looked after my horse. This being done, I was conducted into a very fair room ; there did I make my apology in the best rhetoric I had, for I perceived she was endued with ingenuity, by the quaintness of her expressions ; *Ex pede Herculem.* Many things I forged, as that the ways being dangerous I was fearful to adventure any farther, having a great charge upon me.

Such was her urbanity that laying aside all niceties, she bore me company till it was time to go to bed, entertaining me all this while with what the house afforded, which was beyond my expectation. Every glass of wine or bit, almost, that I committed to my mouth, she ushered thither with some apothegm or other. The whole of her discourse was composed of nothing but reason or wit, which made me admire her ; which she easily understood, I perceived by her smiles, when she observed me gaping, as it were, when she spoke, as if I would have eaten up her words. As her soul was beautiful, sparkling with celestial ornaments, so was the cascanet that contained it very fair, and enriched with

Nature's chiefest gifts.   She was very clear skinned, well-bodied ; a sharp piercing eye, a proportionable face, an exceeding small and white hand ;   and then she lisped a little, which became her so well that methought it added a grace to the rest of her internal and external qualifications.

Being about ten o'clock, she advised me to repose myself, supposing I was weary.   I condescended, though with much regret to leave her so soon ;   but good manners would not permit me to do otherwise.   She conducted me to my chamber, where bidding me good night, she betook herself to her own chamber.   That night I could hardly sleep, not so much for pure love as the heat of lust.   Next morning, very early, I heard her stirring, which made me wonder ;   but she told me afterwards that she got up so soon, fearing I should have gone away, and she not take her leave of me.

About eight in the morning, the maid brought me up a sack posset ; and a little after, her mistress came, courteously saluting me, and enquiring how I slept.   I returned an answer, in as handsome terms I could utter.   Her eyes plainly discovered to mine that she had more than a common respect for me.   Having left me a while, I arose, and made myself ready for my journey.   After several discourses which she had engaged me in, purposely to delay time, with much gratitude I took my leave, she attending me to the court.   My horse being brought out, halted down-right (she had caused him to be pricked in the foot, to the intent I might stay longer).   Not knowing what to say or do, ' Well, Sir,' said she, ' since the unhappy accident hath fallen out so unexpectedly, make use of my house, and what is in it, till your horse be recovered of his lameness.'   This was a proposition that my soul longed for ;   wherefore I could not but shew much satisfaction in the acceptation of this proffer. We walked in again, and prosecuted for diversion sake our former discourse, interlining it with some love-touches at a distance, which she would frequently descant on pleasantly.

We in this short time became intimately acquainted ;   which need not be much wondered at, considering the greatness of sympathy between us ;   so that now the conquest of her appeared not any ways difficult. Having talked ourselves weary, ' Come,' said she in a very familiar manner, ' I will shew you the product of some idle hours ' ;   and with that brought me several epitaphs, elegies, anagrams, anacrostics, epigrams, &c. of her own composition, too many here to relate ;   but for their wit, deserved to have each line characterized in gold.   Some I would here insert, were not the radiant lustre of her conceits so great and glorious that they would absolutely extinguish the dim-sightedness of my fancy.   Having viewed them, I could not but applaud them, as their due merit ; and I was glad I had this happy occasion to vent my own thoughts, which I tacitly insinuated in these lines, reflecting on her from what I had read :

> Sisters thrice three I've read of, and no more,
> Till your quick wit completed half a score :
> Since you are one, let me persuade you then,
> Be kind to me, for they are kind to men.
> Dearest, be like them, they are soft and blithe ;
> Let who will love the nine, give me the tithe.

These lines so powerfully wrought upon her that she could not forbear to tell me that she was much obliged to me for what I had writ. ' You cannot Madam,' said I, ' cancel your obligation till you have made some recompence.' With that, said she smilingly, ' What will content you ? ' ' The continuance of your favour, Madam, is the utmost ambition of my desires.' ' You have it Sir ; neither can I deny any deserving man a thing so inconsiderable.' ' By your favour, Madam, love, I mean.' ' I never was so uncharitable,' said she, ' to be out of love with any.' I was glad to hear her reply so merrily ; for a fort which so capitulateth, is half surrendered. Since I had broke the ice, I was resolved to prosecute my design ; wherefore in plain English I told her that I loved her from the first interview, so ardently that my constancy should prove the reality of my affection. She desired me to leave that to the test of time ; that should she believe me suddenly before she had made trial, she should not only lose the good estimation she had gained by the prudent and discreet management of her affairs, every one accusing her for too much credulity, but thereby it may be involve herself in a labyrinth of all manner of troubles. ' Trial,' said I, ' you shall have.' And knowing the manner of courting a widow, a trial I gave her, knowing that parleys operate little on a widow, and there is nothing sooner gains a conquest than a storm or a resolute assault.

This action made her so firmly mine that I durst not speak of leaving ; which when I did at any time, her soul was ready to leave its ancient habitation to attend on me. Some two months we spent in all manner of self-pleasing delights, till at last I begun to be tired with her too frequent invitations ; the more I endeavoured to satisfy her, the further I was from it. Not only by her, but by others, this experiment I found, that the oftener I treated them the more eagerly and earnestly they desired it. Being now incapacitated to hold out in this manner longer, I thought it high time to be gone, but not without sufficient recompence for my service. She daily solicited me to marry her, which I promised her from time to time, waiting an opportunity when I might become master of her treasure. One day in a frolic, and the more to encourage me to make a speedy consummation of our loves by marriage, she shewed me all her writings which concerned her estate, by which I found her to be so wealthy a fortune, that I often times cursed my unhappy stars that they had thus debarred me from the complement of so great a bliss. After this, she shews me a trunk wherein was contained her cash. Then taking me about the neck with such fervency of affection that I thought she would have strangled me, and with the repetition of kisses, she smiling, asked me, whether these things satisfied me or not. I told her they did, but they were not to stand in competition with her most affected self. With that she gave me the keys of that trunk wherein her money was, and in retaliation, I vowed to marry her in four days.

In the meantime I studied how I might be gone, but could not contrive a way, she not enduring me to be out of her sight. In fine, I feigned some indisposition of body, and that I would ride two or three miles for the benefit of the fresh air, and return ; with much willingness she consented. Just as I was about to take horse (having furnished myself with as much money as I could well carry without discovery) she wept bitterly (as having, I think, a prophetic spirit). I asked her the cause of her discontent ; all bathed in tears, she answered me with a deep sigh, ' I shall never see you more. Hard-hearted man ; can you thus leave a woman that loves you thus dearly, nay, that dotes on you ? ' I made many protestations to the contrary ; which were not believed. Seeing that I could not prevail on her belief, I bad her farewell, setting spurs to my horse, and was out of sight in an instant. I could not but condemn myself extremely for this inhuman action ; but considering that there is no slavery greater than that of the smock, I soothed myself up in mine own unworthiness. Passing by a little ale-house, I called in, and over a pot of ale I composed these ensuing lines, which I sent to her by a messenger I procured in the house, directed thus :

> Deliver these to the fair hands of *Mrs Pulcheria*
> *Tickleman*, at her dwelling-house, near *Reading*.

The contents were these, or to this purpose.

> MADAME,
> A poetess you are, and prophet too,
> Thus to divine I'm gone from you
> Eternally. 'Tis true. D'ye think that I can eat,
> Though ne'er so choice, always one sort of meat ?
> No, faith. I'd rather wear a porter's frock,
> Than to be shrouded in one woman's smock.
> You say you are with child. Pish, don't complain,
> 'Tis but the product of your fruitful brain ;

Y'are only big with fancy, which may prove .
A witty brat, like *Pallas* sprung from *Jove*.
And have you then conceiv'd ? How can I choose
But write *encomiums* on my fertile muse ?
Mind not the father, nor his brat, for it
Will like the father live (no doubt) by wit :
Let *Pegasus* be godfather, the crew
Of the nine Muses, gossips ; so adieu.

I desired no answer, therefore ſtayed not till the return of the messenger, but rid that night to Maidenhead.

CHAPTER LV

He comes up to London, sends to a particular friend whom he could confide in, to come to him, and requeſts him to compound with his creditors, which he did in a short time : in a short time after, he attempts the robbing of an house, but is taken and clapped up in Newgate *: the miseries of an imprisoned eſtate, with the manner of his escape out of that prison*

THE next day I rode towards London, and about twilight took up my quarters in the suburbs. The day following, I sent for a friend whom I could put confidence in, who came immediately upon the reception of my letter. I communicated to him my intentions, who was very glad to hear of my resolution ; yet I would not acquaint him how ſtrong I was, nor by what means procured. 'Twas enough that I gave him commission how far forth he should proceed, and no farther, which was half a crown per pound. He went (after I had given him a liſt of them all) to every one particularly, and treated with them so cunningly, and they despairing of ever recovering a farthing, condescended to his proposals ; whereupon he gets them all to subscribe, and then brings the paper to me, which I exceedingly well liked of. According to the day appointed, he carried them the money, which every one received proportionably, each man respeſtively giving me his general release from the beginning of the world. They to whom I had confessed judgments, filed according to law their discharges.

But when my creditors, a little while afterward, saw me walk the ſtreets in so splendid a garb, some of them were ready to die with anguish : but that which troubled them moſt was my supercilious looks when I met any of them, and my slighting salutations. What I did in this respeſt,

was only to have the freedom of walking the ſtreets, without the moleſta-
tion of chargeable arreſts. I kept such deboiſt company that the remaining part of my money grew low, and in a very short time after, was all
spent. All my drunken companions failed me, and I having nothing
left me but my clothes, necessity made me to condescend to the enquiry
after the kind-natured gentlewoman, my wife. Her neareſt relations
could not give me any account of her, giving her over for loſt. I
wandered up and down, employing all the powers of my wit and
invention in the search of what might conduce to supply my present
necessities. While I was thus hammering out some new design on the
anvil of experience, I bethought myself where probably I might find my
wife. Firſt, I went to Ratcliff Highway, and made enquiry of Damaris,
&c. the metropolitan bawd of those parts, for a gentlewoman of such a
complexion, ſtature, and age ('twas but a folly to mention her name, for
those that follow that trade change their names as often as they do their
places of abode). But that cart-load of flesh could give me no information, neither was it possible for me to have ſtayed to hear it, she so ſtunk
of ſtrong-waters, ſtronger than that cask that never contained anything else. I went down all along to the Cross. In my way I saw many
whores ſtanding at their doors, giving me invitation ; but being poor,
they could not afford the charge of fucus, so that their faces looked much
like a piece of rumbled parchment, and by their continual traffic with
seamen's breeches, I could not come near them, they smelt so ſtrongly
of tarpawlin and ſtinking cod. Yet ſtill no tidings of her I sought for.

From hence I went to Fleet Yard, but there they were so dawbed or
plaſtered with paint, and botched with patches that had I seen her there,
it was impossible for me to have known her. Away I went to Lukeners
Lane, Sodom, and Dog and Bitch Yard ; but the pox, it seemed, had not
yet fitted her for those places. From hence I went to Whetſtone Park,
where I saw my madame ſtanding at the door. Her frequent trading,
and those many shots she had received between wind and water in the
service, had so altered her countenance and disproportioned her body
that I knew not whether this frigate was English or Flemish built. But
at laſt, hailing whence she was, I boarded her, and made her lawful
prize. Miſtake me not, I rummaged not in her hold, fearing she was a
fire-ship. The sight and knowledge of me made her shed some Babylonish tears, which I took little notice of, knowing them to be either
cuſtomary to that sex, or the effects of a moiſt brain.

In we went together, where we had, according to the cuſtom of the
house, pint black pots of small ale for twopence, and quarterns of
ſtrong water half filled for sixpence, with biscuits ; which as soon as
brought, everyone broken, though not a bit afterwards eaten. We muſt

be smoking, too, though the pipe muſt be thrown down carelessly, and often broken as soon as put to the lips. One of the plyers being gone down to draw some more drink, she begged me to conceal myself for the present, and comply also with the cheating cuſtoms of the house, and she would willingly pay all. I had hardly smoked two whiffs more, but that a fellow came where we were, swearing 'Damme, why do you ſtay with this fellow, and leave me thus, you unconſtant quean? Have I spent my eſtate on you, and muſt you now grow weary of me?' And with that drew his knife, making a proffer to cut her nose off.

I was so amazed at what I heard, and so irritated by passion, that I knew not which of them to be revenged on firſt. 'Sir,' said I, 'I have been longer acquainted with her than you, and may juſtly claim a better title and more privilege; but as you have affronted me, so I shall require satisfaction inſtantly, not referring our difference to be decided by the field, an umpire that cowards frequently make choice of.' So drawing my knife also, and seizing on his nose, which I intended to have divorced from his face, I was prevented, for it dropped off into my hand. This accident so aſtonished me, and withal being much affrighted at the sight of his death's-head, I durſt not meddle with him any further, leſt handling any member, it would have dropped off in the same manner. He made a blow at me, but inſtead of ſtriking me, I expected when his fiſt would have flown from his body into my face. He kicked at me, but that leg being up, the other was incapable of supporting his body, and so he fell down.

The old bawd hearing this diſturbance, ran to us as faſt as the vaſt bulk of her body would give her leave, whose pace was not much swifter then a snail in his full career, who having faſted too long, by the conſtant repercussion of the sun-beams on him in a misling morning, forrageth a garden for pillage. From the place whence she ſtarted to that where we scuffled was about six yards diſtance; and from the time of her setting forward, to the time she came to us (not to belie the woman) was about half an hour, and then too, out of breath, for the haſte she made. 'Sirrah, sirrah,' said she, 'come you hither to breed quarrels, and abuse civil gentlemen, and it may be build a sconce too? Get you out of my house, you rascal, or I'll scald you out.' By this time the pimp came to their assiſtance, and so they all conjoined to shove this poor fellow out of doors. And notwithſtanding he had for two or three years frequented the house, yet they neither pitied nor relieved him as a maimed soldier, the marks whereof were a sufficient teſtimony, besides the loss of a member or two.

Having discharged my reckoning, my wife appointed me a place where I should meet her. Having now conveniency and privacy of discourse, we waived everything that tended not to my present design, which was the contrivance of some way to live. At laſt we resolved to take an house and live together. I thought it was as good to be pimp to my own wife, by which means the major part of the gain would be mine, as pimp to another for 12 pence a day and spunging. What we had determined, we soon put in execution; what money she had was laid out in utensils belonging to our trade, as for bedding, linen, chairs and ſtools, &c. The tally-man or broker sells his goods to be paid by 12 d. a pound *per* week. The truth of it is, we found of him, but more especially his servants, excellent cuſtomers; for they would for a private favour, cut off a score, sometimes two or three from the tally. Our ſtock being but small, my wife was forced to be both bawd and whore; but our trade increasing, she goes frequently to the carriers, where at laſt she had picked up a couple of very well-featured country-girls, and brings them home, entertaining them as servants; but shewing as much kindness to them as if they had been our neareſt kindred, purposely to induce them to ſtay. The whore, my wife, intended to have sold their maidenheads at a dear rate; but in truth, I ever loved such things too well to put them to sale, having them in my possession. To be sure thereof, I gathered my rose-buds the firſt night, leſt the infeſtious and contagious breath of some Suburbicarian should blaſt them. In four days' time I fitted them for their occupations, leaving the inſtruſtive part thereof to my wife to season them withal. I never saw two young jades underſtand their trade sooner in my life; for in a month's time they could cant indifferently, wheedle moſt cunningly, lie confoundedly, swear desperately, pick a pocket dexterously, dissemble undiscernibly, drink and smoke everlaſtingly, whore insatiately, and brazen out all their aſtions impudently.

Now did I begin to renew my acquaintance with the tribe of rogues, with whom I grew so intimate that I was seldom out of their company, either at home or abroad. To relate all the tricks and rogueries we committed in one half year were an half year's work; therefore, to be short, we were grown so notorious, and so generally taken notice of, that at laſt my wife and her two maids of dishonour were apprehended by the marshal's men, and carried to Bridewell; I myself narrowly escaping by flight. The next day I boldly went to visit them. Methought their beating of hemp became them excellent well; and in troth I'll say this for them, there hath not been seen in that place a more serviceable ſtrong-dock crew for many years. Looking very earneſtly upon that hemp my wife was beating, a deep fit of melancholy seized me, proceeding only from my imagination; for I fancied that very hemp would make that very rope which should put a period to my life.

P

The time of my visiting them fell out on the day of their correction ; understanding so much, I resolved to stay and see them well lashed, I hoped. My wife being manacled, and the whip ready to encircle her waist ; ' Hold,' said I, and then directing myself to the Masters of Bridewell ; ' May it please your Worships, this woman now under correction is the most impudent brazen-faced whore in the whole town. I have known her a long time, ever since, and some small time before she undid her husband, a very honest man, indeed, and had the good report of all his neighbours. But this confident slut could not then be content without her stallion, whom she maintained by what she purloined from her husband, and so utterly ruined him. Since, she hath been the destruction of several, some in their estates, others in their bodily health ; and now so far from being penitent, she glories in nothing more than in the relation of how many she hath undone here and hereafter. Wherefore, I beseech your Worships, for my friend's sake, that good honest man, and for the good of her own soul, add one half-dozen stripes to the number intended, and let them be laid home.' I had no sooner ended my speech, but I vanished immediately.

Just as I was out of the gate, I met with two of my roguing friends, whom the Devil had sent, I think, to waylay me. They were going, it seems, to see some of their doxies that had that day been committed. Being overjoyed to meet me so accidentally, they would needs have me go to the tavern with them. Over a glass of wine we consulted about divers matters, no goodness to be sure ; the result whereof was, that I should go to such an house and try if by any means I could get into it unperceived, and abscond myself in order to my opening the door for them about twelve o'clock. According to the time nominated I went, and with much facility conveyed myself into a lower room, wherein there was a bed, under which I crept, being confident I might lie there securely till all the household were retired to take their rest. After I had lain about some two hours on the ground, there came into this room a servant. I peeped out, and by the light of his candle, saw that which I thought would have distracted me with fear. He was laying the cloth, by which I understood the master of the house intended to sup there. Soon after, meat was brought in and served to the table ; then came five or six persons, who passing divers compliments (all which needless ceremonies at that time, I wished with their inventors were stark naked upon the top of the snowy alps) every one took seats. Had not there been at that time some small prattling children running up and down, and making a noise, the affright their appearance had put me in, would have betrayed me, for my knees knocked so hard one against the other that they made a noise like a mill-clack, or the striking of two marrow-bones together. For my life I could not prevent the palsy from seizing every limb of me.

My cruel fate had so ordered it that there was a small dog in the room, and a cat, both dearly beloved by their mistress ; who would be continually flinging down something or other, which they continually quarrelled about, jealous and envious upon the distribution of their mistress's favours. At length she threw down a small bit ; the cat being somewhat a more nimble servitor and diligent waiter than the dog, took it and ran with it underneath the bed. The dog ran after the cat snarling, endeavouring to affright her, that she might forsake the purchase. The dog approaching near, and too much entrenching upon her right, she puts him in mind of his duty by one scratch with her claw, and chastiseth him for his rashness with two or three more. This so angered him that he made a furious assault upon puss, who defended herself as well as she could ; but at length they closed, and grappling each other, they made a most hideous noise. The spot in which they fought this combat, was underneath the bed, upon my buttocks. The servant that attended, being over-hasty to quell the noise by parting the fray, snatched up the fire shovel, and throws it underneath the bed. Had it hit my nose with the edge, as it did my breech with the handle, I should have had it pared off even with my face. The cat instantly provides for her safety by flight, but the dog still remained behind grumbling, and now and then barking with such eagerness that he became very offensive to the whole company. Wherefore the servant was commanded to drag him forth, which he did, beating him, and throwing him out of doors ; in the meantime I was left in such a condition as if I had been breathing my last.

As soon as the door was opened again the dog came in underneath the bed with more fury than before. This second alarm did my business (or as they vulgarly say, made me do my business) for running fiercely on me, he had bit me by the nose, but that I snatched away my head from him. But not observing the bed-post behind, I thought I had dashed my brains out against it ; fear also having bereft me of my retentive faculty, I did let fly at one and the same time, which made so strange a noise together that they all rose from the table to see what was the matter. Their noses quickly informed them of some part, for the room was presently strongly scented ; looking underneath the bed, they could see poor Jain Perus giving up the ghost (as dying persons usually evacuate their ordure before their departure) they pulling me forth, quickly revived me, roughly handled me, and then beat me till I was near dead again.

Being taken in the present offence, I could expect no other but to be subject to the rigour of their vengeance ; I could make no plea sufficient to stay their fury, or satisfy their revenge. Having fetched a constable, I was carried before a justice of peace, who with little examination caused my *Mittimus* to be drawn, and so I was sent to Newgate. I was no sooner within, and under lock and key, but fetters confined my legs from struggling, and bracelets were clapped upon my arms. The rogues came all flocking about me for their garnish, which I gave them ; some of the genteeler sort added more to it, so that we had abundance of drink. But never did I hear so confused a din of Damn-me and Sink-me : others singing so loud (*alias* roaring) that I thought myself in Hell, and that these were damned souls that roared through extremity of torments. I thought none had been so wicked as myself, till I came among these Hell-hounds. Not a word came from any of their mouths but what was seconded with an oath, cursing their bad stars, and blaspheming.

The misery of this, or any other prison is sufficiently represented, if by nothing else than want of liberty, that rich inheritance of living souls, as it is the greatest of enjoyments next that imperial gem of health, so the want thereof next to sickness must needs be of all other the most bitter. Since then to be confined to the confines of a gaol is to be in part unmanned, entombed alive, what and how great is that wretchedness that is occasioned not only by a want of liberty, but by a continual dread of shameful death ! The terror of this place full of torture is so exasperated by the imagination of a noble mind, that Hell itself cannot contain more exquisite woes and pains, a continuance whereof were sufficient to punish all offences, if the law dispensed with that debt due to justice, the life of the offender. Your companions are none but licentious wretches, souls which daily surround you with their loathsome persons over-spread with scabs and lice. Here sighing is our air, our comfort coldness, our food despair, our music rattling of chains, our recreation the destruction of vermin ; lastly, our expectation death and damnation. The keeper with the grim aspect of his stern countenance makes us tremble with fear of a new martyrdom, whilst the insulting rascal on the tip-toes of his pride need not screw his ill-favoured face to a frown, for he knows not how to look otherwise ; which so dejects the spirits of us poor imprisoned slaves, that the contrition of our looks seems to implore his smiles, whose flinty heart having renounced remorse, casts a defiance in our sad and piteous faces.

I might insist much further, but that I am hastening to get out of the miserable and soul-excruciating prison. One day after I had exonerated nature, I chanced to view the seat, and found that it was no difficult matter to go down the vault by the help of a rope. A trusty friend coming to see me, I told him what I had observed, and what I wanted.

Some three days before the sessions, he brought me rope enough to have hanged us all. Having a respect unto two more, which I honoured for their admirable good parts, I informed them of what I intended ; which presently we put in execution. First I went down, but I could have wished myself up again ; for I was up to the neck, and knew not but I might be deeper ; but to my great comfort I found to the contrary ; the rest descended after me, with the like good success. Having gotten us to an house, in which we could put confidence, we quickly freed ourselves from our iron tackle.

CHAPTER LVI

He and his two comrades (which he had delivered) disguise themselves :
and having been old experienced gamesters, they taught him all the
tricks on cards, by which they usually cheated their cullies or mouths :
also how to nap, palm, or top a die, with all things thereunto belonging

WE had places enough to send to for change of apparel, as rich as we pleased, or as beggarly again on the contrary, according as our design required. Having lain in lavender about a fortnight in this house, not only to sweeten us, but that the rumour of our escape, and search for us might be over, we got ourselves change of habits. Then did we all consult with our looking-glasses for the change of our faces, not suffering our own judgments to pass without the approbation of the rest. In the first place I got me a coal-black periwig (my own hair being flaxen) and a small false beard suitable, with whiskers in the Spanish fashion. It was no great trouble to black my eye-brows every morning ; then clapping a patch on my left eye, stealing out of the room, while my companions were busied about the same thing, not minding me, and coming in again presently, my appearance did put them all into a very strange confusion. I changed my voice, and asked them what they were doing ; and speaking to them in a tone they were not acquainted with, their chops moved incessantly, but the Devil a word I could understand ; they had got a palsy in their jaws by their sudden surprizal. To have observed the several monkey-faces, and baboon-postures, could not but extract laughter from the severest cynic. ' Why don't you answer me, and that quickly, ye sneaking dumb rascals ? ' Looking most piteously one upon the other, expecting who should speak first, at last said one, ' We mean no harm, we are only preparing some things for a mask, which shortly will be presented to the citizens, and we are persons therein concerned.' I could not hold longer, but burſt forth into an excessive laughter, by which they underſtood their miſtake, not without shame enough, to think that the apprehension of danger so slightly grounded, should so terrify them, being ſtruck dumb, and almoſt dead with a panic fear. To be brief, we very well liked the manner of our metamorphosis ; and having borrowed some money as the necessary tools of our intended trade, we adventured abroad.

The firſt mouth we picked up was in the Long Walk by Chriſt-church, upon the account of a wager. There came towards us a young man, who by his garb seemed to be a merchant's man (he afterwards proved so, and his cashier). I stepped to him and said, ' Sir, if it may not be too troublesome to you, I beseech you resolve me one queſtion : this gentleman hath laid an angel with me, and referred the decision thereof to the next that came this way, whether this next adjacent hospital be St. Thomas's, or St. Bartholomew's.' Said the young man, ' I can assure you it is St. Bartholomew's.' ' Why then, friend,' said I, ' you have loſt. Sir, will you be pleased (if it may not be any great hindrance to your present affairs) to accompany us to the next tavern, and participate of the losings, for I scorn to pocket it ? ' He con-descended, and so we went together. We discovered not anything till the sixth pint, and then my friend, as by chance, found a pair of cards in a corner of the window, which he himself had laid there before. ' Here is a pair of cards,' said he, ' come, to pass away the time, let us play for a pint or so.' I really took up my friend : put was the game. I won of him two or three pints, and ever and anon I would drink to the ſtranger, so that now he began to be warmed, and seemed to take delight in our play, looking over my hand, and sometimes prompting me to see him when he did put to me. At laſt my friend played the high game, as the term of art renders it ; that is, he gave me two trays and an ace, and reserved for himself two trays and a deuce. My antagoniſt puts to me. I pretended I knew not what to do, shewed my game to the ſtranger that looked over my shoulder. He jogs me on the elbow. I ſtill delayed. ' Come Sir,' said my opponent, ' what will you do ? I will hold you five pound on these very cards in my hand.' I received the second jog. ' Will you go halves, Sir,' said I ? He answered me, that he would. But alas, we loſt : it could be no otherwise. This so animated the ſtranger that he persuaded me to play again, and that he would go the moiety of every ſtake.

Sometimes 'twas so ordered that I won ; but in fine I loſt forty pound, my cully being half. He would now give over, being much perplexed that he should thus lose his maſter's money ; but that he might forget the condition he was in, we drank round some half a dozen healths ;

so that now I thought it high time to provoke him again to let down his milk by some new trick or ſtratagem.

Now did we fall to the preaching of the parson, a trick on the cards which hath deceived the moſt curious eye and the wariest of men ; with which we gained from our young merchant, the major part of his money.

Laſtly, to the intent we might without any further delay give him an acquittance for the reſt of his money, we drew out some other implements, *viz.* dice fixed for our purpose, as High-fullums, which seldom run any other chance than four, five, and six ; Low-fullums, which run one, two, and three, &c.

By these means we sent him home penniless and heartless, whilſt we drank healths to the confusion of sorrow.

CHAPTER LVII

From hence he goes, by the direction of his comrades, to a new fashion bawdy house : *he describes it, and relates his own success*

UPON the division we found each man's share to amount to 40 *l.* a piece. Being overjoyed at our firſt good success, we resolved to return thanks for our good fortunes in some private meeting-house, where we might have a siſter to assiſt in the carrying on the work of the day. The Devil in all societies never wants his factor, or one to solicit his business ; for, I had no sooner intimated my desires, but one of my rope-brokers gave me information of a place fit for that purpose, and that the like was not anywhere to be found. Being pricked on with the desire of novelty, and to underſtand the curiosities therein, I went according to my directions solely ; for company in such designs commonly fruſtrates expectations.

They advised me when I came to the door, to pretend I came to enquire out lodgings. At the firſt, I verily thought myself abused by these rogues, or miſtaken in the house, when I saw a porter ſtanding at the door with his tip-ſtaff. To undeceive myself, I confidently, yet civilly asked him whether there were any lodgings to be let there ? ' Yes Sir,' said he, ' which you may view if you will give yourself the trouble of walking in.' I had no sooner entered the door but I was met by a grave matron, who readily underſtood (as I conceived) my approach, by her sentinels above in the windows. ' Madam,' said I, ' I am informed that here are lodgings to be let.' ' There is so, Sir,' said she ; and with that conducted me into her parlour, which was gallantly furnished, there to take a stricter view of me, as to my person, but more especially my garb, by which she might partly judge how well lined my pockets were.

After the resolution of some trivial questions, for discourse sake, she was so well satisfied in me that she shewed me the way up one pair of stairs, into a very large and fair dining-room hung with rich tapestry, and adorned round with excellent pictures, the effigies of divers ladies (as I took them to be) renowned and celebrated in all ages, for the fairest and most beautiful of that sex. A servant brought us up immediately after our entry into that room a bottle of sack, without any order given, as I could perceive; out of which the old gentlewoman drank to me, expressing my welcome. For want of other discourse, because we were both silent a while, for I was contemplating her face, in which I could then see still the goodly ruins of a beautiful and handsome countenance; ' Sir,' said she, ' as you are a gentleman, you may have some knowledge in that noble art of limning, since for its excellency it is in these our days (and hath been in most ages) much studied by the gentry of this nation; wherefore, your judgment, Sir, which of all these pictures is the best drawn, or according to the rules of physiognomy, hath the best features?' ' Madam,' said I, ' I shall freely give you my judgment; which is this, in my opinion (pointing at one), for she hath a full large front, her arched eyebrows are thick and black, without any straggling hairs; her eyes are of the same colour, and by their intuitive faculty seem to penetrate that which they look on; passing her cheeks, which carry in them an excellent air, and her nose, which is neither too long nor too short, view her lips, whose plumpness and redness resemble a double cherry; and then for the dimples in her cheeks and chin, I could make them the subject of an whole day's discourse. What might be said more of this representation, I shall waive, wishing myself no greater happiness than to discourse the rest with the real substance.' ' Which is not impossible, Sir, if you can have but the faith to believe your own eyes '; and so instantly thereupon withdrew herself, leaving me amazed at what I had already seen, my heart the mean time beating an alarm to my passions, to be all in readiness at the approach of this celestial creature.

Hearing a rustling of silks, I drew my eyes off the picture, and looking towards the door, there I saw enter an angel; for I could not believe there could be so much perfection in any one mortal. With profound reverence I stood at a distance, admiring, or rather adoring her person, till she smilingly and familiarly desired me to sit down. Being come to myself, I could talk to her; and in half an hour, confidence had repossessed her ancient seat in me. It will not only take up too much time, but also offend the ears of the modest Reader, here to insert what discourses we had ; therefore I shall waive them, and come to the conclusion.

'Sir,' said she, ' I question not but that you are acquainted with the customs of the house.' I protested to her, I was altogether ignorant. ' Why, you know that you may call for what wine you please, not exceeding four bottles ; and if you please to eat, you shall have some choice bit suitable to the season, &c. If you stay not all night, your expense shall be but forty shillings, and you shall have to boot, the enjoyment of a mistress besides ; but if you stay all night, then thus must you do ' (and with that she drew forth ten pieces of gold) ' whether you fancy me or any else, that matters not, you must deposit before you go to bed ten pound, laying it underneath your own head, and for every kiss, &c., take a piece back again, and if you draw in this manner all your own stake, you may next day be dismissed with a great deal of applause, without expending a penny, but what you shall be pleased to distribute voluntarily among the servants.'

I was stark mad to be at it, and so impatient that I instantly told out ten pieces. Telling my money the next morning, I found I had eight pound of my ten, but I deserved to have had my money trebled : however, for the present, I thought forty shillings was never better spent, nor eight husbanded with so much recreation and delight. By her I understood what manner of cattle they were that frequented that house, though prostitutes and freebooters, yet such as scorned a piece of country dirt : some were persons of no mean quality, which came thither to satisfy (what was impossible to do) their insatiate lusts, and therefore enacted that law or custom of depositing ten pieces, merely to incite such who were confident of themselves to make trial of their skill for the lucre of gain ; and to the intent that it might not be discovered, either by their husbands or such relations or friends that had received causes of jealousy, they had their peeping-holes, where they might plainly and fully see such who came upon the like account. If the gentleman was unknown to that gentlewoman whose picture he elected to bear him company that night, she with much freedom would appear, and tender herself as the subject of his pleasure ; otherwise abscond herself. If so, and the gentleman press hard for a sight of her the picture represented, why then Madam Bawd finds some excuse or other, as that picture she bought casually at second-hand as she passed through Long Lane, or that it was the gift of some friend of hers ; with many other fictions, merely to make him desist from the pursuance of his desires.

Being very much pleased in the satisfaction of my fancy, I took my

leave, not without some acknowledgment thereof, in these consequent
lines.

What is a *bawdy-house*? I fain would know :
It is a thing appears so by the shew.
Is that a *brothel*, or an house of ſtate,
Where tip-ſtaff porters do attend the gate ?
Then there are many noble ones I see,
And palaces may courts of bawdry be.
This was a ſtately house, and yet was such ;
In ſtately houses ladies take a touch.
It muſt be so, th' have little else to do,
Than ſtudy how to answer those that woo.
Such pamper'd flesh muſt yield, and few gainsays
Their own luſts motions, but with formal nays ;
Rather than want that satisfaction, moſt
Stick not to purchase it, though at the coſt
Of health and wealth, delighting thus in sense,
They never think too much the recompence. '
Why should they then fond souls rail at an whore,
Since they themselves are on that very score ?
And damn all *brothels*, too to Hell ; but ſtay
What house is not a *brothel-house* I pray ?
Many I've seen, with this none can compare ;
A new exchange where ladies sell their ware
To none ; they scorn thereon to set a price,
But leave it solely to the chapman's choice.
No sale-shop, but a game at *In* and *In* ;
Throw *In* and *In* but ten times, and you win.
Here by a female council 'twas judg'd fit,
He that reaps pleasure here, muſt pay for it ;
Not with his purse, so much as brawny back,
Solely affecting such who hold them tack.
And to provoke men on, no want of wine ;
Nay, all delights do here in one combine
To raise men's fancy, that he may do o'er
That thing he did but even then before.
Her rosy dimpled cheeks, vermilion lips,
Did blush to see her ivory thighs and hips :
Her round soft belly swelled with pride below
Like a small hill 'twas overspread with snow :
Let a warm hand but touch it, and it will
Its moiſture into pearly drops diſtil ;
We kiſt and parted, I sigh'd, she did sob ;
She for her luſty *lad*, I for my *Mob*.

CHAPTER LVIII

He finds out his two comrades (the gamesters) *and after some consultation had, they resolved to re-assume their* quondam *trade of* padding, *are taken, and committed to* Newgate

FROM this house of pleasure (where I must ingenuously confess I never received more for so little expense), I went in search of my two gamesters, whom casually I met. The next tavern was our council-chamber, where wine was the dictator. We there unanimously concluded it was a thing beneath us to pick up here and there crowns or angels but resolved on have-at-all, knowing that a five hours' adventure might make us possessors of 500 *l.* With this resolution we went and bought us horses, with all things requisite for our intended expedition. Being all ready and well prepared, we took our leave of London for a while. We had not rid above fifteen miles, but we baited ; the hostler knowing me, and what designs I had formerly been upon, and imagining I was steering the same course, whispered me in the ear that he had a desire to speak with me instantly. Taking my opportunity, under the pretence of looking to my horse, he informed me that there were three within, drinking, that on the next morning would travel such a road, and that they had a great charge with them. I thanked him, bidding him come to my chamber at night, where I would discourse farther with him. Then he gave me a summary account of all ; and after a smart drinking bout, with promises to him of reward if we prospered, we betook ourselves to our rest.

In the morning, very early, we called for our horses, and rid in that very road through which those three travellers were to pass, where we planted ourselves very conveniently. About three hours after, we could discern them at a distance. By that time we had made ourselves ready, they were at hand ; just at the bottom of a small hill we bid them stand. They asked us to what intent. We told them that we were younger brothers, and wanted money, and therefore must borrow some of them. With that, they all in an instant drew their swords ; being not unprovided with pocket-pistols, we fired at them, and they again at us. We were all at level coil, and very equally matched ; the second shot killed my horse, and a fourth bereaved my consort of life ; the third rogue ran away.

Being in a labyrinth of perplexity, I thought it the best way to sell my life at as dear a rate as I could (knowing very well that if I were taken I should be hanged). I fought with my sword as long as I could stand upon my legs, wounding both them and their horses ; but at laſt one unhappily ran me through the sword-hand, and thereupon I was disarmed. I was carried by them before the next juſtice of peace, whom they enquired out, and by a *Mittimus* was committed. I could not now expeſt anything but death ; but the next news I heard was, that I muſt be removed to Newgate, there being other things to be alleged to my charge. I was mounted again, in order to my removal, but very ill horsed, being bound thereunto and pinioned. My greateſt grief when I came into London ſtreets was to hear the various descants of the good women on me ; some saying, what a pity it is such an handsome young man should come to the gallows so soon ? Others judged I had deserved it, otherwise I should not have rid to town in that poſture pinioned and so attended with a guard. As soon as the keeper saw me, leaping for joy, ' O Sir, are you come again ? We will take care that you shall not be any more annoyed with smells proceeding from the vault ' ; and so without more ado, laid as much iron on me as there is in some smith's shops, and confined me close prisoner to the dungeon.

> Which made me curse those aſts the Fates have done,
> To cause a setting ere a rising Sun :
> But since my doom is now decreed by Fate,
> I muſt indur't, repentance is too late.

CHAPTER LIX

He much condemns the follies of his paſt aſtions, and in token of his unfeigned repentance, gives some general inſtruſtions to his countrymen, firſt how to know padders on the road, by infallible signs : with other remarks worthy the observation of any traveller, laid down in some consequent chapters

BEING in this terreſtrial Hell (where darkness, horror and despair surrounded me), my conscience ſtarted out of her dead sleep, and demanded of me a severe account of what I had done. My guilt was such I had not a word to speak for myself, but wished my produſtion (as my aſtions were) inhuman. What did not then the apprehension of an approaching and unavoidable death suggeſt to my thoughts ? To have only died (though with the moſt exquisite, terrifying, and soul-excruciating tortures) was not a thing the spirit of man should shrink at ; but the consideration of an eternal punishment hereafter, juſtly infliſted on such who have offended an infinite God, absolutely diſtraſted me. So that methought I already heard the howls and hollow groans of damned souls, which add to the weight of their everlasting misery.

Having somewhat appeased my enraged conscience by a faithful promise and constant resolution to lead a new life, if I should escape the danger of the Law, I determined with myself to shew the first-fruits of my reformation by publishing something to the world that might serve as a guide for travellers, how they might pass in safety on their way. To that purpose I acquainted my keeper with my good intentions ; but that being no particular profit to him, he valued not the public, and therefore rejected my good motion till I greased his fist, and then I had the accommodation of a candle, pen, ink and paper, &c.

The uncertainty of their attire, various disguises, non-constancy of residence, and changeable names, makes me incapable to do what I would ; therefore I will do what I can (according to my small experience, occasioned by my no long continuance among them). Riding on the road (if you have company) it may be two or three shall overtake you, and seem to be much afraid of you. They will pretend to be even now set upon by half a dozen stout fellows, but that they did beat the rogues, forcing them to fly for safety : and this fiction they use to seal with basket-hilt-oaths. Thus by your answers they will find whether you dare fight ; if not, they will wait an opportunity to act their roguery on you ; which having done, as a reward for what unwillingly you have left them, they will pretend to give you a word shall protect you better than your sword, from any injury shall be done you upon the like account ; but this is nothing else than a mere cheat, and no securing charm ; for we valued not words, when our wants were in pursuit of money. Not but that we used some formal words among ourselves, when ready to seize a prize ; and observing other company, either before or behind, to desist a while, by which we knew what we had to do, and the ignorant travellers suspected no wrong.

CHAPTER LX

What is to be taken heed unto, before the traveller begin his journey

MOST respected country-men, and more especially you who frequently pass the road, the most part of my notorious wicked life having been consumed in all manner of cheats and debauchery, and that in part of late maintained by robbing, seeing now the wretchedness of that course of life, and being sensible of the injury I have done my country, I looked upon myself as bound to satisfy the debt I owe to you, to the uttermoſt of my power ; which reacheth to an aĉt not more satisfaĉtory than good advice how to avoid those dangers which too many of late days have fallen into, since Dammee plumes of feathers came in fashion.

Firſt then, if you carry a charge about you, make it not known to any, and conceal the time of your departure in your own breaſt ; for it is a cuſtom no less common than indiscreet and foolish, among some sort of persons, to blaze abroad among their reputed friends the time of their intended journey, and vaingloriously make them acquainted with what considerable sums they should carry with them. By this means the son hath oftentimes betrayed the father, and one friend another, by informing or complotting with some of the padding society, the discoverer sharing (for giving notice of the prize) one quarter or more of the gain he betrays, when but for this foolish humour they had not been waylaid. Again, have a special care, both of the hoſtler, chamberlain and hoſt himself. The two firſt the thief is sure to bribe ; and the laſt, in expeĉtation of a share with them (as it is so ordered) or in hopes that the major part of what they get shall be profusely spent in his house, gives them items where the booty lies.

Especially be sure on the road to associate with none but such as you find inclined rather to leave your company than keep it ; for they are very suspicious persons, and oftentimes prove dangerous, that press into your society, and are very inquisitive to know whither you intend spinning out the time with many impertinent queſtions. But if you would know whether the ſtrangers' intentions be honeſtly inclined, take occasion to make some ſtay. Observe you in the mean time their motion ; for if they make an halt, or alight, so that you may overtake them, follow at a diſtance ; but if their pace be so slow that you needs muſt overtake them, look about you, and provide for your safety ; for there is no surer symptom of an highwayman than such purposed delays.

The other usual marks of such moths be these ; they commonly throw a great leaguer-cloak over their shoulders, covering their faces, or else they have visibly disguised their faces in some manner òr other. Now of late they find very useful a vizard, in every respeĉt (but for the largeness) like the *a-la-mode* vizard-masks so much worn by gentlewomen who endeavour to conceal the shame of their wanton aĉtions by absconding their faces. If you meet with any who have none of these things, as soon as they come somewhat near you, fix your eye full in their face : if they turn their heads from you, keep your diſtance, and ride from them with what expedition you can. But being surprized by any you know, be very careful that you discover it not to them ; for these desperadoes never think themselves secure till they have prevented your giving intelligence, by cutting asunder the thread of your life.

Observe whether their beards and hair of their head agree in a colour, and are not counterfeit ; and be sure to beware of him that rides in a mountier cap, and of such as whisper oft ; or of any one single person that intrudes into your company, for that is one way they have to ensnare the traveller. He will tell you a great many merry and facetious stories, merely to ingratiate himself with you ; which having obtained, he shews himself more than ordinary civil, and so fearful of anything that may prejudice his new acquaintance that he no sooner espies two riding toward them, but he apparently trembles, and will question his new friends what charge they have about them. If little, the best way were to yield to these approaching persons, if thieves, rather than hazard a life ; but if it be anything considerable, he will presently vow to be true to them, and rather than they should come to any danger or loss, he will fight with them as long as he hath breath.

These so causelessly suspected, were perhaps downright honest fellows, but before they had travelled five miles further, 'tis ten to one but they overtake two or three more, one it may be riding aside with twists of hay instead of boots, it may be with a fork, bill, or goad in his hand, like a country boor. It may be your newly-entertained treacherous friend will tell you that he will make good sport with this country bumpkin, and so to that purpose ask him some foolish impertinent question, which the other shall answer as ridiculously ; so spinning out the time till a convenient place and a fit opportunity serve ; then shall this pretended friend seize one of you himself, and my hedge-creeper turn hector, and lay hold on another : and now will it be in vain for you to strive, for nothing but money will ransom you out of their hands.

CHAPTER LXI

Instructions in what manner, at what time, and what road is most safe to ride

THERE are so many ways to rob the innocent, that it behoveth every man to be very circumspect, how, when, and where he rides. If you have a quantity of money about you, choose rather to ride by night than day ; for by this means you are freed from any horseman or cutter whatever. But this course cannot seal your protection from base sheep-stealing penny-rogues, the baseness and lowness of whose spirits will stoop for a noble, though they hang for their pains. Therefore take heed of their long poles, and that they do not suddenly ſtart out and lay hold on your bridle. As for the nobler sort of rogues, this they believe as an undeniable maxim, that none will ride by night that are worth the robbing. Besides, they are obliged to take their inn betimes, leſt through miſtruſt they should be apprehended. Moreover, they hardly dare adventure in the dark, because they cannot discern what dangerous defences the assailed have, as piſtols, or other private weapons in readiness, nor see their own advantages : and withal, it will be no difficult matter to convey in the obscurity of the night, what they have undiscovered, into some ditch. Choose to travel in by-roads, for it is a general rule with highwaymen to keep their ſtation on the greateſt roads, that of the number that pass by they may seleᶜt such as they think will prove the richeſt booties. Here now as a corollary, take notice of a foolish cuſtom ; some when they ride by any place that commonly speaks danger will buſtle up together side by side ; which is the usual overthrow of such. Wherefore take my counsel here, when ere you ride, in fear especially, ride far asunder, at leaſt a ſtone's throw. By so doing none durſt set upon you, fearing leſt this ſtraggling order give some leave to escape undoubtedly, and so raise the country in their pursuit.

CHAPTER LXII

How a man is to behave himself if beset or surprized

WHEN the rogue bids you ſtand, look not about as if amazed, or hoping for a rescue ; for this doth but encourage them to the height of resolution and expedition ; but looking ſternly, as if fear were a ſtranger to you, making your brow the throne of rage and fury, draw, and undauntedly tell them that though you have but little, yet you would willingly sacrifice your life rather than lose a penny ; and add ten more to it (if you had them) than have your reputation ſtained with cowardice. This is the readieſt and moſt certain way to save both your money and credit ; for they fighting with a guilty conscience within and without, againſt country, law, and juſtice, if nobly a man resiſts (this I know experimentally) the ſtouteſt, and moſt undaunted, and higheſt spirit of them all will ſtoop to discouragement.

Some I have known, that durſt out-brave the roaring cannon to the mouth, yet their courage has found an alteration when on this account they have met with a bold and nobly resolved antagoniſt. But if by your own negligence, and the malevolency of fortune, the pleasure of your journey is eclipsed and clouded by a sudden surprizal, and that you see no hopes but that you muſt yield, be not so unwise as to ſtrive when it is too late, but give them the beſt words you can ; and rack your wits to please their ear, moſt devoutly wishing you had more money to supply their present occasions ; and so banishing all dejeƈtedness from your looks, deliver some, and so perhaps they will let you pass without further search.

If they make a second offer, yield freely to it ; then it may be they will sift you soundly. Never in that time lay your hand near your money, and seeming fearless, it will be a means to make their suspicion of a greater sum to vanish. This I have known myself, that when I have taken so much as pleased me well, by men's fear I have had grounds to think they had more, and so made me research ; laying my hand but near the place where they had concealed the reſt, suddenly would they cry out that they were undone, when as yet I had found nothing ; but by their foolish and undiscreet carriage I have found the remainder, which otherwise might have been secure and safe from me.

CHAPTER LXIII

Direƈtions, if robbed, how to follow the thieves ; which way to set Hue and Cry *after them ; how to coaſt, and where to find them*

IF you are robbed, there is no help but to endeavour to surprize the thieves by a ſtriƈt pursuit. Therefore let no Remora or delay deter you from obtaining your wish, and so seize them that so lately seized you. In the firſt place, scour the next road, not ſtraight before, but either on the right or left hand ; for they know Hue and Cries never cross the passages, but go ſtraight along. If in so doing you miss them, then conclude they are sheltered in some inn which you have passed, and therefore you muſt set some careful spies, with a sufficient assiſtance near at hand, and be confident you will see them come that way, without the leaſt apprehension of fear, or fear of apprehension. But this observe, that if they light of any considerable sum, then do they ride that night to their general rendezvous in London, which is too sure a shelter for them.

But observably take notice, for here is as eminent an example of their subtlety as any ever the Devil enriched their knowledge with ; if you are robbed in the eaſtern quarter, pursue them not in the direƈt road to London with Hue and Cry, for by some other way they are fled ; but haſte to the City, and in Weſtminſter, Holborn, the Strand and Covent Garden search speedily, for there they are. If northward they light on

Q

you, then to Southwark, the Bankside, or Lambeth they are gone ; and when you find anyone, seize all with him, for they are all companions that are together.

CHAPTER LXIV

Cordial advice, and infallible inſtruſtions for the innkeeper, *how to know thieves from his honeſt gueſts*

METHINKS the many tragical examples of innkeepers who have harboured and countenanced thieves were sufficient (I should think) to deter those that survive from doing the like ; wherefore my advice to them in general is, that their chiefeſt care be not to wink at any such life-deſtroying aſtions for hope of gain, leſt that sweet be imbittered by future trouble and disgrace. That you may know them, observe these rules : Firſt, they are extraordinary curious about their horses ; they will have them as ſtrangely dressed, as ſtrangely fed, with mashes, bread, flesh, and mingled provender, and that in an unusual quantity. If any wonder at the extraordinary feeding of their horses, they will endeavour to palliate their design therein by telling that their tricks and good abilities deserve it : nay, sometimes they will boaſt that their worthy services will soon repay the coſt ; using the like dark words to that effeſt, which are palpable grounds for suspicion.

It is their cuſtom likewise to ask, Whose horse is that ? or, What is the owner thereof ſtanding by ? of what funſtion or quality ? whither he intends to travel ? how far, and when ? Observe again, that their cloak-bags are for the moſt part empty, carrying them only but to make a show. Next, the chamberlain conduſting them to their chamber, he is at once dismissed ; but let him hearken, and if they are highwaymen, 'tis ten to one but they fall to share what they have purchased that day ; and he shall see every one taking his dividend, as well as hear the money, if he but narrowly pry into the chamber. This they never defer, leſt he which hath the purse should cheat the reſt.

But above all, for their discovery, make this trial ; Cause one to knock haſtily at the gate, giving him inſtruſtions in the meantime that attends on them to observe their carriage then, and he shall see them ſtart and ſtare in each other's face with ghaſtly looks, being ſtruck with fear and amazement. Speak so that they may hear you, seemingly to some or other in the house, asking what officers those are ? what is their business ? or whom do they look for ? or the like. If they seem much frighted, bid them fear not, for none shall search where they are, to offer them any injury ; and that they are as safe with him, as in a well fortified castle. By this means you may pry into their private thoughts and actions so far as that you may gather, not only substantial grounds for more than bare conjectures, but it may be they will confess something too, desiring your concealment and succour, and they shall think themselves for ever engaged. After this you may use your own discretion.

Then again, you may perceive by their loitering and disregard of time, what they expect ; for they only bait but to observe what purchase they can see pass by ; which when they have espied, they will pretend immediate business calls them to be gone, and so mount in great haste. Again, when they come to an inn to lodge, they commonly come in divided, or in several companies, frustrating the Hue and Cry by their number : besides, if one part be surprized, the other may escape ; and when the residue comes in, they seem as strangers one to the other, enquiring of mine host what their companions are, what countrymen, whether he knows them ? And if they find he hath suspicion of any of them, they will feign some business that necessitates their speedy departure. But if you take them for honest men, as they met by seeming chance in your kitchin, so after some formal civil salutations and drinking together, they soon became acquainted, and before they part, shew much familiarity.

Thus as I was farther endeavouring to lay open their devices and deceits, to repair what wrong my country had sustained by me, when word was brought me that I must immediately appear at the bar, and there answer what should be objected against me ; and it was but just that I should be now exposed to the law of justice, since I had so often rejected and slighted the law of mercy.

CHAPTER LXV

He receives sentence of condemnation : he thereupon seriously contemplates death, and considers eternity

APPEARING at the sessions, and seeing so many of my adversaries ready to give in their evidence against me, I concluded myself a leman ; my very countenance betrayed both my thoughts of guilt and despair. In short, I received sentence of death, to be hanged at Tyburn by the neck till I was dead. I thought these sad tidings would have deprived me of my life, and so have saved the hangman a labour. All the way I went back to Newgate I fancied nothing but gibbets stood in my way, and that I saw no other trades but cordwinders.

Being entered the prison, I was forthwith put into the dungeon, laden with shackles. I had not been many hours there before a charitable physician of the soul, I mean a minister, came to visit me, who advised me to repent, since it was high time ; and endeavouring to disburden my conscience by extracting from me a general ingenuous confession of what enormous crimes I had committed. Finding this person to have no other design, but merely for my soul's sake, I dissected the actions of my whole life, not omitting anything that might be accounted sinful. He was amazed to hear such notorious roguery in one man, and so young ; wherefore, before he applied any cordial, he administered his corrosives, and so thoroughly searched every corner of my heart that there was nothing hid from him. In the first place, he made me sensible of the wickedness of my life, and that every, nay, the least evil action deserved the loss of eternal and inexpressible happiness, and instead thereof, torments everlasting and intolerable. It will take up too much time to give an account of every thing this pious man alleged for my information, contrition, and consolation. So effectually and powerfully he delivered his divine message that the obdurateness of my heart was able to hold out no longer, but melting into tears, was willing to have its flintiness broken by the hammer of Sacred Writ.

Finding me in so good a temper, he left me to God and myself for the perfecting of that work he had so hopefully and successfully begun. I began to consider what I was, only a statue of dust kneaded with tears, and moved by the hid engines of restless passions ; a clod of earth, which the shortest fever can burn to ashes, and the least shower of rheums wash away to nothing. And yet I made as great a noise in the world as if both the globes (those glorious twins) had been unwombed from that formless chaos by the midwifery of my wit. All my actions were attended with so much success, and so answerable to my desires, as if I had been one of Heaven's privy-counsellors ; which swelled me up with so much arrogance that I spake thunder, looked lightning, and breathed destruction ; and by the eloquence of my own vanity I persuaded myself that the machinations of my brain were able to unhinge the poles. But it was otherwise decreed, that the ministers of justice should put a period to my boundless pride, to make me know I am but a man, and that mortal too. And having but a short time to live, I thought it very requisite to think of that which must shortly be the means to convey me either to bliss or woe ; by so doing, I seized on death before it seized on me. It was the fittest subject I could busy my soul about, for what more heavenly, than the thought of immortality ? and what so necessary, as the thought of death ? Seneca saith, when he was a young man he studied to live well ; when aged how to die well : but I never practised

Artem bene vivendi, and therefore am so ignorant in *Arte bene moriendi ;* which makes me so fearful that I know not how to be careful of not being found unprepared. Methinks I already hear that doleful saying, *Ite imparata in paratum.*

My sole companions were now despair and fear, for the king of fear is death ; and indeed there is nothing absolutely fearful, but what tends to death, and I am confident, the fear of death is worse than the pains of death ; for fear of death kills us often, whereas death itself can do it but once. Life would not be troubled with too much care, nor death with too much fear, because fears betray, and cares disorder those succours which reason would afford to both ; and though some say he is more sorrowful than is necessary, that is sorrowful before there is necessity, yet that soul cannot be in a good condition, so long as it fears to think of dying. But did I not sorrow now, and juſtly fear that messenger that muſt bring me before the tribunal of Heaven, I should have too little time to wash away so many black spots, especially having nothing but objects of terror and amazement before my eyes ; but I never needed have feared what I should suffer when dead, if I had not deserved it whilſt I lived. Life is not alike to all men. To such a wicked wretch as I am, the beſt had been that I never had been, and the next beſt were to live long. In this condition, it was ill for me that I was born, worse for me that I muſt die ; for without unfeigned repentance, this dying life will bring me to a living death ; whereas a good man is otherwise minded, he counts his end the beſt of his being, for that brings him to the fruition of his hope. Could death end misery, it should be the greateſt happiness I would wish : but my conscience will not let me lie, for I fear the end of my present miseries will be but the beginning of worse ; yea, such as death itself cannot terminate.

Now came into my mind the consideration of eternity ; and with it, I remembered how it was represented by the ancients, which very much helped my present contemplation ; which was thus : a vaſt den full of horror, round about which a serpent winds itself, and in the winding bites itself by the tail. At the right hand of this den, ſtands a young man of a moſt beautiful and pleasant countenance, holding in his right hand a bow and two arrows, and in his left an harp. In the entrance sits an old man opposite, and having his eyes very intent on his table-book, writes according to the diſtations of the young man ſtanding by. At the left hand of this den sits a grave matron, gray-headed, and having her eyes always busied. At the mouth hereof are four ſtairs ascending by degrees ; the firſt is of iron, the second of brass, the third of silver, and the laſt of gold. On these are little children sporting up and down, playing, fearless, and inapprehensive of falling. The sight of this emblem of eternity inculcated into my thoughts this interpretation : The den, which was bottomless, signified to me the incomprehensibility of Eternity ; the circumferating serpent, Time ; the young man, Nature : on earth and hell are her arrows faſtened ; but in heaven there is the harp, fulness of joy, and pleasures inexpressible. The old man I looked upon to be Fate ; the grave matron, Providence ; the ſtairs, diſtinct times and ages ; the children running up and down the ſtairs without fear of danger, do signify foolish men and woman, who regardless of their salvation, sport and play with it so long, till they slip into eternity.

So have I been careless of that which should have been my greateſt care, though I knew (but would not know) that the leaſt and lighteſt touch of death were sufficient, in a moment to translate me from Time to Eternity. Were we all to live a thousand years (whereas the executioner is to put a period to my life in one day longer) we should, before we had ran half our course, in our very nonage, apply ourselves to repentance and newness of life. Now, now is the time, every hour, every moment ; now one part of an hour (as I am informed, to my great comfort) may obtain pardon here, which all eternity cannot hereafter. Therefore, let this now be my time (this one day I have left me) to cancel my debts and trespasses againſt heaven, which I can never do in hell fire, in all the years and times to come hereafter.

Let such who have lived as I, in all manner of wickedness, consider what eternity is, which may make them return like the penitent prodigal. What then is Eternity ? It is a circle running back into itself, whose centre is everywhere, and circumference nowhere, that is to say, infinite. It is an orb that hath neither beginning nor ending ; or it is a wheel,

> *Volvitur et volvetur in omne volubilis evum.*

> A wheel that turns, a wheel that turned ever :
> A wheel that turns, and will leave turning never.

Eternity is like a year, continually wheeling about, which returns again to the same point from whence it began, and ſtill wheels about again. It is an ever-running fountain, whither the waters after many turnings flow back again, that they may always flow. It is a bottomless pit, whose revolutions are endless. It may be compared to a snake bowed back unto itself orbicularly, holding its tail in its mouth ; which in its end doth again begin, and never ceaseth to begin. What is Eternity ? It is a duration always present ; it is one perpetual day, which is not divided into that which is paſt, and that which is to come ; or, it is an age of ages, never expiring and never changing ; or, more properly, it is a beginning continuing, never ending, always beginning, in which the blessed always begin a blessed life, in which the damned always die, and after all death and ſtruggling therewith, always begin again to die. As hell torments are eternal, so will the conscience be perpetually tormented with deep and horrid despair for the life paſt ; their worm shall not die. The poets of old alluded to this place, notably in that fiction or fable of Tytius, whom Virgil feigneth, that a flying vulture every day gnaws and tears his liver, which is every night again repaired and made up that every day the vulture may have more matter to prey upon. What is this vulture, but the worm I speak of ? and what is his liver, but the conscience always gnawn and tormented ? Not only this (as he that preached my funeral sermon told me) but all the torments of the damned shall never have end, because there can be no place for satisfaction. For although these inexpressible torments shall continue many millions of years, yet shall there not one hour, no, nor one minute of respite be granted. Let us then be no longer forgetful of ourselves, and so degenerate into beaſts, but seriously consider our end, and what shall come after.

All men are in the way of Eternity, but I am now almoſt at my journey's end : I sit on the ſtairs of Eternity, expecting when one small thruſt shall plunge me into the bottomless pit, where one hour's punishment shall be more grievous (as Thomas a Kempis saith) than 100 years here in the bittereſt of torments. There they are tortured for infinite millions of ages, and are so far from finding an end, as never to be able to hope for any end. The consideration of these things brought me to that pass that I was content to suffer anything in this life, so that I might not suffer in the life to come. Though a king, I should willingly and patiently have endured what Andronicus did, Emperor of the Eaſt ; who (as hiſtory relates) being overcome and taken prisoner by Isaac Angelo, had immediately two great chains of iron put about his neck ; and being laden with fetters, was brought before Isaac, who delivered him over to the rage of the multitude, to be abused at their pleasure. This rabble being incensed and ſtimulated on by revenge, some buffeted him, some baſtinadoed him, others pulled him by the beard, twitching the hair from his head, dashing out his teeth, dragging him in public through the ſtreets. The insolence of women was such, as to fall upon him, leaving the marks of their nails in his imperial face. After all this, they cut off his right hand. Thus maimed and bruised, he was thrown into the dungeon of thieves and robbers, without either attendance, or the leaſt thing necessary to suſtain life. Some few days being passed, they put out one of his eyes : thus mangled, they put upon him an old rotten short coat, shaved his head, set him upon a scabbed camel, with his face towards the tail, put on his head a crown of garlic, made him hold in his hand the camel's tail instead of a sceptre, and so they carried him through the market place very leisurely, with great pomp and triumph. Here did the most impudent crew and base, among the people, like tigers, after an inhuman manner fall upon him, not considering in the least that not three days before he was no less then an emperor, crowned with a royal diadem, whose frowns were inevitable death, was honoured, yea, adored of all men.

Their rage and madness fitted every one with instruments to execute their revenge. Some struck him on the head with sticks, others filled his nostrils with dirt, others squeezed spunges upon his face soaked in human and bestial excrements : some threw stones, others dirt at him. An impudent woman as he passed, came running out with scalding water in her hand, and poured it on his head. All these indignities which they exercised upon this poor emperor did not satisfy their insatiate revenge, but bringing him to the theatre, took him down from the camel, and hung him up by the heels. Yet did he behave himself like a man, by bearing patiently what was inflicted upon him, being never heard to cry out against the cruelty of his fate. All that he was heard to say, was this, which he often repeated, *Domine miserere, Domine miserere.* Thus hanging up, one would have thought their malice should have ceased ; but they spared him not as long as he lived ; for pulling his coat from his body, they tore him with their nails. One more cruel than the rest, ran his sword through his bowels as he was hanging. Two others, to try whose sword was sharpest, cut him and gashed him in several places ; and so ended his life miserably, but was not suffered to be buried.

Oh, that my condition were as Andronicus, to suffer all that man can lay upon me, that I might not perish for ever ! I should be content to be miserable for so short a time, that I may not be miserable to all eternity. Questionless, he could never have suffered such things so constantly and courageously, but that he had eternity in his thoughts ; and were our minds employed about the same subject, any adversity or affliction we should more easily bear.

From the time of my condemnation till Monday morning I slept not, neither did I eat or drink. Then did I hear my passing-bell (having heard the day before my funeral-sermon) every stroke methought carried my soul one degree higher, being confident I had made my peace above. Whilst I was in the depth of meditation, and my soul breathing out this short ejaculation :

> Is there no hope now of relief,
>   In this extremity ?
> Mercy ere now hath sav'd a thief,
>   And may do as much for me

behold a friend came to me (that never visited me during my imprisonment) but now in the time of need brought me a reprieve. When I
looked thereon at first, I could not believe my own eyes ; I thought
I dreamed, or that grief had so distracted me as that I imagined things
that are not. My friend at length cleared up my doubts ; but I shall
tell you this for a truth, I knew not whether I were best accept of this self-
preserving courtesy. For, methought I had so well settled my eternal
concerns as that I had nothing else to do but die.

About a fortnight after, I was sent aboard, in order to my trans-
portation ; my sentence of death being converted into a steven years
banishment.

CHAPTER LXVI

*Being on board he descants on his ensuing misery, yet draws comfort to
himself from the sufferings of others : he relateth how he was freed from
his intended banishment by a double shipwreck : the manner thereof he
amply declareth*

THE ship that was to transport me lay at Woolwich, about the latter
end of Aug. 1650. I was conveyed aboard a lusty ship, a Virginia
merchantman, and was instantly clapped under hatches ; but I knew they
would quickly call me aloft if there was any fighting work ; as such a
thing might easily be, since the sea was nowhere free from such as would
make a prize of what vessels were too weak to contend with them.
Having pen, ink, and paper about me, I busied my thoughts and pen in
contriving consolation for my disquieted and disconsolate mind, thus :

> Why should not I with patience suffer ? some
> Have kissed what brought them to their martyrdom.
> Many a Saint hath suffer'd on a cross ;
> And our good King endured three kingdoms' loss.
> Shall I (fool) then at any cross take grief ?
> *Tyburn's* the way to heaven for many a thief.
> But must I now to sea ? Well, 'tis no matter ;
> Fortune now frowns, though heretofore did flatter.
> Let not my soul despond, since 'tis my hap,
> I'll scorn that *whore*, and trust to *Thetis* lap :
> Though she may foam with anger, and the wind
> May aggravate her passion, I may find
> Her calm again, and set me on that shore,
> Where I may moor, and put to sea no more.
> *Neptune* may shake his *Trident*, and each wave,
> Or tumbling billow may become my *grave*.

A thundring cannon may pronounce my death,
Or a small shot bereave me of my breath :
All which may throng together in full crowds,
To make m'a *winding-sheet* of *tatter'd shrouds*.
The winds shall sing my *requiem*, and my knell
Shall be a peal of ordnance, they shall tell
My angry fates I'm dead, and the sea muſt
Entomb without the form of *duſt to duſt*.
But I hope better things, and do believe,
My good events will make the *furies* grieve.

About the beginning of September following, we set sail for the Downs. As soon as we had weighed anchor, a thick melancholy cloud encompassed my thoughts, and so much sadness seized my spirits as if I had been not so much taking my leave of my dearly beloved country as leaving the world. Though my soul could not foresee the leaſt danger, nor be troubled at the apprehension of what slavery I was to undergo in my exilement ; yet certainly I found this ſtrange anguish and propassion to be ominous, proceeding from something divine, which is able to unriddle the Apocrypha of nature, and made my soul sensible of some approaching mischief.

Having been about 5 days at sea, one morning, juſt as the sun began to gild our hemisphere with his golden rays, the boatswain made us all turn out, and commanded all hands upon deck. Coming aloft, I could not see a man in whose face there was not written the pale charaćters of fear and amazement ; which were the infallible marks of some sudden and ensuing danger. Upon my firſt coming on board I could discern a great many red-nosed fellows (a drunkard's trueſt *indicium*) but the apprehension of present danger had now extinguished all those flaming torches of their faces, without the help of water. The faces, indeed, of the ſtouteſt amongſt us were so altered by this affrightment that we knew not almoſt one another ; losing our natural complexions through the extremity of passion. One was at his prayers, that never till then knew what a prayer was ; another shedding of briny tears, to make room for more salt water. For my own part, I found myself not much moved, having lately made myself acquainted with death. By this time I underſtood what had passed ; that is, our ship had sprung a leak, and was ready to sink.

Seeing every man in that poſture, and that there required means, as well as prayers for our preservation ; ' Come,' said I, ' Gentlemen, let us not thus cry out, and never lend our assiſting hand. Let us to the pump, and let every one be employed in this grand concern.' Whereupon we all unanimously fell to work. But as is usual in such extremes, we were all busy about doing of nothing. What we began we left imperfect, and fell to another, and so perfected nothing to our safety. Some were sent down into the hold, who quickly returned to us with the symptoms of death in their countenances ; for they all with hesitation and quivering of tongue, with words abruptly or half-spoken, signified to us that our ship's wound was incurable, that the leak could not be stopped, but that we must inevitably perish within some minutes.

These words I received as from a death's-head, which I never heard speak before ; and truly his very looks would have sufficiently declared what message he was about to deliver, *viz.* ruin and immediate destruction. Our inexpressible fears bereaved us of the power of counselling one another ; neither did we know what was best to be done. Our master commanded our long boat to be cast out, and withal ordered some eight guns to be fired, which methought resembled so many tolls of my passing bell, when I was designed to pass by St. Sepulchre's Church in a cart, guarded by fellows whose visages were the true resemblance of the Saracen's Head on Snow Hill, for terror, horror, and merciless proceeding ; as to all which, these cannibals will outvie that inhuman and bloody nation. Every man endeavoured to shift for himself, and I amongst the rest (being loth to be drowned alone) leapt short of the boat, and fell into the sea in *Charontis Cymba ;* but necessity then forcing me to use treble diligence to recover myself, with much difficulty I got into the boat. I was no sooner there, but another leaped down upon me, and had like to have beaten the rest of my breath out of my body : which I took kindly enough, for I would have been content to have borne them all on my back, nay, boat and all, so that I might have escaped with life.

We were constrained to leave many of our friends behind us, and committed ourselves to the sea, driving us we knew not whither. Now were all our hopes dashed, as well as ourselves, by the waves ; for we were almost in despair of human help ; for we were left in the wide ocean, which did not at that time wear a smooth brow, but contending with the wind, swelled into prodigious mountains, which every moment threatened our overwhelming. How could we expect safety in an open shallop, when so stately a castle of wood, which we but now lost, could not defend itself, nor preserve us from the insolency of the imperious waves ?

We were many leagues from any shore, having neither compass to guide us, nor provision to sustain us, being as well starved with cold as hunger. Several bags of money we had with us ; but what good could that do us, where there is no exchange ? We could neither eat nor drink it ; neither would it keep us warm, nor purchase our deliverance.

Therefore we may juſtly eſteem of money in its own nature, as an impotent creature, a very cripple, *inutile pondus*, an useless burden. I could not now imagine anything could preserve us, less than a miracle : and as we were all sinful creatures, especially myself, we could not expeƈt that nature should go out of her ordinary way to save us. The waves indeed carried us up to Heaven,

Jam jam taƈturos sidera summa putes.

Neptune sure at this time was very gamesome, for he played at tennis with us poor mortals, making a wave his racket to bandy us up and down like balls. Sometimes he seemed so proud and lofty, being raised so high, as if he had been about to scale Heaven ; which the incensed Deity perceiving, seemed again to throw us down headlong to Hell, for too much ambition and presumption. Yet I could not see but that the extremity of our condition pleaded for us, crying aloud for pity and compassion. I was now silent, committing myself into the hands of providence ; yet verily believing that the inversion of the old proverb appertained to me, that being not born to be hanged, I should be drowned. Commonly we are not so much moved with a clamorous and importunate beggar, who hunts after our alms with open mouth, and makes Hue and Cry after our charity (as if we had robbed him who begs of us) as with the silence of impotent and diseased lazaroes. Their sores speak loudeſt to our affeƈtions ; *Quot vulnera, tot ora ;* each wound is a gaping mouth ſtrenuously imploring mercy ; the sight whereof, cannot but melt the moſt obdurate speƈtator into a charitable compassion. This was our case, our misery was louder than our prayers, and our deplorable condition certainly was more prevalent than our imperfeƈt devotions.

In this moment of death, when we were without the leaſt expeƈtation of any deliverance, the wind chopped about, and drove back one ship that had over-run us. This was unqueſtionably *Digitus Dei*. This ship made towards us, and we, what in us lay, towards it. The wind blew hard, and the insulting sea, that will not admit of pity, rose high upon us ; so that we were forced to lave the water out of the boat with our hats. It was my chance to sit on the weather side ; fain would I have exchanged my place, but such compliments are useless in a ſtorm ; so that I was conſtrained to endure patiently the indignation of my raging enemy. But now began another despair ; for with all our endeavours we could not reach the ship, nor she us, although she hung on the lee to retard her course. Thus our pregnant hopes brought forth nothing but wind and water (for the ship rode on furiously before the wind, and we came after in pursuit of her as slowly as if an hedge-hog had been running with a race horse) ; so that we which before flattered ourselves with an assurance of safety, were as much confounded with a certainty of perishing. In my opinion it is better to have no hopes at all than be disappointed in them : doubtless it did redouble the punishment of Tantalus, to touch what he could not taste. That mariner who seeing a fatal necessity for it, is contented to die in a tempest, would be exceedingly troubled to perish in a haven, *In Portu perire*. In this very condition were we, having a ship near us, but could not board her for stress of weather ; so that ruin attended us, though all the while we looked safety in the face.

Now did it grow dark, whereby we could not see which way to row. Though this was an evil in its own nature, yet accidentally it became our benefit ; for not seeing our danger, we understood it not, but redoubling our strength, we brake through the waves, and by the assistance of a light which was in the ship, we directed our course truly ; and now did we find we were very near her. As soon as we touched her on the lee side, the seamen, with the rest in the boat, being more dexterous in the art of climbing than myself, never regarding their exiled prisoner (whom they ought to have taken charge of) got all up into the ship in a moment, leaving me alone in the boat. By good hap they threw me out a rope (which once had like to have deprived me of my life, but was now the preserver) which I held fast, to keep the boat from staving off. Our boat was half full of water, and the waves dashed it so violently against the ship side that every such stroke struck me down, so that I had like to have been drowned (and did much fear it) in that epitome of the sea. It would have vexed a man in my condition, to escape by swimming over a large river, and coming ashore, to be drowned in a wash-bowl.

At last with much difficulty I got aboard too. The master, merchants, &c. having saved their lives (even miraculously) one would have thought they should not have been so pensive as they were for the loss of their goods. Those which lost much took it very heavily ; those which lost less, their affliction was greater, having lost all. I was the most glad, joy riding in triumph in my cheerful countenance, having lost nothing, neither could I anything, but my life. Having escaped so miraculously, it was unchristian-like to murmur at any loss ; and as ridiculous, as if a man being restored to life, should complain that his winding-sheet had sustained some damage by lying in the grave.

The ship wherein we were was bound for the Canaries, the wind blowing very fair for that coast. The second night after our deliverance, about ten o'clock, having set our watch, we laid ourselves down to rest, with the thoughts of much safety and security. But it was otherwise decreed, for about one o'clock we were forced to use all hands aloft, a most terrible storm beginning to arise, and the wind blew so furiously that before morning we lost our bow-sprit and mizzen. We durst not bear the least sail, but let the ship drive whither the wind and waves pleased ; and before the next night, we could not endure our remaining masts standing, but were necessitated to cut them by the board. Thus we were tumbled up and down for four days, and as many nights, contending with the waves in a pitched battle, not knowing where we were, till our ship struck so violently against a rock that the horrid noise thereof would have even made a dead man startle ; to which, add the hideous cries of the seamen, bearing a part with the whistling winds and roaring sea ; all which together, seemed to me to be the truest representation of the Day of Judgment.

The ship stuck fast so long between two rocks that we had time enough, all of us, to leap out ; the only means left us for our safety. We all got upon a rock, and the morning star having drawn the curtain of the night, we found that we were a very little distance from the shore. Getting thereon, and ranging to and fro, we at last espied a small house, the sight whereof made us direct our footsteps thither, steering our course solely by the compass of our eyes. Being come to the house, the master thereof stood at the door. We addressed ourselves to him in English, but his replications were in Spanish, which we understood not ; wherefore I spake to him in Latin, in which language he answered me *Tam compte, tam prompte*, both quaintly and readily. In that tongue I made a shift to tell him the sad iliad of our misfortunes. This noble Spaniard understood it better by our looks than my relations ; which made such a deep impression in his soul that his gravity could not forbear the shedding of some few tears, so that one would have thought he suffered shipwreck as well as we. He desired us to come into his house, and refresh ourselves. What little meat he had, stewed in a horse-load of herbs, with some pottage only seasoned by a piece of bacon, that had served for that purpose at least a dozen times, he ordered to be set before us. He was no ways sparing of his wine, better than any I ever yet could taste in taverns ; this good man being not acquainted with dashings, dulcifyings, &c.

Seeing us eat so heartily, he caused another dish to be provided, which was composed of such variety of creatures that I thought he had served us in as a mess, the first chapter of Genesis. This Ola-podrida was so cooked that the distinction of each creature was sauced out of our knowledge. Having satisfied our hungry stomachs, he dismissed all excepting myself, desiring me to accept of what kindness he could do me, for he confessed he took much pleasure in my society and discourse. I was very well contented to entertain his proffer. In some few days he told me he was to go to sea, being captain of a vessel that lay in Perimbana, a small seafaring town near the place of our shipwreck ; and asking me whether I would go with him to the Indies (whither he was bound) I readily consented, and in some few days after we did sail from thence, to perfect our intended voyage.

CHAPTER LXVII

From Perimbana, *a small maritime town on the* Spanish *coaSt, he sets sail with Captain* Ferdinando Velasquez *bound to the* EaSt *Indies : but by the way meets with three Turkish galleys, and by them is taken, miserably abused, and imprisoned*

AN hour before day we left the port, and sailed along the coaSt before the wind ; about noon we discerned three vessels, whereupon we gave them chase. In less than two hours we got up to them, and then we could easily perceive that they were Turkish galleys ; whereof we were no sooner assured, but we betook ourselves to flight, making to land with all speed possible, to avoid the danger that inevitably threatened us. The Turks underStanding our design, hoiSted up all their sails, and having the wind favourable, bore up to us so close, and getting within a small faulcon shot of us, they discharged their ordnance on us, wherewith they killed eight of our men, and wounded as many more ; and so battered our ship beside that we were forced to throw a great quantity of our lading overboard.

The Turks, in the meanwhile, loSt no time, but grappled us ; we on the other side, who were able to fight, knowing that on our valour and undaunted courage depended our lives, or loss of liberty, with perpetual slavery, resolved to fight it out. With this determination we boarded their admiral, doing very eminent execution ; but being overpowered with numbers, we were so overpressed and wearied that we desiSted from making any further resiStance. For, of 35 men we had at firSt, we had only remaining ten, whereof two died the next day, whom the Turks caused to be cut in pieces or quarters, which they hung at the end of their main-yard for a sign of victory.

Being taken, we were carried by them to a town called Mocha, and received by the governor and inhabitants, who expected and waited the coming of these pirates. In the company was likewise one of the chiefeSt sacerdotal dignity ; and because he had been a little before in pilgrimage at the temple of their Prophet Mahomet in Mecca, he was honoured and eSteemed by all the people as a very holy man. This Mahometan impoStor rid in a triumphant chariot up and down the town, covered all over with silk tapeſtry, and with a deal of ceremonious fopperies beſtowed on the people his benedic̄tion as he passed along, exhorting them to return hearty thanks to their great Prophet for this vic̄tory obtained over us. The inhabitants hearing that we were Chriſtians taken captives, flocked about us ; and being exceedingly transported with choler, fell to beating of us in that cruel manner that I thought it a vain thing to hope to escape alive out of their hands ; and all this, because we owned the names of Chriſtians. When I was in England, I juſtly was sentenced to die for my villainy, and now here only for the bare profession of Chriſtianity, I muſt not be suffered to live. The wicked Cadi (as they called him) inſtigated them on to those outrages they committed ; who made them believe that the worse they dealt with us, the more favour and mercy they should receive from Mahomet hereafter.

We were chained all together, and in that manner were we led in triumph ; and as we passed along, we had our heads washed with women's rose water, thrown down upon us from balconies, with other filth, in derision and contempt of the name of Chriſtian ; wherein every one ſtrived to be moſt forward, being inſtigated thereunto by their prieſt. My sufferings then put me in mind of my former wishes, to be as unfortunate Andronicus, miserably afflic̄ted here, that I might escape eternal torments hereafter. I received in part the effec̄t of my *quondam* wishes, no ways acceptable to my present desires. Having tired themselves in tormenting us till the evening, bound as we were, they clapped us into the dungeon, where we remained 21 days exposed to all kind of misery, having no other provision allowed us than a little oatmeal or rice and water, which was diſtributed to us every morning, what should serve us for that whole day. For variety sake, we had sometimes a small quantity of pease soaked in water.

CHAPTER LXVIII

He is brought forth into the market place, and there put to sale : he is bought by a Jew (a miserable avaricious man) and by a ſtratagem he delivers himself from that maſter : is sold to a Græcian, in heart a Chriſtian : the ship being taken, and his maſter drowned, he escaping to shore by swimming, is at his own liberty

IN the morning the gaoler repairing to us, found two of our miserable companions dead, by reason of their wounds, which were many, and not looked into. This made him haſte to the Guazil or judge, to acquaint him of what had happened ; who upon information given, came to the prison in person, attended with officers and other people : where having caused their irons to be ſtruck off, he ordered their bodies to be dragged through the town, and so caſt in the sea. We that remained were chained altogether, and so led out of prison unto the common place of sale, to be sold to him that should give moſt.

By reason of my ſtrength (which those that looked on might argue, from the ſtraightness and firmness of my limbs, being elevated by the pole above a common or middle ſtature) I was firſt bought by one, whom at the firſt sight I could not well tell whether he was man or devil ; for his complexion was of the same colour as the Devil is usually rendered. To say all in short, he was a Jew. He carried me home to his house, where I no sooner arrived but he marked me for his own. My employment was conſtantly to turn a handmill. If I reſted at any time, though ever so little, the punishment he inflicted on me was three or four blows on either the belly, or soles of my feet ; which were doubled or trebled according as he judged of my offence. My diet was such as only served to keep me alive. In general, he used me so cruelly that becoming desperate, I once thought it better resolutely to cut the thread of my life than spin it out longer in so much wretchedness and misery. Revenge too induced me to the undertaking of this attempt, as knowing him to be the moſt covetous wretch living, and therefore would even hang himself when he should lose what he paid for me.

But considering myself, I made choice of a better expedient, which was to pretend (what I intended not) to kill myself. I made choice of such a time, when I was sure some one or other was set to watch me ; who perceiving that I was about to deſtroy myself, rushed in and prevented me, and went forthwith to inform my maſter of what he had seen ; advising him withal to sell me out of hand, otherwise he would infallibly be a loser by me. My maſter taking notice of my countenance and behaviour, resolved to put his friend's counsel in practice ; and so sold me to another, who fortunately proved a Greek, that in show was Mahometan, but cordially a Chriſtian.

Once more was I delivered from miseries that are hardly to be endured, and was embarqued with my new maſter in a ship bound for the Eaſt Indies. In the course that we held, we sailed with so prosperous a gale that in a very short time we arrived in view of the Fort of Diu ; but seeing several vessels lying before that fort, firing againſt it in an hoſtile manner, we shaped our course to Goa, where we arrived in safety. From hence we sailed unto the River Lugor. Juſt as we were entering its mouth, we saw a great junk coming upon us, which perceiving us to be few in number, and our vessel but small, fell close with

R

our prow on the larboard side ; and then those that were in her, threw
in to us great cramp-irons faſtened unto two long chains, wherewith
they grappled us faſt unto them ; which they had no sooner done, but
incontinently some 70 or 80 Mahometans ſtarted out from under the
hatches, that till then had lain lurking there ; and pouring out their
small-shot upon us, clapped us aboard in an inſtant.

Those that knew what it was to be a slave to the merciless Turks,
leapt into the sea, whereof I was one. We were not far from land, so
that it was not long before I got safe to shore. It was my maſter's
misfortune (and truly I think my unhappiness, for he behaved himself
to me as to one of his familiar friends) being wounded, and ignorant in
swimming, to be entombed in the deep. There were some five or six
more that escaped the danger of their enemies and the sea, that wading
up to the waist in mud, landed in safety ; with these I hid myself in the
next adjacent wood. There was hardly one of us but received some hurt ;
and being now diveſted of all hope of help, we could not forbea tor
unman ourselves by weeping, complaining againſt our hard deſtiny,
that should in so short a time bring us into so sad a disaſter. In this
desolation we spent the remaining tragical part of the day ; but considering with ourselves that the place was Moorish, and full of venomous
creatures, we betook ourselves to the ouse, ſtanding therein up to the
middle.

The next morning, by break of day, we went along by the river side
until we came to a little channel, which we durſt not pass (not knowing
its depth) for fear of lizards, plenty whereof we had sight of therein. We
wandered so long to avoid this and the bogs covered with rushes, which
environed us about, till that we were forced to reſt ourselves, being so
weary and so hungry that we could not go one ſtep farther. In the morning awaking, four of our company lay dead, so that there was only one
remaining to bear me company. I now thought my condition worse
than if I had hung at Tyburn, surrounded with a full jury of fellow-
sufferers. My companion and I, with tears, sang the obsequies of our
dead friends, expeĉting hourly our own dissolution. Their bodies we
covered with a little earth, as well as we could ; for we were then so
feeble that we could hardly ſtir, nay, nor speak. In this place we reſted
ourselves, intending to bear our friends company to their eternal reſt.

Some four hours after this resolution, about sunset, we espied a
barque rowing up the river. Coming near us we hailed her, and proſtrat-
ing ourselves on the ground, beseeched those that were in her to receive
us on board. Amazed to see us in that poſture on our bended knees, and
hands lifted up to Heaven, they ſtopped ; our cries for succour reached
their ears, which obtained commiseration from their hearts ; so

taking us in, they carried us with them to Lugor, where about noon next day we landed.

The people are fearful black like the Devil, whom they superstitiously worship, in the form of a bloody dragon. They have many idols amongst them, which they hold in great esteem, as a ram-goat, a bat, an owl, a snake, or dog, to whom they ceremoniously bow or kneel, grovelling upon the earth, and throwing dust on their faces; they offer rice, roots, herbs, and the like, which is devoured by the witches; these devilish creatures being both feared and esteemed by the savages. The female sex, against the appearance of the new moon, assemble upon a mountain, where turning up their bare bums, they contemptuously defy the Queen of Heaven who hath this despite shewn her, because they suppose her the cause of their monthly courses.

They are much given to novelties, amongst which dogs are of very great value with them; insomuch, that whilst I was there, I saw six slaves exchanged for one European cur. They abound with the choicest of Nature's blessings, as health, strength, and wealth, but are very inhuman and uncivil; for they delight much to feed on man's flesh, eating it with more satisfaction than any other food. Upon my first arrival, I did not rightly understand their meaning by feeling my flesh, but when I was informed that like butchers, they felt my flank to know how fat I was, they never touched me afterwards with their fingers but I fancied myself either boiled or roasted, and that their hands, my bearers, were conveying me to the open sepulchres of their mouths, to be entombed in the gut-rumbling monument of their bellies. Whereas other anthropophagi content their appetites with the flesh of their enemies, these covet most their friends, whom they embowel with much greediness, saying they can no way better express a true affection than to incorporate their dearest friends and relations into themselves, as in love before, now in body, uniting two in one (in my opinion) a bloody sophistry. It is a very truth, of which I was an eye-witness, they have shambles of men's and women's flesh, jointed and cut into several pieces fit for dressing. It is usual for some, either weary of life, or so sick they have no hopes of recovery, to proffer themselves to these inhuman butchers, who returning them thanks, dissect or cut them out into small parcels, and so are sodden and eaten.

It is a custom among them, when they would add to their beauties (deformity) to slash their faces in several places. They adore those two glorious planets, the sun and moon, believing they live in matrimony. They are much addicted to rapine and thievery, and they choose to commit any villainy rather by day than night, because they suppose thereby the moon and stars will never give testimony against them.

Their heads are long, and their hair curled, seeming rather wool than hair. Their ears are very long, being extended by ponderous bawbles they hang there, ſtretching the holes to a great capacity. Both men and women hideously slash their flesh in sundry forms ; their brows, noses, cheeks, arms, breaſts, back, belly, thighs and legs, are pinked and cut in more admirable (than amiable) manner.

They contemn apparel, and indeed, the heat of the climate will not permit them to wear any ; very few have nothing on to cover their secrets. Moſt have but one ſtone, the other is forced away in their infancy, that Venus may not too much allure them from martial exploits : wherefore the women take great delight in ſtrangers. One of them so ſtrongly besieged my modeſty that more for fear than love, I yielded to her incontinency. I was displeased at nothing but the sight of her ; for her flesh, no velvet could be softer.

There are in this place great quantity of lions, which in dark weather use great subtlety to catch and eat some savages. They, again, in the day-time dig pits, and covering them with boughs, do train the courageous lions thither, where they receive deſtruction, eating them to-day, who perhaps were sepulchres to their friends or parents the day before. I have seen these well-bred people descend in a morning from the mountains, adorned with the raw guts of lions or other wild beaſts, serving for an hour or two for chains or neck-laces, and afterwards for their breakfaſt ; of which good cheer, if I would not participate, I might faſt for them. So that my squeamish ſtomach was forced to give entertainment to that unwelcome gueſt, to keep ſtarving out of doors.

The ship that brought us hither was now ready to set sail, being bound for Goa, the maſter whereof was a Portugal, who underſtood Latin and French very well, of which I was not ignorant. I addressed myself to him in the French tongue, desiring him to accept of mine and my comrade's service ; which he condescended to with much willingness. At Goa we ſtayed not long, but from thence · passing towards Surat, a vehement and unexpeſted ſtorm overtook us, for three days raging incessantly, so that those which were acquainted with those parts, very much feared an *Hero-cane*, a tempeſt commonly of thirty days continuance, and of such fury that ships, trees, and houses perish unavoidably in it. Once in nine years, it seems, it fails not to visit them. It chanced that my comrade being heedless and unexperienced in sea-affairs, was washed off by a wave into the sea, and so was buried in the large and deep grave of the vaſt ocean ; a sure treasury for the resurreſtion.

The foulness of the weather forced a junk man-of-war, full of desperate Malabars, a bloody and warlike people, in view of us ; but the seas were too lofty for them to board us. After three watches, the sea changed colour and was calmer ; and by the swimming of many snakes about our vessel, the seamen knew we were not far from shore, landing shortly after safely at Surat.

CHAPTER LXIX

From hence he set sail to Swalley Road, *and so from thence coasted till he arrived at* Delyn, *a Town that belongs to the* Malabars : *he gives an account of what he there saw and observed*

SOME two hours after we set sail, we were becalmed, having not the least breeze of wind, the weather withal being exceeding hot and sultry. At length we arrived in Swalley Road where was riding an English vessel ; there we cast anchor. The Englishmen came aboard of us, whom our captain welcomed with the best of his entertainment. I could not forbear embracing my dear countrymen, shewing them so many demonstrations of joy that by their looks, they seemed to question whether I was in my right wits. Their master's mate calling me aside, asked me how I came to be engaged in this vessel ? How long since I came from England ? with many other questions too tedious here to relate. To all which I gave him such satisfactory answers that he seemed very well pleased. I gave him a summary relation of what I had suffered since my departure from my own country ; the report whereof, seemed to extract much pity from him. In fine, I told him, I had a great desire to see England again, and to that end desired him to make use of what interest he could to remove me into their ship. He promised he would ; and accordingly giving a present to our captain, he so far prevailed upon him to let me go, and persuaded the chief of whom he was concerned withal, to entertain me, which they did with much willingness.

I was so like a seaman in this short time that none could distinguish me from one that received his first rocking in a ship. I carried about me as deep a hue of tarpawlin as the best of them, and there was no term of art belonging to any part of the ship or tackling but what I understood. I could drink water that stunk (as if *stercus humanum* had been steeped two or three days in it) as well as any of them, and eat beef and pork (that stirred as if it had received a second life, and was crawling out of the platter to seek out the rest of his members) I say, I could devour it with as much greediness (scorning that my appetite should be ever again taxed with any of those epithets, either nice or squeamish) as if it had been but nine hours, instead of nine months, in salt. And to make me the more complete, I had forgot to wash either hands or face, or what the use of a comb or shirt was, neither did I know how to undress myself ; or if wet to the skin, to make use of any other means than my natural heat to dry myself. I never looked on a hat or band, but as prodigies.

But to return to my purpose, where I left off. In three days' time we set sail for Swalley Road, ſteering our course from thence, all along the coaſt of India, Deccan, and Malabar. I knew not whither they intended, neither did I care now, as thinking myself safe, being amongſt my friends. On the 20 of April, seven days from our weighing anchor in Swalley Road, we came to an anchor at Delyn, a town of the Malabars. We durſt not land, the people being so treacherous and bloody ; yet we suffered them to come aboard us in their small canoes, selling us for any trifles, coco-nuts, jacks, green pepper, Indian pease, hens, eggs, and the like. They brought us likewise oranges of so pleasant a taſte, the rind vying with the juice which shall become moſt grateful to the palate. We had likewise from them plantanes, a fruit supposed by some to be that which Eve was tempted withal ; if a man gathers them green, yet will they ripen afterwards, coloured with a dainty yellow ; the rind or skin will peel off with much facility ; they melt in the mouth, giving a moſt delicious taſte and relish.

These Malabars are coal black, well limbed, their hair long and curled ; about their heads they only tie a small piece of linen, but about their bodies nothing but a little cloth which covers their secrets. Not-withſtanding their cruelty and inhumanity, we manned out our long boat, and 15, whereof I was one, went ashore, carrying some muskets and swords with us, suspeƈting the worſt. Landing, they fled from us, but not without sending good ſtore of poisoned arrows and darts amongſt us. It is no wonder that these people are so black, for they live under the scorching fire of the Torrid Zone. We returned to our ship, finding it no way safe to ſtay here longer ; next morning hoiſting sail, we came to Canavar, where we met with people more civil. Whereupon we landed, and receiving things from the inhabitants of considerable value, for toys and trifles we gave them in lieu, we resolved to ſtay here a while. The better sort of these people are called Nairoes, whose heads are covered with a low tulipant, and their middles with a parti-coloured plaid, resembling a Scotch plaid. The poorer sort have nothing but a small veil over their privities, wholly naked elsewhere ; which veil or flap the women, in courtesy, will turn aside, and shew a man their *Pudenda*, by way of gratitude for any courtesy received, as if they would render satisfaƈtion with that which could never receive plenary satisfaƈtion itself.

They have a ſtrange cuſtom in their marriages, observed among them

by the highest to the lowest : whoso marrieth is not to have the first
night's embraces with his bride, but is very well contented to bestow
her maidenhead on the Bramini, or priests, who do not always enjoy
it, being glutted with such frequent offerings, and therefore will many
times sell them to strangers. Such a proffer I had once made me, and
with shame I must confess I did accept it, forgetting those sacred vows
I made in Newgate, to live a more pious, strict and sober life. The
bride that night, was placed in one of their fanes, as is customary, the
priest or Bramin coming to her ; but instead thereof, according to agreement between this priestly paynim and myself, I went. I wondered to
find her so low of stature, but I did not much matter it then, minding
something else ; which having performed, I departed. The next
morning I had a great desire to see her, but was amazed to see her so
young, believing it impossible (though I knew the contrary) a child
(for I may so call her, being but seven years of age) could be capable of
man's reception at that tender age. Afterwards, I was informed it was
usual for them to marry so soon : first, being extremely salacious and
lecherous, and as fit, nay, as prone to enjoy man at that age as Europeans
at fourteen. Next, they extremely honour wedlock, insomuch, that if
any of their children die whilst very young, they will hire some
maiden to be married to him, and so lie with him the night after his
decease.

So soon as we arrived (which is a custom they use to all strangers, of
what country soever) we had presented us choice of many virgins ;
our boat-swain choosing one he fancied for a small price, she guided
him to a lodging, where if he would have stayed so long, she would have
performed his domestic affairs, as well at board as bed, discharging
her duty very punctually. But he that undertakes any such thing must
be very wary that he be not venereally familiar with any other woman,
lest that she with whom he hath contracted himself for such a time, doth
recompence his inconstancy with mortal poison. At his departure, her
wages must be paid to her parents ; she returns then with much joy,
and they receive her with as much credit and ostentation. The chiefest
amongst them hold it a very great courtesy if any one will save them the
labour, pain and trouble, by accepting the hymeneal rites of his bride. I
should have told the reader that the Bramins are so much respected and
esteemed by the commonalty that if any of them gets their wives or
daughters with child, they believe that off-spring to be much holier than
their own, being extracted from pagan piety.

Their funerals they celebrate after this manner. Bringing the dead
corpse near to their fanes or churches, they consume it to ashes by fire
made of sweet smelling wood, unto which they add costly perfumes in

aromatic gums and spices. If the only wife (for here they will not hear of polygamy) caſt not herself into the flames voluntarily, they look upon her to be some common proſtitute, having not anything commendable in her natural disposition ; but if she freely commits herself to the flames, with her husband's carcase, she from that noble aₑt (for so it is eſteemed of among these infidels) derives to her memory reputation and glory amongſt her surviving friends and kindred. They are deluded on to this resolution by their Bramins, who persuade them by so doing they shall enjoy variety of perpetual pleasures, in a place that is never diſturbed by alteration of weather, wherein night is banished, there being a continual spring ; neither is there wanting anything that shall ravish each individual sense. This was at firſt a ſtratagem invented by some long headed politician to divert them from murdering their husbands (which they were frequently guilty of, by reason of their extreme lechery and insatiate venery) so by that means they were reduced to that good order, as that they tendered the preservation of their husbands' healths and lives equally with their own. For my part, I could wish the like cuſtom enjoined on all married English females (for the love I bear to my own country) which I am confident would prevent the deſtruₑtion of thousands of well-meaning Chriſtians, which receive a full ſtop in the full career of their lives, either by corrupting their bodies by venomous medicaments adminiſtered by some pretended doₑtor's hand (it may be her ſtallion) unto which he is easily persuaded by the good opinion he hath of his wife's great care and affeₑtion for him : or else his body is poisoned by sucking or drawing in the contagious fumes which proceed from her contaminated body, occasioned by using pluralities for her venereal satisfaₑtion, and so dies of the new consumption.

Or laſtly, by pettish and petulant behaviour, she wearieth him of his life, and at laſt is willing to die that he may be freed, not only from the clamorous noise of her tongue, but that the derision of his neighbours, and scandal that she hath brought upon him, may not reach his ears. That all such might be mindful of their duty, I would have (were it at my disposing) these two lines fixed as a motto to their doors.

A couchant cuckold, and a rampant wife,
Are cop'latives disjunₑtive all their life.

CHAPTER LXX

From Delyn *he sailed to* Zeyloon : *with what he there observed*

THE isle of Zeyloon is very famous, and not far distant from the point of India, called Cape Comrein. It abounds with all sorts of odoriferous and aromatical spices ; the people are pagans, not owning a deity ; some, though, have heard of Christ, and others of Mahomet, but such are rarely to be found. They go naked, not compelled thereunto by want or poverty, but mere heat of the sun. They are great idolators, worshipping things in monstrous shapes. On the top of a high mountain they have set conspicuously the idea of an horrible *Caco-dæmon*, unto which pilgrims from remote parts do resort. And upon this account, a king of Zeyloon coming, once derided this idol ; another time, intending to make a second repetition of his former derision, the king was even frighted out of his wits ; for not only he, but his attendants all saw how this *Dæmon* threatened him for so doing, by shaking a flaming scimitar, and rolling his fiery eyes : from his gaping mouth, issued out fiery flames ; whereat this king returns with as much penitence as amazement, resolving by his due respect and worship for the time to come, to make an atonement for his former errors. For my part, had I not believed there was a Devil, the sight of this horrid monstrous representation would have induced me into the belief that this was one really.

They have in another place a chapel, in which they adore the Devil (whom they call *Deumo*). The height whereof is about three yards, and uncovered ; the wooden entrance is engraven with hellish shapes ; within, their beloved Devil or *Deumo* is enthronized on a brazen mount. From his head issue four great horns, his eyes of an indifferent proportionable bigness, having somewhat a larger circumference than two saucers ; his nose flat ; a mouth like a portcullice, beautified with four tusks, like elephant's teeth ; his hands like claws, and his feet not unlike a monkey's. Beside him stand lesser *Deumos* attending on this grand pagod, some whereof are represented or pictured devouring souls. Every morning the priest washeth them, not departing till he hath craved their malediction ; and when he takes his leave, he is very careful of offending the Devil by shewing his posteriors, and therefore goes from him retrograde, stedfastly fixing his eyes on the idol. 'Tis strange that a rational soul should be so much infatuated as to adore such a monstrous and ridiculous thing.

The people in way of mutual love and amity use to exchange their

wives ; a thing, though much hated by the jealous Spaniard, yet would
be - very acceptable to other Europeans, or else to be rid of them
altogether, who are the daily murderers of their content and quiet.
Polygamy, or plurality of wives is here permitted ; and as the men are
granted the liberty to have more than one wife, so are the women allowed
more than one husband. However, the woman hath the disposal left
her of her children, giving them to him she hath the greatest affection
for ; which he receives, not questioning his interest or right (by generation) unto the infant.

> Elsewhere the Fates decreed a cuckold's lot,
> To keep that child another man begot ;
> And by his joy therein he plainly shews,
> He thanks the man that pay'd those debts he owes :
> But these *She-Blacks* in justice thought it fit,
> That he which got the child, likewise keep it :
> Therefore both love and custom made it so,
> On the true father they the child bestow :
> By which good Law unto each man 'tis known,
> That he doth keep no other child but's own.
> Were this observ'd in *England*, I durst swear,
> Some *what-d'ye-lacks* would heirs to lord's appear ;
> And half of what some own, must be conferr'd
> On such who have a father's name deserv'd.
> These *blacks* do tax our women, for they paint
> The Devil white, and make him seem a saint ;
> To let them know, they are far greater evils :
> For fairest females oft are foulest Devils.

We stayed not long here, but having dispatched what we came for,
we sailed along the coast of Coromandel, and landed at Meliapor. The
people are much after the same complexion of those of Delyn, only a
little more dusky, and go in a manner naked, too. Here are likewise
great store of Bramins, who are very busy and industrious to instruct
these poor ignorant souls in the perfect way to damnation ; for which
they have the honour and estimation of all conferred upon them. We
manned out our long-boat and went ashore ; upon our landing, it was
our hap to be eyewitnesses of one of their funerals, which was performed
after this manner. The husband was carried before the combustible
pile ; his most dearly loving wife closely following after, attended by her
parents and children ; music (such as they have, which I cannot compare
to that of the spheres) playing before, behind, and on each side of her.
She was dressed both neatly and sumptuously, to the height of the rude-
ness of their art ; her head, neck, and arms (not omitting her nose, legs,
and toes) each bedecked and charged with bracelets of silver, with jewels

everywhere about her diſtributed. She carried flowers in her hands, which she disposed of to those she met. The prieſts going backwards before her, shewed her a magical glass, which represented to her sight whatever might be pleasing to her sensual appetite. The Bramin all along inculcating to her thoughts the sense-ravishing and affable joys she shall possess after her decease; at which this poor deluded soul smiled, and seemed to be much transported. We followed them till they came to the fire, which was made of sweet odoriferous wood. As soon as her dead husband was committed to the flames, she voluntarily leapt in after him, incorporating herself with the fire and his ashes. We wondered that the ſtanders-by would permit her thus to deſtroy herself, imagining this rash aČtion proceeded from the ardency of her affeČtion; but perceiving her friends to throw in after her, jewels and many precious things, with much exultation and expressions of joy, we concluded this to be the effeČts of cuſtom. Such as refuse to burn in this manner, are immediately shaven, and are hourly in danger to be murdered by their own issue or kindred, looking upon them as ſtrumpets: and indeed many of them are so audaciously impudent that upon the leaſt diſtaſte, or not having their luxurious expeČtations answered, nothing more intended or endeavoured than the lives of their husbands. They are in these parts so extremely idolatrous, and so over-swayed by the Devil, that they adore a great idol made of copper gilded, whose ſtatue is carried up and down, mounted on a glorious chariot, with eight very large wheels overlaid with gold. The ascent or ſteps to the chariot are very large and capacious, on which sit the prieſts, attended by little young girls, who for devotion sake, proſtitute themselves freely to the heat of any libidinous speČtator; for so doing, they are entitled the pagod's children. A very ſtrange zeal in their bewitched or besotted parents, to deſtinate the off-spring of their bodies, from their nonage, to such an abominable liberty; for by letting them know the use of man so soon, it cannot but be very prejudicial to their bodies, but also inveſt them with the thoughts of perpetual whoring. For that woman that shall admit of more than one to her private embraces, will admit of any upon the like account. Nay, such is their blind zeal and superſtition, that as the chariot passeth, some will voluntarily throw themselves under the wheels, who are crushed in pieces by the weight of the idol and its attendants, suffering death without the benefit of a happy (but to them unhappy) martyrdom.

CHAPTER LXXI

From Zeyloon, *he arrived at* Siam : *what there he saw and observed*

SIAM is a kingdom contiguous to Pegu, a part of the East Indies.
And, as the people are included within the burning zone, therefore
far from being fair ; yet are tall of stature, very strong and valiant, and
generally so straight that few are found among them crooked. Formerly
they were much given to sodomy, to prevent which, 'twas wisely
ordered (though strangely), that the males, as soon as born, should have
a bell of gold (and in it a dried adder's tongue) put through the prepuce
and flesh. When the desire of copulation stimulates any of them, he
presents himself to some expert midwives, who advise him to drink
opium, or some such somniferous potion ; which having done in their
presence, he falls asleep ; during which interval, they remove the bell,
and apply to the orifice from whence it was taken, an unguent, which
affords a speedy cure ; then is he free to make use of such as his fancy
leads him to. The young girls are served in a worse manner ; for as
soon as born, their *Pudenda* is sewed up, and only a small *foramen*, or
passage left, as an aqueduct. About eight or nine she is unstitched, and
it is as great a rarity to find a pure virgin here at ten years old, as to find
a maid at sixteen in most places of France, or its neighbouring countries.
And that these young lecherous fry may be capable of that employment
they are destinated unto, they have potions given them to drink which
have the efficacious power as to distend their *muliebria* to such a capacity
as that (if their bells were withdrawn) their males would find too easy
an entrance.

The women here (still the more to allure the men from that detestable
and unnatural act of sodomy) go naked ; (as little a novelty in these parts,
as for Irish and Scotch to wash their clothes with their feet, their coats,
smock and all tucked up about their middles, though twenty men stand by
as (deriding) spectators). I say, they go naked to their middles, where
the better sort are covered with a fine transparent taffaty or dainty lawn,
which by a cunning device is so made to open, that as they pass along,
the least air discovers all, to all men's immodest views. Their priest,
which they call Tallapoi, are seeming very zealously superstitious.
They somewhat incline to Mahometanism ; for they pretend they will
not drink wine, being forbidden it by their law, yet are abominable
hypocrites ; for, though they wear a sheep-skin with the wool thereon,
not suffering any hair to be on their bodies, and in show lead a chaste
life, yet I found the contrary ; as you shall understand by what passed

between one of them and myself. I being on shore with our ship's crew, I chanced to walk abroad, carrying with me a bottle of Spanish wine.

As I entered into a wood, intending not to adventure too far, there came to me one of these Tallapoi or priests, in the habit aforesaid, with a horn about his neck, resembling a sowgelder's, but much less; with which, I was told, they, with the sound thereof, used to convene the people to hear them preach. This holy infidel espying me, blessed himself (as I guessed by his gesture), and approaching near me, I imagined that he prayed for me, by the elevation of his eyes and hands. As a requital, I proffered him some of my wine; and having tasted thereof, liked it so well that by signs I understood he desired his horn full of me. To tell you the truth, I liked it so well myself that I had no desire to part with one drop more of it; but his importunities so far prevailed that I granted his request; which having obtained, he made no more ado but drank if off, making but one gulp thereof; a thing contrary to the strictness of his profession. After this, he seemed to bless me, and so departed. It was but a little while before he again presented himself to my view; and beckoning to me, I followed him. Coming close up to him, he pointed with his finger to a place, where covertly I espied three maidens (as I supposed) to whom he by signs persuaded me to go. Sitting down amongst them, they entertained me with as much civility as they were endued withal, and courted me after their amorous fashion. One of these was the handsomest that I had seen in those parts; though not to be compared, for form of face, with the homeliest kitchin-stuff wench in London. I dallied with her so long, till that lust conquered my fancy; attempting something, and being in a fair way to it, this satyr Goat-Devil (I can't invent a name bad enough to call him by), presently falls down upon us; and taking me thus unawares, lying on my belly, I was not able to help myself, that he had like to have performed his business. He questionless had effected it, but that the two maidens standing by (no ways ashamed at this most shameful sight) assisted me, pulling him off. I presently started up, and seized him; and tripping up his heels, I laid him on his back. Having so done, I bound him; then taking out my knife, I could not find in my heart to spare him one inch; and that he might not have any witnesses left of what was done, I took away his testicles too. The three young girls fled, fearing my rage and revenge might have extended to them. And fearing myself, that they would give information of what I had done, I fled too to my ship's comrades; and giving them account of what had happened, we all judged it the safest way to go aboard; and so we did, with all expedition possible.

CHAPTER LXXII

From hence he sails to Do-Cerne, *so called by the* Portugals ; *who* Adam-*like, give (or, as I may say, take too much liberty) in imposing names on all new places, and things : by the* Hollanders, *it is called* Mauritius : *its general description*

DO-Cerne or Mauritius, is an isle situate within the Torrid Zone, close by the tropic of Capricorn ; but it is very uncertain unto what part of the world it belongs, participating both of America, and bending towards the Asiatic Seas, from India to Java. This isle aboundeth with what the use of man shall require. The landing looking out at sea, is mountainous ; the circuit of this island is about an hundred miles ; it procreates an healthy and nourishing air. The great quantity of ever-flourishing and fragrant trees doth no less lenify the burning heat, when the sun enters into Capricorn, as helped by the sweet mollifying breath of the North weſt wind, when Sol again adheres to Cancer. Now as the temperature of that body is beſt composed, that participates indifferently of all the elements, which either super-abounding or want-ing, begets defeƈt ; what then is the temperature of this place, which is blessed with, and abounds in all, and abortive in none? Water is here very plentiful, drilling itself from the high rocks and trickling down into the valleys, spreads itself into various meanders, till those sweet and pleasant waters disembogue themselves into the lap of the salt ocean. There is so great a quantity of wood, that we could hardly procure passage. But of those many various trees, we found none so beneficial to us as the Palmeto. This tree is long, ſtraight, and very soft, having neither leaves, boughs, nor branches, save at the top, whereon there is a soft pith, wherein consiſts the sole vegetative of that tree ; which cut out, the Palmeto in a very short time expires. Its taſte is much like a kernel of an hazel-nut ; boiled it is like cabbage.

But the chiefeſt commodity that this tree produceth is the wine which issueth from it, pleasant, and as nourishing as Muskadine or Alligant. Thus we procured some thereof ; coming where two or three grew together, with an auger we bored some small holes in each, which immediately the liquor filled ; then with a small cane or quill we sucked the wine out of one tree ; then we went to another, and from that to the third : by that time we had drained the laſt, the holes in the two former were full again. This course we followed so smartly that in less than an hour three of us were so drunk (whereof I was none of the sobereſt) that had not these trees been near the shore, for aught I know, by the morning we might have feaſted the wild beaſts.

Divers other trees there be, ſtrange both in shape and nature ; one whereof (merely out of curiosity) I muſt needs taſte, which for half an hour so bit or ſtung my tongue as if I had had my mouth full of vitriol, or spirit of salt. It is a comely tree to look on, but brings forth not anything that is good. This tree is in a manner naked too, and the body thereof as soft and penetrable as new cheese. The form of the tree, its uselessness, with that hidden ſting it carries in it, together with its softness ; the laſt of which, invites me to cut these lines therein ; which my knife as easily performed, as to write a man's name with a ſtick on the sand. The lines were these :

> Th'art like a woman, but thou want'ſt her breath ;
> Who's fair, but fruitless, and will ſting to death
> If taſted : would I could blaſt thee with my curse,
> Since woman thou art like, for nothing's worse.

There is another tree, which beareth a cod full of sharp prickles, wherein lies hid a round fruit, in form of a dove's egg ; crack it, and therein contained you shall find a kernel, pleasant in taſte, but poisonous in its operation. My sweet tooth longed for a taſte, and being very toothsome I did eat several ; but it was not long ere my guts were all in an uproar, and were resolved in this mutiny, could they have found way, to charge my mouth with high treason againſt the reſt of my members. But they were at laſt content only to discharge their fury through the poſtern of their microcosm ; which they did so curiously that I was much afraid my guts having spent all their shot, they would have marched out after. I had (in plain English) in less than six hours sixty ſtools, besides purging upwards ; and had not we had a very skilful Dr Chirurgeon of our ship, I had unavoidably perished.

Nature in this island shewed her prodigality of water and wood, corresponding also in everything else a fruitful mother labours to be excellent in. Here she seems to boaſt, not only in the variety of feathered creatures, but in the rareness of that variety, which should I run over but briefly, the subjeɕt is so large, that by some I cannot but be thought too tedious. However, I shall lightly touch thereon. Here, and here only is generated the Dodo ; for rareness of shape contending with the Arabian Phœnix. Her body is round and very fat, the leaſt whereof, commonly weighs above twenty pound. They please the sight more than the appetite, for their flesh is of no nourishment, and very offensive to the ſtomach. By her visage (darting forth melancholy) she seems to be sensible of that injury Nature hath done her, in framing so great a body, and yet useless, but to please the eye ; committing its guidance to complemental wings (for so I'm forced to call them) since they are so small and impotent, that they only serve to prove her an off-spring of the winged tribe.

Here are bats also, as large as goshawks. There is likewise great plenty of fish ; among the reſt of more especial note is the cow-fish ; the head thereof not unlike an elephant's, her eyes are small, her body at full growth about three yards long, and one broad ; her fins exceeding little, her flesh (being an amphibious creature, living as well at land, sometimes, as in the sea) doth taſte much like veal. Some say that this fish doth affeᵭ, and takes much delight in the sight of a man's visage. About this island are flying-fish, dolphins, and sharks. One of our men imprudently swimming one day, the weather being very hot, in our sight a shark came and bit off his leg, and part of his thigh, and he thereupon sunk ; we made out to save him, but before we came, he was drowned. Here are tortoises so great that they will creep with two men's burdens on their backs ; but their pace is so slow that they would make but ill porters, going not above ten yards in two hours, when they make their greateſt speed. The birds here are so unaccuſtomed to frights that I have shot five or six times amongſt a flock, letting the dead ſtill lie, and not one of the surviving did so much as offer to fly. The goats here have more of the politician in them ; for they seldom feed or reſt themselves, but they set out their sentinels.

CHAPTER LXXIII

Hence he sailed for Bantam : *by the way he recounts the danger he had like to have suſtained, by ascending a* burning Mountain

WEIGHING anchor, we ſteered our course for Bantam ; but being much ſtraitened by the way, for want of fresh water, we were compelled to make up to the firſt land we descried. Though the darkness of the night blinded our eyes from such discoveries, yet flames of fire not far diſtant from us, gave us perfeᵭ intelligence that land was not far off. That night we caſt anchor, fearing we might run foul of some rock or shelf. In the morning we saw a large track of land before us, not knowing what place it should be. Our captain commanded the long boat to be manned out, to procure water, if any good were there ; amongſt the reſt, I went for one ; for I was very greedy to observe novelties. Coming on shore, and seeing this hill now and then belch out flames, by my persuasions I made my fellows forget for a time their duty or errand they came about, to make some inquisition into this miracle of nature. Whereupon we all resolved unanimously to ascend the hill, and with much difficulty we came so nigh the top, that we heard a moſt hideous noise proceeding from the concave thereof. So terrible it was that we now began to condemn our rash attempt, and ſtood at a convenient diſtance, judging it the only medium of our safety.

Whilſt we were thus in a delirium, not knowing what was the beſt to be done, the mountain was inſtantly possessed with an ague fit, and afterwards vomiting up smoke and ſtones into the air (which afterwards fell down in a shower upon our heads) we thought we could not escape without a miracle. And whilſt we were all ſtriving which way, with greateſt expedition, we might eschew the danger, there rose in the midſt of us such an heap of earth, ashes, and fire, with such kind of combuſtible matter, as that we all seemed as so many moveable burning beacons : and without any thoughts of helping each other, every one endeavoured to secure himself.

And although I was the laſt in the company, yet in this expedition it was much available to me ; for my companions making more haſte than good speed, tumbling down the hill before me, fell several of them together ; which blocks lying in my way, obſtructed my passage, and so saved the breaking of my neck, which otherwise would have been inevit- able. In this prodigious conflict, moſt of us loſt the hair of our heads, not without receiving several batteries upon the out-works of our bodies. At firſt sight we were much afraid ; but the consequence made it appear, we were not more afraid than hurt. We made a shift to crawl down the reſt of the way ; and having fixed our unadvised feet on the bottom of the mountain, we resolved we would never again pay so dearly for our curiosity, but forthwith went in search of some spring, that might serve as well to quench our clothes as our thirſt.

What we sought for we quickly found ; and so filling our empty cask, we made what haſte we could aboard. The captain and the reſt ſtood amazed to see us look so ghaſtly, and were very impatient to know what was the matter with us ; we told them succinctly what had happened, and what great dangers we underwent. Inſtead of pitying us, they only laughed at us for being such adventurous fools. Having thus furnished ourselves with what we wanted, we set sail again for Bantam ; where we safely arrived in a short time.

CHAPTER LXXIV

Going ashore to Bantam, *and observing the merchants what they did, taking up goods upon credit (as it is usual in those parts) till the ship is ready to set sail, he by a stratagem turns merchant, too, and cheats a* Banian, *or China merchant*

AS soon as we came into the harbour before Bantam, we manned out our long boat and went ashore to acquaint the president what we were, and by what authority we came thither to traffic, being empowered by the East India Company. We were received with much demonstrations of joy, and nobly feasted for three days together. Here note, that the house wherein the president dwelleth is the receptacle for the whole factory, each man according to his quality having a dwelling within this house suitable to his dignity; the factors all in general taking their daily repast with the president. In a week's time I learned by observation the custom of the country, and manner or way of trading, our merchant taking up goods daily, and sending them aboard without giving present satisfaction; it being sufficient that he belonged to such a ship, and therefore must pay before he go, otherwise the king will arrest the ship, compelling him to make restitution or payment.

One time I met with a Banian, whom I observed to have a box full of precious stones. I could not sleep for thinking how I should make myself a partner with him. At last I hammered out this invention. I clothed myself in Indian silk, according to the custom of the country; and having so done, I discoloured my face, and clapped a black patch upon one of my eyes. In this equipage I addressed myself to this Banian, who presently laid open his treasure to my view. I was not long in choosing what I esteemed as most valuable; and demanding of him the price, we agreed he should have either so many pieces of English gold within two days, or else take his choice of what commodities I had aboard.

We made a shift to understand each other's broken expressions; and he without the least suspicion of my treachery, delivered his stones into my hands. Taking off my disguise, I went instantly aboard, and hid what I had cheated the Banian of (as I might easily do, for the smallness of its bulk) in the hold of our ship, resolving not to go ashore yet awhile. The day of payment being come, and the Banian nowhere finding me on land, came aboard of our ship, where by signs he made known to our captain his errand; that a merchant belonging to his ship, had bought commodities of him, and promised to pay him on that day. Our captain replied that he verily believed he was mistaken (as knowing what commodities the merchants belonging properly to the ship had bought) and therefore told him he muſt make enquiry elsewhere for satisfaction. The Banian ſtill persiſted, alleging he was not miſtaken, and that he was confident if he might have a sight of all the men, he could out of them select the concerned person.

So wary I was of being discovered, that I acquainted not one soul with my project : for had I committed this secret to any (though ever so dear a friend) it had been mine no longer ; neither could I have promised to myself safety. Hereupon the captain ordered us to be all called aloft ; which was speedily performed. He went all round the company, viewing every man particularly, and very heedfully. At laſt he came to me, and there made a ſtand, which had like to have made my heart ſtart out of my breaſt. He looked upon me on this side, and on the other side ; and to say truly, on every side : and having thoroughly eyed me, he ran to our captain, saying, ' That should be the man ' (pointing to me) ' but that he is a white man, and hath two sees (*id eſt*) two eyes.' Whereupon I was ſtrictly examined ; but for all this sifting, I would not let drop anything of a confession that should convict me of guilt ; but with lifting up hands and eyes to Heaven, I utterly denied that e'er I saw this man, or ever had any dealing with him.

I had now forgot what promises and vows I made to Heaven, when in Newgate, and sentenced to be hanged at Tyburn, what a serious, pious, and honeſt life I would lead, if I escaped that eminent danger the concerns of this life and that to come were then in. Herein I see the old proverb verified :

> *Quo semel eſt imbuta recens servabit odorem*
> *Teſta, diu,* &c. . . .

> That cask will savour of that liquor ſtill,
> With which at firſt the cask a man did fill.

Or according to that thread-bare expression so commonly used :

> *Naturam expellas furca, licet usque recurret.*

> Though man should ſtop his nature from its course,
> It will o'erflow again with greater force.

In short, the Banian, since he could not say positively I was the man, was dismissed, not without a solemn vow he would be revenged of us all in general ; and I was cleared of the indictment.

CHAPTER LXXV

The next going ashore of the seamen, this Banian *(for the injury was done him) caused a* Running a Muck, *that is, he instigated a great many people to kill all they met of that ship : the loss of several men thereupon : but he is out of danger, having cunningly kept himself aboard that time : he afterwards had like to have been killed by a* crease *the* Banian *had hired for that purpose : his enemies being destroyed, he marrieth an* Indian Punch woman

THE next day, a great many of our men went ashore ; and going into China Row (a street so called in Bantam), to drink punch and tea, a great crew of Indians and Chinese (headed by this Banian) fell upon them, killing whom they could (not directing their revenge upon any particular person, which they call a muck). So hot and sharp was this conflict that many were killed on both sides, but more wounded. This accident alarmed the whole town, but most especially the English there resident : but at last, with much ado, this grand uproar was calmed. It was my good fortune that I was not then among them, otherwise I might have been made a sacrifice among the rest of my fellows. But I was fore-warned, having been preinformed that such broils are usual upon such occasions ; wherefore I kept myself out of harm's way for that time.

But not long after, thinking their malice blown over, I went ashore ; and walking with others of our boat's crew in the same Row (where most of our men were used to resort, because of the liquor that was there to be had, and a whore to boot), a fellow came to me, with this Banian I cheated, and both of them with ' Creases ' (a kind of dagger of about a foot and half long), would have stabbed me, had not my friends prevented them by striking up their heels, and afterwards with their own creases stabbed them to the heart. After this, we could walk very quietly without any disturbance, going anywhere without any danger.

Being very hot there, our usual pastime was to go up a little small river joining to the town four or five miles to wash ourselves. The trees so covered it over like an arbour that the beams of the sun could not penetrate it ; by which means it was fine and cool, which very much refreshed our parched bodies. I never came ashore, but I drank very immoderately of punch, rack, tea, &c. which was brought up in great china jugs holding at least two quarts. With every such jug there was brought in a dish of sweetmeats, not of one sort, but variety, and excellent good, for which we paid a shilling English : and if you called for another jug, you paid no more, unless a dish ushered it in.

One house especially I much frequented, for the Indian woman's sake that kept it ; for though she was black, or rather tawny, yet she was well-featured and well-formed, having long black hair (when she untied the tresses) hanging down to her legs. She from the firſt shewed me as much kindness as could be expeſted from that lump of Barbarism ; and I could discern her inclinations in the same manner as a man may from beaſts, when they are prone to generation, but yet it went againſt my ſtomach to yield to her motions. However, she continued her love to me, not letting me pay for anything I called for ; and when there was no necessity of being aboard, she would in a manner make me lie in her house, which, as their houses commonly are, had but one ſtory. The beds they use are a kind of hard quilt ; for were they soft, the hotness of the climate would cause them to be very deſtruſtive to man's body, even melting his very reins. Gold and jewels she had great quantity, with an house richly furnished after the Indian fashion. For this consideration I persuaded myself to marry her ; and with several arguments alleged, I gained so much conqueſt over myself that I could kiss her without disgorging myself ; and by accuſtoming myself to her company, methought I began to take some delight in it. By degrees, intereſt so overpowered me that I resolved to marry her. Thus many, nay moſt, for money, ſtick not to give themselves to the Devil.

Having one night, lying there, seriously considered of my resolution, and liking it indifferent well, I fell asleep ; but wondered when I awaked, to see a thing lie by me all black, as if she had had a mourning smock on. It seems she could hold out no longer. I pretended to flee from her ; but she held me faſt in her arms, using what rhetoric she could to persuade me to the contrary. I asked her what she meant ? She told me in a little broken English she had got, that she would ' Money me ' ; marry me, she meant : ' Aye, money me,' said I, ' that I like well ' ; but without it, let the Devil have married her for me. I asked her several queſtions, to which she gave me satisfaſtion ; and enjoined her several things, which she greedily condescended to : whereupon I gave her the firſt-fruits of her desires. But ere I go farther, take something of my rhyming fancy with you.

CHAPTER LXXVI

He descants on his marrying and lying with an Indian Black : gives wholesome advice to others ; and concludes for this time

AT the firſt sight, her head seemed in a case,
   Or that a *vizard-mask* had hid her face,
Or that she was some *fiend* from hell had ſtole,
Having for luſt been *burnt* there to a coal.
I could not tell what this foul thing should be ;
A *Succubus* it did appear to me ;
A damn'd *black* soul, that was by heaven sent,
To make me of my *blacker* crimes repent.
I ſtarted from her, being much amazed :
The more I was afraid, the more I gazed.
Then she arose, and caught me in her arm ;
Such soft flesh sure intended me no harm.
'Twas time to roar, since that I could not tell,
But that I was *encircled* (now) by *Hell*.
' Stay, ſtay,' said she, ' I am no *hellish fiend*,
I'm flesh and blood, and am thy loving friend :
If my complexion do not please thy mind,
Then close thine eyes, yet love : *Thus love is blind.*'
I underſtood her tongue, and ſtraight did swear
That I would banish this my causeless fear ;
And so betook myself unto the *rug*
On which we lay, and after many a *tug*,
I plighted *faith* with this kind *Infidel ;*
But what we did, my modeſt tongue won't tell.
I would at any time (might I but choose)
The *faireſt white* for this same *black* refuse.
But mischief on't, let me *shoot* e'er so right,
It can't be said that I did *hit the White*.

Intereſt so blinded my reason that I went inſtantly to my captain, and gave him information of my proceedings, desiring his consent in the marrying this Indian, alleging how advantageous it would be to me. He granted my requeſt, upon my earneſt importunity ; and being dismissed from his service, wè were married according to the ceremonies of the Church by an English prieſt, she renouncing her paganism. What money was got by my wife's trade, I laid out in such commodities the country afforded, as calicoes, pepper, indigo, green ginger, &c. and sold them immediately to the ships lying in the harbour, doubling what I laid out ; so that in short time I found my ſtock to increase beyond expectation. Such satisfaction my black received from me, that she thought she could not do enough to please me. I was an absolute monarch in my family; she and her servants willingly condescended to be my vassals; yet though I thus enjoyed the prerogative of an husband, yet I did not lord it too much; which won so much upon my wife's affection, and those that were concerned with her, that as soon as I desired anything, it was immediately performed, with much alacrity and expedition.

I fancied my life to be now as happy as the world could make it, having plenty of everything, and not controlled by the foolish self-will of an obstinate woman. I confess it was at first a great regret to my spirit to lie by a woman so contrary to my own complexion: but custom made her become in process of time as lovely in my eye as if she had been the completest European beauty. I now again considered how he must live that intends to live well; and upon that consideration, concluded upon this resolution, Not to neglect my duty to Heaven, myself, or neighbours: for he that fails in any of these, falls short in making his life commendable. For ourselves, we need order; for our neighbour, charity; and for the Deity, reverence and humility. These three duties are so concatenated that he which liveth orderly, cannot but be acceptable to his maker and the world. Nothing jars the world's harmony more than men that break their ranks; and nothing renders man more contemned and hated than he whose actions only tend to irregularity. One turbulent spirit will even dissentiate the calmest kingdom: so did my past unruly and disorderly life ruin myself, as well as many families. I have seen an orthodox minister in his pulpit with his congregation about him; and since revolving in my mind the comeliness of that well-ordered sight, I have thought within myself how mad he would appear, that should wildly dance out of his room. Such is man when he spurns at the law he liveth under; and such was I, that could not be contained within due limits, living like the drone on others' labours; taking no pains, but only making a humming noise in the world, till justice seized me for a wandering, idle, and hurtful vagabond (an *ignavum pecus*), and so had like to thrust me out of the world, the hive of industrious bees.

Ill company at first misled me, and it is to be feared by my example others have been misled. For he that giveth himself leave to transgress, he must needs put others out of the way. Experience giveth us to understand, that he which first disorders himself, troubles all the company. Would every man keep his own life, what a concord in music would every family be! It shall be my own endeavour to do this, and my cordial advice to others to do the like.

Doubtless he that performeth his duty to Heaven, shall find such a peace within that shall fit him for whatsoever falls. He shall not fear himself, because he knoweth his course is in order ; he shall not fear the world, because he knoweth he hath done nothing that hath angered it ; he shall not be afraid of Heaven, for he knoweth he shall there find the favour of a servant, nay more, a son, and be protected against the malice of Hell.

I know I shall be looked on no otherwise than an hypocrite ; neither will the world believe my reformation real, since I have lived so notoriously and loosely. Let a man do well an hundred times, it may be he shall for a short time be remembered and applauded ; whereas if he doth evilly but once, he shall be ever condemned, and never forgot. However, let me live well, and I care not though the world should flout my innocence, and call me dissembler. It is no matter if I suffer the worst of censorious reproaches, so that I get to Heaven at last ; to the attaining of which, the best counsel I can give myself and others is, *Bene vive, ordinabiliter tibi, sociabiliter proximo, et humiliter Deo :* Live well, orderly to thyself, sociably to thy neighbour, and humbly to thy Maker.

Take this as wholesome advice, though from an ill liver, which hath been in part discovered in the foregoing discourse ; wherein I have endeavoured, by drawing up a list of my own evil actions, to frighten others from the commission of the like. For as there is no company so savagely bad but a wise man may from it learn something to make himself better ; so there is no book so poorly furnished, out of which a man may not gather something for his benefit. Herein I have not minded so much words, as the matter ; aiming at nothing more than how I might completely limn vice in her proper ugly shape ; having done that, I have done what I intended, the reformation of others by my wicked example. For vice is of such a toady complexion, so ill shaped and deformed, that she cannot choose but teach the soul to hate ; so loathsome when she is seen in her own nasty dress, that we cannot look upon her but with detestation and horror. Vice was cunning and curiously painted when I fell into her scabbed embraces ; neither could I have ever known her foulness and rottenness, had I not tried whether her (seeming) fairness and soundness were real. Believe me, she is no ways that she appears to be ; therefore be not deluded by her : but let my life be to the Reader, as a friend fallen into a pit, that gives warning to another to avoid the danger. So admirably hath Providence disposed of the ways of man, that even the sight of vice in others is like a warning-arrow, shot for us to take heed. Vice usually in her greatest bravery, publisheth herself foolishly, thinking thereby to procure a train ; and then it is, that the secret working of conscience makes her turn her weapons against herself, and strongly plead for her implacable adversary, virtue. We are frequently wrought to good by contraries; and foul acts keep virtue from the charms of vice. An ancient poet writ well to this purpose, thus:

> . . . *Insuevit Pater optimus hoc me,*
> *Ut fugerem exemplis vitiorum quæque; notando.*
> *Quum me hortaretur parce, frugaliter, atque;*
> *Viverem uti contentus ea, quod mi ipse parasset:*
> *Nonne vides Albi ut male vivat filius? utque;*
> *Barrus inops? Magnum documentum ne patriam rem*
> *Perdere quis vellit. A turpi Meretricis amore*
> *Quum deterreret, Sectani dissimilis sis.*
> > . . . *Sic me*
> *Formabat puerum dictis* . . .

> . . . Thus my best father taught
> Me to flee vice, by noting those were naught.
> When he would charge me, thrive, & sparing be,
> Content with what he had prepar'd for me;
> Seest not how ill young Albus lives? how low
> Poor Barrus? Sure, a weighty *Item* how
> One spent his means. And when he meant to strike
> A hate to whores, To Sectan be not like.
> > . . . Thus me a child
> He with his precepts fashion'd . . .

There is no better way to correct faults in ourselves, than by observing how uncomely they appear in others. After a fit of drunkenness, my conscience would usually accuse me, and many times, after convictment, would pass so severe a sentence of condemnation on me that my own hands have oftentimes been like to prove my executioners. Considering within myself what should be the cause of this trouble and self-loathing, I found it proceeded from no other reason than the observation of others in the like beastly condition, and how noisome it hath rendered them to all. The first thing that made me abhor a choleric passion, and a saucy pride in myself (of which I was too guilty), was the seeing how ridiculous and contemptible they rendered those that are infested with them. Besides, those that are thoroughly experienced in navigation, do as well know the coasts as the ocean; as well the sands, the shallows, and the rocks, as the secured depth in the most dangerless channel; so I think those that would arrive to as much perfection as they are capable of enjoying here, must as well know bad, that they may abtrude or shun it, as the good, that they may embrace it. And this knowledge we can neither have so cheap, nor so certain, as by seeing it in others: for under a crown you may buy the whole experience of a man's life (as of mine), which cost some thousands ; though me no more hundreds than what I borrowed of the world, having of mine own nothing originally.

If we could pass the world without meeting vice, then the knowledge of virtue only were sufficient : but it is impossible to live, and not encounter her. Vice is as a god in this world ; for as she ruleth almost uncontrollably, so she assumes to herself ubiquity ; we cannot go anywhere, but that she presents herself to the eye, &c. If any be unwittingly cast thereon, let him observe for his own more safe direction. He is happy that makes another man's vices steps for him to climb to his eternal rest by. The wise physicians make poison medicinable ; and even the mud of the world, by the industrious (yet ungrateful) Hollander, is turned to an useful fuel.

·If, Reader, then, thou lightst here on anything that is bad, by considering the sordid stains, either correct those faults thou hast, or shun those thou mightest have. That mariner which hath sea-room, can make any wind almost serve to set him forwards in his wished voyage : so may a wise man take any advantage to set himself forward to the haven of virtue. Man, as soon as created, had two great suitors for his life and soul ; the one Virtue, and the other Vice. Virtue came in this manner, and thus attended ; truth ran before her naked, yet courageous ; after her followed Labour, Cold, Hunger, Thirst, Care and Vigilance ; these poorly arrayed, as looking upon it unseemly to go finer than their mistress, who was plainly and meanly clad, yet cleanly, and her countenance shewed such a self-perfection, that she might very well emblem whatsoever Omnipotency could make most rare. Modest she was, and so lovely, that whosoever looked on her stedfastly, could not but insoul himself in her. After her followed Content, enriched with jewels, and overspread with perfumes, carrying with her all the treasure and massy riches of the world. Then came Joy, with all essential pleasures : Honour, with all the ancient orders of nobility, sceptres, thrones, and crowns imperial. Lastly, Glory, whose brightness was such (which she shook from her sunny tresses), that it dazzled the eyes of her beholders, so that they could never truly describe her. In the rear came Eternity casting a ring about them, which like a strong enchantment made them ever the same.

Vice strove not to be behind-hand with Virtue ; wherefore she sets out too, and in this form. Her precursor or fore-runner was Lying, a painted housewife, of a smooth, insinuating, and deluding tongue, gaudily clad, but under her vestments she was full of scabs and loathsome ulcers. Her words seemed exceeding pleasant, promising to all she met whatsoever could be wished for, in the behalf of her Mistress Vice. On this hypocritical quean Wit waited : next him, a conceited fellow, and one that over-swayed the fancy of man with his pretty tricks and gambols. Sloth and Luxury followed these, so full, that they were even ready to be choked with their own fat. After these, followed some impostors to personate Content, Joy, and Honour, in all their wealth and royal dignities. Close after these, Vice came herself, sumptuously apparelled, but yet a nasty surfeited slut ; her breath being so infectious that he which kissed her was sure to perish. After her followed suddenly Guilt, Horror, Shame, Loss, Want, Sorrow, Torment ; and these were charmed with Eternity's ring, as the former.

And thus they wooed fond man, who taken with the subtle cozenag. s of vice, yielded to lie with her ; whereby he had his nature so empoisoned that his seed was all vitiated and contaminated ; and his corruption even to this day is still conveyed to his undone posterity. It is man's folly, only to look on the fore-runners of Virtue, which are very poor, as Cold, Hunger, Thirst, &c. but not to consider her glorious attendants that follow after, as Content, Joy, Honour, and Glory. We fancy Vice for her outside, not imagining what she is when stripped of all her gauderies.

If you, then, intend to enjoy for your portion a kingdom hereafter, adhere not to the allurements of Vice ; for she will soon persuade you to be an unthrift, to sell your inheritance whilst it is but in reversion. But harken to Virtue's counsel ; she will teach you how to husband all things well, so as to become a purchaser of no less than joys eternal.

Fortune's favours oft do fade,
 To those that in her arms do sleep :
Shelter yourselves in Virtue's shade ;
 She crowneth those that do her reap.
For though darkned, you may say,
 When Friends fail, and Fortunes frown,
Though Virtue is the roughest way,
 Yet proves at night a bed of down.

THUS have I given you a summary account of my life, from the nonage to the meridian of my days. If there be any expressions either scurrilous or obscene, my only design was to make vice appear as she is, foul, ugly, and deformed : and I hope, he that hath sense will grow wiser by the folly that is presented him ; as drunkards are often cured by the beastliness of others that are so. The subject would not permit to be serious, neither would it have been suitable to our merry age, being generally of Tully's mind, when he said, *Lectionem sine ulla delectatione negligo :* He hated reading where no pleasure dwelt.

As the daylight is purest, so have I endeavoured to make my slender wit appear terse and spruce, without the fulsomeness of wanton language. If I have in any place transgresed the bounds of modesty by loose expressions, you need not fear to be offended with their unsavoury breath, for I have perfumed it : but if it should chance to stink, it is only to drive you from my former inclination and conversation. It is probable I may be a little guilty, being not fully cured of that malady I lately laboured under. For as the breaking out of itch and blains shews the body is not clear, so foul and unrinsed expressions are the purulent exhalations of a corrupted mind, stained with the unseasonedness of the flesh.

If any loose word have dropped from the mind's best interpreter, my pen, I would have the Reader to pass it over regardless, and not like a toad, only gather up the venom of a garden ; or like a goldfinder, make it his business to dive in stench and excrements. However, very cautious I was in offending any modest ear (though sometimes it could hardly be avoided, the matter in a manner requiring it), because I look upon obscene expressions as the plague on paper ; and he that comes between the sheets is in danger of being infected. I shall assure you, had I not more respected a general good by displaying vice in general, to put men out of conceit with it, I should not have taken so much pains to be both blamed and laughed at, but should have wrapped up in silence my shame and infamy. For in truth, this book may bear a similitude with the Amphisbena, a serpent headed at either end : one biteth the vicious temper of him that reads it, and the other stings him that wrote it. To conclude, I care not though my wickedness and folly be set up as a monument to make my infamy eternal, so that the reading of my Life may be any ways instrumental for the reformation of licentious persons.